LANCE IN THE FIRE

ALFRED DENNIS

Other Novels By Alfred Dennis

Chiricahua
Lone Eagle
Elkhorn Divide
Brant's Fort
Catamount
The Mustangers
Rover
Sandigras Canyon
Yellowstone Brigade
Shawnee Trail
Fort Reno
Yuma
Ride the Rough String
Trail to Medicine Mound
Slocum
Horseshoeing Tales

~ Crow Killer Series ~

Arapaho Lance - Book 1
Lance Bearer - Book 2
Track of the Grizzly - Book 3
Bear Claw - Book 4
Blood on the Lance - Book 5
Eagle Wing - Book 6
Stalking Moon – Book 7
Arapaho Revenge – Book 8

See more books by Alfred Dennis at:
AlfredDennis.com

LANCE IN THE FIRE

ALFRED DENNIS

KRP
KIAMICHI RIVER PRESS
TUSKAHOMA, OKLAHOMA

LANCE IN THE FIRE
CROW KILLER SERIES – BOOK 9
Copyright ©2024 Alfred Dennis

This novel is a work of fiction. Names, characters, places, and incidents are either the product of the author's imagination or are used fictitiously. Any resemblance to actual events, locales, organizations, or persons, living or dead, is entirely coincidental and beyond the author's or publisher's intent.

The front cover art was designed by Kathleen Baldwin.

Books may be purchased in quantity and/or by special sales by contacting the author via his website: AlfredDennis.com

First Edition, Paperback
Published 2024 by Kiamichi River Press

This book is for my Aunt Thelma
Cousins Nina, Lollie, and Mary
Lovely ladies All

INTRODUCTION

IN THE AFTERMATH of the disastrous Battle of the Little Big Horn and General Custer's death, Jedidiah Bracket, revered among the Arapaho nation as Crow Killer, is summoned to Fort Bridger. He is shown a proposed treaty and reservation papers signed by the renowned General Crook and offered an under-the-table deal to ensure his Arapaho Nation will be given a reservation in their cherished Sweetwater Country of Wyoming rather than the hot arid hills of Oklahoma.

But this offer comes at a dangerously high cost and with a deadly twist.

Crow Killer must rescue Blue Feather, daughter of the great war chief Gall, from a ruthless Pawnee warrior who holds her captive, and ride hundreds of miles through treacherous enemy terrain to deliver the girl to her father in Sitting Bull's camp in the Canadian Mountains. In exchange, Chief Gall is expected to hand over Custer's saddlebags containing some mysterious papers. But will he?

Crow Killer stands to lose more than his life in this daring venture. While undertaking this quest, he learns that his own family and his beloved peaceful valley are being attacked by a disgraced Lance Bearer, who has sworn vengeance on Crow Killer's son.

With the fate of his family and the Arapaho nation hanging in the balance, Crow Killer braces himself for what promises to be his most dangerous adventure yet, and he vows that it will also be his last.

CHAPTER 1

CROW **K**ILLER RODE AT THE HEAD of the small party of travelers as they crossed the mighty Yellowstone River and approached the Arapaho village. The sound of drums pounding in the distance came to him across the few miles still separating them from the camp. With the rhythmic sound of the village drums in his ears, the great warrior of the Arapaho nodded approval. The beating of the drums told him they had been spotted by the camp scouts, and their eminent arrival in the village was known. He knew the people would be waiting anxiously as the camp crier called out his name.

The people of the Arapaho would be elated knowing the great Lance Bearer, Crow Killer, and his family were approaching.

From over the treetops of the cottonwood, oak, and maple trees, Crow Killer saw columns of smoke rising from the many campfires in the village. This was the great yearly gathering of the people for the Lance Bearer Ceremony. The time when the young Arapaho men who had passed their trials of manhood would now be inducted into the warrior society. The Lance Bearer Society were the greatest fighters of the Arapaho. Many regarded them as the bravest and noblest of all the horseback fighters on the plains. Enemy tribes feared them and hated meeting these great warriors in battle. All enemy warriors of the Arapaho knew that when a Lance Bearer plunged his Lance into the ground many of their warriors would die before that warrior would fall. The beautifully carved lance signified no retreat and no surrender until the bearer of the lance was victorious or dead. None were prouder and brave in battle than these mighty Lance Bearers.

Crow Killer remembered his own ceremony when all the villages and many other friendly tribes had come together for the great event. He knew that this time, too, the number of people in the village would swell, doubling or even tripling in size. His senses seemed to tingle, making him anxious to enter the village. Today, all of his friends and relatives would be present for him to see once again.

Gazing up at the great amount of smoke rising upwards into the sky, he could tell that many visitors had already arrived for the ceremony. Crow Killer glanced back to where Red Horse and his soon-to-be bride, Flower Leaf, rode. He could see the excitement in their faces as they looked at each other. Even Grass Bee and Broken Leg seemed eager to see their friends.

Bright Moon rode beside Crow Killer, her dark eyes looked at the sky overhead. "This much smoke shows many new lodges have arrived in the village."

He smiled at the beautiful woman dressed in a light fawn colored dress covered in beads. "Yes. Many have already come to honor our young men, and many more will arrive soon."

"It has always been the greatest ceremony of the people." Bright Moon smiled proudly. "When all will honor these young ones who have passed their manhood rites, soon to become honored men."

"Yes, wife. They deserve to be honored. These are fine young men." Crow Killer sat taller astride his horse, and his chest filled with pride for his son. "They have earned their Lances and all the honors that will be bestowed on them."

"I hope my brother, He Dog, brings his people."

"It has been many moons since we have seen He Dog." Crow Killer thought of the Cheyenne Chief, his brother-in-law. "Yes, it will be good to see him."

"Yes, my husband. It has been a while."

Crow Killer frowned slightly as he looked at the long-haired, beautiful woman riding straight-shouldered and proud beside him. "But do not be too disappointed if he doesn't come this year."

"You think He Dog worries about the white eye soldiers attacking his village?" Bright Moon turned to him. "My husband thinks this will keep He Dog away from the ceremonies?"

"Yes. Since the fight on the Greasy Grass and Long Hair Custer's defeat, the hostile tribes have separated into the winds. They wait in hiding. They know that soon the white soldiers will ride into their lands, searching for them, to drive the people of the plains onto a reservation."

Bright Moon shrugged with irritation. "Did the whites not learn their lesson with the death of so many of their pony soldiers?"

It was very hard for Crow Killer to make Bright Moon or any of the others understand his words when he told of the great numbers of whites living in the East. Or how the pony soldiers of the whites would hate all Indians for Custer's defeat at the Little Bighorn Battle. He alone knew the strength and numbers of the whites and how they would strike hard at the Plains tribes. To lose more soldiers meant nothing to the white generals as long as the Indian was subjugated and put on reservations to be counted like cattle. No matter how hard he tried, his people just could not understand that one major city of the whites held more people than all the tribes combined.

"No, Bright Moon. The whites in the east know only that they must destroy the tribes and move them on to reservations."

Deep in thought, the plodding of the horses on the dusty trail sounded faint to her. "But this is the land of the Arapaho. It has always been so."

"Yes, once it was." Crow Killer nodded slowly. "But I fear the day of the Arapaho People is finished. I know the white man's heart. He will ride here soon against the people."

"And our valley?" Bright Moon looked over at him, her face drawn with worry. "The whites will take that, too?"

"No." Crow Killer shook his head. "Even though I am Crow Killer to our people, the Arapaho, to the whites, I am Jedidiah Bracket. Thanks to Oliver, we have registered a claim of ownership to our valleys."

"Then our people can come live there in our lands."

"No, the whites would follow what they consider hostiles even into our valleys."

"Then what will our friends and relatives do, my husband?"

"We haven't heard anything from the east for several moons now." The drums grew even louder as they neared the village. "We will wait and talk to Wolf's Head and the elders to find out what they have learned."

"I fear for them." Sadness marked Bright Moon's delicate features. "What can they do if the whites are as many as you say?"

She spoke the truth. Crow Killer winced. He remembered the old saying he had heard many times as a youngster, might makes right. Even the once proud and mighty tribes of the Sioux and Cheyenne were few in comparison to the pony soldiers of the whites.

Trying to resist such a powerful enemy would be the death of their people. Crow Killer hated the thought, but he knew the Arapaho had no choice but to heed the words of the whites. Along with the other tribes, they would soon be forced to sign worthless treaties. Then, they would be penned onto reservations like cattle. He wondered how these proud people would suffer such degradation. Crow Killer's stomach tightened. He knew the way of the free-roaming hunters and great horseback peoples of the plains would soon come to an end.

The drums' rhythmic pounding grew thunderously loud as

Crow Killer stopped his people at the edge of the village. Already, hundreds of people were moving busily amongst the beautifully painted lodges. Suddenly, several warriors mounted on their fleet ponies surrounded them, yelling and screaming, brandishing their war lances. Crow Killer smiled as several pushed closer, milling about him, grinning happily and screaming their welcome.

"It is good to see the Crow Killer once again." Wolf's Head reined in beside Crow Killer's Appaloosa stallion.

Crow Killer smiled and took the extended arm. "It is good to see my friend Wolf's Head, Chief of the Arapaho."

Wolf's Head studied each of their faces before turning back to Crow Killer. "I do not see Little Antelope."

"No, my friend. Our little princess has gone to be with her ancestors."

His dark eyes opened wide. "Little Antelope is no more?"

Crow Killer answered solemnly. "She is only in our thoughts now."

Wolf's Head lowered his eyes for a moment before responding. "We will talk of this sad thing later." He turned and greeted Eagle Wing, Broken Leg, and Red Horse. "Come. The people will want to greet the great Crow Killer and his people."

"And we are anxious to see them again." Bright Moon smiled as Wolf's Head nodded at her.

"It is good to see Bright Moon again." The chief turned his horse. "Come. The people already know you are here and are waiting for you."

Drums beat steadily through the night as the villagers moved about from lodge to lodge, talking and greeting old friends. Grass Bee invited Bright Moon, Flower Leaf, and Crow Killer to use Little Antelope's lodge. Ellie, Oliver, Morning Dove, the baby, and Eagle Wing had placed their camp gear in Crow Killer's vacant lodge. Broken Leg touched Grass Bee's shoulder gently, then retreated with Red Horse to his own lodge.

Wolf's Head and Crow Killer stood talking under the large oak that shaded the lodge of Walking Horse and Little Antelope. "We have lost so many loved ones."

Crow Killer looked over at the young chief and nodded. "Yes, my friend, we have."

"I fear there is more death ahead for our people."

"Wolf's Head speaks of the Long Knives of the whites?"

"Yes, the Cheyenne sent news from Sitting Bull and Gall."

"Tell me."

"First Crow Killer will tell me of the loss of Little Antelope." Wolf's Head looked over at the warrior expectantly. "Then we will mention her no more. But I wish to know about the death of the woman who was the Princess of our people. And such a Princess she was."

Crow Killer nodded. He understood the feelings Wolf's Head had for Little Antelope. She was as a mother to all the tribe. After telling him of the fight on the mountain and her death, Crow Killer shook his head.

"What a sad day for the people." The young Chief nodded sadly. "Did the killer of Little Antelope pay for her death?"

"He did."

"Tell me of her daughter, Grass Bee." Wolf's Head gestured towards the lodge. "Do the evil ones still fill her mind?"

"No. With the death of the one that killed her mother, Grass Bee has returned to her people." Crow Killer spread his hands out open wide. "Now, the people can accept her back into their village."

Wolf's Head nodded his head in agreement. "It will be as you ask."

"That is good." He drew in a grateful breath.

"I saw Broken Leg riding close to her when they entered the village."

"I believe soon Grass Bee will be the wife of Broken Leg." Crow Killer glanced over at the warrior. Dressed in full leather leggings and a black breechcloth, the tall young Chief was proud and aristocratic. Crow Killer knew he had chosen well when he had picked Wolf's Head to be Chief of the Arapaho people.

"Yes. I have seen the look that passed between them."

Crow Killer smiled at Wolf's Head, appreciating the perception in one so young. "Their marriage will be a good thing."

"Crow Killer speaks wisely. With Grass Bee as Broken Leg's woman, none will dare question her."

"That is what I think also."

"Tell me of Flower Leaf." Wolf's Head frowned slightly. "She, too, has returned to the Arapaho Village from her people, the Nez Perce."

"After the Lance Bearer Ceremony, Flower Leaf will become the wife of Red Horse."

"You are sure she wishes to become the wife of Red Horse?"

"Yes." But Crow Killer didn't miss the frown that crossed the chief's face. "Is something wrong?"

"No." Wolf's Head shook his head as if confused. "We will speak of this after the ceremony."

Crow Killer could tell something bothered the warrior. "Tell me, my Chief."

"I am Chief, but it was you, Crow Killer, who made me Chief." Wolf's Head met his steady gaze. "You are wise and strong. It is the Crow Killer who should be Chief of our people."

"I cannot be chief and live so far to the north." Crow Killer shrugged. "Wolf's Head is now leader of the Arapaho, and you will be a great Chief."

Wolf's Head acknowledged the truth of this with a resigned grunt.

Crow Killer studied the warrior carefully. It was time to get down to the trouble coming at them. "Tell me about the Sioux and Cheyenne? Has something happened to He Dog's people?"

"No. Their scouts tell me the whites have not come this far west. The pony soldiers are hunting for Crazy Horse and his Oglala people in the badlands to the west."

"And Gall?"

"Not long before you arrived, a rider brought news that the people of Sitting Bull and Gall have taken sanctuary in the Grandmother's Land to the north."

"Sitting Bull is in Canada?" It shocked Crow Killer to hear that the great leaders of the Sioux had retreated to the North Country. "That means no Sioux stand between you and the Cheyenne to keep the whites back?"

"Yes. Only Crazy Horse remains, and he only has a few hundred warriors riding with him." Wolf's Head shrugged. "They say even the great Oglala hides from the pony soldiers now."

Crow Killer shook his head sadly. He knew it was going to happen, but he didn't think it would happen so soon. "All are gone?"

"To the south, the white hunters kill the buffalo and leave their bodies to rot." Wolf's Head frowned. "Soon, there will be no meat to feed our bellies. The people will starve."

"Do the white pony soldiers head this way?"

"The scouts of the Cheyenne say no, we are farther west. But when the hostile Sioux and Cheyenne are beaten, and those that remain alive are driven onto reservations, then I think they will come to our lands."

"What about the Crow and my brother, Red Hawk?"

"Bah. The Crow dogs are safe. They, along with the Rees and Pawnee, scouted against us for the Long Knives." Wolf's Head voice was bitter. "The whites give them the Greasy Grass and much of our tribal lands to place their lodges on. The reward for their treachery is our lands, and they will be supplied with food by the whites while we starve."

Crow killer thought of his friend and blood brother, Red Hawk. So much had happened in such a short time. It had only been a few moons since Custer had been defeated at the Little Bighorn. Rumors about the aftermath of the battle had drifted to him from travelers who had passed through Bridger. He'd heard that Sitting Bull and Gall, along with Crazy Horse, had led thousands of warriors against the yellow-haired General. He'd found it hard to believe that Sitting Bull was being chased by the pony soldiers, and Crazy Horse had retreated and was hiding somewhere in the badlands. Until now, he doubted all these rumors.

Wolf's Head jarred him from his thoughts. "Tomorrow, we must hunt for meat to feed the people for the ceremony. Perhaps Eagle Wing, Red Horse, and your white son will join us for the hunt?"

"We will be honored to join our brothers in the hunt."

Wolf's Head looked sadly over at Crow Killer. "This may be our last Lance Bearer ceremony. A defeated people will no longer need warriors."

"The Arapaho people are not defeated yet, Wolf's Head."

"With the Crow and Pawnee pushing against us, I feel defeated." The Chief shrugged. "I fear that soon, the white pony soldiers will ride with our enemies against us here."

"Have the Crow fought with the Arapaho?"

"No, there has been no killing, but their young warriors feel strong now with the whites behind them. They raid our horse herds and taunt our young warriors."

"And Red Hawk says nothing?"

"Many times, he has returned our horses, but even the great Red Hawk cannot be everywhere at once."

"I will talk with Red Hawk when he comes for the ceremony."

"I do not think he will come here." Wolf's Head shook his head. "You do not understand Crow Killer. The truce is broken, the Crow are again our enemies."

"Red Hawk will never be my enemy."

"No, but he is still a Crow, and he must do as his people want."

"We will talk of this more when we will hold council with the elders after the hunt tomorrow."

"I fear talk will do no good." Wolf's Head shook his head.

"You will call a council? We must talk of this."

"Yes."

The next morning, Wolf's Head, Black Bird, and Broken Leg waited at the small creek crossing as Crow Killer, Eagle Wing, Red Horse, and Oliver walked their horses toward them. The morning was beautiful. Birds sang from the tall branches, and furry squirrels and chipmunks watched and scolded them from the treetops. The small creek bordering the village gurgled as cold, clear water rippled, flowing unchecked across the clear rocky bottom.

Whippoorwill sounded their cries up and down the tree-lined bank of the small creek as the warriors greeted each other. The morning was cool with no wind, perfect for a buffalo run. Black Bird and Fox Ear had already located a small herd only a few miles from the village. So far, the filthy white hunters hadn't dared to move farther north and hunt shaggies in the lands of the Arapaho. The mighty Arapaho Warriors were still a feared enemy. Until the white soldiers moved the Arapaho Lance Bearers onto reservation lands, the buffalo hunters would remain to the east in safety along the Missouri.

Leading the hunters to the south, where Black Bird reported seeing the small herd, Wolf's Head reined in as several Arapaho warriors emerged from the bordering thickets.

"It is Spotted Elk, younger brother of Two Eyed Dog and some of his followers." Wolf's Head turned to where Red Horse set his horse.

As the riders stopped their horses beside Wolf's Head and his men, Spotted Elk pushed in alongside Red Horse and looked the younger warrior over coldly. Kicking his bay horse, the muscular warrior moved back beside Wolf's Head. "My Chief has come to hunt the shaggies?" His voice was sarcastic.

"Will Spotted Elk join us to bring in meat for the celebration?"

"It's not a celebration, just a bunch of children becoming warriors." The warrior glared hard at Red Horse and jutted his chin into the air. "Bah! Let them hunt their own meat."

"You, too, were once a young man waiting to be honored as a Lance Bearer." Broken Leg glared at the warrior. "Has Spotted Elk forgotten his vows?"

"I forget nothing, Broken Leg." The tall warrior snarled. "I am a Lance Bearer, but first, I am a man."

Crow Killer knew this warrior. Unlike his brother, the jovial Two Eyed Dog, this one had a cruel streak in him. Several times, he'd ridden the war trail with him and Eagle Wing. He had been at the fight on the Blue River when Eagle Wing had killed the Pawnee Chief Strong Otter. He could see the glare in the warrior's eyes as he looked across at Red Horse. He had always seemed strange at times, always full of hate. But he didn't understand what was causing the warrior to act as he was this morning.

"Will my brother Spotted Elk help us gather meat for our village?" Black Bird spoke up.

"I said no." Spotted Elk frowned at Black Bird. "Brother, you are not my brother."

"Then we will talk no more." Wolf's Head pushed his horse in front of Spotted Elk's horse and stared hard at the warrior. "Leave this place, warrior. Leave us now. Your Chief has spoken."

"We will leave, but we will talk again after the ceremony when this one becomes a man." Spotted Elk pointed his rifle at Red Horse. "Yes, we will talk, just me and this woman stealer."

Crow Killer quickly raised his own rifle but dropped it back across his horse's withers as the warrior and his followers whirled and rode away with several hoarse screams. Watching as the riders pounded away towards the village, he uncocked his Henry and looked over at Wolf's Head.

"Tell me, Wolf's Head, what was that all about?"

"Someday, I will have to kill that one."

Crow Killer shook his head. "You know a Chief of the

Arapaho cannot kill another Arapaho and remain Chief."

"Nor can you be a Lance Bearer, my Chief." Broken Leg's dark eyes watched as Spotted Elk rode out of sight. "It is forbidden for a Lance Bearer to kill another Lance Bearer. But, I would enjoy killing him for you."

"Enough of this talk, my friends." Wolf's Head shook his head. "We are all Arapaho Lance Bearers. Unless Spotted Elk causes his own death, his empty talk will cause no harm."

Broken Leg scowled. "It causes my ears harm."

"We will speak of this after the hunt." Wolf's Head raised his arm. "Now, we have meat to bring in for the village. Come, my friends. We hunt."

Crow Killer could tell by the actions of Wolf's Head there would be no chance of talking with the Chief until after the hunt. He would have to wait, but something was amiss. Spotted Elk had the same as challenged Red Horse with his looks and actions. Crow Killer didn't understand. Two Eyed Dog and Eagle Wing had been as brothers, and Spotted Elk knew this. What could have made the warrior turn against his friends as he had this morning?

The surround of the small herd of shaggies had been successful. Several carcasses lay about a flat meadow where squaws from the village were carving the meat up for transport back to the cooking fires for the ceremony. Red Horse's arrows had found three of the young cows and one bull before Wolf's Head had stopped the killing.

A young squaw smiled bashfully up at the handsome young man as she returned his bloody arrows to him. "Your arrows, Red Horse." Her dark eyes held a shy smile as she handed him the arrows. "You are a great hunter."

Red Horse looked down at the pretty girl and smiled. "Thank you."

"He is very handsome, is he not, Young Doe?" An older

woman chided the pretty young girl when she returned to her skinning.

"Yes. He is very handsome."

"And very taken." Pretty Eyes, another young woman laughed. "He soon will be the husband of Flower Leaf."

The bloody knives flashed in the early morning sunlight as the older woman worked over the dead buffalo. "Perhaps, but I have heard Spotted Elk has spoken differently."

"Spotted Elk will not dare challenge the son of the great Crow Killer." Young Doe looked at the woman. "Or his brother Eagle Wing."

"They would kill him if he dared do this." Another woman spoke up. "No warrior would dare stand against the bear medicine of Crow Killer."

"Spotted Elk is himself a mighty warrior." Pretty Eyes shrugged. "And Crow Killer has grown old."

"Even at his age, no warrior is the equal of the bear killer or his son Eagle Wing."

Pretty Eyes grew solemn and looked over to where the men were sitting on their horses, watching over the women. "Spotted Elk is not like Two Eyed Dog was. He is crazy and cruel, and he wants the Nez Perce woman for himself."

"She is very beautiful for a Nez Perce." Young Doe looked across the meadow at Red Horse. "I do not think Spotted Elk is warrior enough to stop their marriage."

"I have heard the warriors that follow him talk. They say Spotted Elk will challenge Red Horse after the ceremony when he becomes a full-fledged Lance Bearer and considered a man."

"Why?" Young Doe peeled the heavy hide back, exposing the meat. "Why would he do this thing?"

Pretty Eyes glanced sideways at the older woman. "Tell her, Mother."

"It is the custom of our people that the wife of a dead brother will become the wife of the surviving brother." The older squaw shrugged. "Spotted Elk thinks she is his property and will demand that the elders and the medicine men give him the woman. It is his right. He must do this to save face."

"He will force the young handsome one to fight?" Young Doe's hand trembled.

"Spotted Elk feels he has been dishonored." The older woman frowned. "If he is to have honor amongst the people, he will have to. The coming marriage is already common knowledge in the village. It will be a fight to the death for one, maybe both."

"The Nez Perce woman has no say in who she is to belong to?"

"She was a captive before marrying Two Eyed Dog." The older woman shook her head. "No. She has no choice in this."

"Still, there is the Crow Killer?" Young Doe looked over at the woman. "Would Spotted Elk really dare challenge a son of the great bear killer?"

"If the young cub is challenged as you say, perhaps the old bear would fight for him." Pretty Eyes eyed Red Horse.

"This cannot be. The young one would lose face if his father fights in his place." The older squaw shrugged. "No, it will be Red Horse who must fight."

"But why must they fight?" Young Doe hacked at the carcass. "Why kill each other over a mere woman, a Nez Perce squaw?"

"Men like to fight over women." Pretty Eyes laughed. "And the Nez Perce is a beautiful woman."

"I told you Spotted Elk is crazy to have the Nez Perce, and he feels she is his by tribal law." The older woman shook her head again. "She could be ugly as mud, but he feels she belongs to him."

"But, a Lance Bearer that kills another Lance Bearer is no longer allowed to carry the Lance or belong to the Society of Lance Bearers." Young Doe argued. "Surely he would not do that."

Pretty Eyes laughed again. "The Lance does not keep a man warm at night or cook for him."

"There are many young women that he could have." Young

Doe sliced through tendons separating the hind quarters so they could be loaded onto a pack horse.

"I told you, it is Spotted Elk's pride. He feels the Nez Perce woman is his property." Pretty Eyes wiped her forehead. "I smell death on the wind and not from these shaggies."

"It is so stupid to kill over a woman and be removed from the society of the greatest warriors." Young Doe slashed with her knife. "I do not think this will happen."

"Yes, it is stupid, but men are stupid sometimes." The older woman wrapped a hind quarter in the wet hide. "Where women are concerned, men are strange creatures."

"Well, Young Doe, you only have two days left before you find out." Another squaw shrugged. "If the young one isn't killed and only wounded, then maybe you can nurse him back to health, and he will be yours."

"I do not think Spotted Elk can defeat this young warrior in battle." Young Doe shook her head. "Look at the muscles on him."

"Hah, Spotted Elk is older and more experienced in battle than the young one." The old woman spoke again. "Muscles do not win battles. I think Spotted Elk will hurt Red Horse bad, or perhaps even kill him."

"No, he is too proud. I do not believe he can be defeated." Young Doe looked to where Red Horse talked with another warrior. "I have heard the young one has already counted many coups in battle. If Spotted Elk is so foolish to challenge him, he will die."

"Well, the ceremony is two sleeps away. We shall soon find out, won't we?" Pretty Eyes laughed again. "Two sleeps Young Doe, you won't have to wait long. Now we must all get to work, the day will be hot soon."

Crow Killer and the warriors flanked the heavily laden pack animals as the squaws led the horses back towards the village. Even though these were traditional Arapaho hunting grounds, since the defeat of Custer, danger lurked everywhere. The white generals wanted revenge for their fallen soldiers, and the Crow and Pawnee tribes living nearby took advantage of their friendship with the whites. The young hotheads wanted to fight and take coups from their traditional enemies. With the new rifles provided by the whites, the Crow and Pawnee had grown brave and daring in their raids. Always, when away from the village, the women had to be protected from any raiders that could be lurking about.

Crow Killer rode up alongside Wolf's Head as they led the procession back to the village. "Now Wolf's Head will tell me what that was about this morning with Spotted Elk."

"I will tell you. After the ceremony, Spotted Elk intends to claim the captive woman Flower Leaf as his property."

"So that's it." Crow Killer had forgotten all about Flower Leaf being a captive before becoming Two Eyed Dogs wife. He knew by tribal custom she would become the property of Spotted Elk if he claimed her. "Then Spotted Elk will claim her?"

"He will claim the woman. He bragged about this long before you arrived in the village." Wolf's Head shook his head. "And he already has spoken with Two Bears, the medicine man, and the elders about this."

"And the elders, what do they say?"

"The elders respect you, Crow Killer. In your honor they will not take sides. They have said it will be Two Bears who must decide this."

"What does Wolf's Head think his decision will be?"

"Crow Killer knows by our tribal customs the woman belongs to Spotted Elk." "Two Bears must follow the law."

"Yes, I know this to be the law."

"Your son will not be permitted to marry Flower Leaf." Wolf's Head looked over at Red Horse. "While Spotted Elk lives, by our laws, she belongs to him."

"Red Horse will not give up the girl. He will fight." Crow

Killer frowned. "I think he will die before he would give Flower Leaf up."

"I fear this, too. A proud son of Crow Killer has no choice. To keep the woman and his pride, he must meet this challenge."

"It has nothing to do with Red Horse being my son or his pride. He is a man who cares much for a woman."

"More for a squaw, than his own life?"

"Yes. Red Horse is wild, but he is in love with the woman."

"Spotted Elk is a mighty warrior, and he is older and much more experienced in fighting."

"I will give Spotted Elk many spotted horses if he will turn down his claim to the girl."

"I have already offered him horses."

"And?"

"He says he already has many horses. He wants the woman." Wolf's Head shrugged. "Never will he give up his claim to the Nez Perce."

"Does he want to die?"

"Spotted Elk is a cold-hearted, cruel warrior, but he is also a Lance Bearer and a mighty warrior. He has no fear of dying."

CHAPTER 2

THE AIR WAS THICK with the savory aroma of buffalo meat cooking on the hot fires that dotted the village. The festive mood of the people showed in every face. Groups of warriors gathered in front of the lodges as stories were told and the great deeds of long-ago warriors were re-lived. Children laughed and hid behind their mothers as the older storytellers told the tale of the Coyote and the Rabbit and how the people came to live on the land. It always caused a great roar of laughter when the speedy little Rabbit somehow escaped the wily Coyote's fangs.

With all the whispers in the village of Spotted Elk's threats, Red Horse and Flower Leaf wanted to be alone. Walking away from the village, they strolled along the banks of the small peaceful creek, listening to the calls of the night people. The slow-moving water rippled over the protruding rocks of the stream, whispering to them from the dark. Flower Leaf kept casting her eyes about in the shadows of the tall trees, looking for danger. The hoarse croaking of frogs and a fish leaping from the water to catch a lightning bug making a splash as it re-entered the water were the sounds that came to their ears. The call of the Whippoorwill and the hoot of a great northern Owl echoed through the night.

"It is so peaceful here along the water, just the two of us." Flower Leaf squeezed his hand. "But the sounds from out of the dark are frightful."

"Do not be afraid, little one." Red Horse held her hand. "It is only the night people speaking to us. There is no danger here."

"There is danger. I have heard the women speaking." Flower Leaf shook her head. "After the ceremony, Spotted Elk will demand that I be returned to him."

"It is just talk."

"No, I remember Spotted Elk. He is crazy and cruel. He is unlike Two Eyed Dog." Her dark head shook. "The women say by tribal law it is his right to claim me."

Red Horse shrugged. "He is just a man."

"He is a great warrior. I fear for you." Flower Leaf looked about the dimness. "He could be out here."

"No, he will not do anything before the ceremony."

"Why does he wait?"

"He wants me to become a Lance Bearer, which makes me a man in the eyes of the people."

"You must become a man before he kills you. Is that what you are saying?"

"We will wait and see what Two Bears, the medicine man, says. Perhaps then we will worry." Red Horse took her by the shoulders. "Tonight, we will enjoy the evening and being together."

"You are impossible, Red Horse." Flower Leaf turned to him. "I know already what the old medicine man will say. I cannot enjoy the night when I know you are in danger."

"I do not feel I am in danger." The warrior smiled down at her. "Flower Leaf will be my wife. That is all that matters."

"Let us leave this place now and go back to our valley where we can live in peace." She looked about in the darkness. "Please, Red Horse, take me away from this place. There has been enough death over me."

"I wish we could, little one." Red Horse shook his head in the duskiness of the dying day. "But you know I cannot do this thing."

"Why? Many times, you have proven your bravery in battle. You have many scars on your body to prove this."

"If I run from this place, it would dishonor my father and brother." Red Horse grabbed her small shoulders. "Flower Leaf must not ask me to do that. I would rather be dead than dishonor Crow Killer."

She couldn't see his eyes clearly, but she could read his thoughts. Hugging him, she trembled. "Forgive me, but I love you so."

"It will be alright." Red Horse turned back towards the village. "Come. We will go join the people and enjoy the evening."

The afternoon of the ceremony, He Dog, Crazy Cat, and a few of his people rode into the Arapaho Village amongst the howling and cheering of the people. Slipping from his great yellow horse, the Cheyenne War Chief greeted Crow Killer and Eagle Wing. Then he lifted Bright Moon high and smiled up at her. "You have grown heavy to me, my sister." The Chief laughed as he set her down softly. "Or maybe I have grown old."

"You are not old, brother. So, I must have gotten heavier." Bright Moon laughed as she greeted He Dog's wife, Meadow Lark, and their two children and ushered them toward the lodge. "You men talk, we will prepare food."

"She is still the bossy one." He Dog shook Crow Killer's hand, then followed him to the shade of the great oak. "My sister hasn't changed one bit."

"Bright Moon has always been so since childhood." Crazy Cat shook hands with Crow Killer as they sat down. "When we were young, she could outrun and out-wrestle all of us boys."

"Crazy Cat should not tell these things." He Dog laughed again. "But it is true, she could."

"Yes, she's a fighter for sure." Crow Killer remembered when Bright Moon, many years ago, had killed the two white hunters while she was in labor with Eagle Wing and Ellie.

"Yes, our father says she should have been a boy."

Crow Killer looked across at the two Cheyenne Warriors. "I did not think He Dog would bring his people this year."

"You think of the white soldiers?"

"Yes, the whites and the hostile tribes that roam across the lands."

"The whites, I fear. The Pawnee and Crow, I do not." Crazy Cat flattened his hands. "I spit on the cowards."

"Have you heard any news about the pony soldiers?"

"Soon, the cold time will lay its hands across our lands. Then, I think their chiefs will mount a force of Long Knives to come into our lands to hunt down Crazy Horse and his people."

"Does He Dog know where Crazy Horse is?" Eagle Wing asked.

"Our scouts say the great Chief hunts for winter meat up on the Madison."

"The medicine men of our village say this cold time will be very bitter." Crazy Cat lit up his pipe. "Harsh."

"And Crazy Horse has many mouths to feed." He Dog frowned. "Our scouts have spoken with the Sioux scouts. They say the wife of Crazy Horse, Black Shawl, is very sick with the coughing sickness."

Eagle Wing nodded. He remembered the wife of the quiet war chief from when he had visited the village of Crazy Horse. He remembered her as being quiet but very proud and erect. It saddened him to hear she had the coughing illness. With no white man's medicine, few survived the terrible sickness.

"Will Crazy Horse surrender to the whites?"

He Dog shrugged. "I know the star General Crook has sent delegates from Red Cloud and Spotted Tail Agencies to talk with Crazy Horse, but we have heard nothing yet."

Eagle Wing also remembered the proud Oglala. He didn't think Crazy Horse would surrender until he got what he thought were fair promises from the whites: a fair treaty. What the Sioux

Chief would ask for, he didn't know.

"Crazy Horse wants his own reservation." He Dog looked off across the village. "To surrender one's people to live like whipped dogs, this is a hard thing for one who has lived free all of his years. Also, to live on the same reservation and under the rule of his uncle, Spotted Tail, would be a humiliation to one such as Crazy Horse."

"I am glad He Dog and his people are here, my friends." Crow Killer smiled. "But I fear for the safety of your people while you are away from your village."

"I wanted to see my nephew earn his War Lance. My warriors will watch closely for the Long Knives in my absence."

"We may have a problem, my brother." Crow Killer looked over at the two warriors. "And I don't want you to get involved if it happens."

Crazy Cat looked across at Crow Killer. "Tell us, brother. What problem does Crow Killer speak off?"

"As you know, my son Red Horse has come here for the Ceremony of the Lance Bearers and to receive his war lance. But he has also come here to be married by the medicine man, Two Bears, to the woman, Flower Leaf."

"I remember her. She is a comely woman." Crazy Cat shrugged. "What is this problem?"

"The girl was a captive before she married into the Arapaho Tribe."

"Yes, I remember now." He Dog nodded. "She was married to Two Eyed Dog, who was killed by the Nez Perce in a cowardly ambush."

"Yes."

"And now Red Horse wants her for his woman?"

"Yes, but I fear Spotted Elk, brother of Two Eyed Dog, will claim the woman as his property." Crow Killer shrugged. "Flower Leaf, being his dead brother's wife, makes her his by tribal laws."

He Dog dropped his head thoughtfully. "This is indeed a

problem."

"My youngest is very proud and thinks much of the girl. I know Red Horse. He will not give up the girl even if the medicine man, Two Bears, decides in Spotted Elk's favor."

"Would Red Horse challenge Spotted Elk to fight for the girl?" Crazy Cat shook his head. "Arapaho law forbids two Lance Bearers to fight if they are to keep their Lances, does it not?"

"It does."

He Dog looked over at Crow Killer. "I think this one is much like the young Crow Killer, very proud and unafraid of anything. He will not give up the girl."

"I fear he is." Crow Killer agreed. "If Spotted Elk demands the girl to be turned over to him, Red Horse will fight."

"For one squaw he would lose his right to carry the Lance of the Arapaho that he has worked so hard to earn?" Crazy Cat shook his head. "This is crazy. There are many pretty young squaws in the Arapaho Villages who would be willing to marry your son."

"Maybe crazy, but it doesn't matter. He cares only for Flower Leaf."

He Dog scratched on the ground with a pointed stick. "You cannot offer Spotted Elk gifts to give up the woman?"

"He has been offered horses already."

"And he refused them?"

"Yes."

"Offer him rifles and bullets." Crazy Cat shrugged. "Every warrior wants more rifles."

"He wants the woman, nothing else."

"To refuse such gifts means then this one just wants to fight." He Dog shook his head thoughtfully. "What does Spotted Elk hold against your son, Red Horse?"

"Nothing that I know of, except that he wants the woman."

"What will Eagle Wing do?"

"My son has said nothing. But, if Red Horse is killed, I know Eagle Wing. There will be much bloodshed."

Crazy Cat smiled. "Eagle Wing is a mighty warrior. Spotted Elk must want the girl really bad to risk his life in such a foolish way."

"I do not know this one's mind. Except, for some reason, he wants to fight Red Horse."

"If I were Red Horse, I would not give up the girl." Crazy Cat frowned. "It would cause him to lose face in front of the people."

"To carry the Lance without honor is to carry empty air in one's hand." He Dog agreed. "All we can do is wait and see what the old ones say tonight after the ceremony. We can do nothing more now."

Bright Moon summoned the three warriors to eat, and the subject was dropped. Crow Killer knew that tonight, after the ceremony, decisions and actions would have to be made. He knew Red Horse and Eagle Wing would not back down. They were too proud. And he did not think Red Horse would give up the woman, even if it meant he would lose his right to be a Lance Bearer.

The day passed slowly, and every thought was about what would happen after the ceremony. With the late evening, some anticipated the coming trouble with curiosity, while others dreaded it.

Now it was time. The village crier rode about the lodges on his horse, summoning the people to come to the great council fire that burned in the middle of the encampment. Hundreds of people found seats where they could watch as each young honoree was summoned forward to be celebrated in the traditional Lance Bearer Ceremony. Ten young men stood naked before the fire except for their breechcloth covering. Each of the young warriors was covered in his own color of medicine paint, a color that was shown to them in their vision quest. And each held a single Eagle or Hawk's Feather in his left hand.

All were slim, well-muscled, and stood proud and straight as an arrow. Red Horse was the oldest and the most heavily muscled of the young men. He was a magnificent-looking young man with long black hair falling across his broad, straight shoulders. Rippling powerful muscles and a flat stomach belied his young age. Scars of previous battles covered his smooth skin in places. The young women of the village looked at him in awe, and their eyes betrayed their admiration of the handsome warrior.

Ghost Man, the elder medicine man of the Arapaho, stood before the council of elders as they sat in an arc in front of the villagers. Wolf's Head, as Chief, sat in his place of honor before the elders, stoically watching the proceedings. One by one, the young men were positioned in their appointed places before the elders. Each warrior was called forward, his name was lifted up before the villagers, and the Lance, bearing his medicine helper carving, was presented to him. The Lances were beautifully engraved, painstakingly carved from the most beautiful of hardwoods.

As his name was called out, Red Horse stepped forward and received the coveted Lance with the carving of a horse head at the top. The horse's eyes were blood red and seemed to blaze as if they were alive as they stared out at the crowd. Red Horse had worked hard with Walking Horse as his mentor and was proud to receive the Lance. But he knew when the ceremony was finished, he would have to decide whether he wanted the beautiful carved Lance or Flower Leaf.

He saw the hateful eyes of Spotted Elk. When the ceremony ended, the warrior would demand that the woman be given over to him according to tribal dictates. If he fought Spotted Elk, Red Horse knew he risked death, but if he won and killed the warrior, he would lose the right to carry the honored Lance. But what choice did he have? If he declined to fight, everyone would think he feared the warrior and Red Horse would lose face. If he fought and killed Spotted Elk, he would lose his right to carry the Lance, and he would be shamed before the village.

Red Horse hefted the hard smooth shaft of the heavy Lance. It seemed to rest so easily in his hands. He thought of Walking

Horse and how proud he was to have earned the weapon with his tutorship. Now, he was about to be called upon and forced to shame the Society of the Lance Bearers by fighting another Lance Bearer, one who was the same as a brother. Looking across the fire to where his family stood proudly watching him, Red Horse looked into the eyes of his father, Crow Killer. What was this great warrior of the Arapaho trying to tell him?

Turning his gaze to Flower Leaf, he could see the worry in her beautiful eyes. He knew her thoughts already. He knew in her heart she would rather go and be the woman of Spotted Elk than chance Red Horse being killed.

All of the young men were turned and presented to the village as the newest of the Lance Bearers. For centuries, they had been the protectors of the people. After several minutes of listening to the screaming and adoring calls from the people, Ghost Man dismissed the young men and asked them to go to their families. Then, the medicine man raised his arms and pronounced it was time for the villagers to start the festivities and partake of the great mounds of cooking meat that had been laid out on the cooking frames.

Red Horse had moved to where Crow Killer, Bright Moon, and the others surrounded him. He was being congratulated by everyone when a thunderous roar went up before the elders and the medicine men. The voice of Spotted Elk boomed out threateningly, frightening the villagers, who pulled back and quieted. The warrior stood belligerently before the elders, completely covered in black war paint and brandishing the dreaded war lance of the mighty Lance Bearers.

Clad only in a loin cloth, the tall warrior glared down at the medicine man, Two Bears, and the seated elders.

"Give me your decision, old one." Spotted Elk pointed his lance menacingly. "Tell this insolent pup that the woman is mine by right."

"Put down your lance warrior." Wolf's Head stood up from

where he had been sitting. "Show respect to your Chief and your elders."

"The Great Wolf's Head, friend of Crow Killer and his whelp, Red Horse, speaks." The warrior's loud words rattled everyone's ears. "Have Two Bears give us his decision now, oh great Chief."

"You show no respect for your elders, warrior." The oldest of the medicine men stepped in front of the tall warrior. "I do not like these words I will speak. But I speak for the people and the Arapaho Law."

"Then speak, old man."

"Before I speak, I say this. Warriors of the Lance Bearer Society all know that to fight or to kill another Lance Bearer means you will be shunned from the Society and will live in shame, never to ride into battle again as a Lance Bearer."

"All Lance Bearers know this law, old man." Spotted Elk screamed so all could hear. "Speak!"

Two Bears glanced sadly to where Red Horse and Flower Leaf stood. "The captive woman known as Flower Leaf, the wife of our departed brother, Two Eyed Dog, is by law the property of Spotted Elk. This decision is mine alone. The elders have chosen to remain silent in this."

A jubilant yell went up from Spotted Elk and his followers as they all celebrated the decision. A sudden quietness crept over the shouting warriors as Red Horse's sharp-bladed bone-handled skinning knife stuck in the ground at Spotted Elk's feet. Staring down at the knife, the tall warrior grinned, then looked up at Red Horse and pressed the blade flat with his foot.

"This cannot be." Two Bears stepped in front of the people and held up his hand. "Don't do this thing. You both know the penalty."

"Be quiet, old man." Spotted Elk snarled. "You all see, I have been challenged. I must defend myself. I cannot lose my Lance for defending myself."

"Spotted Elk will not have any more use for his lance when

he is dead." Red Horse stepped forward onto the newly cleared ground in front of the elders and pushed his newly acquired Lance into the ground at Two Bears' feet. Seeing the beautiful Lance sticking in the ground, a sign of no retreat, the villagers let out a slow groan of despair. They all knew the son of Crow Killer, and they all loved him as a son of the people.

Flower Leaf lunged forward, trying to stop the fight, but was restrained by Bright Moon, Morning Dove, and Ellie. Struggling in their grasp, she begged Red Horse not to fight.

"I will go with Spotted Elk!" Flower Leaf screamed. "Please, Red Horse, do not fight him."

"The woman, Flower Leaf, speaks. The woman wants to be my woman." Spotted Elk leered over at Red Horse. "She wants a real man, not a mere boy."

Two Bears stepped between the two combatants and held up his hand to quiet the yelling people. "The Lance of Red Horse has bit into the mother earth. If no one will cut it free, the challenge must be finished."

"Move and let us fight, old man." Spotted Elk glared. "After I kill this one, then I, Spotted Elk, will cut the thong that holds his lance."

"If you two will not heed my words but demand to fight for the woman, then the fight will commence with the coming of the new sun."

"No!" Spotted Elk screamed out. "We will fight now. Then tonight, after I kill this dog, you will marry us. And I will celebrate with my woman and enjoy all the food the women have prepared."

Two Bears looked over at Red Horse and shook his head. "Do you agree, warrior?"

"I am ready, Grandfather. Turn this evil one loose."

Nodding, the old medicine man pointed at the lance of Spotted Elk. "By your actions here, you have forfeited your right to be a Lance Bearer. Cast your Lance into the fire now, or do not fight. You are no longer a Lance Bearer of the Society."

Spotted Elk shook his head. "No, I will not do this. After I kill this dog, the elders will decide the fate of my lance."

Red Horse pulled his war axe and faced Spotted Elk. "Let the big mouth keep his lance, Grandfather. It means nothing now. It will mean less when he no longer walks the land."

Eagle Wing handed Red Horse his own sharp skinning knife to replace the one at Spotted Elk's feet, then stepped back beside Crow Killer and Bright Moon. Placing his hand on Flower Leaf's shoulder, he shook his head to stop her from struggling. "Be still young one. Red Horse's mind must be on his enemy, not on you at this time."

As Two Bears and the elders moved away from the two combatants, Red Horse shifted his weight and faced the black-painted face of the tall warrior. Spotted Elk was a few inches taller than he was but not nearly as powerfully built. Muscles bunched in both fighters' bodies as they faced each other.

"Well, Young Doe, you might get your young man after all. He may be dead, but you'll get him." Pretty Eyes whispered as they watched the fighters face each other. "Red Horse has no chance against such a warrior as Spotted Elk."

"We will see." Young Doe's face was animated in anticipation of the fight. "I think you are wrong, Pretty Eyes. No, I won't get him, but he will live."

Spotted Elk brought first blood, and a yell went up from the people. A small trickle of red ran down the forearm of Red Horse as the snake-like strike of Spotted Elk's knife bit into his arm. Parrying blows, Red Horse jumped back as the taller warrior's long arms reached out with his sharp knife. Red Horse stayed out of reach of the flicking blade.

"You are very slow for a horse." Spotted Elk laughed as he lunged forward, his blade barely missing Red Horse's stomach.

The sound of their war axes banged and reverberated across the village as the two fighters lunged back and forth, trying to strike a killing blow. The fight raged back and forth as each fighter tried to kill the other with his blade. Red Horse smiled slightly as he noticed Spotted Elk was starting to open his mouth to bring in air. He knew that when a man started to tire while his opponent was still fresh, he would become afraid and make mistakes.

Spotted Elk was a Lance Bearer, which meant he was supposed to be brave, but that was all Red Horse knew of him. He hadn't ridden in battle with Spotted Elk as Eagle Wing had, so he knew nothing of the warrior's courage. Wanting the man to use more energy and sap his strength, Red Horse pushed forward harder, lunging back and forth out of reach of the warrior. Several small spots of blood appeared on each man's arms where the blades had bitten, but as yet, no serious wound had been inflicted on either fighter.

The heavy war axe of Spotted Elk began to droop, and his knife strikes started to slow as Red Horse darted forward then retreated back out of range of his opponent's dangerous knife. In a lightning-like rush, Red Horse sprang forward, leaving a long, shallow gash across the chest of the taller man.

Eagle Wing smiled as he looked over at Crow Killer. "Your son plays with Spotted Elk."

"Yes, I see. He could have opened up his stomach if he had wished."

"Spotted Elk is nothing, all mouth." Crazy Cat laughed.

Oliver watched the deadly fight intently. "Will Red Horse kill him?"

Crow Killer shook his head, relieved. "The warrior is already dead, but Red Horse will let him live, I think."

"What does Crow Killer mean?" Flower Leaf asked as the women released her.

"Red Horse will let him live if he drops his weapons, then Spotted Elk will have lost everything and be an outcast to his people."

"He would die before dishonoring himself." Flower Leaf

looked across at the bloody fighters. "I know this evil one."

"I do not think so, young one." Crow Killer nodded. "I think Spotted Elk would prefer life to death."

"That would make him a coward to the people."

"Well?" Bright Moon shrugged. "That is what this one is."

Red Horse moved in again and left a long slash across Spotted Elk's arm. Retreating quickly, he acquired a cut on his own forearm, but nothing serious. Looking down at his arm, he lifted his war axe and moved in for a killing blow, knowing he must end the fight quickly. The tiring warrior could get in a lucky blow at any moment. The time for playing was finished. Now was the time to finish the fight. Spotted Elk was a dead man unless he dropped his weapons.

Looking over at the bloody heaving chest of Spotted Elk, he flourished the heavy war axe. "The time has come, Spotted Elk. Drop your weapons now or meet your ancestors."

"This I cannot do." The words were hoarse. The warrior was exhausted, not used to fighting on the ground and using his legs as young Red Horse was. "I will never drop my weapons."

"Then, Spotted Elk, prepare yourself to go on the long journey." Red Horse pushed his heavy war axe and skinning knife forward and moved in deftly. About to lunge forward for the killing blow, Red Horse hesitated. He stopped his attack as the weapons of Spotted Elk fell to the ground.

Red Horse stepped forward triumphantly, placed his sharp skinning knife against Spotted Elk's bloody chest, and cut a thin line, causing more blood to flow. "Now, you will tell the people that you give up your claim to Flower Leaf."

Nodding weakly, Spotted Elk looked shame-faced down at the ground. "I give up my claim."

Pointing at the skinning knife he had thrown at Spotted Elk's feet, Red Horse waited as the warrior picked it up and handed it to him.

"Wipe the dirt from it." Red Horse took the cleaned weapon

and then pointed for the warrior to leave. "Walk away in shame, a warrior with no Lance."

"Wait." Two Bears walked to where the defeated warrior stood. "Spotted Elk must first throw his lance into the flames. Then he will leave the village in shame."

Red Horse watched as Spotted Elk laid his lance on the burning flames and turned away shame-faced. He shook his head to see a fellow Lance Bearer in such disgrace. "This fight was all for nothing."

"Not for nothing, Red Horse. Pick up your lance." Two Bears cut the rawhide thong, binding the lance to the warrior. "The elders will agree you did not want this fight with another Lance Bearer. The fight was pushed on you, and still, you did not kill him."

Red Horse smiled tiredly. "Then, Grandfather, am I still a Lance Bearer of the people?"

"And you will be a great Lance Bearer. Walking Horse, our beloved Chief, would be proud of you this day."

Red Horse retrieved his lance, wiped the beautiful red horse head clean, and raised it to the cheering people of the Arapaho.

CHAPTER 3

TWO DAYS AFTER THE FIGHT with Spotted Elk, Two Bears performed the marriage of Flower Leaf and Red Horse. Afterward, they held the naming of Eagle Wing's small son. Soon, the people who had come for the celebrations packed up and departed to journey back to their own lands. The teeming Arapaho village was once again left with only its own villagers.

He Dog and his warriors left, too, after sitting in council with Crow Killer and Eagle Wing. Crow Killer had spoken of his concern for the safety of the Cheyenne People. The pony soldiers knew the Cheyenne had participated in the battle of the Greasy Grass against Custer. He figured they would soon ride against the closer villages and take their revenge. He Dog listened and heeded the words of caution. He understood how relentless and dangerous the Long Knives were. Promising he would move his village deeper into the forested mountains, He Dog said a solemn goodbye to his sister. Parting that day had been deeply sad for Bright Moon and He Dog. Crow Killer knew this might be the last time he would see his friends and relatives riding as free men, masters of their own fate.

Shaking hands with Wolf's Head as they prepared to leave the village, Crow Killer declined the escort the Chief offered. If possible, he intended to visit the Crow Village of Red Hawk while he was this far south. Wolf's Head had warned him that crossing

Crow lands could be dangerous. The younger Crow Warriors were hot-headed and eager to show their bravery against anyone who crossed their lands. And now, some were armed with powerful rifles the whites had given them.

"I know that Red Hawk is your brother," the Chief argued, his voice marked with concern. "But these young Crow Warriors have grown bolder since Custer's defeat. They believe the pony soldiers will soon invade our lands, and now, armed with rifles, they are ready to fight against us."

"Thank you, my friend." Crow Killer took the Chief's extended hand. "We will be safe in Red Hawk's Village. His warriors would not dare challenge his words."

"I did not think they would dare to go against his word and raid our lands, yet they have."

"I will speak to Red Hawk. If Wolf's Head needs us, send word."

"Thank you, Crow Killer."

Eagle Wing sat his horse beside Broken Leg as the small column started from the village. "Have you heard anything of Spotted Elk since he left the village?"

"No, my friend, we have heard nothing. Be careful and watch for him on your journey home." Broken Leg frowned. "He has lost everything. Be on guard for him to strike. He hates Red Horse, and he wants Flower Leaf. Spotted Elk will seek revenge on them and anyone who helps them, and I think he knows where the valley of Crow Killer lays."

"How many ride with him?"

"His youngest brother, Bold Knob, and maybe ten others with their women." Broken Leg shook his head. "Not many, but it only takes one to kill you."

"Yes, my friend. It only takes one."

"The times have changed." Broken Leg frowned thoughtfully. "Now, we are no longer safe in our own lands. We were once mighty. Now, we must watch over our lodges like a dog over a bone."

Eagle Wing's horse stamped impatiently. "Yes, my friend. The whites have changed everything. Long Hair Custer may have lost the battle, but in a way, he has won. He turned the white eyes against the people."

Broken Leg stared off into the distance. "The medicine men and elders speak of this in council. They no longer see our future in this new world that is coming against us."

Eagle Wing shook his head sadly. "When will you and Grass Bee be married?"

"Soon." Broken Leg smiled. "She asked for a short time to prepare, and I will give her that time. She has been through much. She is a good woman, worth waiting for."

"Yes, my friend, she is." Eagle Wing clapped him on the shoulder. "If things get bad, you are welcome at my lodge. There you can live in peace."

"Maybe one day I will show up at Eagle Wing's lodge." Broken Leg frowned as Grass Bee left Bright Moon and Morning Dove's side and walked over to where they stood. "But first, I must see that the people are safely settled."

"You think the whites will try and move the Arapaho to a reservation?"

"The elders think so, and the ancient one, Two Bears, has seen this in his visions. I fear the time of our free-roaming people is soon to end."

"I am sorry for our people, Broken Leg." Eagle Wing shook hands with his old friend and turned his great Appaloosa stallion. "Remember, you are always welcome at my lodge."

"Thank you, my brother." Broken Leg waved. "Crazy Cat has spoken of a distant land, a hot land, where they have sent others."

"Yes, I have heard of this place." Eagle Wing shook his head sadly. "They call that land Oklahoma Territory."

As Crow Killer figured, several Crow riders were watching

them from the high banks when the small caravan stopped at the edge of the Yellowstone River. He raised his hand and waited. Then, seeing the young watchers wave back, summoning them across, he kicked his spotted horse into the warm water. The powerful horses swam easily across the wide river. Every horse except the horse carrying the baby's cradle board had no rider. All had slipped from their horse and hung onto the animal's mane, letting the powerful strokes of the animal carry them safely across.

Crow Killer rode dripping wet from the river and waited on the banks as the young Crow riders rode down to greet them. He studied the riders as they rode up, knowing by their thin frames that they were all youngsters and not of warrior age. As they neared the riders, Crow Killer greeted them, paying close attention to the young man who seemed to be the leader.

"You are Crow Killer?" the boy asked.

"You know me?"

"I have been told of you all my life." The youngster nodded slowly. "I am Little Tree, son of Red Hawk, your brother."

"Well, I'll be. Little Tree has grown much since I saw you last." Crow Killer smiled at the youngster. "Where is Red Hawk?"

"My father is there, camped up on the flats." The young one motioned towards the high banks. "He says I am to bring you to him."

"We will follow Little Tree."

The youngster studied the riders, letting his eyes rest for a minute on Red Horse. "This one is the warrior that fought with the warrior Spotted Elk over a woman?"

Crow Killer was shocked. "You know of this fight already?"

"The Crow know everything." Little Tree turned his horse. "Come, my father is anxious to see his brother."

"How old would this boy be now?" Bright Moon studied the dark back of the youngster.

"About fourteen, I would think." Crow Killer shook his head. "Time passes too quickly."

"How could the Crow know of the fight with Spotted Elk?"

"They probably had scouts watching the ceremony."

"Why would they do this?" Bright Moon questioned.

"Wolf's Head says the younger Crow warriors now have no fear." Crow Killer shrugged. "They keep a close eye on the Arapaho."

"This could be dangerous if they are discovered near the village."

"Very dangerous."

Red Hawk greeted the visitors with a shout as he and Ellie Medicine Thunder met them in front of a huge lodge. A young girl waited quietly beside her mother as Crow Killer dismounted and was greeted by Red Hawk. The Crow Chief had aged some but was still strong in appearance. The muscled frame carried the scars of battle but still showed the strength and vitality of his youth. The smooth face smiled as he greeted everyone and welcomed them to his lodge.

"I wanted to come to my brother's village before we rode on to our valley." Crow Killer took the extended hand. "Wolf's Head warned me of danger there."

"He is right. This is why I meet you here." Red Hawk shook his head sadly. "Crow Killer, my brother, would be safe from the older warriors, but the young ones cannot be trusted to show respect for my friend and his family."

"Would they dare disobey your words?" Crow Killer shook his head. "Is it that bad, my friend?"

The greying head shook slowly as he shook hands with the others. "I fear it is."

"I am sorry for both our peoples."

Red Hawk laughed. "Forgive me, I am not being a good host. We will speak of this later, but now we will sit and eat and talk about the better days of old."

All afternoon, the warriors sat around before a small fire and spoke of past adventures they had shared. Oliver was awed. He never had heard of the many battles Red Hawk and the Crow Killer had fought. He never realized how close these two great leaders were. Now, hearing their words and laughter, he understood. Only men who had lived through the dangers and adventures they had endured could become so close. He could see in their words and actions these two truly were brothers.

Alone here, with just their families, the women were allowed to take part in the talks. Bright Moon had been with her husband through many of these adventures, and she had heard of the rest. At first, she had disliked the haughty Crow Warrior known as Red Hawk, but over time he had also become like a brother to her. She remembered Little Antelope saying the same thing about the handsome warrior.

"Red Hawk is arrogant, he is haughty, and he is aggravating." She remembered Little Antelope saying as she talked about Red Hawk. "But he is a proud, brave, man and we are lucky to have him as a friend."

Bright Moon knew Red Hawk was all of these things, but she also knew if he was your friend, he would willingly die for you. He had proven this numerous times over the years when he helped Crow Killer through his many perilous adventures. Risking his own life, he had rescued Little Antelope from enemy warriors on two occasions.

She watched quietly as the two warriors talked. She could see the deep respect they had for each other. Taking her son's baby, she handed him to Red Hawk. Red Hawk looked down into the little one's face and smiled. "He looks like his Father."

"He'd better." Morning Dove laughed as Red Hawk held the baby over his head. "After all the pain he caused getting here."

"What is he called?"

"The medicine man Two Bears gave him his baby name." Morning Dove smiled at the small black-haired baby. "Porcupine."

"What kind of a name is Porcupine?" Red Hawk grinned.

"Look at the way his hair sticks up like Porcupine quills." Red Horse laughed. "It is a good name, I think."

"Oh, but he is so pretty." Morning Dove laughed at the way Red Hawk was holding the little one.

Red Horse smiled. "A mother always thinks their baby is the prettiest."

"Hush, Red Horse, or I will stick you with a real porcupine quill." Morning Dove glared at her brother-in-law.

Red Hawk nodded as the baby's small black eyes stared brightly up at him. "This one will be a strong warrior. His eyes stare boldly into mine."

Lowering the little one, Red Hawk looked over to where Eagle Wing and Red Horse were sitting. "My nephews have grown into magnificent warriors. Has Eagle Wing recovered from his fight with Strong Otter on the Blue?"

"I have, Uncle."

Crow Killer took the baby from Red Hawk and handed him back to Morning Dove. "Tell me, brother, was it really too dangerous for us to ride into your village?"

Staring into the fire, Red Hawk shook his head sadly. "Times have changed since the defeat of Long Hair Custer."

"How is that?"

"My young warriors do not listen to my words as they once did." The Chief nodded. "They now listen to their new friends among the Pawnee."

"This is a very bad thing."

"Very bad."

"Wolf's Head say they raid the Arapaho horse herds."

"I have told them not to do this thing, but like I said, the young Pawnee hotheads tell them how weak the Arapaho have become."

"You know the Arapaho are not weak, my brother." Crow Killer shook his head. "They will fight if they have to, and if this happens, many will surely die."

"Yes, the Lance Bearers are great warriors. I have ridden many times into battle with the Arapaho. But sometimes, the young ones have to find out the hard way. I fear this is what will happen."

"Can't you stop it?"

"I have spoken, and the elders and the medicine men have spoken against this foolishness." Red Hawk shrugged. "But our young men are eager for battle, eager to count coup. They know nothing of death."

"The day of the true warrior, true honor, and true dignity is finished."

"I have spoken these same words to them."

"But your young men won't listen?"

"The whites that trade for our furs tell them how strong they are and give them the firewater that makes them crazy."

Crow Killer's shoulders heaved wearily. "Trying to provoke a fight."

"Yes." Red Hawk nodded. "The whites want to start trouble, so the pony soldiers will move the hostile tribes onto reservations."

"If any Arapaho are killed, then I fear Wolf's Head will ride against the Crow." Crow Killer thought of the young Chief's words as they were leaving. "But he does not want this."

"I know it is only the fear of bringing the pony soldiers against his people that keeps Wolf's Head from riding against the Pawnee now." Red Hawk shrugged. "Many times, they have stolen his horses and threatened his young hunters."

"Yes, he waits, but do not be deceived. His fear is only for his people."

"I know this."

For two days, Crow Killer and Red Hawk sat about the small camp on the Yellowstone, talking of bygone days. Eagle Wing, Oliver, Red Horse, and Little Tree hunted the banks of the river for the elusive deer that grazed its banks. The camp was small, but it still took several deer to keep the cooking pots full. Early on the morning of the third day, as Bright Moon boiled the much-desired white man's coffee over the small blaze, a lone rider was spotted coming across the flat lands at a fast pace. The rider was coming too fast. Something was wrong.

Sliding to a hard stop, the rider slid from his horse almost into Red Hawk's lap. "What is wrong, Yellow Moon?"

Handing a rolled-up parchment wrapped in oilskins to Red Hawk, the warrior stepped back. "A Pawnee rider for the whites has brought this for the eyes of Crow Killer."

After studying the parchment for several seconds, Red Hawk passed the parchment to Crow Killer. Unrolling it, he read the white man's writing and then slowly rerolled it. "I thank my friend Yellow Moon for bringing the white man's words."

"I have done this for you, Crow Killer. You are still a good friend of the Crow People."

"Thank you, my friend."

"The one who brought the message rests in my lodge. Do you want to send a reply?"

"No, I will reply to the message when I return to my lodge."

"I will tell the Pawnee this." Yellow Moon swung upon his horse. "Does my Chief need me?"

"No, Yellow Moon. Do you need a fresh horse?"

"No, I will ride this horse slowly back to our village."

Watching the warrior ride away, Crow Killer turned to where Eagle Wing waited. "Prepare the animals. We leave as soon as we have eaten."

"Is there something wrong, my father?" Red Horse glanced at the parchment.

"The message is from General Crook. One of his sub-chiefs waits for Eagle Wing at Bridger. He wants him to come as soon as he can."

"Who sent the paper?" Oliver questioned.

Crow Killer looked down at the rolled parchment. "The

signature on the paper is General Crook's."

Red Hawk shook his head. "The whites know Eagle Wing fought with Gall and Crazy Horse on the Missouri. They know he killed a white scout in the battle. Perhaps it is a trap."

"I don't think this is a trap." Crow Killer unconsciously tapped the parchment. "No, I don't think it is."

Oliver was doubtful. "Then what do the whites want with Eagle Wing?"

"We won't know until we ride to Bridger." Crow Killer finished his coffee and handed the cup to Ellie Medicine Thunder. "We must go. This message says Crook wants us there as soon as possible."

"It is always urgent if the whites want something, my friend." Red Hawk took Crow Killer's arm. "Use caution. Be wily as the fox. If you need me, send word."

Crow Killer met Red Hawk's steady gaze with a grateful smile. "I will do this, my brother."

"You will ride with Eagle Wing on to Bridger after you return your people to the valley?"

"Yes, with all haste."

"I don't trust the white man, any white man." Red Hawk walked with him as the horses were led forward. "They only think of their own people."

"I have heard this General Crook wants only good for all of us, red and white."

"Crook is white."

"Does my brother forget I am white?"

"You are Crow Killer. My father loved you as one of his own." Red Hawk shook his head. "Your skin is partly white, but your heart is red."

"As I loved him, but I am still white." Crow Killer smiled.

"No, my brother. In your heart, you are as red as I am."

Crow Killer pushed the horses hard to reach the big river, riding down into his beloved valley as fast as the baby and women could travel. The parchment in his hunting pouch bothered him.

What could possibly be so important for Crook himself to ask for an urgent meeting with Eagle Wing? Crow Killer doubted it was a trick of any kind. If the Army wanted to capture Eagle Wing, someone at Bridger could tell them how to find his valley. Still, Red Hawk's parting words bothered him. So many times, whites had lied and tried to destroy his family. He would ride into Bridger, but he would be wary at all times. Alex Caldwell, the old man who owned the store, and the blacksmith, Otis McGraw, were his good friends. He knew they would warn him of any treachery. At the first sign of danger, he would return to his valley.

Chalk Briggs stood in the yard of the cabin as they splashed across the small creek and rode up to the cabin. A huge smile crossed the old wagon master's face as they dismounted at the pole corral.

"I thought you would be gone much longer." Briggs helped Bright Moon from her horse. "It is good to see you."

"It is good to be home." Bright Moon thanked Briggs.

"What brings you back so soon?"

Crow Killer pulled the hackamore from his spotted horse and slapped him on the rump. "We've got business at Bridger."

"If it's business at Bridger bringing you home, it must be urgent."

"It is. We'll be riding out as soon as we change horses and grab a bite to eat."

"I'll put some grub on." Briggs turned for the cabin with the women and the baby.

Sitting around the outside oak table Crow Killer looked about the cabin and the herd of horses that grazed out on the flats. The little mule seemed even grayer in color than she had when they left. He knew it was only his imagination as they had only been gone from the valley a few days. Sipping on his coffee, he looked over at the baby in Bright Moon's arms.

"Chalk, I'll need you to help Red Horse look after the women while Eagle Wing and I ride to Bridger."

"I wanted to ride with you and see our old friend, Caldwell." Bright Moon frowned, disappointed. "It has been many moons since we saw him, and he is getting old."

"Fort Bridger is a far piece, woman." He knew she wanted to go with him because of the letter he carried. "You have come far, and you are tired. No, you will stay here. We will be riding fast over the mountains."

Oliver cleared his throat, trying to get his father-in-law's attention. "If you don't need us here any longer, Ellie and I need to be getting back to Baxter and our business."

"You go, Oliver. Thank you for going with us to the ceremony."

Oliver laughed. "We wouldn't have missed Red Horse becoming a Lance Bearer for anything."

"Yes, but the rest of it we could have done without." Ellie looked across at Red Horse. "Some people never change."

Briggs saw the look that passed between the siblings. "Did I miss something interesting again?"

"Nothing much." Ellie frowned. "Just Red Horse being Red Horse."

"That bad, huh?" Briggs chuckled.

"Almost."

Red Horse shook his head at his sister, then looked over at Crow Killer. "I will ride with you to Bridger."

"I think you should stay here with the women and help Chalk with the chores."

"Chores?" Red Horse knew it wasn't chores that his father spoke of. The letter the Pawnee had brought from Crook was suspicious. Not trusting the whites and why they had sent the message, he knew Crow Killer wanted him to remain behind and watch over the women and valley. "I will do as you ask."

Leaning from his bay horse to take the bag of dried meat Bright Moon handed up to him, Crow Killer pulled her up in his lap and kissed her. Looking about his beloved valley he lowered the beautiful woman back to the ground gently.

Looking over at Red Horse, he nodded slowly before turning his horse. "Stay alert, Red Horse, and don't get far from the cabin until we return." Crow Killer's words were hard. "Do not even hunt unless you run out of meat."

"We will." The young warrior nodded. "Don't worry for us. I will stay close and watch over the valley."

Eagle Wing looked down at his brother and Briggs. "Listen for the mule. Make sure you watch the passes."

"We'll be watchful. You can count on us." Briggs shook his head.

Red Horse knew Crow Killer was reminding him of the threat of Spotted Elk. The warrior hadn't been seen or heard of since his departure from the village after the fight. Spotted Elk was cunning and a dangerous warrior. No matter what he had done, he had been an Arapaho Lance Bearer, the most dangerous of all warriors. The warrior hated Red Horse, and it was doubtful he would easily forget about the embarrassment of being shunned from the village. The warrior knew where the valley of Crow killer was. He could come north into these lands for revenge. Or he could come from the south pass. One never knew what a man with such hatred was capable of doing.

CHAPTER 4

THE LONG TRAIL ACROSS THE MOUNTAINS and the fording of the Snake River at Black Horse Crossing had been uneventful. If he hadn't been preoccupied with the letter he carried, Crow Killer would have enjoyed his time on the trail with Eagle Wing. Neither man had spoken but a few words until the palisades of the old Fort came into view. Nothing had changed much. The stockade walls and gates looked older, turning grey with age, but the buildings were much the same as they were on his last trip to the fort.

Curious women stood in front of their lodges as he and Eagle Wing passed. None greeted them, but Crow Killer heard his name whispered as their horses slowly walked past. Most were Arickaree squaws. Some were from other tribes camped about the post. As they passed, Crow Killer looked closely for the lodge of the Silent One's mother, but he couldn't see it.

Their horses were tired from being ridden hard with little rest across the mountains. The paper he carried had asked Eagle Wing to come as quickly as possible on an urgent matter. From the valley, Crow Killer had pushed the horses much harder than he normally would as he was anxious to see what General Crook thought was so important. Crow Killer knew the Army, and anything that would cause the two-star pony soldier to send such a message had to be important. He wondered if Crook himself would be at the post.

The letter had requested only Eagle Wing's presence at the fort. Crow Killer, knowing how treacherous some whites were, wouldn't let him ride into the fort alone. Camped outside of Bridger were people from many tribes, mostly hostile Arickaree, and he was worried for his son's safety. Some Assiniboine, Blackfoot and Pawnee were also visible, but these tribes were here mostly to trade for the supplies they needed.

Passing through the gates, Crow Killer studied the hostile gaze of the fort loafers who idled their time away sitting alongside the stockade walls. Smoke floated over their heads from the rolled smokes that Bridger provided them from time to time. He wondered if these post loafers ever hunted or how they now lived. He knew Bridger was tight-fisted and wouldn't let them run up much of a tab for the things they needed. The women made buffalo robes and coats, but buffalo were becoming fewer in numbers now that white hunters were moving farther west and killing the shaggies for their valuable hides.

The great wagon trains still rolled past the fort, stopping to refill their supply wagons and rest their teams. Now that the tribes had been somewhat subjugated, there seemed to be an endless line of the large Conestoga wagons heading west. The Indian women camped outside Bridger sold their jerked meat, moccasins, and warm coats to the westbound settlers.

Dismounting at the dilapidated hitching post in front of the trader's store, Crow Killer was about to step upon the porch when the old trader, Alex Caldwell, stepped through the door.

"Jedidiah Bracket, is that you in the flesh, you old reprobate?" The trader was elated to see his old friend. "And Eagle Wing, it's good to see you both."

"It's us, alright, Alex."

"Sakes alive. Let us take a good look at you." The store man smiled. "You've rode a far piece and mighty fast by the looks of you and your critters."

"We have." Crow Killer patted his horse's neck. "We're pert near done in."

"What brings you here so fast? Is it trouble?"

"Don't know for sure. I got this dispatch from the pony soldiers." Crow Killer reached for the parchment in his bag. "That is to say, Eagle Wing did."

"Who sent you the paper?" Caldwell eyed the rolled-up oil skin skeptically.

"The Pawnee that brought it said it came from General Crook himself."

"You don't say?" Caldwell scratched his head. "Weren't aware y'all were on speaking terms with the Pawnee?"

"We ain't." Crow Killer shook his head. "But I reckon they scout for Crook and do his bidding. Anyways, one of them brought this paper to Red Hawk's Village."

"And you happened to be there?"

"We'd been attending the Lance Bearer Ceremony."

"That's right. It is that time of year."

"Yes. It is always in the time of the brown grass moon, before the meat taking time, and the cold days arrive."

"I'm surprised Red Hawk attended this year." Caldwell nodded. "I hear the Crow and Arapaho Warriors have had trouble."

"You have big ears, Alex."

"No, sir. Jim does." Alex grinned. "His eyesight is failing, you know? But there ain't a thing wrong with his ears."

"I didn't know Bridger was having eye trouble." Crow Killer frowned. "I'm sorry. In the shining times, him and ole Lige Hatcher were the greatest of mountain men."

"Those two were a pair, alright." Caldwell smiled. "They danced with the devil and seen the elephant."

"What's an elephant, Alex?" Eagle Wing didn't know the word.

"Just never you mind, young man." Caldwell laughed and winked at Crow Killer. "Your pappy and old Red Hawk had their days, too. If'n I remember rightly."

Crow Killer cleared his throat, tapped the parchment, and frowned at Caldwell.

"Important, huh?" Alex looked curiously at the paper and nodded. "Never knew the great Crow Killer to pay much attention to anything the white man thought was important."

"Usually, I don't, but somehow this seemed different." Crow Killer glanced over at Eagle Wing."

Caldwell motioned for a young Indian and told him to take the worn-out horses over to the blacksmith shop. "Tell McGraw to tend to them, then come over here."

"We could have done that, Alex."

"Nonsense. You're my guest." Caldwell turned for the doorway. "Let's go inside and get you some refreshments."

Crow Killer hesitated, gripping the letter. "This may be important, Alex. Is General Crook here?"

"No, not the General, but his man is." Alex stuck his chin out. "He's been here for most of a month now."

"Only his man? This paper said the General himself would be here." Crow Killer glanced about the old store. "That's why I come on the run."

"Reckon, you'll have to talk with his man." Caldwell placed glasses on the counter and filled them up with spring water. "I'll have the women put on some buffalo hump for you."

"Thank you, my friend. We could use a feed, alright."

"Yep, a high-falluting Army Captain from Crook is over there in his room." Caldwell motioned in sign language at an Indian girl, then turned back. "I don't like it at all."

"What don't you like, old friend?"

"I don't know what that letter of yours is all about, but I don't like anything about this Captain that Crook has sent." He set the bottle down with a hard plunk. "Nothing."

"How so?"

"His eyes. He's the shifty-eyed sort. Can't look at a man without acting like the cat that ate the canary. No sir, I don't cotton to him at all."

Crow Killer smiled at the old man. "Well, Alex, we can't all be perfect, can we?"

"Reckon we can't. Tell me, how are my girls?" Caldwell looked towards the back door expectantly. "Why ain't they here with you?"

"They wanted to come see you." Crow Killer sat down tiredly. "But we rode a long way fast, and they were just too exhausted to come any further.

Eagle Wing sipped on his water and lowered his cup. "And the baby is still too small to make such a journey?"

Caldwell turned his head. "What baby?"

"I have a son, Mister Caldwell." Eagle Wing smiled.

"Well, I'll be dog-gone." Caldwell lifted a glass and smiled. "Seems like only yesterday you were just a yonker yourself. Congratulations, Eagle Wing."

"Thank you."

"But that ain't your only reason for leaving them in your valley, is it?" Alex could tell Bracket had another reason. "You smell something and didn't want them here this time. Under these circumstances, I don't blame you nary a bit. No, siree, not one bit."

Crow Killer had hardly taken one bite of his buffalo tongue when heavy boots sounded on the back porch, and the old door creaked open. The dark woolen uniform and the bars on the shoulders identified the man standing in the doorway as an Army officer. The man stood ramrod straight as he stared across at the two Indians sitting at the table.

Crow Killer could tell the Army man was surprised. No doubt, he expected to find a white man, but instead, he found two Arapaho Warriors staring up at him.

Caldwell seemed tickled at the Captain's surprise. "Captain, let me present you to Jedidiah Bracket and his son Eagle Wing." He gestured gentlemanly-like at Crow Killer, then back at the Captain. "This here be Captain William Lawrence, sent here by General Crook himself."

Crow Killer had to hold back a grin as the officer looked them up and down. He could tell the man was definitely surprised to find two long-haired warriors dressed in leather britches and deer hide vests decorated with porcupine quills, and wearing moccasins on their feet. Abruptly, the blond-headed officer snapped to attention and nodded sharply. That surprised Crow Killer. He didn't know whether he was supposed to salute or bow.

"Captain William Lawrence at your service, uh, sir." Lawrence seemed to gag on the words. "You are Eagle Wing the Arapaho?"

"He is." Crow Killer stood up slowly.

The man looked back and forth at the two, confused. "Then, you are?"

"Jedidiah Bracket, Eagle Wing's father." Jed nodded slowly. "Some call me Crow Killer, but whites call me Jedidiah Bracket."

"Oh yes, Jedidiah Bracket. I've heard the name many times." Lawrence nodded. "I believe you've met the General once before?"

"Yes, once years ago back in St. Joe, Missouri."

"And this man, uh, warrior, is Eagle Wing?" Lawrence studied the two men. "His reputation proceeds him, sir. A deadly fighter, I've been told. But you, I was told you were white?"

"Yes, I'm white. But I am also what you people back east call a squaw man, Captain. I have lived with the Arapaho many years." Crow Killer shrugged. "But we are civilized, at least, I am. Can't speak for my son."

"Yes." Lawrence cleared his throat. "As I said, your son's reputation is well known to General Crook."

Crow Killer presented the rolled parchment. "This paper says General Crook wanted me here quick."

Lawrence looked over where Caldwell was standing and shook his head. "Perhaps we should talk in private."

Crow Killer laughed lightly. "Captain, Mister Caldwell here probably already knows what you want with my son. But if you want to talk private-like, let's go find us a shade tree and get to it."

"Y'all just do your talking right here. I've got work to do in the front." Caldwell started from the room but stopped and turned. "Mister Army man, I've known Jedidiah Bracket for many a year. He's one of the most honest men I've ever known. If you're smart, you'll respect his word as gospel."

"Is that right, Mister Caldwell?"

"That's right, Mister Army man." Caldwell stomped away.

"I didn't mean to hurt the old man's feelings, but the General said to keep this between us for now."

"You'll find nothing stays secret for long out here, Captain Lawrence." Crow Killer sat back down at the table. "You hungry?"

"No, thank you."

"Alex's squaws cook up some good buffalo tongue."

Lawrence frowned. "I know; I've been eating on it for a month now. But thank you, I'm not hungry."

"Well, Captain, we rode many days to get here. So why don't you spit it out while we eat." Crow Killer cut into his steak. "What does the general want from my son?"

"General Crook has a proposition for Eagle Wing." Lawrence sat down at the table uncomfortably. "This proposition will benefit the hostiles that you think so much of."

"And what hostiles would that be?"

"If my information is correct." Lawrence pulled out a piece of paper. "You live with the hostile Southern Arapaho under a Chief Wolf's Head camped on the upper Yellowstone River."

"Not camped, sir. They have lived there for years."

"No matter. At this time, they are considered hostile by the war department." Lawrence laid out a large flat envelope. "They may not live there for much longer unless, of course, we can come to an understanding."

"So, the war department intends to place them on a reservation somewhere?" Crow Killer looked over at the paper the man held. "Tell me, what terms would these be exactly?"

"They will be sent to Oklahoma Territory in the near future unless you agree to do a service for General Crook and the Army."

"Oklahoma!" Crow Killer looked up. "That's a long way from the Yellowstone Country."

"Unless you see fit to cooperate, that's where they're headed after we get Crazy Horse and his bunch corralled." Lawrence nodded smugly. "Some of the Southern Cheyenne have already been headed that way."

"You mean herded, don't you?" Eagle Wing frowned.

Crow Killer thought of He Dog and his people. "Not all of them?"

"No, not all of them yet." Lawrence frowned. "In another few days, the Army will be scouring Wyoming and Montana Territory for every hostile they can find."

"You enjoy displacing people, Captain?"

"I enjoy displacing murdering hostiles, sir."

"You're referring to Custer, I presume?"

"Custer was a great man, a great fighter." The Captain shook his head. "They cut him and his men to pieces."

"Well, I reckon that depends on who you ask." Crow Killer nodded slowly. "Seems like he came looking for that little fight."

"Two hundred fifty men butchered." Lawrence glared across the table. "That, sir, is how I look at it."

"They were all full-grown men."

"I'll not bandy words with you, Mister Bracket." Lawrence unfolded the paper he held. "If you agree to work with the General on this, I think you and your friends will be nicely compensated."

"That's a big word for us heathens: compensated. Tell me exactly, Captain, what does the general want from us?"

Lawrence poured himself a shot of whiskey from a dusty

trade bottle and swirled the glass in his hand. "I understand your son, Eagle Wing, knows Gall and Crazy Horse? He fought with them on the Missouri."

Hesitating, Eagle Wing looked down at the paper for several seconds. "I know Chief Gall and Chief Crazy Horse."

"Admit it, Mister, you fought with him on the Missouri two years or so back." Lawrence glared hard at Eagle Wing. "We know you killed a scout named Howard, who was leading the horse soldiers in that fight at Skull Canyon."

"I told you, pony soldier, I know Chief Gall."

"Do you know Gall has retreated into Canada with Sitting Bull and his people?"

"No, we have not heard this." Crow Killer shrugged. "We stay in our valley for the most part."

"That is unless you're out killing white scouts?" Lawrence sipped the whiskey. "Isn't that right?"

"Tell us what you want, white eye." Eagle Wing stared hard across the table.

"Your answer is as I expected. I guess you don't know where the great Crazy Horse is hiding either?"

"This is not getting us anywhere, Captain." Crow Killer held up his hand. "Tell me, what exactly does your General want from my son?"

Lawrence pushed the wrinkled envelope across to Crow Killer and waited as he read it. "I guess you can read Mister Bracket?"

Crow Killer ignored the question and read the document carefully. "Is this true what this paper says, Captain?"

"It's true enough." The man tasted the whiskey again and made a face. "It is against my wishes, but if you'll help the Army, the General will try to help you in return."

"What does Chief Gall have that is so valuable to the Army?"

"We have been informed that he has Custer's saddlebags containing a book with some papers and orders, that sort of thing.

Plus, a few of his personal items that Mrs. Custer would like to have returned."

"Mrs. Custer wants them?" Crow Killer stared hard at Captain Lawrence. "Or General Crook?"

"This book holds orders about the battle, maybe?" Eagle Wing asked with a knowing smile. "Could it be that what is in these papers will embarrass some white eye?"

Lawrence shrugged. "Let's just say it would be problematic if it should fall into the wrong hands."

"How would Gall know what he has is valuable?" Eagle Wing shook his head. "The Chief can't read or even speak English."

"There are missionaries up north, you know." Lawrence bristled. "Gall may be a heathen, sir, but he is also a smart man. He defeated Custer and the U.S. Army in open battle. For some reason, he didn't destroy this book before he had someone tell him what it contained."

"And you are saying if my son gets this book for you, Wolf's Head and his people will be given their own reservation when they come in?"

"Yes, sir. You have the General's word."

Crow Killer slowly re-read the paper. "I want it in writing, not just his word."

"The General anticipated you might." Lawrence produced a flat sheet of paper and presented it across the table. "When you get me the book, or, I should say, Custer's diary, the treaty lying before you will be honored."

"Are you certain of this, Captain?"

"You have the General's word, and this treaty signed by him has several very important witness signatures on it."

"It doesn't say where this reservation will be."

"It says on or near the Yellowstone, in Wyoming Territory."

"That's a pretty big piece of ground you speak of." Eagle Wing shrugged.

"You can pick any ground you want within reason."

Lawrence grinned. "Yes, it is a big territory."

"I understand the Crow have been given a reservation near the Big Horn River in Montana Territory?"

"They haven't been relocated there yet." Lawrence seemed surprised Crow Killer would know this. "Who told you this?"

Crow Killer ignored the question. "So, if my son gets Custer's book for General Crook, will the Arapaho people be guaranteed these lands?"

"Let's first wait and see if he gets the book."

Eagle Wing placed his finger on the paper. "Chief Gall isn't going to just give me this book you want. The Arapaho aren't his concern. What does Crook have that Gall would be willing to trade it for?"

"Were you at the battle of the Little Big Horn last summer?" Lawrence sneered directly at Eagle Wing. "Tell me the truth, mister. It's not you we're after."

"No. He was not there." Crow Killer glared at him. "We didn't even know a battle had been fought for several moons."

"Moons?" Lawrence shook his head. "Speak English, man."

"Months, white eye."

"I didn't think you'd own up to being there."

Eagle Wing started to rise. "I do not speak with a forked tongue, pony soldier. I am not like some whites. Do not call me a liar."

"Alright." Lawrence stood and stepped back after noticing Eagle Wing's dark hand move near the long skinning knife at the warrior's side. "Alright, you weren't there." He'd heard tales of this one, how he had killed the white scout, Howard. This warrior was not one to push too far. "Gall lost all of his family, his wives, children, everything in the battle."

"What does he wish to trade for?" Crow Killer repeated. "Tell us, Captain."

"We have a captive."

"A captive?" Eagle Wing tilted his head and squinted at the

white eye Captain.

"Yes. The Pawnee took Gall's daughter, Blue Feather, captive during the battle." Lawrence swallowed as Eagle Wing set back down and relaxed. "We were able to trade her from the Pawnee. She was wounded, but now she is fine. Now, we have her, and our scouts informed Gall she still lives."

"Blue Feather." Eagle Wing nodded. He remembered the pretty little girl.

"Turns out he wants his daughter back." Lawrence shrugged. "You might say she is his only living kin."

Crow Killer didn't understand the white eye's indifference. "Wouldn't you want your daughter back, Captain?"

He waved the question away. "Yes, if she was the captive of hostile savages."

"Who holds her captive?" Eagle Wing asked.

"Bull Coat, the Pawnee."

"That devil." Crow Killer leaned back and shook his head. "He's the meanest warrior of the Pawnee."

"You are sure it is Blue Feather?" Eagle Wing looked over at Lawrence. "The pretty one?"

"The Pawnee say it is Blue Feather." Lawrence grinned smugly. "Gall spoke with our scouts and said he will trade the diary and Custer's saddlebags for her."

Crow Killer shook his head and looked over at Eagle Wing. "Do you know this girl?"

"I know her."

"You would recognize her?" Lawrence questioned Eagle Wing. "If she were standing here?"

"Yes, she is tall and very pretty. Her mother was Gall's third wife, the aunt of my woman."

"Gall's woman was Cheyenne?" Crow Killer blinked. "I did not know this."

"Yes."

"I don't care what breed of Injun she is as long as she is truly

Gall's daughter." Lawrence shook his head. "You must be sure."

"I won't know this for sure until I see her."

"I will bring her here to Bridger in the morning."

"Bring her." Eagle Wing shrugged. "I will see this girl."

"Then, do we have a deal, Mister Bracket? Your son will get the book for the General in exchange for this girl?"

"General Crook must want this book very badly to go to so much trouble?"

"He does. Do we have a deal?"

"Where is Gall now?"

"Our scouts report he is with Sitting Bull at a place called Wood Mountain in Saskatchewan Territory. That'll be Canada."

"I know where that is." Crow Killer tried not to glare at the white eye. "Will he come here for her?"

"No. He knows the Army patrols the boundary line looking for hostiles." Lawrence shook his head. "We must take the girl to him."

"We? That'll be a mighty long ride across Montana Territory."

"And Wyoming, sir, don't forget Wyoming." Lawrence looked down at the table. "Close to six or maybe eight hundred miles, I would guess."

Eagle Wing looked across at Crow Killer. "That will take at least two moons there and two moons back. That is if there are no problems."

"If we get it, where do we bring the book and saddlebags?"

"Fort Robinson."

"Tell me, Captain, do you plan to ride with us on this trail?" Crow Killer studied the tall white.

"No, Mister Bracket. The Army has more important things for me to do."

"No, huh?" Crow Killer crossed his arms. "You know Robinson will add at least another full moon riding back here."

"The cold times come soon." Eagle Wing spoke up. "If we

get caught in the storms, it will slow us down even more."

Lawrence shook his head. "It is mid-summer now. You have plenty of time to cross into Canada and get back before the snow flies."

"And if the snow comes early as it sometimes does?" Eagle Wing studied the treaty paper. "And we don't get back before bad storms come?"

"Just get the book, Mister Bracket." Lawrence shook his head. "And don't let anyone get their hands on it. Do you understand? No one!"

Crow Killer looked again at the paper, studying the layout of the reservation lands. The whites had already divided the lands up like they were cutting a piece of cake. He knew the Captain did not lie about sending the tribes to the hot lands of Oklahoma. This might be the only chance the Arapaho people had of staying in their homelands in the north.

"This will be a long trail, Captain." Crow Killer rubbed his face. "Will the Arapaho be left in peace until we return?"

"I guarantee it, even if I have to send troops to watch over them." Lawrence nodded. "The Arapaho will be safe."

"Where is the girl?"

"Close by and in good health."

"I will speak to my son and give you my answer tonight."

"I will be waiting in my quarters." Lawrence turned and then stopped. "Just you remember, Gall has made it very clear that he will only give the book to Eagle Wing. If and when your son brings the girl."

"We heard you plain enough, Captain."

Crow Killer walked with Eagle Wing over to McGraw's to check on the horses. Each knew what the other was thinking as they crossed the compound. If they agreed to Lawrence's proposition, this would keep them away from their families for many moons. The cold times were coming as the meat-taking times were. The old blacksmith McGraw met them at the corrals with a huge smile across his face.

"It's good to see the great Crow Killer and his son again." McGraw laughed as he shook their hands. "Did old Chalk make it to your valley in one piece?"

"He did for a fact." Crow Killer nodded as he looked into the corral at his horses. "He's gonna be staying with us from now on."

"Have you met with that sassy Army gent yet?"

"We have."

"Are you going to work for him?"

"Work? What work?" Crow Killer shook his head. There were definitely no secrets at Bridger.

"I weren't hatched yesterday, old son." McGraw laughed. "That Army feller has been here nigh on a month now. He wouldn't have stayed so long if he didn't want you for something. Something big, I'd say."

"Well, you're right. He wanted something, alright." Crow Killer admitted good-naturedly.

"Figured so." McGraw looked over at the corral. "Fed your nags, where's my mule?"

"I left her home, Otis. She's getting a mite old to be traipsing across the rough mountain trails anymore."

"Yeah, I reckon she is at that. I'll bet she's done turned herself snow white by now."

"She's getting there, alright. Ain't we all?" Crow Killer shook his head. "Otis, tell me something, old hoss."

"What?"

"Why did you always want that little mule so bad?"

McGraw laughed. "I wanted her, alright, but I wanted more to watch you squirm when you turned down five or six good horses for one bandy-legged little mule."

At that, Crow Killer had to grin. "Well, old son, I did have to give it some thought every time you offered so many horses for her."

A soft whistle and gesture from Eagle Wing brought the two men to the back corral. Standing at the rough-hewn pole fence, they looked to where Eagle Wing was pointing at a red roan horse with four stocking feet.

"What is it?" McGraw was curious about the way Eagle Wing was looking at the animal.

"Does my Father not remember this horse?" Eagle Wing pointed again.

"No. Should I?"

"It is the horse Spotted Elk was riding the day I fought Strong Otter on the Blue."

Looking closer, Crow Killer nodded. "It is the same animal. No other could be marked as he is."

Eagle Wing turned to where McGraw stood. "Where did you get that horse?"

The old blacksmith could see the seriousness in the young warrior's face. "I bought him and those other five from an Arapaho warrior two days ago. He said he needed money to buy supplies and cartridges for his rifle. Told me he was going hunting."

"He give you his name?" Crow Killer studied his friend intently.

"No." McGraw could see Eagle Wing and Crow Killer were agitated about something. "Why? Is there something wrong?"

"Tell me, Otis, what did this warrior look like?"

"I don't know, mostly like any other warrior, I reckon. No offense intended, Eagle Wing." McGraw rubbed his chin. "He was taller than most. Kinda slender but well-muscled. Arrogant customer, he was, though."

"Anything else you can tell us?"

"Well, for a young'un, when he dismounted and moved about, he acted like he was real sore or something."

"It was Spotted Elk." Eagle Wing shook his head. "Were any

others with this one?"

"None that I saw." McGraw shook his head. "He put the ponies in the corral, took his money and skedaddled."

"Where did he go?"

"Like I told you, he walked over to the sutler's store to get his supplies, I reckon." McGraw looked in the corral at the horses. "They are good-lookin' horses. He must have needed those supplies pretty bad."

"You say he left here on foot without a horse?" Crow Killer stared across the open grounds towards the store.

McGraw snapped his fingers. "By golly, come to think of it, I never thought of that. No Indian would sell all his horses and walk home on foot."

"Spotted Elk goes hunting all right." Eagle Wing shook his head. "He hunts for us and our valley."

"Come, Eagle Wing." Crow Killer gestured to his son. "We'll see you again before we leave, Otis."

"You need anything, you fellers just holler."

Crow Killer walked with Eagle Wing back to the trading post porch. "Stay here and wait for the Captain."

"Where are you going?"

"If it was Spotted Elk, we need to know where he headed or if he's still here at the post." Crow Killer frowned. "I know someone who just might tell us."

Eagle Wing frowned. "Red Horse should have killed this evil one, so we don't have to worry about him anymore."

"True, he should have killed Spotted Elk, but he didn't. I don't have the slightest idea what he's doing this far from Arapaho lands."

"He hunts Red Horse. What else would bring the disgraced one here to Bridger?"

"If it was him, I think you are right. He hunts for our valley and Red Horse. If so, I need to find out what direction he took."

Crow Killer walked to the front gates past the sitting warriors. He could feel their hostile eyes on his back as he passed. Here, on the grounds of the post on what Bridger considered his property, there was nothing to fear from the Arickaree. Bridger's word was law, but outside and away from the post, he knew they would attack him if they got the chance. There had been too much bad blood passed between the Arapaho and the Arickaree.

Searching out the small lodge of the Silent One's mother, Crow Killer walked amongst the many lodges that dotted the post grounds. Finally, down along a small creek, he located the small lodge he remembered by the lightning slash mark on the faded hides of the lodge.

Clearing his throat, he waited until the small woman appeared in the doorway. Her small frame was bowed, and she had aged more since he had seen her last. It had been only two summers, and the little squaw, even at that time, was old. The deep wrinkles in her withered face showed much age now, as did her thin frame.

"It is good to see the mother of the Silent One again." Crow Killer crossed his hands in respect. "How are you, little Mother?"

Outside in the afternoon sunlight, the old woman squinted, trying to adjust her eyes to the brilliant light. Then, recognizing Crow Killer, she grinned a toothless smile. "Is it truly you, Crow Killer, my son's friend?"

"Yes, it is me, Mother." Crow Killer smiled. "Am I welcome at your lodge?"

"The friend of my son is always welcome." The old one motioned for him to sit beside the lodge out of the sun. "You, too, are as a son to me."

"How have you been, Mother?"

"Life is good but fleeting, I fear."

Crow Killer smiled. "Do you have everything you need?"

"An old woman needs very little."

"But you do get whatever you ask for?"

"Yes, the store trader gives me anything I need." Her nod

was slow. "Thank you, Crow Killer. If not for you, I fear I would be a long time with my ancestors."

"You have many years left, young lady."

The smile came again. "You do not lie so well, my son."

"Tell me, Mother, have you seen any Arapaho Warriors ride this way the last few days?"

"These old eyes don't see very well anymore."

"Nothing?"

"I have seen no Arapaho Warriors pass by my lodge. As I say, these old eyes don't see so well anymore. But I will find out these things you ask and send word."

"Thank you, Mother." Crow Killer stood up. "I will be at the trader's store."

"When do you leave the fort?"

"I do not know, Mother, maybe soon."

"I will ask, then send word." The old head nodded. "Are these warriors friends or enemies of Crow Killer?"

"I fear they are not friends."

"But you are Arapaho."

"Yes, I am Arapaho." Crow Killer shook his head. "But they are not Arapaho any longer."

"I will let you know, my son."

"Thank you, Mother." Crow Killer smiled down at the old woman. "Go to the store man if you need anything."

Looking up, she smiled. "I have everything an old woman needs. I soon go to be with the Silent One."

He acknowledged the truth of her words with a solemn nod and an honoring glance. "You will be missed, little Mother."

"Goodbye, Crow Killer."

When he returned from the old woman's lodge, Crow Killer found Eagle Wing in the corral checking over their horses. He and Eagle Wing thought the same way. If it was Spotted Elk and he had left the post heading west, they would have to ride back to the valley with all haste. If the crazy outcast had ridden south, Red Horse would have to be warned of the warrior's presence in their mountains. Spotted Elk did not ride all this way to go hunting as he had told McGraw.

There was a chance Spotted Elk had only been purchasing supplies for the winter and shells needed to hunt deer and elk. Since he had been driven from the Arapaho Village, he and his followers were solely dependent on themselves to survive the cold times. Still, the thought of the dangerous warrior and his followers riding into his valley without warning bothered him. He would take no chances. Red Horse, Chalk Briggs, and the women would have to be warned of the warrior's presence this far to the north. Crow Killer was sure that until one of them was dead, bad blood would always exist between Red Horse and Spotted Elk. The hatred of the warrior would keep him seeking revenge. He wanted Flower Leaf and would kill anyone standing in his way to claim her.

"Did the old woman know anything?"

"No, she is old now. Her eyes see poorly." Crow Killer ran his hands over his tall bay horse, checking for any soreness. "She will send word when she hears anything."

"It doesn't matter." Eagle Wing shrugged. "One of us must ride back to the valley and warn the others."

"I will not let you ride to the north alone. It is far too dangerous a trail, and it is a long ride."

"Yes, it is a long trail," the warrior agreed. "But I do not fear Gall or his people."

"It is not Gall I worry about." Crow Killer looked over at Eagle Wing. "The white pony soldiers will be as thick as fleas on a dog between here and the Grandmother's Land. If you are spotted, they will only see an Indian."

"If we are to help the Arapaho people, one of us must go." Eagle Wing patted his Appaloosa. "And one of us must return to our lodge to give the warning."

"We could send a rider."

"Tell me, would my father really trust our people's lives with someone we don't know?"

"No."

"Gall knows me. He does not know you, only your name." Eagle Wing argued. "His people could kill you before they find out who you are."

"We will wait and see what the old woman learns."

"And we must also see if this girl is really Blue Feather."

Walking back to the post, they were both shocked to find Broken Leg and Black Bird standing in front of the trading post. Looking at each other, they hurried to where the two warriors were waiting.

"What do you do here, my brothers?" Eagle Wing was elated. "How did you get here?" Clasping each other's arms, the warriors laughed and smiled. They didn't notice the glares from the Arickaree men loafing about the stockade.

"Tell us why you are here." Crow Killer couldn't believe his eyes. "This is a good sign, an answer to my prayers."

Holding up his hand for silence, Broken Leg smiled. "Red Hawk sent word you were coming to Bridger's and asked us to meet him here."

"Red Hawk is coming to Bridger?" Crow Killer shook his head. "Why would he do that?"

"All we know is this is the word he sent." Black Bird looked around the post grounds. "He is not here?"

"No. We have only been here ourselves since this morning."

"If he told you to meet him here, he will come." Crow Killer frowned. Why would his friend make such a journey this far from his lands? Even for the great Red Hawk, this far north was a dangerous trail. Until the warrior arrived, he would have not only Red Horse and his valley to worry about but also his brother, Red Hawk.

"Look." Eagle Wing motioned towards the stockade gate.

"Pawnee Warriors bring the girl."

Crow Killer leaned close to his son. "Is it Blue Feather?"

"I cannot tell for sure at this distance." Eagle Wing studied the oncoming warriors. "I must wait until her face becomes clearer."

Captain Lawrence walked out of the store onto the porch beside the warriors. "There. They have brought the girl."

"We see that, white man." Eagle Wing glared at the Pawnee Warriors. "Stay close to your Pawnee Dogs, so there will be no trouble."

"I guarantee there will be no trouble unless the Arapaho start it." Lawrence studied Broken Leg and Black Bird. "I guess these are your reinforcements."

"You want the book back, Captain." Crow Killer frowned. "They are here to help."

"How many does it take to carry a small book back across a river?" Lawrence glared at the two Arapaho. Crow Killer could tell the Captain wasn't happy seeing the two mighty Lance Bearers here at Bridger's.

"It would depend on how heavy the book is, wouldn't it?" Eagle Wing shrugged.

"Mister Bracket, this is supposed to be a secret mission." Captain Lawrence raised his chin with a look of considerable irritation. "It was to be kept confidential between us, not told to the whole Arapaho tribe."

"I figure it is confidential, as you say, Captain." Crow Killer smiled. "I don't believe these warriors can read."

Lawrence turned red in the face. He stomped away, motioning for the mounted Pawnee riders to follow him behind the store. Crow Killer and Eagle Wing moved quietly through the breezeway, leaving Broken Leg and Black Bird waiting in front of the store.

CHAPTER 5

CROW KILLER STEPPED IN FRONT of Eagle Wing as the Captain and one of the Pawnee Warriors walked through the back door of the kitchen post with the girl between them. One Pawnee shoved the girl roughly ahead of him, but the girl refused to raise her head and jerked away as the warrior tried to force her to show her face. Crow Killer took a deep breath to quiet his anger. There was no doubt she had been treated badly as a captive. Her clothes were as filthy as her face, and she stared down at the floor sullenly.

"Well, Mister Bracket." Lawrence pointed at the girl in disgust. "Is this girl Gall's daughter?"

Crow Killer stepped aside as Eagle Wing moved forward and removed the filthy rawhide rope from the girl's neck. He glared threateningly over towards the tall Pawnee when he found the bloody rope burn around the girl's delicate neck.

"Blue Feather, it is me, Eagle Wing, the good friend of your father, Chief Gall." The warrior leaned over and looked into the round black eyes of the pretty girl. "I have come here to take you back to your father."

Looking up at the warrior, she seemed to recognize him. The girl nodded slightly. "I remember the great Eagle Wing from when you came to our village many moons ago."

"It is good you remember." Eagle Wing nodded. "Do you trust me, Blue Feather?"

"Yes, but I don't trust these Pawnee dogs." She frowned at her captors.

"I don't blame you, little one," he whispered. "I don't trust them either."

"You do not lie? You will really take me to my father?" Blue Feather trembled. "I have not seen him in many moons."

"Yes, but it will be a long trail. First, you will have food, a bath, and some rest. Then we will leave."

"A long trail does not matter." The girl glared at the large Pawnee warrior and hissed. "What does matter is the death of this dog."

"He cannot die today, little one." Eagle Wing shook his head. "We cannot have trouble with the Pawnee at Bridger. It is not allowed."

"Tell me, warrior. The Pawnee boast that they have sent all of my family to meet their ancestors." Blue Feather stared into his eyes. "Is this true?"

"I will not lie to you, Blue Feather. Only your father still walks the land."

"My mother. The small ones." She moaned and hung her head, slumping down at the table. It was some moments before she could speak. Finally, though her face was streaked with grime, she lifted her chin with great dignity and looked up at him. "I thank you, Eagle Wing, for speaking the truth."

Lawrence wrinkled his nose, moving away from the filthy girl. "Well, Mister Bracket, your son seems to know the girl. Do we have a bargain?"

"Yes, I know this girl." Eagle Wing turned on the Pawnee. "I don't like the way she has been treated."

"She's just a captive hostile." Lawrence shrugged. "And she's alive, that's what counts."

Crow Killer shook his head in disgust. "She's a human being, mister."

"Really? You sure couldn't tell it from the dirt all over her."

"Lawrence should be a captive of his Pawnee friends for a few sleeps." Eagle Wing clenched his fist. "You might change your thinking, white eye."

Crow Killer carefully studied the signed treaty once more, running his fingers over the document. He knew this paper was the only chance the Arapaho might have of staying in the Yellowstone Country, the land of their birth. With the buffalo facing extinction, starvation and sickness would soon follow. Even Crazy Horse would have to surrender and take his people to a reservation. Then, the pony soldiers would turn their full might on the smaller tribes of the Cheyenne and Arapaho. This document from Crook might be the only way for his people to avoid death and devastation on the long journey to Oklahoma Territory.

Crow Killer knew he only had Crook's word and this document to guarantee the Arapaho Nation a future. It would be a reservation, not the broad plains and vast high country that they now roamed freely and considered their hunting grounds, but at least they would be in the cooler climate of the north, near their ancestral homeland. This is the only way his Arapaho people would survive the coming of the white man's plow.

He nodded solemnly to himself. He had no choice. He could only hope that this treaty wouldn't turn sour like so many others had. As long as the grass grows and the rivers flow, had been the wording on the other treaties. Well, the rivers were still flowing, and the grass was still growing, but the treaties had blown away like smoke in the wind. They were nothing but worthless pieces of paper.

"We'll get your book, Captain." Crow Killer looked over at Eagle Wing. "I hope your word is good and that this paper speaks the truth."

"You have my word as an officer representing the United States Government."

"The word of a white man?" Eagle Wing shook his head.

"How many times has the red man heard this?"

Lawrence ignored Eagle Wing and looked over at Crow Killer sarcastically. "There is one other thing, Mister Bracket."

"And what would that be, Mister Army Man?"

"I repeat, Gall insists that it must be your son who brings his daughter north to him personally." Lawrence stared at Eagle Wing coldly. "That means in person."

"I think we know enough of the English language to understand what it means." Crow Killer didn't bother to disguise the bitterness he felt as he stared back at the arrogant captain.

Eagle Wing squared his broad shoulders and took a step toward Lawerence. "I will take Blue Feather to her father. I owe him that much."

"Then I will leave this, uh, young lady in your care." Lawrence hesitated. "You do realize if you fail in your mission, the Arapaho will be the ones who suffer."

"Mission." Eagle Wing paused and stared down at the white eye. "You mean if I don't bring back this book you're so nervous about, my people will be herded off to the Oklahoma Territories."

"That, sir, is exactly what I mean." Lawrence sneered. "You'll go too, Mister Eagle Wing, if I have my way."

Crow Killer frowned. "Just remember this, Captain Lawrence. You gave your word, and I'll hold you personally responsible if the Arapaho are betrayed in any way."

Lawrence sniffed and looked away. "You bring that book back, and the Arapaho will get their reservation."

"For your sake, they better." Crow Killer stared hard at Lawrence. "Or I'll make finding you my mission."

Lawrence frowned and exited the room. The heavy-built Pawnee warrior who had pushed the girl into the room cast a hateful glare at Eagle Wing before he followed the Captain out.

"You remember him?" Crow Killer watched the warrior walk away.

"Yes. That one is called Bull Coat. He sat behind Chief Strong

Otter on the Blue."

"Yep, he's the one that wanted to attack you after you killed Strong Otter." Crow Killer nodded. "But Red Hawk said their old medicine man stopped him."

"I think he still wishes to attack me."

"He won't dare attack you here at Bridger's. For now, we must not risk fighting with the Pawnee. We cannot chance losing this treaty for our people."

"I know, but the Pawnee deserves to die." Eagle Wing took a deep breath and gave his father a quick nod of agreement.

"We will leave this place with the coming of the new sun." Crow Killer looked over at the girl. "It will be a long hard trail. We must let Blue Feather rest tonight. I'll get Alex to have his woman give her a bath and a good meal." Crow Killer looked down at the ragged girl. "And some new clothes."

"I will stay close. I do not trust the Pawnee."

"They will cause no trouble. It is Spotted Elk that I worry about."

"We will speak of him after Blue Feather is in her sleeping robes."

"Have Broken Leg and Black Bird stay close."

"My father does not trust the Pawnee either?"

"I do not trust any warrior here, Arickaree, Assiniboine, Pawnee, any warrior."

Leaving Caldwell and his workers to watch over Blue Feather, Crow Killer, Broken Leg, Black Bird, and Eagle Wing gathered around a small fire near the corrals. The blacksmith, McGraw, sensing they wanted to be alone, retired to his bed. Crow Killer studied the dark faces of his friends as the firelight reflected on them. He had known these warriors since they were in their cradleboards. All were Lance Bearers, and none were braver in battle or more trusted.

"My friends, we must decide quickly what we are to do with

the coming of the new sun." He laid another small piece of wood on the fire.

Broken Leg shrugged. "Speak, Crow Killer, and we will do as you ask."

"Yes, speak. Tell us what you will have us do." Black Bird added.

"With the new day, Eagle Wing will take the girl, Blue Feather, to the north country." Crow Killer stared at each face. "We must decide now who will ride with him."

"Someone must ride back to our valley and tell Red Horse of Spotted Elk's presence here." Eagle Wing looked around the small circle. "He has to be warned."

"Does Crow Killer think Spotted Elk will ride against his people in the valley?"

"I do not know this." Crow Killer shrugged. "But it is likely. He hates my son, Red Horse, and he wants the woman, Flower Leaf."

"He is crazy enough to try to raid your lodges." Broken Leg spoke up. "I have known the warrior since before we could walk. This one cares only for himself."

"Only one is needed to carry the warning." Black Bird looked over at Eagle Wing. "One can take the word as good as two."

"What Black Bird says is true." Crow Killer stirred the fire. "But I would feel better if two rode to give the warning to Red Horse."

"I think my father, Crow Killer, should carry the message to Red Horse." As Eagle Wing spoke, the fire crackled, and sparks shot up into the night air. "Let us younger ones make this long ride to the north."

"Will it be a long trail?" Broken Leg asked.

"The store man, Caldwell, says it will take many sleeps to ride there." Crow Killer shrugged. "At least two moons."

Black Bird looked into the fire thoughtfully. "That is a long journey."

The warriors stared into the fire until a slight noise from the dark drew their attention. They all turned as Red Hawk led his Appaloosa horse into the dim light of the fire. Busy talking, the warriors had not heard the approach of either the warrior or the horse. The light nicker of greeting from several horses in the corral now alerted them of the spotted stallion's presence.

"Red Hawk, my brother." Crow Killer scrambled to his feet and greeted the warrior. "Why have you come so far from your village?"

"Crow Killer, it is good to find you here." The big warrior smiled. "As usual, I have come to keep you out of trouble."

"But Ellie Medicine Thunder and the children?"

"They are well protected."

Broken Leg smiled. "We were beginning to worry when Red Hawk didn't come."

As Red Hawk neared the fire, Eagle Wing noticed blood on his arm. "My Uncle has been in a fight."

"Not a fight. Some coward sent an arrow my way as I neared the post. It was already dark, so I didn't see who it was."

Crow Killer thought of the Pawnee Bull Coat who had brought Blue Feather to the post. It had to have been an Indian. Whites didn't use bows, and nobody around Bridger would have known of his coming or had any reason to kill the Crow. What reason would any warrior have to try and kill Red Hawk except the Pawnee? Lawrence had said the Pawnee were working with the Army to try and get Blue Feather back to her father, but were they? The Pawnee would have remembered Red Hawk being at the Blue River with Eagle Wing. The desire to get revenge for a dead Chief was strong amongst the tribes. Many times, bitter tribal rivalries that lasted for years started with a single killing.

"Come, we will have the squaws at the post tend to your wounds." Crow Killer looked over at Eagle Wing. "We will return and talk more as soon as Red Hawk has eaten and his wound cleaned."

Red Hawk glanced down at the gash in his arm and shook his head. "This wound is nothing."

"We will tend to your arm, my brother. We need you healthy, not with an infected arm." Crow Killer turned towards the store. "And you need to eat."

They awakened Caldwell from his bed, and he roused his hired women. One doctored Red Hawk's arm while the other woman warmed up some leftovers. Looking in on Blue Feather, Crow Killer found her in a deep sleep with another squaw from the post watching over her. He was about to leave the room when the woman motioned for him to wait.

Stepping close, the woman whispered quietly. "The old woman sends word that the Arapaho you seek rode to the west following the immigrant road early this morning."

"Did she say how many rode with him?"

"Many. Maybe this many." The squaw held up her open hands two times. "Many warriors, many squaws."

Nodding his thanks, he retreated to where Red Hawk was eating. "Eat quickly, my brother, then we must go."

Red Hawk sensed Crow Killer's anxiety and quickly gulped down his plate of food. Thanking Caldwell and laying money on the table, Crow Killer and Red Hawk hurried back to the blacksmith shop. Quickly, he told of Spotted Elk's departure earlier, heading west along the immigrant road. The cut-off to Black Horse Crossing was only a few miles from Bridger. He wasn't sure Spotted Elk knew of the shortcut or would ride on to the southern trail that crossed the Snake River leading to his valley. He knew the warrior would know his valley lay somewhere off to the east from the immigrant road. A few Arickaree warriors knew of his valley, and hating the Crow Killer the way they did, they would be willing to tell anyone how to find the valley. But would they tell another Arapaho? The Arickaree hated the Arapaho, but they hated Crow Killer and his sons even more. Crow Killer knew the greedy Arickaree. If Spotted Elk offered them a few rifle cartridges or some smokes, they would eagerly tell him.

Spotted Elk and his warriors left Bridger heading west. That could only mean he intended to raid the valley. Crow Killer couldn't believe it. Was the warrior so obsessed with the girl and his hate for Red Horse so strong that he would ride into Crow Killer's mountains? Yet there would be no other reason for Spotted Elk to ride west. Many before him had ridden into the Bear Killer's lair, intent on raiding and killing. And all were now buried or hung on scaffolds feeding the vultures. Crow Killer's face hardened as he thought of all the dead ones that had died deep in the high meadows. He vowed that if Spotted Elk rode into his mountains bent on raiding and killing, his bones would soon be bleaching with the rest of the intruders.

Crow Killer looked around the fire. "Someone must leave tonight and carry a warning to Red Horse."

"It will be hard to slip past Spotted Elk on the trail that leads to our valley." Eagle Wing shook his head. "It is very narrow and steep in places."

"Black Bird says he remembers the trail to your lodge well." Broken Leg shook his head. "Let us ride to your lodge, Crow Killer. We will find a way to stop Spotted Elk."

Eagle Wing said nothing. He waited, watching his father closely. Would the Crow Killer dare trust the safety of his people to anyone but himself? Could he ride north on this errand to find Gall, not knowing if Bright Moon and the others were in danger? Leaving the safety of his loved ones to Broken Leg and Black Bird would be a hard thing for a warrior like the Crow Killer to do. But the Arapaho tribe's future depended on them getting Blue Feather back to her father and exchanging her for the book General Crook wanted so badly.

Red Hawk waited, too, but not as patiently. He leaned in and asked, "Will my brother ride back to his valley or north to the Grandmother's Land?"

Crow Killer studied the two warriors solemnly. It was a

difficult decision, but he had to choose now. Time was of the essence. Spotted Elk had at least a twelve-hour lead on them already. He hoped that because the warrior had women with him, he would think he had plenty of time and might take his time riding slow and making camp during the dark times. If that happened, Broken Leg and Black Bird, riding hard, could pass them before they reached the valley.

"It is a good plan. You are true and brave, Lance Bearers. I trust the Broken Leg and Black Bird to warn Red Horse and the others." Crow Killer knew how dangerous the path to the valley could be and hated to ask either warrior to go, but there was no other choice. Red Horse had to be warned. "I thank Broken Leg and Black Bird."

"If you reach the valley and they are warned." Eagle Wing shook his head. "With Chalk Briggs and Red Horse, there will be plenty of rifles to stand off Spotted Elk if needed."

"When you catch up to Spotted Elk, you will have to slip by him somewhere along the trail while they sleep." Crow Killer looked toward the two young Lance Bearers. "You have to reach the valley first."

"Does Black Bird remember the shorter trail across Black Horse Crossing? If Spotted Elk doesn't take this path, you and Broken Leg take it, and you will reach the crossing of the Snake easily before he does. Then it will only be another day's ride over the mountain to warn Red Horse."

Black Bird smiled. "I remember the path Crow Killer led us on the last time I rode to the valley."

Crow Killer nodded, impressed with the warrior's sharp eyes and memory. "Good, but if you can't get by Spotted Elk on the trail, do this. Stay hidden behind him until you reach the high ledge where you can look down on Crow Killer's lodge. When Spotted Elk starts down the steep trail, fire shots," Eagle Wing added. "That will give Red Horse plenty of warning."

Eagle Wing sketched the layout quickly in the dirt. "With the

Henrys you carry, they will be trapped on the trail between you and Red Horse."

Crow Killer agreed. "Stay behind the large boulders at the top of the pass."

"It is a good plan." Black Bird agreed. "I remember the high place you speak of. From there, we can look down upon your lodge, and Spotted Elk will be caught like a fish on a hook."

Broken Leg looked over at Crow Killer. "Do we let them leave your valley?"

"They come into our mountains to kill and raid." Eagle Wing studied the two warriors. "I do not think you should let them leave."

"And the women?" Black Bird asked.

Crow Killer frowned. "We do not make war on women. Let them leave the valley."

"We will ride now. The moon will soon be bright and show us the trail." Broken Leg stood up.

"Be careful, my friends." Eagle Wing stood back as the warriors entered the corral for their horses. "Spotted Elk was once a Lance Bearer. He is still dangerous."

"Do you need shells or food?" Crow Killer asked as the warriors swung up on their horses.

Shaking his head, Broken Leg raised his rifle. His bow and quiver of arrows, along with the lance, hung across his back. "We have plenty of both."

"What will you have us tell Red Horse and the women?" Black Bird looked down from his horse.

"Tell them if things go bad to use the cave and fight from there."

"Tell them to stay watchful." Eagle's Wing added.

"And what of yourselves?"

Crow Killer squared his shoulders. "We have a long trail ahead, but we will return safely. Tell them not to worry for us if we are gone for several moons."

"These words we will tell them." Black Bird nudged his horse forward. "We will ride like the wind Crow Killer."

"Have no worry, Crow Killer, your loved ones will be warned and protected from any enemy while you are in the north." Broken Bow touched his lance. "Spotted Elk will have to ride over our dead bodies to reach your lodge."

The warriors rode out of the corral and headed for the post gate. "And if we can, we will kill Spotted Elk before he reaches your valley. "Or at least a few of his warriors." Black Bird's strong words came back to the three still standing by the fire.

"They are good friends." Eagle Wing watched the two warriors disappear into the dark. "And brave warriors."

"The best," Crow Killer agreed. "Now, let us get some sleep. We have a long trail ahead of us."

Red Hawk looked at the face of his brother, knowing no words would ease the worry he carried. Crow Killer had no choice. If he was to help the Arapaho, he had to make this long trail.

Eagle Wing and Red Hawk loaded the supplies of food and shells needed for the long journey on a pack horse. Crow Killer went inside the store to speak with Caldwell about the best trails to take on the long ride north to what the Indians called the Grandmother's Land. The old storekeeper explained to Crow Killer that it was a rough passage, mostly across uncharted and unmarked trails. The old-time mountain men and the Indians, for the most part, had followed well-worn buffalo trails that led across Wyoming and the Montana Territories. At one time, in his youth, Caldwell had hunted and trapped all over the North Country with Jim Bridger. Too many close encounters with hostile tribes in his youth contributed to his decision to remain safe behind a sales counter at Bridger's Post. Jim Bridger was just the opposite. He was too fiddle-footed to stop his trapping and wandering to settle down for long at Bridger. He always wanted to see what was over the next mountain. Leaving Caldwell to run Bridger's Post, he would sometimes be gone for several months.

"I've been north with my old friend Gabe a few times." Caldwell scratched his head while drawing on a piece of paper. "But I grew fond of my topknot and decided trapping weren't for me. No, sir, we had some hair-raising experiences. I mean literally. Those Blackfeet could snatch a man's scalp quicker'n you could twitch an eye."

Crow Killer remembered his own experiences in the shining times. Many a man, both white and red, had tried to lift his hair. "I remember those days myself, Alex."

"That Army Captain is asking a lot of you, my friend. It's a long ride to Canada from way down here in Wyoming Territory. A mighty long ride."

"Just how long you figure it'll take us." Crow Killer watched as the old trader drew on the crude map. "Two, three months?"

"Maybe. Even with the best of weather and provided you don't run into trouble." Caldwell scratched his chin. "Now, mind you, Jim and me were trapping and hunting, just taking our time as we moved north across that country."

"How long, Alex?"

"Providing your horses don't break a leg, and you don't get snake-bit or ate by a grizzly. I'm figuring at least two months, maybe a mite more just to reach the Grandmother's Land. And that don't count trying to find Sitting Bull."

"That long?"

"You're gonna be crossing two territories, old son." Caldwell shook his head. "That's a fer piece to tromp across on a four-legged animal."

"Yeah." Crow Killer rubbed his forehead.

"I don't like it a bit, Jedidiah. I don't know the particulars other than you're taking Gall's daughter back to him. But something about this smells rotten to this old chicken thief."

"I know, Alex." Crow Killer clapped his friend on the shoulder. "But I've got to try. It's a chance to help my people."

"You're speaking of the Arapaho, I reckon?"

"Yep."

Caldwell smiled sadly and handed the rolled-up map across to him. "If you won't change your mind, old hoss, then you'd best keep your eyes on the horizon and your face to the winds."

"I will, old friend. I will."

"Remember this, the Arickaree tell me there's soldiers out there everywhere hunting for hostiles." Caldwell frowned. "And if you're spotted, they'll figure you for hostile. I reckon they'll shoot first and ask questions after you're dead. You'll be having no friends out there."

"I'll remember."

"Yes, siree, that Captain is asking a lot of you and Eagle Wing." Caldwell shook his head and cussed. "If'n were me, I wouldn't do it."

Crow Killer rubbed the back of his neck. "Yeah, you're probably right. The Captain is asking an awful lot."

Caldwell stared up at him. "Why not just let old Gall come fetch his own daughter?"

"That wasn't our deal."

"Neither is getting yourself done in out there."

"I've got to try. This could get the Arapaho a reservation." Crow Killer looked down at the paper, wincing at the thought of his Arapaho people suffering in the dry winds of Oklahoma. "I've gotta try."

"So that's it, is it? Good gosh, man, you surely don't believe that bull?" Caldwell spit in disgust. "Them politicians in the east ain't about to give the Arapaho a decent reservation. Those blackguards wouldn't give their own mothers the sweat from their brows."

"It's worth a try."

"Well, old son, I reckon it's your hair." Caldwell tapped the rolled-up parchment. "That there's the best I can remember. It's been a spell since I rode those northern trails."

"Thank you, old friend."

"I 'spect you sent word to my girls about how long you'd be gone?"

Crow Killer smiled at the old trapper calling Bright Moon and Morning Dove his girls. "I sent word with Black Bird and Broken Leg."

"And I s'pose they'll warn Red Horse about the Arapaho, Spotted Elk?"

Crow Killer drew back. "How'd you know about that one?"

"I'm old, but I ain't deaf." Caldwell chuckled. "I hear things."

They shook hands, and Caldwell followed the powerful warrior out onto the porch. He watched them finish loading the pack animal and offered one last piece of advice. "Remember, boys, watch your hair. Lots of folks out there will be hankering for it."

Eagle Wing had traded for a small bay mare from McGraw for Blue Feather to ride. The little horse was small in stature, but her size was deceiving. The mare had a running walk that could cover many miles a day without its rider feeling the bouncing and bone-jarring they would normally feel riding a Mustang. A squaw's saddle had been thrown in with the price of the horse. Warriors on a war trail rode bareback, but on a long trail like this, they used a buffalo hide or trade blanket to sit on to protect the horse's back. Women of the tribes normally rode a squaw saddle made of bone or wood covered with deer or elk hides.

Leaving the safety of Bridger with a final wave, Eagle Wing took the lead while Crow Killer trailed the small group at a good distance, making sure they were not followed. He'd noticed the Arickaree loafing around the fort, watching too closely as Eagle Wing and Red Hawk packed up. He didn't like their wolf-like stares. He figured they might try to follow and find out where they were headed. They knew that only three warriors and one young girl had departed the post and were riding the trail north alone. The warriors that hung around the fort were a lazy bunch, but the Arickaree were a danger not to be underestimated.

When his party was farther out on the prairies, away from Bridger, Crow Killer knew the Arickaree might risk bringing a war party against him. If they came in big enough numbers, it would destroy any chances of getting Blue Feather back to her father. So, he hung back, and if he spotted anyone following them, he intended to discourage them quickly before they could lay an ambush for them.

Away from Bridger, alone on the prairie, they would only have themselves to depend on. In the wilderness north of the trading post, there were many dangers that could kill a man, wild animals, bears, snakes, and even buffalo. But of all those threats, hostile warriors bent on stealing horses, women, or weapons were the most dangerous. On the plains or in the mountains a man only had his wits and his rifle to keep him safe from danger. Crow Killer kept a close watch on the trail behind them, doubling back at times. He was not going to let a band of raiding Arickaree take away the chance of a reservation for the Arapaho.

Luckily, at this time of year, water and grass for the horses were plentiful. Buffalo herds were fewer now, and the grass covering the prairies wasn't grazed down as in the past. Some of the old buffalo trails had become completely grown over, making them difficult to follow.

The first night on the trail Eagle Wing made camp in a pocket of mountain cedar that protected them from being discovered if an enemy should pass close by them. Since the Battle of the Greasy Grass, white pony soldiers were as likely to be found here as were the native tribes that were here hiding from the whites. If they were discovered, Crow Killer hoped it would be by one of the hostile tribes, not whites, who thought every native warrior was a hostile. As Caldwell said, the pony soldiers would most likely shoot first and ask questions later. Most of the tribes still roaming the north were hostile, but they were friendly to the Arapaho. And most of these tribes were on the run from the pony soldiers. All were trying to hide out in these dense mountains rather than risk crossing the flat prairies that lay ahead.

"It was a good trail today." Red Hawk bit into some jerked meat and biscuits Caldwell had made up for them. "We made good time."

"How is the arm?" Crow Killer set across the small fire.

"It is nothing."

On the trail away from the hated Pawnee, the girl had started to talk, seeming to be enjoying herself now that she had prospects of being reunited with her people. "How long will it take us to reach my father's village?"

"This I do not know, little one." He studied the crude map Caldwell had drawn up for them. "I have never been in these northern mountains and plains before."

"What does your paper show?"

"Well, it would take Bridger himself to translate this thing." Crow Killer scratched at his chin. "Caldwell said it could be a long trail, maybe two moons or more to reach the Canadians."

"That is a very long trail." The girl sighed.

Red Hawk studied the tall sturdy-built girl. "Can Blue Feather ride that far?"

"I will ride as far as it takes to be with my people." Her dark eyes looked over at him. "Don't worry, I won't slow you down."

Crow Killer rolled up the map. "From what I see on this so-called map and from what Caldwell told me, we oughta be coming out of the mountains into open plains by noon tomorrow."

"Is that good?" she asked.

"Yes, in ways." Red Hawk nodded. "The horses won't have to work so hard on flat ground."

"In ways?"

Crow Killer tucked the map away. "What Red Hawk means is that when we leave the safety of these mountains, we'll be out on the wide-open plains."

Blue Feather nodded. "And an enemy searching for hostiles could easily spot us."

"Yes, there's not much out there to hide behind."

"Then we will have to be extra careful." The girl lifted her chin bravely. "Or fight."

Eagle Wing looked at the girl. "Fight? With just three warriors and one girl?"

"All of my life, I have heard of the warriors Red Hawk and Crow Killer. And my father brags about his friend, the great and fearless Eagle Wing. I am not afraid."

With a slight grin, Eagle Wing shook his head. "I'm glad you have such confidence in us."

"I will fight too if I have to." Blue Feather shook her head. "I will never become a slave again. Never."

Eagle Wing took the first watch and patrolled the camp, moving about as silently as a mountain cat. The fire had been extinguished, but he knew a good scout would be able to smell the remaining ashes of the fire for hours. With so few to guard Blue Feather and with such an important reason to deliver her safely, much caution had to be taken.

Crow Killer had spoken the truth. By midday the next day, the country had leveled out onto flat grassy plains where deer, elk, and antelope were plentiful. A baby fawn lay nestled in the tall grass, hidden by its mother. As Blue Feather's pony passed close by, the fawn spurted out from its hiding place, spooking the little mare, making her jump sideways and dump Blue Feather unceremoniously into the grass on her backside.

Dismounting quickly to see if the girl was hurt, Crow Killer let out a sigh of relief when she stood up and laughed. "Blue Feather, don't do that to an old man. I can't have you hurt before you reach your father. We can't slow down."

"It was nothing, Crow Killer. I am not hurt, and you are not an old man.”

"Times like this, I feel old," he grumbled.

"Blue Feather only said that because she doesn't want to hurt your feelings." Red Hawk laughed. "Compared to these young ones, we are old, brother."

"I never lie." Blue Feather pursed her lips, pretending to pout.

"What happened?" Eagle Wing heard the commotion and rode back to see why the girl was off her horse.

Crow Killer caught her horse. "Blue Feather tried to catch a deer and fell from her horse."

"Were you that hungry, Blue Feather?"

"No." The girl seemed to blush. "And I did not try to catch the deer. I frightened it."

The day passed with only the sound of the horse's hooves scraping through the thick buffalo grass as they passed. Tops of the heavy cane and grass brushed roughly against their moccasins and leggings. Pushing through the high grass, the taller horses of the warriors weren't being worked as hard as the short-legged little bay mare. Trying to help her horse navigate through the maze, Blue Feather kept the mare directly behind Red Hawk, following in the path he made as he plowed through the thick stalks.

Eagle Wing stopped, waiting for the others to catch up. "We will come out of the growth of tall grass and weeds soon." The trail he had made pushing through the jumble of tall weeds on his big Appaloosa had helped the other horses, but it was still rough going.

Eagle Wing had been right, by mid-afternoon the hard trek through the long grass was behind them. As dark descended on the column, the warrior found a large buffalo wallow deep enough to hide their fire from hostile eyes. Hobbles were placed on the horses, and they were allowed to graze and water from a nearby seep-hole of water.

Settling down in the dark around the small fire, the travelers suddenly found the light attracting flies to them like a magnet. The wallow was soon swarming, covered with a thick swarm of biting heel flies. Finding the horses, the large bee-like flies settled like a black cloud on the animals, keeping them swishing their tails, stomping, and slapping at the buzzing pests with their heads. Red Hawk pulled out a bag of bear grease and rubbed it across his face and arms.

"It will not keep them all away, but it'll help." The warrior offered the bag to Blue Feather. Seeing her wrinkle her nose, he smiled. "Yes, little one, it does smell."

Crow Killer nodded in admiration as the girl smeared the foul-smelling grease across her face. The grease didn't just smell. It stunk enough to make one's eyes water. But the tough little girl bravely applied the foul-smelling goop. He figured that, after being captive of the Pawnee, the girl could tolerate almost anything. He heard the horses snorting and stomping about, trying to escape the swarm.

"Catch the horses." Red Hawk stood up, swatting at the buzzing insects. "We don't want the flies to stampede them."

"This wallow has too many flies." Eagle Wing brushed at his face, trying to keep the flies out of his nose and mouth. "We go."

After an all-night passage under a full moon, the flies finally left them. Red Hawk had seen an infestation of flies like this many times. Usually, it was caused by the close presence of a buffalo herd, which was always accompanied by the red-headed biting flies. He had seen many times a buffalo herd break into a stampede, trying to avoid the pesky things. As the new sun came up after an all-night ride Eagle Wing called a halt beside a small fast running stream to let the horses have a much-needed rest and graze.

Seeing the girl look disgusted as he handed her another piece of jerky, Eagle Wing took his bow and walked down the stream. Crow Killer hobbled the horses while Red Hawk kept watch from a small rise. In these strange lands, they didn't want any unwanted surprises. An hour had passed before Eagle Wing reappeared carrying a heavy catch of fish on a willow reed.

"Build a fire, woman, and we'll have a fine dinner." He held up the brook trout. "That is if you are still hungry."

"I'm starved." Blue Feather hurried to the creek bed, looking for small twigs to gather for a fire. "How did Eagle Wing catch so many?"

"A bow is good for many things."

"Don't build too big of a fire, little one." Red Hawk warned. "Out here, the smoke can be spotted for miles."

Cooked over the small flame, the fresh fish were delicious. Hungry as she was, Blue Feather quickly consumed two by herself. Smiling, she was about to thank Eagle Wing, but suddenly froze, her eyes growing wide as a figure stumbled into sight across the creek. The figure went to his knees then pitched forward on the sandy bank.

Grabbing their rifles, Crow Killer and Eagle Wing splashed warily across the stream while Red Hawk watched for more enemies. Turning the small frame over, Crow Killer brushed hair from the dark face.

"He is Sioux." Crow Killer studied the face closely. "He's only a boy."

"What does he do out here alone?" Eagle Wing looked over the still figure. "He has no wound, no blood."

"Looks starved and dried out, is all. Let's move him to the fire."

Carrying the limp form across the creek, they placed him on a robe beside the fire. Washing the boy's face and putting water to his pale lips, they saw the dark eyes flutter open in fright. Trying to rise, Crow Killer pushed the youngster back down.

"Lie still, warrior." Red Hawk placed his hand on the young one's shoulder. "You are among friends."

"If you are friends, what tribe are you?"

"I am Crow, and these others are Arapaho." Red Hawk looked

at the girl. "She is Sioux, the daughter of Chief Gall."

The body seemed to relax as he heard these words. "I am Sioux."

"What is your name?"

"I am Jumping Rabbit." The words were hoarse. "My father is American Horse. He rides with Crazy Horse and Sitting Bull."

"Crazy Horse!" Eagle Wing knew Crazy Horse, and he had heard many stories about the great warrior, American Horse. "Is he camped close?"

"No, I do not think this. I don't know where the people are now."

Helping Jumping Rabbit to a sitting position, Red Hawk motioned for Blue Feather to bring the youngster some fish. Hungrily, the boy devoured the meat and accepted another piece from the girl.

"What are you doing out here alone?" Crow Killer questioned the famished youngster.

Thanking Blue Feather, the boy looked up at the warriors. "The pony soldiers and their Pawnee Dogs attacked our camp many sleeps ago and killed our hunters."

Crow Killer frowned. "How did you get away?"

Jumping Rabbit shrugged. "The white eyes were so busy killing and robbing the dead that they did not see this one crawl away in the grass."

Eagle Wing squatted down beside the boy and asked, "Was American Horse killed?"

"My father was not there. Only a few young warriors were out hunting for the shaggies."

"Was American Horse still with Crazy Horse when you left with the hunters?"

"My father was, but Sitting Bull and Gall took their people north many sleeps ago."

"Were their villages attacked?"

"I do not know what has happened since I went on the hunt,

but the pony soldiers are everywhere. They search for our villages every day." Jumping Rabbit shook his head. "Our warriors have to guard the old and sick. They cannot hunt for meat to feed the people. They are starving. Sitting Bull had no choice. He took his people to the Grandmother's Land to the north."

"That's a long way from here." Crow Killer hoped the youngster would know how far away it was.

"Yes." The boy accepted some water from Blue Feather. "My father says it is many sleeps away to safety in the north."

Eagle Wing thought of the young war chief. "Did Crazy Horse and American Horse decide to stay in these lands?"

"Yes." The young brave lowered his head. "But I do not know where they are now."

"So, you and your party were out hunting when you were attacked?"

"We were hunting shaggies. The sun was not yet high when the older warriors of our hunting party discovered the Long Knives and their Pawnee scouts had us cut off from our people to the north." Jumping Rabbit frowned. "Wild Pony, our leader, tried to ride west and circle around them."

Crow Killer guessed at what had happened next. It was an old soldier's ambushing trick. Anger rumbled inside his chest. "That's when the pony soldiers caught you?"

"Yes." Jumping Rabbit bowed his head. "Our horses were very tired from running. We stopped to let the animals rest, and they came at us from all sides, firing their rifles."

"Aren't you a little young to be out hunting?"

"I am fourteen summers old." The youngster looked up and frowned at Red Hawk. "The people of American Horse go hungry. They are starving. We are eating our horses. My father sent me with the hunters to help with the meat."

"How many died?"

"This, I do not know." Jumping Rabbit shook his head sadly. "Our party was small. I think maybe all died."

"Maybe some escaped, like you did?" Red Hawk offered hope.

The youngster looked strangely at Red Hawk. "You say you are a friend? The scouts that led the white eyes against us were Crow and Pawnee."

"He is a friend, Jumping Rabbit. My friend." Crow Killer shook his head. "Not all Crows are enemies."

"I do not think Crazy Horse would call him friend."

"I have been to Crazy Horse's lodge, and I think he would call Red Hawk friend if he were here." Eagle Wing spoke up. "You can call him friend, too."

"I thank you for the food, but I do not believe this. The Crow have always been our enemies."

"Rest, Jumping Rabbit. You will ride with us when the horses are rested."

"I must return to my father and tell him what has happened." The youngster protested.

"You are weak. You cannot travel on foot." Red Hawk shook his head. "You will ride with us to Sitting Bull's lodge to the north. There, maybe we will also find American Horse."

"My father will worry for me."

"You must go with us. We do not have a spare horse to give you to return to your people." Crow Killer stood and brushed off his hands. "Soon, you will be with him again."

Eagle Wing studied the youngster. "How far do you think Crazy Horse is from here?"

"This I do not know. After the attack I became lost and wandered for several sleeps."

"Then how do you expect to find your father? No, you will ride with us." Red Hawk insisted with finality. "Perhaps on the trail ahead, we will come across some of your people out hunting."

"We must be careful. The pony soldiers are everywhere." Jumping Rabbit looked out across the flats.

"Rest, young one." Crow Killer shook his head. "My son Eagle Wing's eyes are sharp like the Hawk."

CHAPTER 6

FOR TWO DAYS, EAGLE WING led the small party north. They encountered riders on the second day but silently concealed themselves in dense brush. A party of soldiers led by the hated Pawnee scouts passed within earshot from where they sat hidden. Fearing the soldiers' horses would sense the presence of their horses, Crow Killer had his gun ready and watched closely, expecting the Pawnee to turn on them at any second.

All tribes had excellent trackers like Black Bird. It was uncanny how they could sense the nearby presence of an enemy. The pony soldiers themselves were of little threat without their Indian scouts.

As they passed from sight, Jumping Rabbit sneered scornfully. "Pawnee, hah. They are like the blind. They see nothing."

Looking over at the youngster Red Hawk scolded him, "Be silent, Jumping Rabbit. You are the one that is blind, you are acting as a child would."

Eagle Wing leaned in and added in a low serious voice. "The Pawnee are great warriors. Their ears are as sharp as the fox. Their eyes quick like the hawk. Never underestimate your enemy, young one."

"I am sorry." He lowered his face. "I became excited."

"Excitement with an enemy close by can get you killed." Red Hawk shook his head. "And I, for one, wish to live another day."

"I said I was sorry."

Eagle Wing swung up onto his Appaloosa. "I will follow and make sure they don't return to this place."

"Does Jumping Rabbit know how far to the north the Grandmother's Land lies?" Crow Killer studied the wrinkled map, trying to decipher Caldwell's scribbling.

"I am not sure." The boy rubbed his arm absently. "When Sitting Bull and Crazy Horse separated, my father said Sitting Bull's people would have a long ride before they reached the safety of the Canadians. Maybe a full moon, or even more."

"So when you left to hunt, you were much farther north?"

"Perhaps." Jumping Rabbit shrugged. "I wandered very far. Maybe in circles. Here on the flat plains, everything looks the same."

"When you left for the hunt, were the Long Knives hunting the small villages hard?" Red Hawk watched as Eagle Wing disappeared into the tall grass.

"Very hard. Two times, we heard shooting. They were attacking the people somewhere out on the prairie. We had no time to hunt. All we could do was run and hide from the dreaded pony soldiers of the one they call Miles."

"Did this Colonel Miles hold council with Sitting Bull and try to get him to surrender and come into a reservation?"

"My father said they held council once, but Sitting Bull did not trust the white eyes, so we continued into the badlands to find Crazy Horse." The youngster frowned. "The pony soldiers followed close behind and attacked us many times."

Crow Killer rolled the map. "If you're right, that means it could still take us two full moons to reach the Grandmother's Land."

They had been headed north for five days now, making good time, but the horses could not keep traveling at this pace. They would have to stop to rest and graze. The only thing he knew for certain was that the boundary of the Canadians was many sleeps to the north. He wasn't exactly sure where Sitting Bull and Gall were camped. They would just have to cross into Canada and search for them.

Crow Killer didn't know anything about the tribes that lived in the Grandmother's Land. Would they be hostile or friendly? He didn't figure they would be friendly since Sitting Bull and his people had come into their lands uninvited and were killing the buffalo they needed for their own people.

Until they found the lodges of the Sioux, they would have to keep out of sight of any mounted riders. Crow Killer remembered the dreaded Assiniboine people he had encountered many moons ago. They were great warriors and would fight any trespassers in their lands.

Returning, Eagle Wing and Red Hawk reined in beside Crow Killer. "They ride on to the west. The Pawnee scouts are looking for something."

"We were lucky they didn't find our tracks."

"When they passed by us, they seemed to be in a great hurry." Red Hawk pointed back the way they'd come. "The grass was very thick. They probably mistook the trail we left for deer or buffalo."

Eagle Wing looked over at the youngster. "I think these are the ones that attacked Jumping Rabbit's hunters. They were leading several horses, and I saw many things tied to their backs. Two of the horses were much larger than the horses of the Sioux."

Red Hawk swung upon his horse. "They were probably horses captured from Custer. My warriors say the Sioux and Cheyenne captured at least seventy or eighty horses from the Long Knives at the Bighorn."

"You think they search for the boy?" Crow Killer asked his son.

"Not just Jumping Rabbit. I think they search for others who have escaped."

Crow Killer kicked his horse. "Well, we've got a fer piece to ride yet today. Let's get to it." They just needed to be cautious like the coyote and make their way through hundreds of miles of hostile lands without being spotted.

Shaking his head, he looked back at Red Hawk. How many times had they been in similar trouble before? He smiled to himself. Many times, but they'd been much younger in those days.

Riding mostly at night and resting during the daylight hours, they were able to travel for another week without seeing any riders out on the wide prairies. Scouting ahead alone while the others waited out of sight and rested in a small windbreak of brush and cedar, Eagle Wing saw the dark silhouette of trees on the far horizon. Turning his horse, he rode back to where the others were waiting. Dismounting, he hobbled his tired stallion and moved to where Red Hawk and Jumping Rabbit were skinning a small doe that Red Hawk had been able to kill with his bow.

"What have you seen, nephew?" Red Hawk pulled a handful of grass and wiped his bloody hands.

"A night's journey will bring us into many trees." Eagle Wing motioned ahead with his hand. "It seems to be a deep forest, but I could tell no more than that."

"When the dark comes again, we will build a fire and cook the meat." Crow Killer watched as Red Hawk pulled the heart and liver from the animal and sliced them up into small pieces. "It will slow us down reaching the forest, but the horses need the rest."

Red Hawk passed the raw meat out, smiling as Blue Feather made a face. "It will keep the hunger away until we can cook the meat."

"I think the jerky and biscuits would taste better." The girl took two pieces of the warm meat and put one in her mouth.

Eagle Wing laughed lightly. "Maybe they would, but they are all gone."

Jumping Rabbit was about to speak when he suddenly knelt down and put his fingers to his lips. Pointing to the prairie, he made the sign for the enemy. Crow Killer and Eagle Wing raised enough from the tall grass to see three riders following the stomped-down trail they had left as they passed through. Far out on the prairie, they looked like ants. Too far away to tell what tribe they belonged to, Crow Killer figured they had to be enemy scouts. The Sioux would not be trying to follow trails as they were too busy trying to keep out of sight of the pony soldiers that were searching for them.

"We cannot ride away." Crow Killer shook his head. "They would see us and bring the soldiers after us."

"Then they must die." Red Hawk shrugged. "We have no choice."

"And if they are Crow Scouts?" Eagle Wing looked over the warrior. "What will we do?"

"If they are Crow, I will ride out and speak with them." Red Hawk looked out across the vast prairie. "Soon, they will come close enough to see what tribe they are."

Eagle Wing looked over at the older warrior. "If they are Crow, Uncle, will they listen to you and leave us in peace?"

"This, I do not know. There are many bands of Crow. We will just have to wait and see which band these are and if they are indeed Crow."

"Every Crow Warrior has heard of Red Hawk." Crow Killer studied the far riders. "But since becoming scouts for the white pony soldiers, these young ones don't have the pride and respect for their elder Chiefs as they once did."

"They are Pawnee." Jumping Rabbit peeked above the tall grass, then dropped back down out of sight. "Their heads are shaven except for their top knots."

Eagle Wing looked across the flats. "He is right. The young one has sharp eyes."

"If the riders keep coming, we will use these." Crow Killer motioned with his bow and pointed at the oncoming riders. "We cannot miss. If one gets away, he will bring the Army down on us."

"Jumping Rabbit will stay back with Blue Feather until this is finished." Red Hawk looked sternly over at the youngster. "Go now and hold the horses out of sight."

The trail through the stomped-down grass was easy for the sharp-eyed scouts to follow. Two watched warily ahead and to the sides as the third followed the track. Their top knots told Crow Killer that the boy had been right. These were Pawnee. Slender and lean-limbed, wearing only the breechcloth, moccasins, and beaded armbands of their tribe, they were definitely Pawnee. All three warriors were armed with the Springfield Army issue rifles. Heavy shell belts were strapped around their slender waists, along with a long skinning knife. The traditional long bow and a quiver of arrows hung from their backs. Crow Killer could see the war paint covering their faces. These warriors were on the hunt, looking for hostiles.

Eagle Wing studied the cruel faces of the warriors and shook his head. Killing them would be easy, for he knew that if these Pawnee had discovered his party first, they would kill him, his father, Jumping Rabbit, and even the girl. One rode a bay horse with the U.S. brand on its shoulder. He knew it must be another of Custer's horses taken from a dead Sioux Warrior. Eagle Wing shook his head as he notched an arrow. These Pawnee would kill no more Sioux.

The warrior in the lead stopped his horse and studied the trail suspiciously. The warrior was a scout. His instincts must've told him something was amiss. For several minutes, the Pawnee sat his horse and stared at the trail. Finally, finding nothing wrong, he kicked his horse forward. Crow Killer raised his bow as the riders came abreast of where they waited. Three arrows hissed out of the tall grass, knocking all three Pawnee from their horses. Quickly, Eagle Wing and Red Hawk grabbed the dragging rein of the rope hackamores to keep the horses from getting away.

Crow Killer checked the scouts. All three were dead. The razor-sharp arrows protruding from their chests had done their job. Red Hawk's strong bow had sent his arrow almost completely through the body of one thin warrior. Retrieving the bloody arrows, Jumping Rabbit handed them back to Red Hawk and Eagle Wing.

"We must go now. We cannot wait for the safety of the dark." Crow Killer turned to where Blue Feather stood holding the horses. "There may be others following behind these."

"One good thing." Red Hawk examined the horses he held. "Now we have extra horses so ours can rest."

Handing Crow Killer his arrow, Jumping Rabbit smiled. "And now there are three more good Pawnee."

Crow Killer looked once more at the dead bodies and shook his head. Killing from ambush was not his way, but the Pawnee would have killed them the same way if they had of gotten the chance. The cavalry had armed these Pawnees with rifles, so now they rode bravely against a tribe that they normally feared. How many Sioux and Cheyenne had they already killed scouting for the pony soldiers? He was thankful they hadn't been Crow warriors. He didn't know if Red Hawk would have killed one of his own people, but he and Eagle Wing would have had to. The girl had to be returned to her father at any cost. His Arapaho people needed that reservation. He hated helping Lawrence and Crook, but he had no choice. He had to get Custer's book returned to the General.

With the extra horses, Eagle Wing was able to push the animals faster. Riding the captured horses, they were able to let their own horses rest. Traveling without a rider was a lot easier on a horse than carrying live weight on his back. The far timber he had seen had been reached just after the setting of the sun. Luckily, Eagle Wing had found a natural camping place at the edge of the forest just as full dark set in. Dismounting beside a small stream, they watered the animals and then hobbled the horses on a growth of good grass. Blue Feather and Jumping Rabbit had quickly started a fire to cook the deer meat.

Crow Killer had found leather saddlebags used by white soldiers lying strapped across the horses of the dead Pawnee. Each bag contained biscuits, dried meat, extra shells, and white man matches. The vile Pawnee scouts were well supplied with food from the white man's mess hall. A leather pouch holding several scalps of dead warriors, squaws, and some little children was also discovered. Crow Killer's stomach tightened with disgust. He shook his head. No longer did he regret having to ambush and kill the scouts. Killing an enemy was something he had to do many times, but he had never scalped.

Blue Feather had the deer steaks spitted and sizzling over a small flame on green sticks. They were hungry. All they'd had to eat that day was the small pieces of heart and liver from the deer right before the Pawnee had ridden into sight. At first, the raw meat had turned the girl's stomach, but as the day grew longer and hunger ate at her insides, the raw meat began to sound better. She found riding horseback all day, with nothing to eat, made even raw liver taste better.

While waiting for the deer to cook, Eagle Wing trotted on foot back to the edge of the timber and looked out in the dim sunset for any enemy. Finding nothing dotting the prairie, he sat down beside a small oak and studied the darkening lands. Nothing moved out on the wide prairie, only the slight swaying of the grass in the winds. Satisfied that no enemy approached, he returned to the small camp.

Lying back with full stomachs after eating fresh deer and the white man biscuits, the small group listened to the hobbled horses grazing on the grass alongside the stream. For days now, they had been on the trail. All were tired from the constant riding and the hot sun beating down on them. Their stomachs full, Blue Feather and Jumping Rabbit had already fallen asleep on their trade blankets. Crow Killer, Red Hawk, and Eagle Wing, after extinguishing the fire, sat about in the darkening shadows of the night. The deep timber was full of noises from the night animals that roamed the forest looking for a meal. The Ring-tailed Coon walked the stream looking for fish in the babbling stream, while the possum dug in the soft soil beneath the trees looking for roots. The call of the great Northern Owl sounded as it watched for prey from its lofty tree limb perch. Rabbits and squirrels were easy targets. The smaller animals had no chance against the stronger predators. The owl's large red eyes missed nothing, penetrating the darkest of nights. Their huge talons were razor sharp, strong enough to capture even a grey fox in their grasp.

The dark of the night served as a safety blanket for some animals, but it was also a time for hunting and death. For Crow Killer and his small band, the dark gave them a sense of security and a time for rest. With the coming of a new day, once again, they would be moving and on the alert for any enemy. Eagle Wing took the first watch, letting the older warriors get some much-needed sleep.

The scream of a mountain lion coming from deep in the forest brought Eagle Wing to his feet. Moving nearer to the creek to be closer to the horses and keep them calm, Eagle Wing sat back against a tree. Horses had few enemies, but the mountain cat and grizzly were two. They could spook the horses enough to make them try to run, even with hobbles. He knew if they spooked while hobbled, some could be lost or crippled. To lose any of the horses, even for a short spell, could be disastrous for the party.

The soothing call of the whippoorwill seemed to calm the horses, so the warrior made another circuit of the camp. Finding nothing, he returned to the horses, where Red Hawk joined him.

"You should rest, Uncle."

"I have rested enough. Now it is your time to sleep."

"Tomorrow, we should be able to make good time with the trees to hide us." Eagle Wing looked off into the dark. "The horses we captured are fresher than ours. We will ride them with the new day."

Red Hawk glanced sideways at his nephew. "I think the Pawnee are looking for more than just hostile Sioux and Cheyenne."

"What does my uncle mean?"

"I think they are searching for you, nephew."

"For me? Why would they search for me?"

"These warriors search the prairie for something more than hostile warriors." The handsome chief crossed his arms and stared meaningfully at Eagle Wing. "I have a feeling it's you."

"The Pawnee scout for the Army and General Crook." Eagle Wing shook his head. "Why should they look for me?"

"This I do not know." He shrugged and let his arms drop free. "Maybe I am wrong."

But Eagle Wing studied Red Hawk. The man was wise. "My uncle may be right. The big Pawnee, Bull Coat, was with the Army Captain back at Bridger. When he brought in the girl, he listened closely as we spoke. He knows we are taking her north to her father, Chief Gall. And this Bull Coat was there when I killed the Pawnee Chief, Strong Otter, on the Blue."

"You think maybe he hunts for you for revenge?"

"The look on his face back at Mr. Caldwell's store was pure hatred."

"Perhaps that is why he searches for you." Red Hawk shrugged. "He would like nothing more than to see you fail and the Arapaho people not get their reservation."

"Yes. The Pawnee have always been enemies of the Arapaho." Eagle Wing frowned. "My uncle could be right."

"I don't think the warriors we killed yesterday scout for the pony soldiers." Red Hawk looked over at the horses. "I think they look for us and scout for this warrior you speak of."

"But they had supplies from the Long Knife camp."

"Yes, but any Pawnee could ride into the white man's camp and pretend they were scouting for them and get supplies." Red

Hawk scoffed. "The Long Knives don't know one Indian from another."

Eagle Wing leaned against a dead log. "They hunt us like animals, but yet they don't know us."

"I also think this Pawnee has many warriors with him."

"Why do you think this, Uncle?"

"If this was not so, would the Pawnee dare ride against the Crow Killer and his son?" Red Hawk shook his head. "They are not that brave or foolish."

"But why would Bull Coat do this?" Eagle Wing looked over at the horses. "Why would he disobey Lawrence and ride after us?"

"If this warrior kills you and stops the girl from reaching her father, he will earn much prestige from his people."

"And maybe become Chief?"

"Yes, Chief of all Pawnee." Red Hawk nodded in the dark. "Maybe this is what brings him here, far to the north."

"If Crook and Lawrence find this out, he will be hunted as all the other hostiles are."

"If we are dead, who would tell them?"

"If this is true, we must ride with much caution." Eagle Wing could not keep his fists from tightening into hard knots. "This Bull Coat could be very dangerous."

"What are you two talking about?" Crow Killer appeared beside them from out of the dark.

Eagle Wing quickly told him what Red Hawk had said. If Bull Coat's warriors were following their trail, they would have enemies in front and in back of them. His Pawnees would have no fear of the Army, who would think they were friendlies and let them ride where they wanted without fear of being attacked.

"Our trail will be hard to cover here in the soft ground under these trees." Crow Killer shook his head. "I never thought about Bull Coat quitting the Army to follow after us."

"Red Hawk thinks he comes for me and the girl."

Red Hawk glanced up at the dark sky. "With the coming of

the new sun, we must ride fast and stay ahead of them."

Crow Killer shook his head. "I doubt we can outrun them with Blue Feather and the boy."

"What do you want to do?"

"When we have the chance, we must try and throw them from our trail."

After eating a cold meal of biscuits and deer steaks, Eagle Wing led the small group through the tangle of the oak, maple, and cedar trees that made up the timbered forest. Crow Killer hung back, watching their trail. The timber was so thick in places he couldn't see far behind them. He relied mostly on his sharp ears and the horse's natural instinct to smell other horses in the deep woods.

Traveling quietly, with only the sounds of the rustling dried leaves under their feet, the riders moved silently, not speaking. Nothing had been seen or heard all morning of any riders behind them. Hopefully, Red Hawks's fear of Bull Coat following would be wrong. While Crow Killer watched to their rear, Eagle Wing kept a lookout for any riders in front of them. His sharp eyes missed nothing as they moved forward. Riding up to a small stream of water knee-deep on the horses at midday, Eagle Wing turned his horse into the water. If there were riders on their trail, it would take hours for the trackers to search out where the trail left the small stream. Eagle Wing and his party would lose time deviating to the east, but traveling through the stream would slow their pursuers.

For two hours, Eagle Wing held to the water, then finding solid ground to leave the stream, he turned back to the north. The wet tracks would show where they had splashed out of the water, but with any luck, the ground would dry before any Pawnee trackers would have time to discover it.

Switching horses, Crow Killer didn't slow the urgent pace to the north. They needed to place many miles between them and the

Pawnee who were following them. If Bull Coat and the Pawnee were on their trail, they would have already discovered the dead warriors. He had the urge to ride back to see if they were being followed, but he couldn't take the chance of running into them unexpectedly.

He shook his head, thinking it was foolish to worry about an enemy he didn't even know for sure was following. But then, he remembered Walking Horse teaching him many years ago that it was better to be safe than sorry.

Darkness found the small group at another stream of water that meandered through the heavy timber. Eagle Wing slid from his horse and waited for the others to ride up.

"We will stay at this place tonight."

Blue Feather dropped tiredly from her horse and looked fearfully about the small clearing. "Shouldn't we ride on?"

"No, we can't ride through these woods in the dark time." Eagle Wing could sense her fear of the Pawnee. She must've overheard Red Hawk's warning. "The horses could step in a hole or brush one of us off under a low limb."

"Don't worry, Blue Feather, the enemy cannot follow our tracks in the dark times." Jumping Rabbit smiled at the girl. "Build us a fire, my stomach growls."

"You gather wood, and I'll build a fire."

"Gathering wood is woman's work, not a warrior's."

"You? A warrior?" Blue Feather giggled. "You're still a boy, not long out of your cradleboard."

"That is not true. Soon, I will be a warrior."

"When that day comes, then I will gather wood for your fire."

"Here." Red Hawk dumped an armload of dry sticks at their feet. "We do not have time to decide who is a warrior and who isn't."

"I am sorry, Great Chief." Blue Feather blushed. "I was just teasing this young one."

"Both of you listen. This is a serious matter, and we do not have time to tease each other."

Both youngsters quickly had a small fire burning. The fire spread its warm glow about the camp. Crow Killer finished hobbling the horses, who quickly started biting hungrily at the grass growing along the creek. Meanwhile, Eagle Wing had retreated on foot, backtracking along their trail. Stopping some distance from the camp, he sat down and listened for several minutes. Nothing came to him on the wind. Regaining his feet, he returned through the pitch black to the camp.

"Nothing?" Crow Killer asked as Eagle Wing moved into the light.

"No. The woods are quiet. I found no one following."

As Blue Feather and Jumping Rabbit quieted and fell asleep, the warriors huddled close by the fire and talked. Each could almost read the other's thoughts. They were deep in strange lands with enemies all around. They didn't know for sure if they were actually being followed or if it was the uncertainty of not knowing that bothered them. At night, the deep stand of Maple, Spruce, and Aspen trees towered over them, so dark and quiet that they gave off an eerie feeling.

Red Hawk poked at the small blaze absently with a dead stick. "If we are being followed, it would have taken the best of trackers many hours to find our tracks after leaving the water."

Eagle Wing stared into the flame. "Many hours, but it could be done."

Crow Killer sat back and stretched his weary shoulders. "All we can do is stay alert and watch closely for any enemy."

Eagle Wing turned to his father. "One of us could remain behind here and see if riders do follow our trail."

"No, my son. We will stay together. If they catch up to us, then we will fight."

Red Hawk agreed. "This is the best plan. We cannot separate in these strange enemy lands."

Again, Crow Killer unrolled the wrinkled map and studied it

by the dimming glow of the fire. "If this map of Alex's is anywhere close to accurate, we should be out of these woods in two days, then it is open prairie again."

Eagle Wing glanced down at the map. "Woods or plains, we are still in danger."

"Yes, but in the open, we can see if anyone follows." Red Hawk gestured at the thick trees surrounding them. "Here in the woods, we cannot see an enemy in hiding until he is on us."

"Neither can we be seen by an enemy following us." Eagle Wing argued.

"We've no choice. If this map is right, we will be out in the open grasslands soon."

Eagle Wing looked over at the horses. "If we have to ride fast to escape an enemy, our horses are strong."

"I know the Pawnee. I have fought them many times." Crow Killer tucked the map back away. "They don't have the stomach for a hard fight. They are not like the Lance Bearers of the Arapaho. They are afraid to die."

Red Hawk chuckled to himself. "Yes. And they will not ride hard to catch up unless they have us outnumbered badly. Many dogs on a bone makes them brave."

"Bull Coat's Pawnee only have the old single-shot rifles the Army gave them." Eagle Wing patted his Henry. "If we are found, our rifles will kill many."

"If we discover them before they find us." Crow Killer warned.

"When we leave these woods, we must watch for anything that moves." Red Hawk squinted as he gazed into the fire.

"Yes, we will be watchful." Crow Killer agreed.

Red Hawk shook his head. "This still does not make sense to me."

"What, my brother?"

"You said the Long Knives want you to bring back a paper to this General Crook, yet their Pawnee scouts hunt for us." The warrior shrugged. "Why is this?"

"That is a good question." Crow Killer admitted. "Only time will tell."

"What could they want, Uncle?"

"If my son is what they want. Wouldn't they have laid an ambush earlier instead of following us out here?"

Red Hawk shook his head. "This I don't know, but something makes me think they come for Eagle Wing."

"Maybe it is like we talked about before. Bull Coat wants to be chief and wants to count coup on me so that he will be chosen as the Pawnee's new chief."

"This doesn't make sense. It would be against this Captain Lawrence's orders." Crow Killer shrugged.

"This Bull Coat is a Pawnee. I think he could care less about what the white eyes want." Red Hawk shook his head. "I do not think Gall has any such book as this pony soldier speaks of."

"I've got the treaty paper giving the Arapaho a reservation if we get them this book." Crow Killer argued. "Why would Lawrence lie?"

Eagle Wing laughed lightly. "He's a pony soldier, isn't he?"

"Soon, we will see." Red Hawk shrugged. "But I think the white eye treaty is like smoke in the wind. It blinds the eye."

"Perhaps my brother is right. But until we figure this out, we'll keep heading for Sitting Bull's camp in the Canadians."

The open plains came into view on the second day, just as the map had shown. Riding from the scrub brush that separated the timber from the open plains, Eagle Wing waited for the others to catch up. Far out in the tall grass, he spotted the dark forms of a small herd of buffalo. His sharp eyes searched the plains for any sign of riders.

Jumping Rabbit reined in his horse beside Eagle Wing. "The shaggies do not run. There are no hunters nearby."

"How can you be sure, young one?" Red Hawk studied the

distant herd. "There could be hunters on foot, creeping through the grass."

"This is true, Uncle, but I don't think this." The youngster shook his head. "The herds have been hunted hard by our people and the white eyes. If anything was close, they would be moving about nervously."

Red Hawk smiled. The youngster was smart about this. "Thank you, Jumping Rabbit."

"We will pass by the herd on the downwind side." Crow Killer pulled his bow from his shoulder. "We need meat. Be ready if we get near enough to a calf or sleeping deer for a shot."

Red Hawk looked over at Jumping Rabbit and Blue Feather. "You two watch closely for enemies."

Two hours later, Jumping Rabbit's words came true as the herd caught the smell of humans on the wind and started drifting away to the east. Riding in the lead, Eagle Wing had sighted a small calf asleep in the deep grass. The twang of his bow was faint as it flew true to the small form, killing it quickly. Quickly gutting the red calf, Eagle Wing tied it across the back of the pack horse.

"We will fill our bellies tonight." Jumping Rabbit laughed as Blue Feather declined the cut of heart Eagle Wing offered her. Grinning, he smacked his lips as he bit into the bloody warm meat. Seeing Red Hawk frown at him, he turned his face away.

Jumping Rabbit's prediction came true as the small group sat around a small fire eating the tender calf meat. The buffalo herd smelling the riders had drifted away and were no longer in sight. The deep wallow they camped in this time didn't have the swarm of heel flies the other had. Eagle Wing had already checked out the deep buffalo wallow for flies before motioning the others down into it. No water was close by for the horses, but they had watered earlier in the afternoon, so they would be okay for the night.

Feeling the presence of Eagle Wing as he knelt beside him in the early dark of the wallow, Crow Killer whispered quietly. "What is it?"

"The light of a fire shows itself far out on the grasslands."

Rising quickly, Crow Killer stood looking out across the plains with Red Hawk and Eagle Wing. The small twinkle of a campfire could barely be seen far out across the prairie.

"The light is many miles away." Eagle Wing studied the faint light.

"Yes, I think it is near where we killed the calf."

Red Hawk strained his eyes. "I think this, too. Whoever follows us has camped where we killed the calf."

"Why would they be so foolish as to let their fire show to our eyes."

"They found the dead ones, and they know we have found out they follow." Crow Killer stared out over the flats. "It means they probably outnumber us, and so they have no fear."

"To ride blind like this is no good. We must find out who the ones are who follow us."

"Yes, my son. But to do this, we must let them get close."

"Not all of us, just one."

Red Hawk shook his head. "That would be dangerous for the one who stays behind."

"It is the only way." Eagle Wing pointed to a large clump of brush off to the east. "I will wait there, hidden in the tall weeds and brush, as they pass this place."

"This is not a good plan, my son." Crow Killer didn't like the idea of letting the followers catch up. "It could mean your death. I do not like it."

"We must see who follows our trail."

"You would have to ride hard to overtake us." Red Hawk shook his head. "If we ride all night, with the new day we would be a great distance ahead of you."

"And you would have to get past them to reach us." Crow Killer added. "How would you do this and stay out of their sight?"

"I will circle around them after I find out who follows. The spotted horse is powerful and strong. If I am discovered, he can outrun anything they ride.”

"He cannot outrun a bullet. And how will you find us later?"

"When they sleep tonight, I will sneak close enough to see who follows. Then I will slip away and ride through the night."

"They will have someone watching their camp," Red Hawk grumbled. "And how will you find us in the dark?"

"You will ride north through the night and into the new day. When the sun is high overhead, watch for me on the prairie. Give the call of the meadowlark when you see me appear."

"My son, this is a dangerous game you play." Crow Killer shook his head. "I do not like this plan."

"There is no other way."

"He is right, Crow Killer. No horse could catch the Appaloosa if he is discovered watching them."

"Wake Blue Feather and Jumping Rabbit, and ride from this place quickly." Eagle Wing turned. "I will find you with the new sun."

"We go." Crow Killer loaded up the remaining meat and sleeping blankets and grasped Eagle Wing's arm. "Be careful, my son."

Eagle Wing clasped his hand over his father's. "I will find you when the new sun is overhead."

CHAPTER 7

EAGLE WING LISTENED until the sound of the horses' hooves moving away in the dark slowly faded from his hearing. Leading the Appaloosa, he chose his path carefully as he moved away from the buffalo wallow, hoping any sign he left in the tall grass wouldn't be noticed by the oncoming warriors as they passed. Leaving through the west end of the wallow, where the grass wasn't as tall, he tried to leave as few signs as possible. He hoped the warriors on their trail were weary from their long day's ride and wouldn't take time to closely examine all the tracks in the wallow.

When he first noticed the fire far out on the prairie, it had been only a speck to his naked eye. He knew the tiny orange glow had to be several miles from the buffalo wallow. Only the dark of the night had made it possible to be seen. Eagle Wing expected the ones following might stop at the wallow as they had and camp there for the night. The tall, rough buffalo grass and stubble were uncomfortable to sleep on, and after sleeping in the tall brush, the soft dirt of the wallow would seem inviting to any warrior. But their decision whether or not to stop there would depend on how badly they wanted to catch up to the ones ahead.

Out on the open prairie, a beat-down trail through tall thick-bladed grass wasn't difficult for even a young warrior to follow. Hopefully, their pursuers would think they had plenty of time to catch up to the ones ahead and would stop at the wallow and rest their animals.

Eagle Wing knew the Pawnee wouldn't ride until the coming of the new sun so they could follow the trail across the flats. It would be several hours before the warriors would reach the wallow where he waited. Hobbling the spotted horse behind a thick stand of thickets less than a half mile from the wallow, he made sure the horse could not be seen. Unrolling his sleeping robe, he curled up for a much-needed rest, knowing he would not sleep soundly with the oncoming warriors near, but any rest would be welcome.

The afternoon sun was starting to wane when Eagle Wing stood up slowly and gazed out across the open prairie. He was shocked to find mounted warriors so near to where he waited. Somehow, they had reached the wallow much quicker than he thought they would. Ducking low, he took a quick count of the riders as they stopped at the wallow. Looking cautiously about in a circle where he stood, he made sure no lone warrior had circled behind him.

He noticed the stallion's ears perked up, having smelled the new arrivals from where he was picketed. Moving to the stallion, Eagle Wing placed his hand on the soft muzzle. He wanted to make sure the horse didn't nicker a greeting to the newcomers. From where he crouched, the wallow was too far away for Eagle Wing to be able to recognize any individual. He could tell by their top knots they were definitely Pawnee, but nothing else could be affirmed. He hoped they would settle down for the night at the buffalo wallow, letting him creep nearer for a closer look at their faces.

Eagle Wing got his wish. The Pawnee Warriors settled in for the night, laying their sleeping robes in the soft dirt of the wallow. Pulling a piece of dried buffalo meat from his pouch, he chewed on the meat patiently and waited for the sun to set. Today, the long ride through the tall dusty grass of the prairie would have been dry and hot. He didn't figure the warriors would sit around and talk long before falling asleep. They were rugged Pawnee warriors, but they were still flesh and blood and needed rest just like anyone else.

The sun slowly set in the west as he wrapped a piece of rawhide around the stallion's muzzle to keep him from whinnying. The horse had been trained since he was young not to move about when he was hobbled or try to whinny when he was muzzled. Still, Eagle Wing knew a stallion was unpredictable when strange horses were near.

As the sun set and darkness covered the land, he patted the horse's neck, hoping he wouldn't make any sounds to give away his position. Allowing time for the warriors to fall asleep, Eagle Wing took up his rifle, but left his lance, his bow and arrow quiver behind with the Appaloosa. Moving slowly, he crept silently through the tall grass like a ghost towards the wallow. Smoke coming from down in the deep place drifted out over the prairie, filling the grasses with its smell. He felt out every step before he placed his foot down firmly, careful not to make a sound. There were no wood branches out on the prairie to snap under his foot, but some of the heavier dried stalks of grass could crackle and give away his presence.

Moving towards the fire, downwind of the hobbled horses, Eagle Wing eased to the lip of the wallow and looked down into the camp. His sharp eyes counted twenty-one warriors lying around the small fire. Two others sat atop their robes, watching over the sleeping ones. The watchers themselves were slumped over like they were half asleep. Eagle Wing's sharp eyes studied each sleeping form closely, then frowned. Below him lay the large frame of Bull Coat. Suddenly, he stiffened. Next to the big warrior slept the unmistakable blond-headed form of Lawrence, the white Captain who had sent them on this trail for Crook. What was the Army man doing so far out on the prairie with the Pawnee?

Eagle Wing didn't know how, but Red Hawk had guessed right.

There must be a reason the Captain was here, but what could it be? Eagle Wing wondered if the book Gall was supposed to have might only be a pretense to lure him out here to this vast land alone. But why? The thought kept running through Eagle Wing's head. Why?

Maybe it wasn't Captain Lawrence after all. Eagle Wing looked again. The trade blanket covered the man enough that the uniform he wore couldn't be seen, but the man's face and blond hair showed him, without a doubt, to be Lawrence.

Touching the knife at his side, Eagle Wing was tempted to slip in and finish off both Lawrence and Bull Coat. But if one sound was made and it woke up the others, there would be too many for him to fight alone. No, he couldn't risk it. He would be needed if the rest were to reach Sitting Bull's Camp in the Canadians safely. They couldn't turn back to Bridger. They had no choice. Blue Feather still needed to be returned north to her father. Gripping the rifle hard, he shook off the urge to kill these enemies. No, the girl would be delivered first, and then he would hunt down Lawrence and confront him. Taking one last look at the sleeping Pawnee and white eye, Eagle Wing retreated back to the hobbled stallion.

All through the night, the Appaloosa picked his way carefully across the flat grasslands of the prairie. He kept a slow pace as he didn't want the stallion to accidentally step into a prairie dog hole or plunge into a buffalo wallow in the dark. Daylight found the warrior and the great stallion still moving steadily to the north. With the new rays of light showing the way, Eagle Wing urged the horse into a slow lope. The trampled-down trail through the tall grass made it easy for him to follow the ones ahead, and it would also make it easy for the Pawnee to follow. He knew their pursuers were probably just now rousing from their robes, but still, he had to find the others quickly. Out here on the flat grasslands, a rider could be spotted by a sharp-eyed scout from a long distance away.

At midday, with the sun high, he surveyed the surrounding grasslands to his front and rear. Reining in, he kept the Appaloosa quiet, listening closely, but only the rustling sound of the tall grass could be heard. Then it came to him across the flats, the familiar whistle and warble of a meadowlark. Returning the call, he reined the horse off to his right. Several minutes elapsed before he spotted the smiling faces of Red Hawk and Crow Killer as they appeared out of the grass riding towards him.

Relief spread over the smiling face framed by long greying black hair as Crow Killer rode up and clasped Eagle Wing's hand. "It is good to see you, my son."

"It is good to see my father and Red Hawk."

Red Hawk studied the broad prairie. "Did Eagle Wing find what he looked for?"

"Yes, Uncle. But we must talk of this later. Now, we need to ride from this place quickly."

"The ones that follow are near?" Crow Killer's dark eyes turned questioningly to the west.

"Hopefully, they rested in the wallow until the new sun." Eagle Wing glanced behind him. "They should be a half day behind us if they didn't ride in the dark as I did."

"How many follow?"

"More than twenty. In the dark, I counted maybe twenty-two or three." Eagle Wing drew in a breath, trying to conceal his anger. "We will speak of this when we make camp."

Crow Killer turned as Blue Feather and Jumping Rabbit appeared out of the tall grass. "We go."

Eagle Wing had ridden through the night with no sleep, so he let Red Hawk take the lead when he offered. Changing horses to let his spotted horse rest from the long night's ride, he swung up on the big Army horse they had captured from the dead Pawnee. Riding in line behind Jumping Rabbit, he let the plodding motion of the animal lull him into a light sleep.

Crow Killer brought up the rear of the small column, watching for any enemy to appear. Eagle Wing had said the enemy was close behind them and following, but how close, he wondered?

As dusk started to cover the plains, Red Hawk stopped on the banks of another stream and looked up and down the shallow waterway. No tracks other than that of the four-legged forest animals showed on the banks. Sliding from his spotted horse, he let the animal drink.

"We will camp here tonight." He spoke quietly to the others as they approached. "There is good water and grass for the horses."

Blue Feather and Jumping Rabbit quickly had a small fire going as Crow Killer and Red Hawk hobbled the horses along the creek bank. Sitting close, the three warriors watched as the youngsters heated up the last of the dried meat.

"Now, tell us, my son, what you have seen?"

Eagle Wing looked over at the two warriors. He had been able to sleep and rest a little as they had ridden through the day. To sleep on the back of a moving horse had been learned from an early age as a young horse tender when the village moved from one campsite to another. After falling from a horse and hitting the hard ground many times, he had learned to keep his balance even in his sleep. It wasn't total sleep, but for his young body, it was sufficient to get him through the day.

Eagle Wing quickly told of what he had seen. "Twenty-two Pawnee following our trail, twenty-three counting Bull Coat. He and the pony soldier, Captain Lawrence, lead them."

"Lawrence!" Crow Killer's head jerked up in surprise. "The Army Captain rides with those that follow us?"

"Yes. It is as Red Hawk feared back when we left Bridger."

"I don't understand this. Why would he follow after us?" The strong hand of the warrior slapped at a fly on his buckskin sleeve. "He insisted that we bring back this book Gall is supposed to have."

"This I don't know." Eagle Wing shrugged. "But there is no mistake. It is Lawrence that I saw with them."

"There is only one answer." Crow Killer nodded slowly.

"Lawrence said Gall insisted that only Eagle Wing was to bring Blue Feather back to him."

"Yes, I remember his words exactly. His words were that Gall wanted me to bring Blue Feather to him personally."

"Lawrence lied to us to get you out here on the prairie." The broad face scowled. "It is plain, Lawrence and Bull Coat are after you, my son."

"They used the girl as bait and convinced us the Arapaho would get a reservation of their own if we delivered Blue Feather to her father."

The hawk feather in Red Hawk's top knot moved as the warrior shook his head. "But why didn't they just try to take Eagle Wing back at Bridger or ride into your lands to capture him?"

Crow Killer's eyes glimmered like flames as he looked into the fire. "The answer is simple, my brother. They know there are more warriors in our valley, and they have heard of what happens to enemies who enter our mountains to raid. Lawrence knows the law of Bridger. No fighting is allowed around the post. This little ruse they have pulled was the safest way for the cowards to get Eagle Wing out here."

Red Hawk crossed his arms and shook his head. "But the Army is different. They do as they wish."

"No, Uncle, they do not go against Bridger and Caldwell." Eagle Wing shook his head. "Bridger has much authority with the warriors camped near his post. The Arickaree and many other tribes need his trade goods. They don't need the Army, and they would fight if Bridger asked them to. Lawrence would not dare try to take me at the post."

"That must mean Lawrence lied about the book of Custer and about the reservation as well." Crow Killer frowned. "It was all a lie and a trick to get you out here."

"I think this, too." Eagle Wing shook his head.

"But why would Lawrence do this thing?" Red Hawk shrugged. "I understand why the Pawnee Bull Coat wants to kill

Eagle Wing. By doing this, he would gain much esteem from his people. They would make him Chief of the Pawnee."

"You're right, Uncle. Bull Coat thinks killing me will make him Chief of the Pawnee, and it probably would. But Lawrence and the Army, this I don't understand."

"He hides something." Crow Killer growled.

"Well, I'm not dead yet."

"The Pawnee has no warrior that can kill you, my nephew." Red Hawk smiled.

"And the whites?"

"Neither do the whites, my son. We will deliver Blue Feather to Gall, then we will hunt down Lawrence and find out why he has done this thing."

"I remember Crow Killer's words at Bridger. You warned him what would happen if he tried to betray us." Eagle Wing looked over at the powerful warrior.

"If the pony soldier has lied to me just to lure you out here, then he is a dead man. I, Crow Killer, swear this on my lance."

"And the Pawnee, Bull Coat?" Eagle Wing asked. "What will happen to him?"

"This Pawnee dog will also pay for what he tries to do."

"They will pay if they don't find us first." Red Hawk laughed lightly. "I think twenty-three to three is pretty good odds on their side."

"They are bad odds for a Crow maybe, but not for Arapaho Lance Bearers." Jumping Rabbit spoke up, having been listening as he brought the hot meat.

"The young one has big ears." Red Hawk frowned at the youngster. "Maybe this Crow will cut them off of the young warrior."

"I only joke, Uncle." The youngster laughed as he handed Red Hawk the meat and biscuits. "I have heard how great a warrior you are."

"From who did you hear this, young one?"

"The prairie winds spoke to me." Jumping Rabbit pointed out into the dark. "Who else?"

"And the young Sioux doesn't lie either?"

"Never, Uncle. A Sioux never lies."

For a solid week, Eagle Wing led the small group steadily, only deviating from their northward passage to hide their trail in the small streams or a rocky shelf they crossed. He knew he couldn't lose the sharp eyes of the Pawnee scouts from finding his trail for long, but at least he could slow them down. As yet, no sightings of the Pawnee had been seen following behind them as they neared another large river. Eagle Wing was astride one of the large horses with the US brand on its shoulder as they hit the deep water. The horse proved to be a strong swimmer as they crossed the swift river and waded out onto the gravelly banks.

"I wonder what the river we just crossed is called." Water dripped from Red Hawk's doe-skin leggings as he looked back at the swift stream.

Crow Killer shook his head. "I think maybe it is the river Caldwell told me about that divides Montana Territory and Wyoming Territory. He called it the Clark or the Yellowstone, but I don't know for sure."

"We have been on this trail almost a moon." Eagle Wing studied the river. "We have been making good time. Perhaps you are right. We should be out of Wyoming territory by now."

Red Hawk laughed. "When we return to Bridger, we should give the store man a lesson in how to make marks on paper that a warrior can follow."

"That would be a good idea." Crow Killer smiled at Red Hawk's joke. "But first, we've got to get ourselves to Sitting Bull and back there."

"We have been in worse fixes than this, my brother."

"Yes, I know, Red Hawk. I just can't remember when."

Leaving the broad river, they found themselves once more nearing timbered country. It was not as dense as the forest they'd ridden through miles back, but it still had a heavy growth of spruce, maple, and cedar trees. Crow Killer saw no signs of anything except the wild four-leggeds in the soft ground of the game trails entering the forest. After crossing the river, Crow Killer had the riders again switch horses to let the ones they had been riding recover from the strain of swimming.

"The horses of the ones that follow have to be getting tired from this long journey." Eagle Wing patted his spotted horse on the neck. "I saw no extra horses with them. I do not think their horses could still be as strong as ours."

Crow Killer slid to the ground as they neared the edge of the timber and hobbled his bay gelding. "The young ones will cook up some of the meat Red Hawk killed this morning while the animals rest."

Eagle Wing could still see the river and its smooth-moving current from where they stood. Nothing showed on the flats on the other side except miles of empty prairie. Glancing up at the afternoon sun, he looked back across the river. "We have plenty of the day hours left. We don't want to become careless."

"Their horses have to have rest the same as ours." Crow Killer looked over at Blue Feather and Jumping Rabbit. "And the young ones need food and rest."

Red Hawk nodded and held up his rifle. "The river is wide. If the ones who follow are foolish enough to try and cross with us here, we will have the advantage."

"They wouldn't do such a foolish thing." Crow Killer wiped his face. "Even the pony soldier Captain is smarter than that."

"He is a white eye." Eagle Wing shook his head. "He was foolish enough to follow us out here."

"Lawrence thinks he has numbers on his side."

Red Hawk smiled. "How many lay dead over the years for thinking this?"

"Too many, brother, far too many."

"I do not think they are close." Eagle Wing leaned forward on his horse. "Unless Army friends have brought them more, or they have been able to steal some from the hostiles, the animals they ride have to be very tired."

"Still, we will keep a sharp watch." Crow Killer studied the river. "As you say, they could have met up with an Army patrol somewhere behind us."

"I do not think this, but it is possible." Eagle Wing shrugged, then moved to where Blue Feather was cutting up the fresh meat of a small deer Red Hawk had killed as they neared the river. "The meat will taste good, little one."

Blue Feather looked up at him. "I am sorry for causing so much trouble for you and Crow Killer."

"Gall, your father, is my friend. It is a good thing to help a friend."

"I thank Eagle Wing." Blue Feather smiled as the handsome warrior walked back to the horses.

"You know, woman, he is married." Jumping Rabbit laughed.

"Red Hawk is right. You have big ears and a very long nose."

"And sharp eyes that can see." The youngster dodged a rock that the girl threw his way. "And I am very quick-witted."

"Go drown yourself, child."

Crow Killer had the riders up and mounted with the coming of the new day. They ate a breakfast of cold meat and hard stale biscuits as they rode onto a trail leading due north into the deep woods. Jumping Rabbit, sitting backward on his horse, munched happily on his food as he looked back at Blue Feather. "We will have much to tell our fathers when we reach Sitting Bull."

"If we reach Sitting Bull," she muttered quietly.

"You have no faith, woman. Don't you know we have the greatest fighters of all the tribes here to protect us?"

"I know, but I heard Eagle Wing say there are twenty-three

Pawnee dogs following us." Blue Feather turned on her horse and looked over her shoulder. "And right now, my fear is stronger than my faith."

"Do not forget the pony soldier, Lawrence." Jumping Rabbit laughed. "Does Blue Feather fear only twenty-three warriors and one white eye?"

"I fear one Pawnee more than the white eye and all the others. And that is Bull Coat."

"He can die just like any other."

"Yes, but when?"

"Did Blue Feather have good dreams in her sleep?" Jumping Rabbit laughed and spun around on his horse. He could feel the dark eyes of the girl penetrating the buckskin vest he wore.

The glare from the pretty dark eyes was enough to silence Jumping Rabbit for a while, not long. The brashness of youth kept the young Sioux from staying quiet. Only the harsh look given the youngster by Red Hawk for talking again on the trail closed his mouth.

With the coolness of the morning air, the horses had a spring in their trot. They seemed fresh from the long night's rest and the grass they had been on all night, so Eagle Wing led them in an easy trot all morning. The timber had thinned out as they rode out on another open pasture that was covered with high grass. Eagle Wing reined in hard as several riders appeared suddenly out of the grass ahead. Looking around for the others, he waited until Crow Killer and Red Hawk rode up to him.

"Eight riders come." Eagle Wing pointed his chin. "They have already seen us."

"What tribe are they?" Crow Killer held his hand up to his eyes to keep the sun's rays out.

"They are too far away to see."

"We cannot turn back, so let's ride out to them." Red Hawk checked the loads in his Henry. "Be ready."

Both parties moved slowly forward, each watching their sides to be sure no others appeared. As they neared each other, Eagle Wing recognized the warriors to be Sioux from the Oglala people. Holding up his hand in greeting, he circled his horse, the sign for a council. The warriors were wary. They didn't recognize Crow Killer and Eagle Wing, but they knew the tall scalp lock of Red Hawk as Crow. Again, Eagle Wing circled his horse and held up his hand.

"Wait here." Eagle Wing handed Crow Killer his rifle. "They do not recognize us from where they sit. I will ride out and speak with them."

Riding his Appaloosa forward, Eagle Wing reined his horse to a stop in front of the warriors. One of the warriors nodded as he recognized him.

"Eagle Wing, it is good to see you." The warrior turned to the others. "My friends, this is the great Eagle Wing of the Arapaho Lance Bearers."

One of the warriors looked across to where the others waited and pointed. "Why does Eagle Wing, an Arapaho, ride with a Crow?"

"It is good to see my friend Straight Arrow again." Eagle Wing ignored the warrior's question and greeted Straight Arrow. Looking back at where Red Hawk and Crow Killer set their horses, he pointed. "You know of my father, Crow Killer. The Crow Warrior with the hawk feathers is his brother, Red Hawk."

"I have heard many tales of this great horse stealer." Straight Arrow laughed. "If he is the friend of Crow Killer, then he is our friend as well. Just watch your horses, my friends, when he is here."

A large warrior shook his head. "Even the great horse stealer Red Hawk cannot steal a horse you're sitting on."

"This is not what I have heard from the Cheyenne." Straight Arrow laughed again making the other warriors break out in laughter.

Raising his arm, Eagle Wing motioned the others forward. "We cannot talk here. We have enemies following us. We must get back into the cover of the forest."

"Enemies?" Straight Arrow looked about the large field. "Who are these enemies you speak of?"

"Pawnee."

"We know the Pawnee, and we know the Crow. They scout for the pony soldiers." Big Smoke scowled. "Even now, they search for our people everywhere."

Eagle Wing quickly introduced the Sioux Warriors to Crow Killer and Red Hawk, then followed the warriors back to the north towards a heavy stand of timber. Straight Arrow recognized both Blue Feather and Jumping Rabbit, but didn't speak. Out here in the open was not a good place to talk. A sharp eye could spot them from afar.

Riding into a shady clearing, the two groups slid from their horses. Straight Arrow sent a young warrior back to watch over the flats that led to the river. Shaking hands with the three warriors, he smiled over at the two youngsters.

"What do you two do here?" The warrior asked Blue Feather. "Your people are north in the Grandmother's Land."

"Eagle Wing is taking us to our families." Blue Feather dropped her eyes shyly. "Have you seen my father?"

"No, with all the pony soldiers hunting for them, Gall took his followers and retreated north to the Grandmother's Land with Sitting Bull."

"And Straight Arrow?" Eagle Wing looked at the squat warrior. "Why are you here?"

"Our Chief Crazy Horse sent us here looking for the shaggies." The warrior nodded. "Our people are starving."

"Is Crazy Horse close?"

"He hides to the northwest, maybe one sleep."

"We saw buffalo across the river." Crow Killer nodded. "But there are many pony soldiers and Pawnee scouts there also."

Straight Arrow nodded solemnly. "Since the Battle on the Greasy Grass, the Long Knives search for us every day."

"We have meat from a fresh kill." Eagle Wing pulled the hide holding the deer meat from the pack horse. "Blue Feather, build a fire so our friends can eat."

"We thank you." Straight Arrow looked over at Red Hawk and held out his arm. "It is good to meet the great Chief Red Hawk."

Red Hawk nodded and took the arm. "It is good to meet Straight Arrow."

"Come sit and tell us of the ones that follow you." The warrior motioned to a flat shaded area. "We will smoke and speak of this."

For two hours, the warriors talked of the battle and the Long Knives. Straight Arrow told of the continual pursuit of the hostiles by the pony soldiers. Since the Battle of the Greasy Grass, the pony soldiers under Crook and Miles had pursued the hostiles across the territories, killing any they found. Only Crazy Horse had been able to stay hidden, but he had no supplies, no food. Soon, he would have to find meat or surrender to the hated white eyes.

Blue Feather and Jumping Rabbit brought steaming meat from the small fire and handed it out to the hungry warriors. As they ate, Eagle Wing told of Blue Feather's captivity and how they had found Jumping Rabbit lost out on the prairie.

"Tell us about the ones who follow Eagle Wing and Crow Killer to this place?"

"Many Pawnee warriors, a pony soldier named Lawrence, and a Pawnee named Bull Coat leads them." Crow Killer answered. "They have tracked us all the way from Bridger's Post."

"Why?" Straight Arrow frowned. "That is many sleeps from here."

"Almost a moon."

"Why do they follow such a small group?" The warrior bit into his meat. "They normally do not waste their time on such a few. They want to kill many and take scalps, horses, and plunder."

"I think they follow my nephew for another reason." Red Hawk shrugged.

"We think we know why the Pawnee, Bull Coat, follows Eagle Wing, but the white, we don't understand." Crow Killer added.

"Eagle Wing fought with Gall on the Missouri." Straight Arrow nodded. "I remember two summers ago when he came to our village to meet Crazy Horse."

Crow Killer wiped his face with the buckskin sleeve of his hunting shirt. "I do not think him fighting so long ago with the Sioux is why they come for him."

"Then why would this white follow you this far north?"

Another older warrior named White Robe spoke up. "This pony soldier, Lawrence, you speak of. Tell us what does this one look like?"

Eagle Wing looked at the warrior. "He is tall, slender, with blue eyes and yellow hair."

"Yellow like Long Hair Custer's?" Straight Arrow asked.

"I never met Custer. But yes, this one's hair is yellow."

"Eagle Wing killed a white scout when he rode with Gall at the place of the bones called Skull Canyon." The older warrior spoke. "Does he not remember this one?"

"Yes, I remember the white eye scout. His name was Howard."

"Did he not have the same yellow hair as the one that follows you now?"

Eagle Wing thought back of the scout, Howard. The white eye did have yellow hair, but that's where the similarities of the two men ended. Howard was stockier and shorter with a broad face.

"What does White Robe say?"

"At the Laramie Treaty signing, two blond-headed white eyes were there. "One was a scout, the other a pony soldier chief. They were brothers."

"Brothers!" Eagle Wing looked up.

White Robe continued, "The two-bar pony soldier was arrogant and belligerent toward the people."

"And the scout?"

White Robe shrugged. "I think if he had not scouted for the pony soldiers, he would have been a good man."

"Is White Robe sure these two men were brothers?" Crow Killer looked across at the warrior.

"All I know is Eagle Wing killed a blond-headed white eye, and now another blond-headed white eye follows him here far to the north." The warrior shrugged. "This is what I know."

"Revenge. If they were brothers, that could be why Lawrence follows us here." Red Hawk thumped his fist against his thigh. "Revenge."

"Do you still take Blue Feather and Jumping Rabbit north to the Grandmother's Land?" Straight Arrow looked to where the youngsters were sitting.

"Yes, I will follow this trail." Eagle Wing shook his head. "I have promised the girl, and Gall is my friend."

"There are many Long Knives here on the prairie." White Robe looked from Eagle Wing to Crow Killer. "There is no safety for us, and there will be none for you, my friends."

"We must go now." Crow Killer looked over at the grazing horses. "Lawrence could be coming."

"Ride to Crazy Horse's Village and stay with him." Big Smoke pointed off to the northwest. "At least there, you will be safe there for a while, and you can rest."

"Your people are hungry. We would be just more mouths to feed." Crow Killer declined the offer. "We will continue north and find Gall."

"We can stay here and intercept the ones that follow you." White Robe shrugged.

Crow Killer shook his head. "No, my friends, they have more warriors than you do."

"They are Pawnee. We are Sioux. Numbers do not matter." Straight Arrow laughed.

"If you see these warriors, do not try to stop them. Let them come on." Eagle Wing looked over at the warriors. "After we deliver the girl, then we will find this white eye Lawrence and deal with him."

"As you wish, Eagle Wing." Straight Arrow stood up. "Then we will ride on and try to find a herd of shaggies."

"I wish you luck, my friends." Crow Killer pointed. "There is a small herd across the river, but that is also where the Pawnee were."

"We will need luck. The pony soldiers are as thick as the flies that follow the shaggies." Straight Arrow spoke sadly. "I think the times of our people are over. Crazy Horse's woman, Black Shawl, has a coughing sickness. I think soon he will go to Fort Robinson and surrender his rifle to Crook."

Crow Killer never thought he would hear himself say the words. "The pony soldiers will hunt Crazy Horse relentlessly. Maybe it is for the best if he surrenders on his own terms."

Straight Arrow agreed. "We have spoken of this many times."

"I am sorry, my friends."

"Does my father, American Horse, still ride with Crazy Horse?" Jumping Rabbit looked over at Straight Arrow.

"No, young one. He, too, has taken his people to the Canadians with Sitting Bull."

Waving, the two small parties separated to go their own ways. Crow Killer watched the proud backs of the Sioux Warriors disappear off to the south and shook his head. For decades, the Sioux were the lords of the plains, a great people. Now, they were almost helpless before the hordes of whites pursuing them. As the seasons changed, he knew the Sioux would also have to change. No longer would they be free to roam the lands and hunt the buffalo as free men. It was a sad time for the people.

CHAPTER 8

A full day after leaving Crow Killer and the others at Bridger's, Black Bird and Broken Leg reined in at the cut-off to Black Horse Crossing. Studying the small, almost hidden trail that forked off south from the immigrant road, they found no new tracks. Fresh tracks of the horses they had been following all day headed straight to the west towards Baxter Springs. The signs of horses on the sandy road were plainly visible. Black Bird didn't even bother to dismount to read them. Pointing south towards Black Horse Crossing, he looked over at Broken Leg.

"We can take the cut-off here and maybe reach the upper crossing of the Snake ahead of Spotted Elk if we ride hard."

"It is good you know the trail." Broken Leg nodded. "We go."

The crossing at Black Horse was refreshing after the hurried ride from the immigrant road. Both warriors clung to their horses as they swam across the river. The water felt warm as it flowed around them, washing the dust of the trail from their bodies. Swinging back on their horses, they headed up the narrow path that followed the river to the west. There was no reason to be watchful, as no other tracks showed on the trail, and the riverbanks along this part of the rocky path were almost impassable. Rocks, boulders, and steep banks covered with log jams kept most four-leggeds from crossing anywhere along this part of the river.

Black Bird had only ridden this trail one time when he had

come this way with Red Horse and Crow Killer. They had been in pursuit of the three whites that had taken Grass Bee captive at the Blue. The young Arapaho Lance Bearer had eyes like the Hawk, that's what made him such a great tracker. Plus, his sharp mind never forgot any trail he had ridden.

Broken Leg had never ridden this trail before. "How far is it to the crossing Eagle Wing spoke of?"

"Crow Killer rode hard when we passed this way." "Three sleeps will take us to the crossing of the river if we camp in the dark times." Black Bird studied the rough trail. "The horses will have to rest, and this is a dangerous path to ride. We will need to camp when we can no longer see the trail."

"Then we will be three sleeps reaching the upper crossing." Broken Leg frowned at the rocky trail. "We must do all we can to reach the crossing ahead of Spotted Elk."

"Spotted Elk has women with him. They will slow him down." Black Bird's horse pawed at the ground. "I think he will be in no hurry to reach the valley of Crow Killer. From the crossing, the lodge of Crow Killer is just a long day's ride over the mountain."

"Is it as rough as this trail?"

"The same until the crossing, but the trail over the mountain is much steeper."

"I think Spotted Elk will want to ride slow and keep his horses strong." Broken Leg frowned. "He would not like to ride into the raid on tired horses."

"When we reach the crossing, do you think we will ride on to the lodge of Crow Killer and warn Red Horse?" Black Bird looked over at Broken Leg. "Or should we let Spotted Elk pass us and catch him and his warriors between us and Red Horse?"

Broken Leg thought for a moment. "If we catch Spotted Elk between us, we can keep him from escaping back over the mountain." His horse tossed his head impatiently. "Then, he will never be able to ride against the Crow Killer and his people again."

"But, if we follow Spotted Elk now, we will not be able to

warn Red Horse."

"Red Horse will be warned when we fire our rifles from the high ridge." Broken Legs face turned hard. "Given the chance, Spotted Elk would do the same to us."

"I, too, do not like to kill our people from ambush, but Broken Leg is right. Spotted Elk would do the same to us if he had the chance."

Late on the afternoon of the third day, on the rocky trail leading to the crossing of the Snake, Broken Leg and Black Bird rode onto a small glade of open pasture. Heavy brush and small boulders lying ahead of them littered their path, making the trail ahead difficult to see. The river's steep dangerous banks lay only feet alongside the trail near where they now passed. Leaning sideways on his horse, Black Bird peered over the side of the deep gorge at the river below. The steep drop was at least thirty feet to the water. Dead logs and snags floated in the river, and a huge log jam in a sharp bend downstream kept the water moving very slowly.

"I would not like to swim in this place."

"Nor I." Broken Leg shook his head. "Today, I have no intention of swimming anywhere."

"The crossing is not far ahead now."

Neither warrior heard the heavy crack of several rifles firing, only the impact of the bullets striking their horses. Both horses fell dead on the trail. Broken Leg crawled to where Black Bird was pinned under his dead horse.

"Are you hit Black Bird?" Broken Leg ducked behind the dead horse as several more rounds again smacked into the dead body, splattering flesh and blood across his face. Examining the grey face of Black Bird, he could see where blood showed in two places.

"Yes, hot iron hit me. But the horse took the worst of it."

"We must get the horse off of you, little brother."

"Save yourself, Broken Leg." Black Bird shook his head. "Red

Horse must be warned."

"Where would I go?" Broken Leg pushed against the dead horse. "When I push, try to pull your leg free."

"I will try."

"Now, push hard with your good leg, Black Bird." The warrior strained with all his strength. "Push warrior."

Only a moan came from Black Bird as he came free of the heavy body. Luckily, only his foot and lower leg were caught under the weight of the horse. Lying back on the ground as Broken Leg examined his wounds, the warrior frowned.

"My friend, I don't think we beat Spotted Elk to the crossing." Black Bird tried to joke.

"We got careless." Broken Leg mumbled, angry at himself, as he wiped away his friend's blood. "We were talking instead of watching."

"Yes, and Spotted Elk is cunning. He guessed Crow Killer would send someone to his valley to warn Red Horse." Black Bird looked down at his wounds. "He reached the crossing faster than we thought and sent someone to watch this trail."

"But he did not take the shorter trail as we did." Broken Leg frantically tried to stop the gushing blood. "We should have reached the crossing first."

"He did not camp in the dark times as we did." Black Bird grimaced. "And he pushed his horses harder. That is why he arrived at the crossing ahead of us."

"Maybe one of his warriors was out hunting and discovered us."

Black Bird shook his head. "Spotted Leg had a warrior watching this trail."

"Perhaps, but it matters little now." Broken Leg peeked over the horse to try and figure out where their attackers were. "Spotted Elk has us in a bad way, my friend."

"You can escape. Get my rifle, and I will keep them back while you go back downriver."

"Your wounds are not serious." Broken Leg frowned. "I will not leave you."

"Leave me while you can."

"They can't get to us unless they come across the open ground." The warrior peered cautiously over the horse. "They are where the brush is so heavy alongside the trail. I can see the barrels of their rifles pointing at us."

Black Bird pulled his leather pouch to him and opened it. "If you will not leave me, hard head, then plug these holes before all my blood runs from my body."

The tall warrior took the cloth and rabbit skin and placed them over the wounds. "One has only grazed your side. I have stopped the bleeding there."

"And the other?"

"It hit you in the fatty part of your leg." Broken Leg dabbed at the wound. "It tore your skin where it entered and left your leg. You were lucky, my friend. The bullet did not stay lodged in your leg. You will be sore, but you will live to see your grandchildren be born."

"My leg doesn't feel lucky." Black Bird tried to smile. "You never told me how the hot iron burns when it bites you."

"You were not supposed to try and catch the hot lead."

"Well, it seems I did."

"Then I will tell you, now." Broken Leg smiled. "If you get shot, Black Bird, the iron that hits you will burn like fire."

"That is not funny."

"No, but if you feel pain, you are still walking this land."

"Broken Leg." The gruff voice carried across the open field. "Do you still live, my brother?"

"It is the voice of Spotted Elk." Broken Leg whispered.

"Do not answer." Black Bird held his finger to his lips. "They may get curious and try to cross over to find out if we are dead."

"If they do this, then they will feel the hot sting of our lead when they get close."

"Answer me, Broken Leg." The voice came again. "We don't want to kill you. Answer us, and we will go and let you live."

"He doesn't want to kill us?" Black Bird hissed. "Bah, he should look at my leg and my horse."

Broken Leg peered over the horse again. "They do not move."

"Maybe they will show themselves. Then we will get a chance to shoot them."

Helping Black Bird onto his side, Broken Leg handed him the Henry. Minutes passed, and still, only quiet sounded out across the flats. The rifles' firing had carried loudly down the river, silencing the singing birds that lived in the branches. Nothing was heard. Complete silence covered the field. The day was deathly quiet and held a tense eerie feeling.

"If you will not answer, Broken Leg, then we will have to come and see if you still walk the land." Spotted Elk yelled out again. "But if you make us come to you, my friend, then you will die."

Again, after several minutes passed, Broken Leg peered over the horse, but still nothing showed out on the flats. Black Bird started to sweat heavily. The hot sun, along with the wounds, heated his body. The dead horse lay atop one water skin, and the other skin lay on the other horse and couldn't be reached without showing themselves.

Peeking barely above the carcass of the horse, Broken Leg dropped down and nodded over at Black Bird. "Spotted Elk sends the young warrior, Sparrow, across the flats."

"I remember Sparrow." Black Bird shook his head. "He is just a boy. He is not even a Lance Bearer yet."

"A rifle in the hands of a boy kills the same as in the hands of a warrior."

"This is true, my friend."

"I do not wish to kill a boy, but if he gets closer, he will force me to shoot." Broken Leg was peering over the horse, watching the slender youngster moving slowly towards them.

"You will have no choice. Spotted Elk is a coward to send a boy."

"They have spread out along the trail." Broken Leg could see the movement of the warriors. "There are many more of them than Crow Killer thought."

"How many?"

"I see at least eight warriors moving into sight." Broken Leg shrugged. "I think more could still be hiding behind the brush."

"Does the boy still move this way?"

"He nears." Broken Leg cocked the Henry. "Be ready, Black Bird. We cannot hold back so many when they come at us."

"What will we do?"

"When I shoot, be ready. We are leaving this place quickly."

"Where are we going?"

"Into the river."

"That's a long jump, my friend." Black Bird looked over towards the edge of the bank. "And we are not birds."

"We will be today." Broken Leg smiled. "What do we have to lose?"

"Our lives, maybe." Black Bird shook his head. "I think we should just remain here and kill as many as we can."

"Put your bow over your shoulder and leave the rifle behind. It is heavy and will be worthless after it goes into the water."

"If we reach the water." Black Bird remarked. But he laid the rifle down and strung the bow and quiver over his shoulder.

"When you jump, brother, I'll almost guarantee you'll reach the water. "Here we go."

The discharge of the heavy Henry crashed out across the flats, knocking Sparrow backward onto the grass. Screams of outrage came from several throats and the keening of several squaws set up a racket. Several warriors came out of the brush and charged across the flats towards the dead horses. Grabbing Black Bird powerfully under his arm, Broken Leg helped him to the high ledge of the river, and with a scream of defiance, both warriors disappeared from sight.

A mighty scream of rage came from the warriors of Spotted Elk as they raced to the edge of the bank and peered down into the river. Raising their rifles to fire, they looked for the two warriors and then lowered their guns. Only the disturbed surface where the two had plunged into the river showed. They could see nothing else, only ripples spreading across the water.

"Let us climb down." A warrior stared hard down into the river. "They hide somewhere."

"No, the jump has killed them." Spotted Elk held his warriors back. "They no longer live. There is no sign of them down there anywhere."

"We should look for them."

"No, Wild Horse. We waste no more time here." The tall warrior shook his head. "We will leave this place. We go to the lodge of Crow Killer."

"But, what of Sparrow?" The warrior argued. "Is he not to be avenged?"

"Sparrow is dead. So are the ones down there." The dark eyes turned on the warrior with a glare. "I give the orders here, Wild Horse."

Broken Leg and Black Bird lay hidden, partially submerged behind a huge floating log, listening as the warriors on the overhanging ledge above them argued. They did not dare rise up from the water for fear of being seen. All they could do was keep low, still, and listen. Finally, after what seemed like hours but was actually only minutes, quiet finally came from the banks.

"They have gone," Broken Leg whispered.

Broken Leg shivered. "We should wait here awhile in case it is another trick of Spotted Elk's."

"I do not think it is a trick, but we will wait." Broken Leg wiped the water from his eyes. "Spotted Elk thinks we are dead.

Or if not dead, he thinks we are helpless, no longer a danger to him."

"We are alive. We are Lance Bearers. As long as a Lance Bearer lives, he is not helpless."

"We've got to get you out of this water and dry before you catch a fever." Broken Leg noticed Black Bird's lips had turned blue.

"If that crazy leap from up there into the river didn't kill me, nothing will." Black Bird looked up at the high ledge. "I can't believe we didn't land on one of these rocks or a log."

"The Great Spirit was watching over you, my friend. Come, we go."

"Which way?" Black Bird looked up at the tall clay banks.

"Up there, we must reach our horses. Perhaps Spotted Elk overlooked something we can use."

"I don't think we'll be able to ride them." Black Bird tried to smile at his own joke before taking a deep breath. "Okay, my friend, I am ready."

"Hold tight to my back." Broken Leg patted his soaked hunting shirt. "Do not turn loose. This river has a strong undercurrent."

"Don't know about the current, but that bank over there looks awfully steep."

"You are a Lance Bearer, Black Bird. That bank is nothing for you."

"My leg wants to argue with you."

The current was strong. It tugged at the two warriors powerfully as Broken Leg battled to cross the river. Dog paddling from log to log, then resting, they fought the river's powerful drag with every kick of their legs. Black Bird held onto Broken Leg's shirt and bow quiver and kicked with his good leg to help the warrior fight the current. Resting on a huge boulder as the water rushed around them, the warriors nodded.

"From here to the bank will be the worst part." Broken Leg pulled air into his lungs. "This is a fish's work. I am not used to swimming like this."

"I told you to leave me."

"If we go under, we go under together."

"Then swim hard, my friend." Black Bird wiped water from his eyes. "I will help all I can."

"It is narrow here. The current will be strong from here to the bank." Broken Leg pointed at a down tree that had fallen from the caved-in banks. "If we get close, grab a limb of that tree as we are swept by."

"And you?"

"Without the extra weight pulling me down, I can swim out okay."

"I am ready." Black Bird took a firm grip on Broken Leg's arrow quiver.

"Here we go."

The final swim from the boulder to the dead tree was the worst. The river, forced into a narrower channel from fallen trees and boulders, churned with a violent current. Broken Leg stroked powerfully, trying to reach the tree limbs that stuck out from the bank. Pulled under by the current as they neared the limbs sticking from the tree, both warriors were completely submerged. Frantically, Black Bird grabbed for the limb that he felt as it brushed up against his face. Luckily, his hand closed on the limb, letting him turn Broken Leg loose. With both hands free, he worked himself partially up onto the fallen tree. Weak and totally exhausted, he was about to be swept down river when he felt the powerful hand of Broken Leg pull him mightily from the water.

Leaning against the muddy bank, he smiled weakly. "You have saved me again today, brother."

"Black Bird would have done the same for me."

The exhausted warrior could only nod and mutter his gratitude. "Thank you."

"Come, we must climb this bank before we stiffen up."

For an hour, the warriors slowly scratched and pulled themselves up the steep and slippery incline of the banks. Climbing from one handhold to another, Broken Leg would reach back and help Black Bird across to another limb or outcropping of rock. The going was slow and dangerous. One slip could land both of them back in the river. If they fell, they both knew that even if they survived, they wouldn't have the strength to climb the bank again. Black Bird, weak from his wounds and totally exhausted, lay propped up against a limb, trying to summon the strength to climb higher.

Only a few feet separated them from the top, but that last stretch would be the hardest. Standing on the roots of the tree with only his head and neck showing above the lip of the bank, Broken Leg could see over the top, but he found nothing to grab ahold of. He could see the dead horses and the open field several yards back from where he stood. The soil on the banks had been loosened from the heavy rains and blowing winds that had brought down so many of the trees. Trying to get a handhold of the dirt, he felt it crumble and come loose in his hands. Desperate, he looked about for a way over the lip. If the ground crumbled and gave way from the ridge, he knew he would fall. The precipice here was even steeper than where they first went into the river.

Broken Leg looked around for any means of pulling himself over the lip of the bank. In vain, he studied his situation. Looking back down the way they had ascended the bank, he shook his head. Black Bird was just too weak to make another climb. He had to figure a way over the edge from where he stood.

Black Bird saw their predicament. He looked around and tugged at a large root sticking from the bank. The limb seemed strong enough to hold him. "Climb on my shoulders, Broken Leg. From there, you can pull yourself up over the edge."

Broken leg glanced down at him. "No. You are too weak to hold my weight."

"This limb is strong I will lock my arms around it." Black Bird showed him what he meant to do. "Hurry, my friend, before I change my mind."

"Don't you fall when I stand on your leg."

"Just go. Get over the edge, then you can pull me up." Black Bird tightened his grip on the heavy limb. "Hurry, Broken Leg. I will not let go."

Placing his foot gingerly on the wounded leg, Broken Leg eased his entire weight onto the injured warrior. Rising higher with the help of Black Bird, he was able to lift himself above the muddy lip. Now, as long as the whole ridge didn't cave in under his weight, he would be able to pull himself over the top. With a final heave, he rolled safely over the edge of the bank.

"Quickly, give me your hand, Black Bird."

Heaving with all his might, Broken Leg was able to pull the injured warrior over the ridge and up beside him. Both warriors lay back on the flat ground and regained their breath. Black Bird's leg had started to bleed profusely. Quickly binding the leg tighter, Broken Leg helped Black Bird over to the horses. The warriors of Spotted Elk had taken everything, their rifles, sleeping robes, and all the food. Luckily, the water flask beneath Black Bird's bay horse had been overlooked.

"I'm surprised they didn't eat the horses too." Black Bird shook his head weakly and tried to ease himself.

"I will move you to the safety of the trees, and then we will build a fire and eat."

"Eat what?"

"Like you said, Spotted Elk was kind enough to leave us some fresh horsemeat." Broken Leg grinned. "Come, Lance Bearer, think good things. We will eat our fill tonight."

Black Bird looked at the small bag that held Broken Leg's flint and steel and nodded. "We were lucky we did not lose our fire-maker in the river."

After bathing and wrapping Black Bird's leg again, Broken Leg finished cooking the thick steaks he had cut from a horse. The soaking in the river water seemed to have helped the wounds. At least they were clean. Broken Leg cooled the grease from the horse meat and rubbed a mixture of fat and grease onto the wounds. Placing Black Bird's buckskin leggings and leather vest across a long branch to dry, he looked over at the warrior.

"How does Black Bird feel?"

"My leg burns, but it is better with the grease on it."

"Tomorrow, it will be stiff and hurt even worse."

"Thanks, my friend, that is great to hear." Black Bird frowned. "I have heard Crow Killer and Eagle Wing speak of their wounds. I thought they were just telling stories."

"Wounds are serious, my friend, any wound."

"Yes, I believe Broken Leg."

Grease from the spitted meat fell with a hiss into the small fire, making smoke curl up into the night sky. It didn't smell like buffalo tongue or back strap, but tonight, the warriors were hungry enough to eat anything. Turning the meat slowly, Broken Leg looked over to where Black Bird had his eyes closed.

"Do not go to sleep before you eat." The warrior warned. "The meat will give you strength."

"Then give me a lot of it." The eyes didn't open, but the lips moved. "I need strength."

Cutting bark from a maple tree, Broken Leg placed the steaming horsemeat onto the green bark and handed it to Black Bird along with the water flask. He could see the slight shake of the warrior's hand as he accepted the meat with a slow nod.

"Chew slowly, Black Bird."

"Where do you go?"

Broken Leg pulled his skinning knife and started towards the dead horses. "Your shirt and leggings are still wet. You will need to keep warm when the cold of the night comes on us. The horses no longer need their hides."

"What if an enemy sees the smoke from our fire?"

"It is dark. They may smell the meat, but they surely can't see the smoke."

"And if they do?" Black Bird bit into the meat. "We do not know how far Spotted Elk has traveled from this place."

"If his warriors come back, we will push our lances into the earth and die like Lance Bearers."

"You could leave this place."

Broken Leg shook his head. "If I was going to leave, Black Bird, I would have left you in the river instead of almost getting myself drowned getting you out."

"This is true. Thank you, my friend."

"One day, you will repay me, maybe."

CHAPTER 9

LEADING THE SMALL GROUP, Eagle Wing once again turned the horses to the north towards the Canadians. Straight Arrow had studied Caldwell's crude map and shook his head. Motioning to the north, he made the sign of a moon with his fingers. Crow Killer took the sign to mean that if they had no trouble, the small party should reach the Canadians in less than a moon. They had also learned from the warrior that Sitting Bull said he would camp at a place called Wood Mountain.

Before riding away, the warrior had warned them of the Assiniboine, Cree, and Blackfoot tribes that claimed the northlands as their own. Crow Killer believed Straight Arrow. He knew the ferociousness of these tribes. All warriors of the northern country were fearless fighters, very protective of what they thought were their tribal lands.

Eagle Wing stopped for the night at another small stream with plenty of grass for the horses. Luckily, as their meat had been depleted by the hungry Sioux Warriors, Eagle Wing, in the lead, had been able to bring down a small deer that they had surprised earlier in the day. The horses were almost atop the resting buck when the twang of the bow sent the arrow through the air, hitting the bounding deer through his chest as he tried to flee.

Blue Feather had a small fire going and Jumping Rabbit quickly spitted the back strap of the deer over the fire. After seeing to the horses, Crow Killer, Red Hawk, and Eagle Wing seated themselves against tree trunks alongside the creek.

Eagle Wing could see his father was preoccupied with something. Never overtalkative, tonight he was quieter than usual. He knew he worried about Bright Moon and the ones back in the valley. Had Broken Leg and Black Bird been able to warn Red Horse of the impending danger of Spotted Elk? Were they all safe? These thoughts he knew were in the mind of the Crow Killer, for they were in Eagle Wing's mind as well.

"My father is worried about the valley?"

"Yes, I worry about whether your mother and the others are safe. It is a full moon again. By now, Broken Leg and Black Bird will have reached our valley."

"I wish you and Red Hawk had stayed behind and ridden to the valley." Eagle Wing's thoughts were of Morning Dove and the baby. "I have faith in Broken Leg and Black Bird, but they are not the Crow Killer and Red Hawk."

"I know, but whatever has happened is done."

Eagle Wing shrugged. "Yes, but I wish we knew."

"I wish I could be there also." The older warrior tried to smile. "But the ones in the valley should be safe even if our friends were not able to warn them."

"You're thinking of the small mule?"

"Yes, and Red Horse. He is a great warrior and has been taught to always be wary. He and Chalk will protect them."

"I think this also."

"If it would ease your mind, brother, you can return to the valley." Red Hawk looked over at Crow Killer. "I will remain with Eagle Wing and the children."

"I thank Red Hawk. But even if the treaty paper for the reservation is a lie, I must help the children reach their families."

"That treaty paper is like all the others. It is forked tongue talk of the whites." Eagle Wing tossed a small rock into the water. "The white man will promise anything to get what he wants."

"And this time, I fear they want you, Eagle Wing." Crow Killer sent a rock skipping across the surface. "Another reason I can't ride back to our people until this is finished. I cannot leave you two here alone to face such enemies."

Several roasted deer steaks had been consumed when the sound of horses came to their ears. The warriors' hobbled animals alerted, their ears pointed down the trail they had ridden in on. Sending the youngsters to hide, the three warriors grabbed up their rifles and quickly moved behind trees. They had acted carelessly, thinking they were safe for the night. Crow Killer shook his head. He knew better. In a hostile land such as this, one should know never to let his guard down.

The sound of many horse hooves on the forest floor quieted as whoever was riding towards their camp reined in their horses. The click of the hammers cocking on the Henrys sounded as they waited for the riders to show themselves.

"Eagle Wing, it is Straight Arrow." The voice came to them out of the dark. "I am coming into your fire. Do not shoot."

A sigh of relief came from Eagle Wing and Red Hawk as two riders leading several spare horses approached the fire. Sliding to the ground, Straight Arrow and Big Smoke looked about as the three warriors stepped from behind the trees.

"What does Straight Arrow do here?" Eagle Wing couldn't believe the two warriors were standing in front of them. "I am glad it is you, not the enemy."

"We smelled your meat, and Big Smoke is always hungry."

"You are welcome to our fire and to share our meat, my friends." Crow Killer welcomed the two warriors.

Eagle Wing watched as the two accepted the offer of the deer meat. "Now tell us, why you are really here?"

Between bites, Straight Arrow looked over at the three warriors. "I think the paper you carry will not get you to Sitting Bull in the Canadians. We have come to show you the way to his village."

"What about Crazy Horse?"

"We were lucky. We killed ten shaggies after we left you. There'll be enough fresh meat to fill the stomachs of all the people, at least once anyway."

"And then?"

"The hunger will return as it always does." Straight Arrow shrugged. "I think my Chief will take his people into the reservation at Robinson. I will not go. I wish to live free in the Canadians with Sitting Bull."

"You have no families?"

"My wife and children were killed by the blond-headed Pony Soldier and his Pawnees on the Bad Water plains." Big Smoke shook his head. "Straight Arrow only has an aunt. She will be fine."

Crow Killer studied the warriors. "Thank you, my friends. Your help leading us to the Canadians will be appreciated."

Eagle Wing looked pointedly at his father and Red Hawk. "It will not take five warriors to get the youngsters to Sitting Bull."

"What does my son say?"

"I wish for you to take Red Hawk and ride fast for our valley. Very fast. I fear, as you do, for the safety of our people."

"As my brother has already said, whatever has happened has already happened." Red Hawk shook his head. "It is a far ride back to Bridger and Crow Killer's valley."

"You won't have the children to slow you down. You can take extra horses and ride day and night." Eagle Wing argued.

Straight Arrow bit into his meat. "If you go now and don't stop to rest, you can reach Bridger's in ten sleeps, maybe less."

"That would be some hard riding."

"If the pony soldiers see you and give chase." Big Smoke chuckled. "Then you will ride even faster."

Crow Killer shook his head. "We cannot leave you out here alone."

"I will not be alone. I have Straight Arrow and Big Smoke, two great Sioux warriors, to help protect the children. It is our people who are alone, our women and children. My father must ride and ride fast."

"And they have me." Jumping Rabbit stood up.

Blue Feather frowned at the youngster. "A lot of help you would be."

"You will ride the big horses of the pony soldiers." Straight Arrow motioned at the larger horses. "I give them to you."

Big Smoke laughed. "And Red Hawk can tell around the fires this winter how he stole them from the Sioux."

"I never steal a horse. They just follow me home." Red Hawk acted hurt.

"I have heard this story." Crow Killer smiled. "Many, many times."

"If Crow Killer rides back to Bridger." Red Hawk grew serious. "I will only take one. I will ride the Appaloosa. He is still strong."

Straight Arrow pointed over at the horses. "There are four pony soldier horses we took from Custer. Take them if you wish."

"They are long-limbed and heavy-chested for endurance, Crow Killer." Big Smoke gestured at the big horses. "They will outlast anything the Pawnee have."

"I thank my friends, Straight Arrow and Big Smoke, for the gift of the horses." Crow Killer looked over at the two warriors. "But to leave you all out here, this I cannot do."

"Go, Crow Killer. We know these lands like the back of our hands. The Pawnee and white eye pony soldiers hunt everywhere for us. But they haven't found us yet, and they won't."

"Take Red Hawk." Big Smoke grinned and winked over at Red Hawk. "A Sioux cannot be seen in the light of day riding with a Crow."

Eagle Wing encouraged the hesitant Crow Killer. "I will not worry so much for Morning Dove and the baby if you return to the valley."

Crow Killer walked away from the fire and stood amongst the

horses for several minutes. Turning, he walked back to where the warriors stood, waiting for his decision. Both Eagle Wing and Red Hawk knew Crow Killer was torn in two different directions.

Looking over at Red Hawk, he shrugged. "I have decided to ride on to the Canadians."

Eagle Wing studied his father's face. "If this is what you think is best. I will say no more."

"It is. But after we deliver the children, I will ride on to Fort Robinson and speak with General Crook." Crow Killer patted the leather pouch hanging from his side. "I have the treaty paper promised by Lawrence. Maybe Crook will honor it and give the Arapaho a reservation. I have ridden this trail too far to turn back now."

"So, my brother no longer believes Gall has such a book?" Red Hawk asked.

"No, I think now it was a trick to get Eagle Wing out here away from Bridger. It doesn't matter now. I must speak with General Crook about this treaty."

"And Spotted Elk?"

"What Red Hawk said is true. We have been on this trail for over a moon. Whatever has happened back in our valley has already happened."

"If this is my brother's decision, I will ride with him."

"It is. Perhaps I can persuade Crook to help my people."

"So be it." Eagle Wing kicked dirt on the small fire. Once tonight, he had been taken by surprise, but no more. Now, even Jumping Rabbit would help. He would take a turn being on guard for any enemy during the dark times as the older warriors did. The youngster was still too young to fight, but his ears and eyes were keen and sharp.

"With the new sun, we will ride to the Canadians to find Sitting Bull." Crow Killer looked around the group.

"Then it is settled. We will rest tonight. Tomorrow, we follow Straight Arrow and Big Smoke to the Canadians." Eagle Wing sat down against a tree trunk.

"I know Eagle Wing wants to return to his own lands. Yet you stay. Why?" Straight Arrow asked as Crow Killer and Red Hawk rolled into their sleeping robes. "Is it the white pony soldier you seek?"

"Yes. I will return to my lands only after Lawrence and Bull Coat are dead." Eagle Wing frowned. "The white Captain has put my family in danger. Now he will pay."

"Then you will follow them wherever they ride?" Big Smoke asked.

"I think soon, if they don't find us out here, they will search for us near Fort Robinson. We will deliver the children to Gall first, and then I will ride on to Fort Robinson with the Crow Killer. But I say this: wherever the yellow-haired Captain and Bull Coat ride, I will follow."

The large Sioux nodded solemnly. "This is good. I, Big Smoke, will ride with you on this quest. No matter where it leads."

"With the new sun, we will take the shortest trail to Sitting Bull." Straight Arrow watched Big Smoke walk away. "We will ride fast."

Big Smoke was typical Sioux: powerfully built, thick through the shoulders, and slightly bow-legged, as were most horseback Indians. Long black hair cascaded down his shoulders, not kept in braids as most warriors wore theirs.

Eagle Wing looked over at Straight Arrow and shrugged. "Why does Big Smoke wish to ride with me?"

"It was the Pawnee and the white pony soldier, Lawrence, who led the raid on his small village, killing his wife and two children. They did terrible things to the people that day."

"He knows it was them?"

"He knows. The men were out hunting for buffalo when the pony soldiers and Pawnee rode down on the village. The survivors told of seeing Bull Coat and the tall white two-bar pony soldier with the yellow hair."

Eagle Wing thought of the raid on his lodge by the Nez Perce that almost cost the life of Morning Dove. He had taken his revenge for that raid. He could understand Big Smoke's feelings. He hadn't lost Morning Dove that terrible morning, but she had almost died from her wounds. He understood very well the warrior's need for revenge after losing his wife and two innocent children to these killers.

"He is welcome to ride with me wherever this trail leads."

"That is why we are here, Eagle Wing." Straight Arrow shrugged. "We knew from the way you and the Crow Killer spoke that you would be riding after the yellow-hair Captain and the Pawnee.

"What has Straight Arrow lost?"

"The woman of Big Smoke was my sister." The warrior's fist curled tight, shaking as he spoke. "They did terrible things to her. They will pay with their lives even if we have to follow them to Fort Robinson."

"We will deliver the children, then my friend, we will hunt for Lawrence and Bull Coat." Eagle Wing swore. "They will pay for their butchery. This, my friend, I promise."

"If we run into any pony soldiers on this trail, we do not run. We fight." Straight Arrow looked over at Eagle Wing in the darkness. "Any way we can. This one is tired of running."

Eagle Wing could sense the fury in the warrior. He knew that losing one in such a way makes a man's blood hot, wanting vengeance. Still, he knew all whites weren't killers. Eagle Wing wouldn't kill any he came upon in cold blood just because they were white. The Pawnee were different. Like Bull Coat, they butchered and killed for no reason. He felt no remorse for killing Pawnee as he had the three back on the trail.

Straight Arrow seemed to sense his thoughts. "Big Smoke and I will kill the pony soldiers. Eagle Wing can have the Pawnee dogs."

"Let's get some rest. Tomorrow, we ride hard." Eagle Wing

eased back against the tree, wondering how long it would take for their small party to reach the Canadians. It was a hard thing not to know, but he knew he had to finish this trail before he could return to Morning Dove and his people. Looking up at the bright star-covered sky, he swore this would be the last time he would leave his family for any reason.

The early light came quickly, waking Eagle Wing from a troubled sleep. He and the others had taken turns watching over the camp. Jumping Rabbit had thrown out his chest proudly as he had been told to take a turn standing watch while the others slept. The night had been peaceful. Only the night critters were heard walking in the creek or sounding their night calls. With the break of day, Crow Killer took the youngsters off to the side and told them what would be expected of them. They would be riding hard with little rest. This would continue even through the dark times until the Canadians were reached.

Both Blue Feather and Jumping Rabbit nodded in anticipation. They knew the faster they rode, the quicker they would reach their families.

The lands they crossed were open prairie, dotted in places with juniper, fir, spruce, and several kinds of pine trees that partially hid them at times. The prairies were beautiful, the fresh morning air sweeping the flats, the birds calling out, flying up from under the horse's feet. If it weren't for the danger of enemies, this trail would be enjoyable. When they were out on the open prairie, all they could do was keep a close watch for any enemy. Straight Arrow, practiced in the run-and-hide tactics the Sioux used to evade the slower pony soldiers, took the lead. Every two hours, he called a halt to let the riders change horses and give the animals some rest. All five warriors led two extra mounts. The youngsters led one apiece.

They maintained a slow lope throughout the first day and slowed to a trot after the sun set over the land. They were making good time, and no enemy had been spotted yet. Eagle Wing kept a close watch on Blue Feather to make sure she didn't sleep and fall from her horse in the darkness. He didn't worry about Jumping Rabbit, who had been riding since before he could walk. After hitting the ground hard a few times, youngsters learned to sleep on their horses without losing their balance and falling off. As he grew older, Jumping Rabbit's job was to guard the huge horse herds of his people. A brash youngster, scared of nothing and eager to make a name for himself, Jumping Rabbit was thoroughly enjoying himself. Around the council fire, when he grew older, he would tell of the long ride with the great Lance Bearers, Crow Killer and Eagle Wing, and the famous Chief Red Hawk and how they evaded the murderous Pawnee and pony soldiers.

Straight Arrow led them due north, occasionally moving to the west when a deep arroyo offered them cover from seeking eyes. Raised here, hunting the buffalo in the mountains and prairies of these lands long before it was called Montana, the two Sioux warriors were familiar with every dip and hollow of the land.

When the sun was high overhead on the fourth day, Straight Arrow had ridden down into a large waterhole sunken in a deep gorge. He knew Blue Feather needed a rest, even if it was a short one. The horses, ridden almost constantly except for water and an occasional stop to let them graze, were tiring. Straight Arrow had no choice. Rest was needed.

Sending Big Smoke to scout the long gorge leading to the west, he had Jumping Rabbit build a small fire to warm what was left of the dried deer meat. Today, no game had been found within bow shot along the trail they rode. The blast of a rifle here on the plains would be heard by every enemy in the vicinity. Crow Killer turned his horse, checking their back trail before following the rest down into the gorge. Nothing moved out on the flat plains that he could see. A few four-legged tracks were found around the waterhole where they dismounted, mostly coyote.

"Soon, we will have to slow down and hunt." Red Hawk

looked over at the youngsters. "They are young. They will weaken without food."

"Tomorrow, we will cross a river the white eyes call the Musselshell." Straight Arrow nodded. "The Sioux call it the Thayyunga. There will be game there."

"Good. There we will hunt."

"Only for a short time." Straight Arrow warned. "These are very dangerous grounds."

"Dangerous?" Red Hawk shrugged. "Everything out here is dangerous."

"Many pony soldiers ride this land looking for hostile Indians, as we are now called." He thumped his chest. "We are the hostiles, yet we lived on this land always, long before the white eyes even knew this land existed."

"They have the strength, my friend." Red Hawk felt sorry for the once free-roaming warrior. "And the whites believe might makes right."

Looking up as Big Smoke raced up the gorge, Eagle Wing whistled to get Jumping Rabbit's attention. Something was wrong! Or else the warrior wouldn't be pushing his already-tired horse so fast. He signaled for the youngsters to extinguish the fire and cover the burnt wood with sand.

"Enemy." The big Sioux slid from his heaving animal. "Pawnee warriors ride this way."

"Pony soldiers?"

"No." He shook his head. "Maybe they follow behind them. I didn't see any."

"What else?"

"There must have been a fight somewhere." The warrior swung his huge arm. "They lead many horses."

"How many Pawnee?"

"Maybe six." The warrior waved his arm excitedly. "That is all I saw before I turned back here."

Straight Arrow looked over at Crow Killer. "What do we do?"

Looking around at the deep-sided banks, Crow Killer called to the youngsters. "We will move back to the canyon mouth and wait for them there."

"They will see our fresh tracks here by the water." Big Smoke spread his hands at all the evidence. "We should fight here."

"No, my friend. If they see our fresh tracks, they will ride fast to see who is here. They will look for an easy kill."

"And run right into our rifles." Straight Arrow grinned. "It is a good plan. We go."

They had hardly reached the path where they had ridden down into the deep gulch when they heard the Pawnee scream come from the waterhole. As Big Smoke had predicted, their tracks and the still-warm ashes of the fire were quickly discovered by their lead scout. Eagle Wing knew the Pawnee would be coming fast, hoping they had more helpless Sioux or Cheyenne fleeing from them down the gorge. He knew the Pawnee would be anxious to catch up to their small band. Thinking they had an easy kill and anticipating more plunder would make the Pawnee more careless than usual.

The oncoming warriors had discovered their tracks. With the children, they wouldn't be able to outrun them out on the flats. Crow Killer knew he and the other warriors would need to stand and fight in the gorge, and he wanted it to be at a place of his choosing. Big Smoke hadn't known exactly how many men were in the Pawnee war party. Since there was to be a fight, their best chance of surviving would be to catch them by surprise.

He raced them to a place farther up the gorge and motioned Blue Feather and Jumping Rabbit into the narrow side passage out of harm's way. Then Crow Killer, Straight Arrow, Big Smoke, Red Hawk, and Eagle Wing quickly spread out across the ravine. Both of the Sioux were armed with the repeating rifles they had carried in the battle with Custer. Eagle Wing, Red Hawk, and Crow Killer raised their Henrys and waited for the Pawnee to ride into view.

Only minutes passed before they heard the sound of pounding

hooves coming fast down the gorge.

Crow Killer had placed them well. A slight curve in the walled passage kept them hidden until the oncoming warriors were right on them. Galloping through the gorge, the Pawnee rounded the bend and came unexpectedly under the rifles of the five waiting warriors. They tried in vain to stop their horses, but they were too late. The rapid fire of rifles echoed up and down the passage, knocking several Pawnee from their horses. With a scream, Eagle Wing charged the two remaining mounted Pawnee, racing his horse forward into the surprised warriors. Both tried to turn their horses from the fierce warrior, only to be toppled to the ground by the war axe of the Lance Bearer.

Straight Arrow shook his head as he watched Eagle Wing swinging his battle axe. He had heard tales of the fighting ability of this Lance Bearer from Gall and others, but he had never seen it. Today, he witnessed for himself the powerful warrior in battle. He saw Eagle Wing duck under the rifle of a Pawnee and, with his heavy axe, take off the head of the screaming warrior, then he spun around and nearly cut the other Pawnee in two. Never had Straight Arrow seen a warrior fight with such ferocity and daring.

Big Smoke whirled his horse and pointed back down the gorge. "I will see if any more come this way."

Straight Arrow called to the youngsters, "Gather their horses and weapons." But Blue Feather and Jumping Rabbit stood in a trance, having watched Eagle Wing's ferociousness in battle, and they had to be called a second time.

"He is like a demon in battle." Blue Feather muttered, unable to take her eyes from Eagle Wing. "Beautiful!"

"Look. One still lives." Jumping Rabbit knocked a wounded Pawnee back to the ground as he tried to rise. "I don't think for long, though."

Eagle Wing walked to where the warrior lay. "Who do you ride with?"

Only hate came from the dark eyes. The warrior had a bad

belly wound that exposed his insides. Moaning slightly, the warrior tried his best to spit at Eagle Wing.

"Tell us, Pawnee, who do you ride with?" Jumping Rabbit touched the man's wound, making him flinch in pain. "Speak warrior, or I, Jumping Rabbit, will push this arrow clean through you."

The warrior's head raised slightly as if he tried to speak, then fell back dead.

Blue Feather looked down at the warrior. "He is a good Pawnee now."

"Why does Blue Feather say that?" Jumping Rabbit frowned. "He did not tell us anything."

"He didn't have to speak." The girl glared at the dead man. "I know this one. He rides with Bull Coat."

Eagle Wing looked over at the girl. "Is Blue Feather sure?"

"I'm sure. This one always kept me tied tightly to his rope when I was a captive in their camp."

Crow Killer stared at the dead warrior. "Then Bull Coat and Lawrence should be close."

"This one, they called Bald Man. He was always with Bull Coat."

"Maybe this one and these others ride ahead of the main party." Straight Arrow watched as Big Smoke came into sight.

"Maybe. Let's see what Big Smoke has seen."

All watched expectantly, waiting as the big Sioux warrior slid from his horse. "No more come."

"Is Big Smoke sure?"

"I am sure." The warrior shook his head. "These are alone. They left the horses they led back at the waterhole."

Crow Killer noticed the uneasiness on Big Smoke's face. "There is something else?"

Big Smoke looked at him gravely. "Two pony soldier horses carry packs loaded with things they took from our people."

Straight Arrow turned. "We'll ride back there and catch the

freshest horses. Ours are worn out."

"I will be along." Big Smoke pulled his skinning knife and turned towards the dead Pawnee.

Blue Feather and Jumping Rabbit quickly caught the dead warriors' horses while Eagle Wing gathered any usable rifles and ammunition. As Crow Killer rode down the gulch towards the waterhole, he glanced back and saw Big Smoke bending over the dead bodies, taking scalps. Crow Killer shook his head, but he understood the hate the warrior felt. He would feel the same if something ever happened to Bright Moon.

Eagle Wing handed Jumping Rabbit an almost new Winchester Rifle and a bone-handled skinning knife he took from one of the dead Pawnee. The youngster smiled happily as he examined the rifle. "These are for me, Eagle Wing?"

"A warrior needs a good rifle when he becomes a man. And today, Jumping Rabbit has become a man."

Blue Feather smiled shyly at the youngster as he proudly threw out his chest. "That was a brave thing you did, Jumping Rabbit, counting coup on a live enemy."

"Jumping Rabbit will have a new name when we reach his father, American Horse." Straight Arrow walked up. "I think he should be called Pawnee Killer."

"That is a good name." Big Smoke agreed as he touched the youngster on the shoulder. "I agree."

Crow Killer and Red Hawk returned, leading several of the fresher horses they had exchanged for their worn-out animals. Big Smoke had been right, two of the horses were loaded with hides full of food and plunder taken from unlucky villagers. A few scalps found in the pack were quickly buried beside a small maple tree. Big Smoke looked at the bloody scalps he held and flung them to the ground.

Crow Killer understood the warrior's feelings.

CHAPTER 10

BROKEN LEG FINISHED SKINNING both dead horses and dragged the heavy hides back to where Black Bird lay beside the small fire. He knew the hides would stiffen without being worked, but for tonight, until his clothes dried, they would keep the wounded warrior from getting cold. He knew a chill from the night air could bring on a bad fever that might kill his friend. Quickly wrapping Black Bird snugly in the hides, Broken Leg added wood to the fire and laid his knife in the coals.

"What do you do?"

"I am sorry, my friend, but the wound has to be closed, and this is the only way." Broken Leg started removing the bandages wrapped around the leg.

"You are going to burn me?"

"This will help. It will keep the bad spirits out of your wounds."

Black bird's dark eyes stared at the reddening blade. "I think this is going to hurt somebody."

"It'll hurt me more than it hurts you."

"Somehow, I do not think this is true." Black Bird forced a half-smile. "But you must do what is necessary."

"It has to be done if you wish to keep your leg and maybe your life." Broken Leg picked up the red-hot knife and looked down sadly. "Are you ready, my friend?"

"No."

"Remember, you are a Lance Bearer with the strength of the grizzly bear."

Looking at the red glowing blade, Black Bird struggled to smile. "I do not feel like a bear right now."

The stench of burning flesh filled the air as the blade seared the wound, touching it front and back. The body of Black Bird stiffened in pain as the blade touched his flesh, but not a sound came from the wounded man. Heavy sweat beaded on Black Bird's head as Broken Leg quickly covered the wound with fresh fat and grease from the horse meat, then rewrapped the wound.

Black Bird slept fitfully for a few minutes, then woke up to see Broken Leg putting his still-damp leggings and hunting shirt back on. Adding a few more sticks of wood to the fire, he looked down at his friend's pain-racked eyes.

"You said the crossing is close."

"Very close, I think, maybe just over the next hill." Black Bird spoke faintly. "Where do you go?"

"I must find out if Spotted Elk and his people are still camped at the crossing or if they have moved on to Crow Killer's valley."

"If they are not there, start up the trail that leads over the mountain." Black Bird winced painfully. "Beyond the crossing up the hill, a short way is a hidden trail that Red Horse used when he slipped away from us while we were following the whites who had Grass Bee."

"A hidden trail?"

"Red Horse told me later after the battle with the whites that he discovered it while out hunting." The sweaty brow moved. "I rode horseback across the mountain pass with Crow Killer, but still, Red Horse beat us to the ridge overlooking the lodge in the valley."

"There is a shortcut to the cabin of Crow Killer?" Broken Leg mused. "That is good."

"Not to the lodge, Red Horse says the trail comes out just below the high ridge. He says the trail is dangerous in places, but it is mostly downhill."

"I will scout the crossing first, then try and find this trail." The warrior stood up. "Perhaps we will still beat Spotted Elk to the valley in time to warn Red Horse."

"I remember a bent pine tree grows where the hidden trail starts." With what little strength he had, Black Bird drew the shape of the bent tree in the air. "Find this crooked one, and you will find the trail."

"I will return as soon as I can." Broken Leg handed the water flask and some meat to the wounded man. "Try to eat. The meat will help you regain your strength."

"I will try. Be careful, my friend, remember Spotted Elk is a crafty one."

"I think we already found that out." Broken Leg gave him a sideways grin. "Stay put."

"I don't think I will be going anywhere."

Dark covered the land as Broken Leg moved up the narrow rocky road, carefully searching for any warrior Spotted Elk might have watching the trail. Black Bird spoke the truth. Spotted Elk was a wily leader. A warrior who had passed the Lance Bearer tests was not an enemy to be taken lightly. No matter if he had turned his back on his tribe and his lance, the man was still very dangerous. Topping out over the smaller mountain, Broken Leg looked down the steep, dark trail. Black Bird had said he thought the crossing of the Snake lay at the base of this mountain. Studying the trail for several minutes, he could see nothing of a fire in the darkness. He had only his instincts and hearing to go by until the moon rose enough to give him light to see by.

He couldn't waste time waiting for the moon's light to show him the path, so he started down the mountain. He had to get to the crossing and find out if Spotted Elk and his warriors were still camped there. Moving carefully down the rocky trail, he let the soles of his moccasins feel for any loose rock that could roll away beneath his feet. Almost at the bottom, as the ground leveled out, he spotted the glow of the fire. Slipping alongside the trail as the moon started to throw its light across the mountain, Broken Leg searched closely for scouts watching the trail.

Moving closer, he could tell both warriors and women were there. He could smell the smoke of their fire and hear faint voices coming up to him from the crossing. Moving cautiously, he crawled on his stomach closer to where he could see the fire and the warriors sitting around it. Spotted Elk was speaking as he came within hearing of their words.

"We will let the woman rest here one more day, then we will ride on to the lodge of Crow Killer." The nasal voice of the warrior was familiar to Broken Leg. "There is no hurry. The Arickaree squaw said Crow Killer and Eagle Wing would ride north."

"Yes, the Arickaree woman said this." Wild Horse spoke up. "But we don't know if it is true that they went north or not."

Spotted Elk raised his voice loudly in anger. "Argue, argue! That is all you do, warrior. I told you, I am the leader here. Go back if you do not like my plan."

"We have been here two days."

"And we will stay two more days if I say so." Spotted Elk spoke again. "I told you we will let the woman rest another day before crossing the mountain."

Broken Leg recognized another warrior. Coyote Man grumbled. "Women have had little ones for many years without stopping two days to rest, my Chief."

"She is not just any woman." Spotted Elk growled. "This is my sister, Two Baskets, wife of my brother, Bold Knob."

Broken Leg listened closely. He knew both Spotted Elk's and Wild Horse's voices. They had disliked each other and had fought over who would lead since they were children. The only reason Wild Horse had followed Spotted Elk into this folly was because of his deep dislike of Wolf's Head, now head Chief of the Arapaho.

"Where is Bold Knob?" Coyote Man asked. "He should speak for his woman. Not you, Spotted Elk."

"He watches the trail while we sit here and argue over his woman and child." Wild Horse shook his head. "You are right, Coyote Man. He should speak for his own woman."

Broken Leg stiffened at the words. Somewhere, the warrior Bold Knob watched over the camp. In the gloom of the darkness, he had missed seeing the warrior. Luckily, the warrior must not have seen or heard him as he passed. Quickly retreating away from the fire, he retraced his steps carefully, studying every place Bold Knob could be watching from. He knew this one. Bold Knob was still young, but he was a Lance Bearer, a dangerous foe. Easing quietly through the brush as he circled the camp, he finally spotted the warrior sitting on a large boulder.

Broken Leg shook his head in disgust. The warrior was letting his silhouette be seen plainly in the shadow of the moon. Any youngster would know better. Broken Leg touched the sharp skinning knife, then let his hand drop. He would slip past the warrior and let him live. If the warrior was found dead or didn't show up in camp on the coming day, Spotted Elk would have his warriors looking for his killer. He couldn't take the chance of the Arapaho warriors discovering Black Bird.

Spotted Elk planned to stay at the crossing until the woman recovered from having her baby, and Broken Leg didn't want them to change their minds. One day might give him the time he needed to get the wounded Black Bird past the crossing unnoticed. If he was lucky, he would find the trail Black Bird spoke of and hide him there. Or perhaps with a day's rest, Black Bird would be able to walk, and they could take the hidden trail to the lodge of Crow Killer. Black Bird's injured leg would be sore, but the warrior had a strong heart, and maybe he could walk despite the pain.

Slipping silently around Bold Knob, Broken Leg moved away from the crossing. Just as he started up the steep grade, he dropped behind a rock outcropping and watched as a squaw hung a freshly killed deer high in a tree. Broken Leg smiled, watching as she hoisted the carcass up out of reach of the night hunters. Creeping closer after the woman walked away, he quickly cut a large chunk of meat from the deer. He was afraid to take more of the meat. The squaw would miss it and set up an alarm. Gripping the meat, he turned away from the camp and back toward the mountain. If he didn't find the hidden trail, at least he and Black Bird would have a good meal.

Broken Leg turned up the trail again and balanced the hunk of meat on a high limb. He hoped he wouldn't be gone long enough for a meat scavenger to discover it. If he was lucky and found the crooked pine Black Bird spoke of, they might still be in time to warn Red Horse. Only a short way from the crossing and out of hearing of the running river, Broken Leg turned onto the rocky trail. It quickly became very steep. The mountain trail was strewn with loose rock, making it difficult to walk. The path was hard, much harder on a warrior used to riding.

He remembered Black Bird saying the trail of Red Horse was only a short distance up the mountain from the crossing. How long had he been climbing? How far had he come in the darkness? Kneeling, he looked up through the trees in the moonlight, trying to locate the bent pine Black Bird had described. How much longer did he dare linger on the mountain? He needed to slip past the watcher and the camp at the crossing before the new sun came up. And he had to have time to retrieve the deer meat he had placed in the tree.

He knew trying to pass the camp in the daylight could be disastrous. With the coming of a new day, the warriors of Spotted Elk would be out hunting or tending to their horses. He could take only a few more minutes to locate the hidden trail, and then he would be forced to retreat back down the mountain. Minutes later, just as he had decided to turn around, he spotted what he thought Black Bird had described. The tree was a pine, and it was bent awkwardly, just as the warrior had described. Now, he had to try and find if a trail existed at the base of the crooked pine.

Barely visible by the light of the moon under the brush and trees, there it was, the hidden trail of Red Horse. Feeling with his feet and what his eyes could tell him, Broken Leg was sure it was the trail. With no time to explore the trail further, he retraced his steps to the mountain trail and started back down to the crossing.

Grabbing the meat and moving cautiously past the camp and back up the smaller mountain, Broken Leg reached the top. The early morning sun had just started to show a slight hint of daylight in the east. Now able to see the rough trail plainly, the warrior broke into a faster pace back toward where he had left Black Bird. Reaching the camp, he found the fire had gone out, but the wounded one was awake and seemed in good spirits as he trotted up.

"Broken Leg has been gone a long time." Black Bird greeted the tired warrior. "I thought Spotted Elk might have caught you."

Broken Leg was surprised, he figured to find Black Bird weak from his wounds. "I found the trail you spoke of."

"By the crooked pine tree?"

"Yes." Broken Leg pulled out his flint and steel and struck sparks into the squaw wood he had piled up for a new fire. He also produced the freshly killed deer meat. "And I have this for your breakfast."

"Where did you get that?" Black Bird smiled.

"Spotted Elk and his warriors killed it for us."

"You went into their camp and stole the meat?"

"Well, young one, it sure didn't walk out to me."

"And you found the trail of Red Horse?" Black Bird shook his head. "How did you do all this in the dark?"

"It wasn't easy. Without such a bright moon, I wouldn't have."

"What is your plan now?"

"I heard Spotted Elk say they will remain at the crossing today, then will move on to Crow Killer's valley with the second sun."

Broken Leg had the fire burning brightly as he spoke. "If you can walk, we will move near their camp before dark, then pass them while they sleep."

"This is a good plan." Black Bird watched as the spitted meat dropped grease into the flames. "But won't they have watchers out after darkness comes?"

"They only keep one warrior watching the camp." Broken Leg touched the skinning knife. "With any luck, it will be Spotted Elk this time."

"I hope I will be able to walk such a trail with my leg." He tossed a stick into the fire, sending sparks floating up into the dark night.

"If the trail is too steep, I will hide you and come back for you after I have warned Red Horse."

"I will try to go with you." Black Bird shook his head. "But that trail will be very dangerous in the dark."

"I have already seen it is too steep to walk in the dark. We will only walk the trail a short way. Then we will wait out of sight for the new sun."

"This will give me one more day to rest."

"You will be able to make it."

"I know. I am a Lance Bearer."

"You are."

The day came and passed as Broken Leg kept a close watch on the trail and tried to feed Black Bird as much deer meat as he would eat. Re-bandaging the wound, he nodded, pleased. The wound was sealed and looked good, only it had to be very painful. Broken Leg hated that Black Bird would have to walk on it, but they had no choice. He had to get the warrior past the camp and onto the hidden trail. Then, at least, he would be safe from discovery if he had to leave him behind.

After feeding Black Bird another piece of the deer, Broken Leg helped the injured warrior to his feet. Earlier in the day, he had cut a sapling that Black Bird could lean on and use to help him ease weight off of the injured leg. Pain showed on his face as he took his first few steps.

"The leg will loosen up after you walk on it a few steps. I will carry your bow and arrow quiver."

"No. I will keep my lance and arrow quiver." Leaning heavily on the crutch, Black Bird shook his head. "I might need them if we run into trouble."

"We will move slowly in the dark." Broken Leg held onto Black Bird's arm. "Be careful you do not fall and open your wound again."

"I will do my best."

The full moon burst out from behind clouds as they passed slowly down the mountain. Halfway down, Black Bird was limping badly on his wounded leg, but with Broken Leg's help, he crossed the rough slopes. Reaching the flat ground as the mountain trail leveled off, Broken Leg eased Black Bird down at the base of a large pine. He examined the wound as best he could and found no fresh blood on the bandage.

The wounded leg was painful to walk on but not as bad as Black Bird feared it would be.

"I will leave you here until I locate their guard." Broken Leg pulled the water flask and a piece of deer meat from his shoulder bag and put them in the warrior's hand. "Eat. You will need your strength."

"Thank you, Broken Leg."

"I go now. Try to sleep."

"Be careful, my friend." Black Bird's dark forehead was beaded with sweat. "Remember, Spotted Elk is a crafty one."

"I remember. Stay silent while I am gone."

Broken Leg slipped slowly away, moving cautiously toward the crossing and the camp. He had no way of knowing where the guard would post himself tonight. Crawling across the open spaces, he stayed low, stopping many times to listen for anything that might give away the guard's position. Moving towards the boulder where Bold Knob had positioned himself last night, Broken Leg noticed the light of the fire as he had before. Again, several voices came to him through the dark. Spotted Elk might be cunning, as Black Bird said, but he was foolish sitting here talking around a fire as if he was in his own lands.

Moving away from the fire, he circled to the boulder, and as he had the night before, he found the watcher at the large rock. This time, the warrior was hidden in the shadows of the boulder. If Broken Leg hadn't been looking for the guard, he would never have seen him sitting there. The guard's dark form melted into the shadows, making it impossible for Broken Leg to identify the warrior. Completing a final circle to make certain no other guards were posted around the camp, he moved back where he had left Black Bird.

The night was still young as Broken Leg helped Black Bird bypass the sentry. Only the sound of the night birds made noise as they slowly worked their way to the steep mountain trail. The only sound made by either warrior was Black Bird's heavy breathing. He was weak and exhausted, trying his best to drag himself up the mountain without giving away their presence.

"There." Broken Leg whispered as he spotted the bent pine that appeared out of the dark. "There is the crooked one."

Descending the dark path several yards, Broken Leg helped Black Bird sit back against a slab-sided boulder. "Thank you, my friend. I couldn't have gone much farther without rest."

"I will go erase any tracks we might have left when we turned from the main trail."

Moving back up the small path, Broken Leg stopped as he reached the bigger trail leading to the Crow Killer's valley. Searching out the trail before he moved onto it, he studied the rocky trail. In the dark of the moon, he couldn't discern any tracks they had left on the hard ground as they passed. Finding a pine branch that had broken off in the wind, he brushed the trail to erase any sign he hadn't seen.

He knew that with the coming of the new sun, Spotted Elk planned to ride on to the valley. He doubted the mounted warriors, not knowing of any enemies' presence on this rocky mountain, would look for sign on the trail. Still, Broken Leg didn't want to take any chances of being discovered. Black Bird wouldn't be able to get away from any pursuers if they were discovered.

Broken Leg held the limb and looked down the steep trail. He was tempted to move lower and see what Spotted Elk and his warriors were up to, but he changed his mind. The trail was steep, and he would need all of his strength to help Black Bird along the dangerous trail going down the canyon.

Dragging the pine limb, he tried not to leave any signs that the trail had been brushed over. Hopefully, the new day would bring a wind that would blow away any sign of his passing that he had missed. Taking one last look down the trail, he turned back to where he had left Black Bird.

"Are we followed?"

"I do not think this." Broken Leg took the offered water flask and put it to his lips. "How do you feel?"

"With the new sun, I will try to walk."

"How far do you think it is to the valley trail?"

"This I do not know." Black Bird shook his head. "All I remember is when Crow Killer and I got to the ridge, Red Horse had already gotten Grass Bee away from the whites and was pursuing the one that had taken her."

"Why is it so far horseback?"

Black Bird bit off a piece of venison. "Above the trail is blocked by rocky cliffs, and those on horses have to veer off and circle far around."

"But this trail leads straight down the canyon?"

"This is what Red Horse told me. He also said that in places, it was a difficult trail to walk."

"Soon, the new sun will raise its head. Does Black Bird think he can make the ridge?"

"I don't know. All I can do is try." The dark head shrugged. "If I cannot, then you must leave me behind and go on alone."

"You will make it, Lance Bearer."

"Broken Leg puts a lot of faith in a Lance Bearer."

"No, my friend, I put a lot of faith in your heart."

CHAPTER 11

AFTER THE FIGHT in the gorge, Crow Killer had Straight Arrow take the lead. They left the carnage of the gorge behind them and headed due north. Straight Arrow led two of the spare horses in a slow lope while several other horses were strung out, running tied head to tail by their hackamores and tails. Big Smoke handled the halter rope on the lead horse, and Jumping Rabbit kept the horses bunched together so they wouldn't be dragging the others back. Red Hawk, Crow Killer, and Eagle Wing also led two horses apiece.

Jumping Rabbit seemed to have matured overnight since the fight in the gorge. The repeating rifle taken from a dead Pawnee was carried proudly in one hand, and the skinning knife hung from his side. A belt filled with cartridges was wrapped around his small waist. He was young and small in size, but now the repeating rifle made him the equal of a mature warrior.

Eagle Wing nodded as he watched the proud youngster ride with his chest thrown out and his face set hard. Before leaving the gorge, he had shown the boy how to fire and reload the rifle. He had no doubt that if the youngster was needed to fight, he could be counted on. Only fourteen summers of age, yet no fear showed in this one.

Late in the day, Straight Arrow slowed down to a trot and

turned slightly to the west, riding into a grove of maple and spruce trees. A small creek with crystal clear water flowed before them. He reined in behind a dense stand of spruce and studied the creek for several minutes before moving on down to the cool water.

"We will rest and let the horses graze for a short while, then we will move on."

Crow Killer looked back out across the open prairie. "There has been no sign of Lawrence or Bull Coat."

"They are back there. I can smell them." Straight Arrow frowned. "We must ride with watchful eyes from here to the Canadians."

Red Hawk agreed. "They will follow. They think they have Eagle Wing trapped up here in the north."

"This far to the north, I think now they plan to wait for Eagle Wing when he rides toward Fort Robinson." Straight Arrow slid from his horse. "They think he will not be expecting them there."

Eagle Wing shrugged. "Sometimes the hunter gets caught in his own trap."

"This is true, my friend." Straight Arrow patted his horse. "But there are many hunters on our trail."

Quickly hobbling the horses, the warriors walked to where Blue Feather was preparing the supplies of biscuits and dried meat they had captured from the dead Pawnees. Thanking the girl as she handed him the food, Crow Killer watched as she took her own food and collapsed tiredly on the sandy bank. Moving to where she sat, he smiled. "The water is inviting."

"Yes." Her voice sounded tired. "It is beautiful here with the overhanging trees and the shady banks. And the singing birds make it so peaceful."

"We have time if Blue Feather would like to go downstream and take a bath. It would help take the soreness from your body."

"It would feel good to bathe."

"Go, child. We will wait."

"I thank Crow Killer, but I will bathe when I reach the

Canadians." Blue Feather shook her head. "If the enemy came, I would look foolish without my clothes."

"Then rest, girl." Crow Killer stood up. "We will probably be riding all night."

"Straight Arrow hurries this trail."

"He fears for you and Jumping Rabbit's safety."

"He shouldn't fear for that one." Blue Feather smiled slightly. "Look at the pride in him. The Pawnee should be the ones with fear."

"He is a nice-looking young man, isn't he?"

"Your son Eagle Wing is the nice-looking one." The girl grinned. "But he already has a woman, so I guess Jumping Rabbit will do."

Crow Killer laughed lightly as he walked away. The young woman knew what she wanted and wasn't afraid to speak her mind. She and Jumping Rabbit were about the same age. In a few years they would make a good match.

The sun had just passed its zenith when Straight Arrow tied the horses together again and swung up on his horse. Looking around to see if all the others were mounted, he pointed north. "We will be riding steadily through the night." Straight Arrow turned the big cavalry horse he rode around to face the others. "Tomorrow, when the sun is high, if we don't see any pony soldiers or their scouts, we will camp on the big river and hunt for meat."

"The Musselshell?"

Big Smoke nodded. "That is what the river is called by the white eyes."

Crow Killer studied the rough map and blew out a breath. "We have crossed a lot of prairie."

"And we have many more to cross before we reach the Grandmother's Land." Straight Arrow gestured at the flats. "But if we ride hard, and no pony soldiers attack us, we should reach the Milk River in three or four sleeps."

"Then how far is the Canadians?" Eagle Wing glanced over at

Blue Feather. "The girl tires."

"With no problems, at most two sleeps from the last river we cross."

The moon fell over the land, lighting up the prairie as the small group passed through the waving grasses. Straight Arrow had spoken the truth. He kept the horses moving through the night with only two stops to water the animals. With the coming of day, they found themselves in another deeply wooded area.

Crow Killer had ridden beside Blue Feather through the dark times. He could see the girl was completely exhausted, but she was too brave to admit it.

Following a well-worn game trail through the trees, Straight Arrow reined in near the edge of the timbered land. It was almost midday, and in front of them lay more flat prairie land covered in grass with only a few small scrub trees.

"Here, the ground looks flat, but there are many swells out on this prairie, and the tall grass hides too much." Straight Arrow pointed with his rifle. "We will rest here while Big Smoke searches out any enemies that we cannot see from here."

The warrior rode out in a slow lope and quickly vanished from their sight. The tall grass and the rolling prairie seemed to swallow him and the horse immediately. Crow Killer tried to see the warrior, but Big Smoke and his horse had completely disappeared. "Is the Musselshell ahead of us?"

"Only a short way. There should be four-leggeds here, but I have seen no sign of the shaggies anywhere."

"Nor have I." Eagle Wing studied the surrounding area. "The grass has not been eaten or tromped down by the herds."

"I feel something is not right." Straight Arrow frowned. "Always, since I was a boy, the shaggies roamed these prairies in great numbers."

Crow Killer leaned forward on his horse, staring at the rolling plains. "What does Straight Arrow think?"

"I see nothing, but I smell enemies."

"While the horses rest, Eagle Wing, Red Hawk, and I will hunt and find something to fill our stomachs."

Grabbing Blue Feather as she slid tiredly from her horse, Jumping Rabbit helped her to a place beneath a tree. "I will bring Blue Feather water and a pony soldier biscuit to eat."

"Thank you, warrior, but I am too tired to eat."

"Eat, woman. Then you can sleep until Big Smoke returns."

Blue Feather was exhausted, but she had to grin. Jumping Rabbit was still a boy, but he was strutting with his shoulders back and chest out and already trying to act like a warrior. Still, she enjoyed the attention he paid her and did her best to chew the dry biscuit before falling asleep. It seemed like her eyes had just closed when Straight Arrow announced they were riding again. Never again would she listen when the squaws of the village said warriors never worked, just played. Those squaws had never been horseback for a full moon with little rest.

Straight Arrow sat his horse excitedly in front of the others. "Big Smoke has discovered a pony soldier camp to the east."

"How many soldiers?" Eagle Wing looked over at the warrior.

"Their lodges are many." Shrugging, the stocky Sioux opened his hands many times. "Too many to fight."

"That explains why there are no four-leggeds here." Crow Killer nodded. "We hunted, but could find nothing."

"We'll have to circle to the west around them." Straight Arrow motioned with his hand. "Watch closely for our enemies. They can be anywhere. We go."

"Are we taking all the horses with us?" Big Smoke spoke up.

"We will." Straight Arrow kicked his gelding. "Be ready to turn loose the extra horses and run if we are discovered."

Straight Arrow kicked his horse into a slow lope and turned to the northwest. Big Smoke had given the lead rope to Eagle Wing and, after changing horses, had ridden out ahead of them. Crow Killer was thankful the summer grass was almost belly-deep on the smaller horses. It made it harder to ride through, but their chances of being discovered were greatly diminished.

All that appeared on the horizon were more vacant grasslands and not a four-legged in sight. Ten years ago, Straight Arrow had said there would have been thousands of buffalo grazing these prairies. Deer, antelope, and even some elk would have been found on the prairies and in the forests. Now, there was nothing. Soon, Crazy Horse and his people would have to make a choice: either starve or move to a reservation. There, given the white man's rations, at least they could survive.

There used to be a few herds to the south, but the pony soldiers had burned the prairie and ran off all the northern herds. Civilization, Crow Killer shook his head. That's what the whites called it: starving people and killing off their food source if they couldn't subjugate them by force. He thought of his valley and how fortunate he was to have it. One day, he, too, might have to fight invaders trying to take his land. For now, though, the high mountain valley was still remote. And the deed paper Oliver had given him was proof of his ownership of both valleys. It should keep his lands safe. For now.

Ahead, as they topped a small rise, they saw the sheen of the sun reflecting off of the Musselshell River down below. Straight Arrow reined up in a small stand of trees and sent Big Smoke ahead to scout the river. The big river was less than a mile ahead. Straight Arrow thought pony soldiers might be patrolling its banks, looking for hostiles trying to reach the Canadians, just as they were doing. They all tensed as they waited and set their horses, ready to flee, watching for Big Smoke to reappear.

When they saw the smile on his face as the big Sioux loped his horse back to them, they all relaxed, knowing no enemy had been found. Waving his rifle over his head, he seemed to be enjoying himself.

"Big Smoke has found something that makes him smile."

Eagle Wing shrugged. "What could he have found out here?"

"I think maybe something to eat." Straight Arrow laughed. "Big Smoke likes to eat, and we haven't eaten anything but dried pony soldier bread today."

Reining in, the warrior held up a bloody arrow. "I have found no enemy, but I did find a large deer that wanted to feed us."

"See?" Straight Arrow looked over at the others and grinned. "I told you why he smiled. Let's ride to the river and cook this deer."

"You think it'll be safe?" Blue Feather glanced warily out across the flat lands. "The enemy could see our smoke."

"Woman, would you rather die by an enemy bullet or by starving?" Jumping Rabbit shook his head as he rode by her. "Women."

She tossed her chin up. "I'd prefer not to die from either."

The deer lay on their side of the river, very near the bank. Big Smoke gutted the big deer and slung the carcass across a horse's back. While the warrior loaded the deer and lashed it down, Eagle Wing and Red Hawk crossed the Musselshell River and found a secluded spot along its banks to safely build a fire. The crossing before them had been shallow enough for the horses to wade without swimming. Waving the others across, they kept a close watch as the crossing was made.

After crossing, Blue Feather removed her moccasins and let the warm water wash around her feet as they waded in the river.

Jumping Rabbit grinned. "Blue Feather has pretty feet."

Frowning, the girl turned her dark eyes on him. "Don't let your eyes fall out."

He laughed. "They won't."

Crow Killer hobbled the horses on good grazing and sent Jumping Rabbit and Straight Arrow to stand watch on each side of the camp while the deer was being cooked. Tired as she was, Blue Feather helped Big Smoke skin and quarter the heavy deer, then cut it into steaks. This was a woman's work. Almost from the time she could walk, she had learned how to butcher deer with the grain. This would guarantee the meat would be tender and almost melt in your mouth.

Crow Killer watched along the riverbank for any unseen enemy. This was a wild and desolate land, with enemies, both red and white, roaming the prairie. Danger could come at them at any time. With the Canadians and safety so near, he wasn't about to drop his guard.

"We will finish our meal, then move away from this camp farther into the forest lands." Straight Arrow swallowed. "When the horses have watered and eaten their fill of the deep grass, then we will go."

Crow Killer remembered the warrior's sense of danger when Big Smoke had discovered the soldier camp. He trusted this warrior's instincts just as he did his and Red Hawk's. "As soon as we finish eating, we will ride."

"This is a good plan." Red Hawk agreed.

"Can Big Smoke get on his horse?" Straight Arrow laughed lightly.

In ways, the big Sioux Warrior reminded Crow Killer of another warrior who had been killed back on the big river many moons ago. Both were strong men with a jovial way about them unless they were mad. He remembered Big Owl with sadness but also with good memories. He had been a friend and a great warrior. He knew the warrior was in the happy hunting grounds with his favorite horse running the shaggies. Yes, Big Smoke reminded him of Big Owl, the Lance Bearer.

The days and nights passed in a blur as the tired riders moved northwards towards the Canadians. Several times, patrols of pony soldiers had been spotted out on the prairie. Straight Arrow had used the swells in the open prairie to keep them concealed carefully from the sharp-eyed Pawnee scouts.

Reining in where Big Smoke sat his horse near another line of trees, Straight Arrow studied the far horizon. "You have seen nothing?"

"Nothing, two-legged or four-legged. It is like Mother Earth swallowed up everything living."

"Good. We will rest the horses here until the dark times come again."

Big Smoke slid from his horse. "The last river is just ahead."

"Is this the Milk River?" Crow Killer looked over at the warrior.

"That is what the white eyes call the river."

"Soldiers!" Red Hawk whispered as he spotted several mounted men riding to the north. "White pony soldiers."

Straight Arrow shook his head. "They ride towards the river."

"I saw nothing when I rode there." Big Smoke watched the soldiers as they passed from sight. "The prairie and the swells hide many things."

"It is a small party of the pony soldiers." Eagle Wing looked out from the trees. "We have no worry from these Long Knives. They did not see us."

"And one Pawnee dog." Jumping Rabbit pointed as a lone rider rode through the tall grass straight to where they waited, hidden in the trees. "I don't think he has seen us yet. He just comes here to check this place for us hostiles."

"Jumping Rabbit has eyes like the hawk."

Big Smoke handed his blowing horse to Jumping Rabbit and moved swiftly down the tree line. Notching an arrow to his powerful bow, he knelt on one knee and waited.

"The Pawnee is a dead warrior if he does not turn." The youngster whispered to Blue Feather. "Big Smoke will not miss."

Reining in at the edge of the timber, the Pawnee studied the surrounding trees as he sat just out of bow range. For several minutes, he sat his horse, then turned the animal and followed after the pony soldiers. Big Smoke shook his head and watched the warrior ride out of sight.

"He was one lucky Pawnee." Jumping Rabbit shook his head in disgust. "A few more steps, and he would have gone to meet his ancestors today."

"You have become bloodthirsty." Blue Feather looked over at him.

"They are the bloodthirsty ones." Jumping Rabbit shrugged. "They're not out here hunting for rabbits. Too bad he didn't come closer. He would have made a good Pawnee."

"We will wait here while Big Smoke goes ahead to scout." Straight Arrow slipped from his horse. "I think there will be more pony soldiers riding the prairie patrolling the river."

"We will let Big Smoke rest. Red Hawk and I will scout ahead." Crow Killer swung up onto a small bay gelding.

"Do not ride the Appaloosa." Big Smoke grinned at Red Hawk. "His spots will catch the notice of every sharp eye out there."

Red Hawk swung upon a bay horse. "Thank you, Sioux."

The river Straight Arrow and Big Smoke had called The Milk lay just below the small rise where they waited. The milky water flowed lazily along this section of the river. Riding warily across the flats, Crow Killer and Red Hawk hadn't spotted any riders out on the vast grasslands as they rode nearer the river.

"One of us will wait here and watch for riders." Crow Killer reined in and studied the river closely for many minutes. "I will go." He turned his mount.

"Keep a sharp eye out, my brother." Red Hawk warned. "This is a strange land."

"How is it strange, my friend?"

"There is nothing out here, just grass, more grass and the quiet."

"Red Hawk is right. It is not like our mountains."

"I think the pony soldiers must have driven all the shaggies to the south away from the Canadians."

"I figure it is to starve Sitting Bull into leaving the Grandmother's Land and surrendering to reservation life." Crow Killer shook his head. "An empty stomach weakens even the strongest of warriors."

"A strong fighter like Sitting Bull will never be happy on a piece of land the whites give him." Red Hawk frowned. "His heart is bad for the white man and their reservation life."

Crow Killer looked out across the vast grasslands and then turned toward the river. "It is a beautiful country. If I were Sitting Bull, I wouldn't want to leave these lands either."

"Nor would I. But as Chief, he must do what is best for his people. I am glad I do not have to make such a choice for the Crow People."

"Watch closely, my brother. I will ride for the others."

Riding towards the Milk, Straight Arrow held the small party back from the river. He had them hide in a stand of dense cane breaks that grew thick along its banks. Big Smoke and Eagle Wing rode ahead, making a wide swing up and down the river, checking for soldiers and also looking for a shallow crossing. They all knew that crossing the river in daylight would be the greatest danger. If the sharp-eyed Pawnee or Crow scouts spotted them while they were in the river, they would be helpless. Crossing would be dangerous, but waiting hidden along the banks was also dangerous. At any time, a patrol of pony soldiers with their scouts could ride along the river and see signs of their passing.

Watching as the two warriors kicked their horses into the water, Straight Arrow strained his dark eyes, trying to see movement of any kind on the opposite bank. Trees lined both sides of the river, reaching down almost to the water's edge. An enemy could easily be concealed, waiting until Crow Killer and his small band were mid-stream before opening fire. A sigh of relief came from the watchers as the two warriors splashed up out of the water onto the sandy banks.

Staying concealed, they watched as both warriors disappeared into the shadowy trees for what seemed like an hour. Finally, they breathed a sigh of relief as Big Smoke rode out onto the bank and motioned them across. During the dry times of the browning grass, the river was at its shallowest. This time, the horses had only a short distance to swim before they waded across the last few feet onto the bank.

Crow Killer nodded as he splashed out of the water. "How much farther is it to the Canadians?"

"A hard day's ride from this place, but it will be the most dangerous." The warrior shook his head. "The pony soldiers will watch like rabid wolves for any Indian trying to cross the boundary that divides the Canadians."

"We will rest the horses, then we will ride through the dark times these last few miles." Eagle Wing slid from his horse.

"These lands are very treacherous in places." Big Smoke shook his head. "We should ride now until the sun fades and then rest until the new sun comes over the land again."

"Big Smoke is right. We should be able to see any enemy and hide if one comes into sight." Straight Arrow agreed. "If we are discovered, it will be a running fight to the Canadians, but that is our best chance."

Crow Killer looked over at Red Hawk and shrugged. "What does my brother say?"

"These warriors know this land better than we do. Whatever they wish will be done."

"Then we will ride until the sun goes down."

"For now, we will ride the weakest of the horses." Big Smoke studied the animals. "If we have to run, pick out the strongest and fleetest and mount them."

Looking at Jumping Rabbit and Blue Feather, Red Hawk pointed at two horses they led, a barrel-chested, long-limbed bay and a tall sorrel carrying the US brand. "Ride those if we are seen and have to flee."

Jumping Rabbit raised his rifle and smiled, which made Blue Feather frown. "This is not funny, warrior. This is serious."

"What tales we will have to tell our friends." The youngster shook his head. "If we have to flee with Pawnee dogs on our heels, it will be a great story for the cold nights around our fires."

"If we make it to our fires." Blue Feather frowned. "You are as crazy as the loony bird."

Jumping Rabbit looked down at his rifle and rubbed the stock. "Crazy enough to kill one Pawnee."

"One Pawnee might eat you, boy."

"I do not think this. They would not waste their time." The youngster laughed. "I am far too skinny."

"Crazy is what you are." Blue Feather shook her head. "But at least you are brave, as a warrior should be."

Blushing, Jumping Rabbit swung up onto the smaller horse and smiled over at Blue Feather. "I will protect Blue Feather with my life if we are discovered."

Straight Arrow waved his arm, and they turned to the north, riding the last few miles to the Canadians. Their long days and nights crossing the territories had been difficult and dangerous, but the boundary line lay just ahead. With luck, by the new day, they would be safely in Canada.

CHAPTER 12

WITH BIG SMOKE AND EAGLE WING scouting the broken land ahead for enemies, the small column moved warily toward the Canadians. Big Smoke and Straight Arrow had spoken the truth. This part of the country was broken with gullies and washes, making it too hazardous for the horses to cross during the dark hours. Even in daylight, they had to keep the animals on a slow trot as they rode northward. The land was dotted with large holes deep enough to snap a horse's leg if he stepped into one. Crow Killer figured the holes were made by the black-tailed prairie dogs that Straight Arrow had said were common to these lands. He didn't know of any other land animals that would dig such deep burrows surrounded by mounds.

They rode strung out in a line, and Crow Killer knew they would be easy to spot if any pony soldiers were watching this part of the boundary line. The grass here had been burnt off. He didn't know whether a lightning strike had started a grass fire or if the pony soldiers had burnt off this section of the prairie as they had others. It didn't matter. They had to move north even though it would make them visible to any sharp-eyed scout.

Straight Arrow had said the Canadians were only a hard day's ride away. A hard day, yes, but it would also be a dangerous day if they were discovered. If an enemy spotted them, it would be a running fight to the border. He hated knowing the children might be exposed to gunfire, but they had no choice. To reach Wood

Mountain, Sitting Bull, and the boundary line, these last few miles had to be crossed, no matter the risk.

Crow Killer rode alongside the very tired Blue Feather and Jumping Rabbit and tried to lift their spirits. "If we are discovered, be prepared for a hard race to the Canadians."

Blue Feather frowned over at the youngster riding ahead of her. "Jumping Rabbit, the crazy one, is thrilled at that idea."

"Crazy one?" Crow Killer didn't understand why she called Jumping Rabbit crazy.

Blue Feather smiled. "He thinks because of the rifle, he is now a warrior. He wants a chance to kill a Pawnee and count coup."

"And that makes him crazy?"

"I think it does."

"Well, I guess at his age, we were all a little crazy."

Blue Feather smiled at Jumping Rabbit. "Well, I know this one is crazy."

"I do not tell you this to scare you, but if we are fired on, lean low over your horse's neck." Crow Killer changed the subject. "It will make you a smaller target."

"He is already skinnier than I am."

"Don't worry, woman." Jumping Rabbit threw out his chest. "The Pawnee are terrible shots, but I, the crazy one, will protect the daughter of Gall."

"How would you know if they are bad shots?"

"I have seen them shoot." The youngster laughed again. "Just don't fall from your horse. That is all you need to worry about."

Crow Killer interrupted their teasing. "If Straight Arrow yells, you must change horses quickly and release the others."

Crow Killer knew the boy was right. Running horses across this rough ground could make a horse stumble or fall and cause the rider to tumble off. But if they were spotted, they must either run and maybe fall into one of the deep holes or be shot by their pursuers. If discovered, the youngsters would have to run for their lives.

The sun was low in the west when Big Smoke, scouting the terrain ahead, held up his rifle and waved the riders on. Ahead stood a small stand of pines, big enough to conceal them for the night. The grass fire had singed the trees, but still, the burnt pines were thick enough to hide them from prying eyes. A small gulley of stagnant water, good enough for the horses to drink, lay inside the trees.

Straight Arrow looked about at the scorched trees and shook his head. "No fire. The enemy could be close."

"Keep your fastest horse tied to your arm while you sleep." Big Smoke was, for once, serious. "With the coming of the new sun, we will be riding hard."

Blue Feather stared at the dried tough meat Eagle Wing handed her. "How far are the Canadians?"

"Not far, but we might have to fight our way across into the Grandmother's Land."

Big Smoke took in a deep breath. "It is always patrolled by the pony soldiers and their scouts."

"Pawnee?" Jumping Rabbit asked.

"It could be the Pawnee, Crow, or even our own people now scouting for the whites." Straight Arrow shrugged. "Or it could be the tribes from across the boundary not wanting us to cross into their lands."

Crow Killer looked over at Straight Arrow. "You say Sioux are scouting for the Army?"

"Yes, warriors from Red Cloud's band and some from Spotted Tail's people have agreed to help the pony soldiers against us."

Eagle Wing shook his head. "I never would have believed that."

"I, myself, have seen Sioux riding with the white eyes." Big Smoke nodded sadly. "Even some of my own relatives scout against us. Feed a dog, and he will do your bidding, even fight his own kind."

"What Big Smoke says is true." Straight Arrow waved his arm.

"And here, it could also be enemy tribes from the north who will want to stop us from entering their lands."

"But Sitting Bull and my father are there."

"Yes, they are in the Grandmother's Lands. The local tribes, Assiniboine and Cree, are not happy that unwanted people have entered their lands. Now they try to stop any more from coming into their hunting grounds." Big Smoke shook his head. "We have to be ready to run or fight. We must watch for enemies in front and behind before we reach Sitting Bull's camp."

"What exciting tales we will have to tell around the fire." Jumping Rabbit chewed his meat happily.

Blue Feather shook her head. "You are one crazy boy."

"Warrior." He waved the rifle.

"A rifle does not make a boy into a man, crazy one."

"Blue Feather will see one day."

With the first faint light in the east, Straight Arrow had everyone mounted and ready to ride. A cold meal of dried meat and cold biscuits was their breakfast eaten on the trail. Mounted on the swiftest and strongest animals now, they continued to lead the slower animals. At the first signs of trouble, they would quickly be turned loose. But for now, Straight Arrow wanted to keep the weaker animals. Across the boundary into the Canadians, if affronted by a hostile tribe, perhaps they could be traded for safe passage to Wood Mountain and Sitting Bull. These northern tribes were no different than the plains tribes. Every warrior wanted more horses. Horses made them rich in their tribe's eyes.

Again, Big Smoke and Eagle Wing took the lead as they started across the tree-dotted land. Straight Arrow said there were only a few miles left before they should see the boundary. Eagle Wing didn't know what the warrior meant by seeing the boundary. Perhaps it was marked somehow by a natural landmark. Hopefully, this part of the trail would be free of pony soldiers searching for hostiles.

The sun was high overhead as the two warriors scouting ahead rode up out of a ground swell right into the face of a squad of horse soldiers. The soldiers had been concealed in a belt of timber, relaxing lazily along a small waterway streaming through a small stand of aspen and fir trees. The soldiers were taken completely by surprise at the sudden appearance of the two warriors.

Lunging to their feet, the soldiers scrambled hastily for their horses and rifles. In their haste to reach the horses, one man fell clumsily and scared the animals. The spooked horses broke free, rearing up and lunging back away from the frantic soldiers.

Big Smoke didn't hesitate. He fired his rifle, killing a Pawnee lookout who had managed to swing up on his horse. Eagle Wing levered round after round into the milling soldiers, forcing them to retreat behind cover. Another Pawnee raced on foot after the running horses, only to be brought down by Big Smoke's belching rifle. Complete bedlam sounded along the waterway as racing horses, cussing soldiers, and an officer barking orders added to the confusion and disorder. A spattering of pistol shots rang out, but their excited owners missed their targets completely.

Whirling their horses, Eagle Wing and Big Smoke turned to get out of range of the blazing pistols. Trying to run, Big Smoke didn't see a third Pawnee scout charging toward them, firing his Army carbine. The bullet brought down Big Smoke's horse. Both horse and rider plunged sideways to the ground. Rolling free from the dead animal, Big Smoke pointed his rifle at the oncoming scout and fired. The heavy slug knocked the Pawnee backward. Big Smoke grabbed the dragging rein of the scout's horse and swung nimbly up onto the running animal as it raced past him.

Amazed at his new friend, Eagle Wing yelled in triumph and fired his Henry into the cussing soldiers. Not wanting to anger the white eyes any more than necessary, he didn't aim to kill them, only to cover their retreat.

As they raced away, Eagle Wing grinned at the remarkable Sioux. Catching and mounting the dead Pawnee's horse in full flight was quite a feat for a man the size of Big Smoke. Granted, the trail leading over the rise was narrow and may have made it slightly easier to snare the racing horse, but still, it was an incredible feat of horsemanship.

Racing back over the swell, they found Crow Killer, Red Hawk, and Straight Arrow coming towards them at a run. They'd heard the gunfire and screaming and were racing to their assistance. Waving them back, Big Smoke led the riders in a wide circuit out of range of the revolvers the soldiers were firing. Their rifles were out of reach as they had disappeared with the panicked horses racing ahead of them. Big Smoke reined in and slowed the riders' flight. He knew they would be far away, maybe even over the boundary line, before the pony soldiers could catch their loose horses and give chase. Eagle Wing, riding beside Red Hawk, smiled. He would like to be present when the officer who had been yelling tried to explain to his soldier chief how they had lost their horses and let the hostiles escape.

Scouting the flat burnt grassland for more enemies, Eagle Wing grinned over at Big Smoke. "Straight Arrow should have seen that flying mount you made on the Pawnee horse."

The big Sioux only shrugged. "He would still not believe what he saw."

"Well, Big Smoke, I saw it. And that was the best piece of horsemanship I've ever seen."

"Was it even better than the Crow could do?" Big Smoke grinned over at Red Hawk.

"I believe it was, my friend." Eagle Wing shook his head, still amazed as he thought back on the feat. "Much better than any I have ever seen."

Straight Arrow, who had been listening, looked over at the big warrior and nodded. "I see you have a new horse."

"Yes, my friend, but you didn't see how I got it." Big Smoke patted the horse's neck. "That is the story for the cold times."

"I know Big Smoke. Someday, we will hear all about it."

Straight Arrow grinned over at his friend.

Eagle Wing smiled as he listened to the friendly banter of the two friends and glanced over at Straight Arrow. "I will tell Straight Arrow something else that happened. Today, Big Smoke killed three Pawnee, counted coup, and took the horse he rides."

"It is a fine animal." Red Hawk was curious about what had excited Eagle Wing so much. Nothing short of his newborn son had ever excited the warrior the way he was talking today. "Tell us, my nephew. What really happened? How did Big Smoke get the horse?"

Looking over at the warrior, Eagle Wing grinned. "It is Big Smoke's story to tell."

"You killed three Pawnee today?" Jumping Rabbit stared at the big Sioux in awe. "Really?"

"He did that and more." Eagle Wing nodded as Big Smoke moved his horse back out in front of them. "He is a fearless warrior, that one."

"He is." Straight Arrow agreed. "Also, a sad one."

"Then there are three more good Pawnee," the youngster said proudly.

With a slight smile, Blue Feather shook her dark head. "Jumping Rabbit, I swear you are bloodthirsty for one so young."

"I am, woman. And my thirst has not yet been slaked."

Straight Arrow set his horse, watching Eagle Wing and Big Smoke ride across a flat and circle their horses. At the all-clear signal, he kicked his horse and led the others to where they waited.

"We are in the Grandmother's Land now."

"How do you know this? I see no markers or anything." Crow Killer looked about the grasslands for some kind of boundary marker. Nothing showed him that they had crossed into the Canadians.

"There." Big Smoke raised his huge arm and pointed. "See the cut marks on the pine trees?"

"Someone marked the trees as the boundary?"

"The pony soldiers did this, a sign for them to know not to cross the line into the Canadians and start trouble with the northern whites and the Red Coats." Straight Arrow nodded. "The Metis are always wishing to make trouble."

"Red Coats?" Red Hawk didn't understand the meaning. "What are Red Coats?"

"They are the pony soldiers of the Canadians." Crow Killer tried to explain to Red Hawk. "They all wear red coats."

"Then there are many of these Red Coats?"

Crow Killer's mother had told him of the Canadian Mounted Red Coats when he was a child. "No, only a very few. Most times, only one Red Coat controls the land."

"They must be very strong if it only takes one to make the tribes honor their law?"

"Very strong, very proud, yes. The hostile tribes listen when they speak in council."

Red Hawk was impressed. "I would like to meet these warriors."

"I imagine you'll get the chance when we find Sitting Bull."

"Let's ride. Now, all we have to watch for are the warriors of the north tribes." Straight Arrow kicked his horse. "The pony soldiers will not follow us across the boundary."

Straight Arrow again sent Big Smoke ahead to scout out the trail to the north. The local tribes would object to their crossing into their tribal lands. Armed poorly, the Assiniboine and Cree had not been able to prevent Sitting Bull's heavily armed warriors from entering the Canadians. But Crow Killer's small party with only a few warriors could easily be ambushed.

In the dimness of the falling sun, Crow Killer rode his horse beside Straight Arrow. "How far are we from the camp of Sitting Bull?"

"One day's ride to the north will get us to his camp at Wood Mountain." The warrior shook his head. "But we wait until the new moon rises to show us the way. The youngsters can use the rest."

Big Smoke looked up at the darkening sky. "The moon will be full tonight and show us the way."

"Will the Assiniboine have scouts out at night?" Red Hawk stared out at the darkening woods around them.

"I do not think this. They like the warmth and safety of their lodges during the evil hours." Big Smoke tugged at the line of horses he was leading. "They have not had to fight like the Sioux have."

Crow Killer knew most tribes were the same. They were superstitious, and many feared the bad omens of the dark times. Some tribes would not fight at night, afraid that if killed, their spirits would forever wander the earth, never to go to their great hunting grounds in the sky. Tonight, if they were lucky, their passage would be unnoticed.

Sliding from their horses, they picketed the animals on what little grass they could find. No water was in the area, so it would be a dry camp until they moved on and found water. Relaxing, the warriors listened to the quiet of the night. Crow Killer had never been this far north. He could feel the chill in the colder night air. He listened for the night walkers, but he heard nothing he recognized.

Blue Feather and Jumping Rabbit, for once, had fallen asleep without the usual bickering. Both were totally exhausted from the miles of riding and the many dangers that they had encountered on their way north. Crow Killer had to admire the youngsters. Both had shown a great deal of strength and fortitude on the journey. Tomorrow, if all went well, they would be in the village of Sitting Bull, where they would be reunited with their families.

Later, under the full light of the new moon, they moved on to the north. With the coming of the new day, Straight Arrow reined in his horse and stared out across the barren ground broken up by heavy stands of poplar trees. The weary travelers gazed towards the dense trees and saw nothing else in sight.

"Have you ever been to Wood Mountain?" Crow Killer asked Straight Arrow.

"No." The warrior stared intently at the stand of poplars. "I have never crossed the boundary into the Canadians."

"I see no mountains. Why do they call it Wood Mountain?"

Straight Arrow shrugged. "Some say the first Metis people gave this place that name because of the trees that grow here."

"It is a funny name for such a place." Red Hawk looked across the barren land. "There is nothing here."

"The village of Sitting Bull is near." Big Smoke looked over at Jumping Rabbit. "I think many Sioux await us in the trees ahead."

Eagle Wing stared across the field. "You think we have been discovered."

"I think Sitting Bull already knows we are here. His visions are strong." Straight Arrow kicked his horse's side. "We go."

Eagle Wing had heard many times of the great Chief Sitting Bull being able to see into the future. People at Bridger's said that he had foretold of Custer's defeat before it even happened. Crazy Horse, Gall, and American Horse were the war chiefs and the fighters, but Sitting Bull was the one who united the tribes into a formidable fighting force. That is why the pony soldiers hated and feared him more than any of the other chiefs.

Crow Killer and his party were barely halfway across the small clearing when several warriors rode out from the tree line and set up a long line waiting for them. Straight Arrow didn't slow his horse. He just walked the animal straight toward the center of the long line and held up his hand.

"I greet the great Chiefs Gall and American Horse."

"It has been many moons since we have spoken, Straight Arrow." The stocky war chief nodded. "It is good you have come."

"The great warrior Crow Killer and your friend Eagle Wing bring something that will please Gall."

Crow Killer moved to the front with Blue Feather and Jumping Rabbit. Gall's eyes lit up and he slid from his horse, running to take the small girl in his arms. "My daughter."

Crow Killer could see tears were about to come into the eyes of the great leader, something that was hard to stop. Never would a warrior show such emotion, but Blue Feather was his only living child. Gall couldn't hold back the tears as he held her.

Releasing the girl, Gall walked to where Crow Killer had slid from his horse and gave him a powerful hug, something else that was also never done. "I have heard much of Crow Killer, the father of Eagle Wing."

"And I have heard much of Chief Gall, the fighting arm of the Hunkpapa." Crow Killer turned to where Red Hawk sat his horse. "This is my brother Red Hawk of the Crow Nation."

Gall studied the broad handsome face and reached out his arm. "If he is the brother of Crow Killer, then he is my brother as well."

A quiet murmur went up and down the line of warriors as the two men shook hands. Never would they have believed they would see such a sight. The great warrior, Chief Gall, gripping the arm of a Crow in friendship.

"I am proud to meet Gall." Red Hawk ignored the murmuring. "I have heard of your deeds of bravery in battle."

"Eagle Wing, my son." Gall embraced the warrior. "How is Morning Dove?"

"She is well, Uncle." Eagle Wing smiled. "We have a new son now."

"A son." Gall smiled. "That makes me proud."

Chief Gall turned to face his warriors and raised his arms. "Hear me. These warriors have returned Blue Feather and Jumping Rabbit safely to their people. Let no harm or word of dishonor come to them."

Rain in the Face kicked his horse forward and looked into Red Hawk's face. "I have fought the Crow against yellow-haired Custer and his brother. But if you are the brother of Crow Killer and the uncle of Eagle Wing. Then, I, too, welcome you, great Chief."

"Thank you, Rain in the Face. I have also heard of the great Sioux warrior who fought against Custer."

"A great battle, but all for nothing." The warrior shook his head. "We hide here in the Grandmother's Land like rabbits."

American Horse, taller than the others, walked forward with Jumping Rabbit and stopped. Reaching out his hand, he nodded happily and thanked Crow Killer.

"I never thought to see my son in this life again." The tall chief smiled. "Thank you, Crow Killer."

"Your son is a brave young man. He earned the rifle he carries and a new name."

American Horse looked down at the rifle and at the long-skinning knife strapped to his son. "The workmanship on the sheath of this knife is Pawnee."

"It is." Eagle Wing admitted. "Jumping Rabbit took it from the hands of a live Pawnee."

Hearing those words, a triumphant yell went up from the mounted warriors.

Jumping Rabbit looked over at Blue Feather and smiled. He was surprised that, for once, the girl returned his smile with no words of criticism.

American Horse smiled proudly down at the youngster. "He will have a new name soon."

"Come, we will go hold council with Sitting Bull." Chief Gall helped Blue Feather up on her horse, then swung up on his. "He will be anxious to hear of the pony soldiers to the south."

The large procession that entered Sitting Bull's camp was greeted with yells and jeers when they recognized a Crow riding in the midst of the warriors. Crow Killer rode close on one side of Red Hawk, and Gall himself rode on the other at the head of the procession. Stopping in front of a large lodge decorated with buffalo skulls, Gall again held up his arm.

"Hear me, my people." The chief whirled his horse, and the crowd quieted. "This Crow chief is my friend and the brother of the great warrior, Crow Killer, the bear medicine warrior. No harm or harsh words will come to him."

A sudden hush swept the people as the squat form of the great medicine man Sitting Bull stepped from his lodge and looked up at Red Hawk. Everyone waited in anticipation of his reaction.

Gall slid from his horse. "Great Chief, this is Red Hawk, Chief of the Crow people." He raised his hand to Red Hawk. "He has helped bring Blue Feather and Jumping Rabbit home to their people."

The voice coming from the sad strong face sounded guttural. "I have seen in the bones the return of Blue Feather and Jumping Rabbit. Red Hawk is welcome in my village and in my lodge."

Those listening heard the words and breathed in awe.

"We will hold council." American Horse announced.

"Yes, feed our guests, and then we will sit and talk." Sitting Bull nodded at Crow Killer and Eagle Wing. "I think the great bear killer has many things to speak of."

Crow Killer had never met the great Hunkpapa Chief, but he was struck with the words. How did Sitting Bull know he had things he wanted to talk about?

"Why are Straight Arrow and Big Smoke here in the Canadians?" Gall looked over at the two warriors as Sitting Bull returned to his lodge. "Why have you left Crazy Horse?"

"We rode here with the Crow Killer to help him bring the young ones home."

Looking hard at Big Smoke, Gall shook his head. "Big Smoke knows we can have no killing here in the Grandmother's Land. The Red Coats allow us to remain here if there is no trouble."

"I will cause no trouble for the people."

"This is good." Gall relaxed. "I know of Big Smoke's hatred

for the pony soldiers, but there can be no killing on this side of the boundary. No trouble."

"There will be none, great Chief." Straight Arrow looked across at Gall. "None. You have my word."

"We will be riding back south in a few days." Crow Killer spoke up. "But, first, we must ask you a few questions."

"Sitting Bull will speak with us tonight in his lodge." Gall pointed at a large lodge. "Rest now. The women will bring you food. After the dark times come, I will send for you. Then we will talk."

"We thank you."

True to his word, after their meal was finished and the sun started to set, a young warrior came to the lodge and summoned Crow Killer, Eagle Wing, Red Hawk, Straight Arrow, and Big Smoke to Sitting Bull's Lodge. The lodge was larger than most. The hides that made up the lodge were old and greying, but they were still strong against the elements. Buffalo are fewer now, here in the north, and their hides to make new lodge coverings were harder to get. Inside, the lodge was roomy, allowing several older warriors and elders to have room to sit in a circle in front of the small fire.

Sitting Bull himself sat on the north side of the lodge along with Gall and American Horse. Crow Killer and the others were greeted cordially. Nothing was said as Gall lit the ceremonial pipe and started it around the circle. Sitting Bull was the last to smoke. As he blew smoke to the four winds, he spoke a few words and laid the long-stemmed pipe aside.

"You have come far, my friends, to return the children." Sitting Bull was the first to speak. "I have seen your coming for a moon now. You are welcome."

"Thank you, great Shaman."

"Straight Arrow says you had difficulty getting across the land with all the pony soldiers after you."

"We had some difficulty."

"Were many pony soldiers killed?" Gall looked across at Straight Arrow.

The warrior shook his head. "Only Pawnee scouts, as far as we know."

"The Red Coats demand that no whites be killed." American Horse spoke up. "They threaten to make us leave this land if any are killed."

"We killed Pawnee only to defend Blue Feather, Jumping Rabbit, and ourselves." Crow Killer shook his head. "No whites were killed."

Sitting Bull's gaze rested calmly on Crow Killer. "This is good."

American Horse looked over at the others. "Crow Killer says my son killed a Pawnee?"

Eagle Wing spoke up for the boy. "Jumping Rabbit counted coup on a live Pawnee. That earned him the rifle and knife of the warrior. I think he should be given the name Pawnee Killer." He nodded respectfully at the Chief.

"That is a strong name for one so young."

"Your son is young in years, but he has a brave heart." Red Hawk looked over at American Horse. "He has earned the honor. He rode bravely with us and helped deliver the girl here safely, as much as the rest of us."

Sitting Bull looked over at American Horse. "It is a worthy name for one such as your son."

"Then he will be called Pawnee Killer." American Horse flattened his hands. "This makes me proud."

Gall looked around the lodge. "Crow Killer says he has other things for us to speak of?"

"I know of these things." Sitting Bull nodded at Crow Killer. "Speak Crow Killer."

"I thank the great leaders of the Sioux for letting me and my friends sit in council." Crow Killer looked across at the headmen of the Sioux Nation. "Does Sitting Bull or Gall know a pony soldier named Lawrence?"

"Big Smoke says he is the brother of the one you killed back at the place we call Skull Canyon," Gall admitted. "We know of him, but his name is Howard."

Eagles Wing shrugged. "This pony soldier called himself Lawrence."

"The white eyes have two names. Lawrence was this blue coat's first name." Gall shook his head. "Both of these were named Howard, and both had yellow hair as Custer did."

"This one who called himself Lawrence sent us here to bring Blue Feather to her father. He said Gall would know we were coming and had something for us to take back to Crook."

"I knew nothing of my daughter being returned here or even that she lived." Gall frowned. "What does he say I have to trade for Blue Feather?"

"A small book with white man marks in it."

"This blue coat lied to you," Gall exclaimed. "I have no such thing."

"I remember this two-bar pony soldier. He is the same one that leads the Pawnee scouts against us." Lone Wolf, an elder, spoke up. "I saw him when we fought his Pawnee scouts on the Greasy Grass."

"He is an evil one." Another elder spoke up, and howls of rage rose up from the sitting warriors. "He kills women, children—anything he sees."

Crow Killer continued as the council quieted. "He says Gall has a book that belonged to Custer and some saddlebags with pictures and small things the yellow-hair's woman wants back."

"I do not have this book you speak of."

Eagle Wing looked over at Crow Killer and frowned. "Gall is right. Lawrence lied to us."

"I do have the yellow-haired Custer's leather bags."

"Are there things of Custer's in them?"

"Trinkets, pictures, papers with the marks of the white man on them, nothing of value to a warrior."

"Would Gall let me see these saddlebags?"

"Crow Killer is welcome to them. They are just something else for the women to carry if we have to leave this place."

"Burn them as we should have burned Custer." Rain in the Face raised his voice in anger. "Do not give anything back to the white eyes."

Sitting Bull raised his hand to quiet the uproar from others who agreed with the warrior's strong words. "The leather bags of Custer are Gall's property for him to do with as he pleases."

"Eagle Wing fought with us against the pony soldiers on the great river." Gall looked over at the angry warriors. "Many times, he charged the pony soldiers and saved many warriors, including the great Cheyenne warrior Stone Fist."

Rain in the Face glared across the fire. "What does Gall say?"

"The leather bags of Custer now belong to Crow Killer and Eagle Wing to do with as they wish."

"Why do you do this thing?"

Gall looked at the hot-headed warrior. "One day, my friends, I fear we will have to cross back into the lands of our youth. Maybe this gesture will soften the heart of the white eye chiefs."

"I will never go back." Rain in the Face shook his head. "Never."

"If the Red Coats drive us out, we will have no choice."

"Why would they do this thing?" Lone Wolf spoke up. "We have caused no problems here."

Gall nodded. "No, but the buffalo herds are too few here to feed our people and the people of the north. The Assisboine, Cree, and Blackfoot think that they may starve if we stay here in these lands. Soon, they will demand that we leave this place."

Rain in the Face looked over at Sitting Bull. "What does our headman see in his visions?"

The old Medicine Man shook his head sadly. "What Gall says

may come true, but I will never leave this place unless the Red Coats drive my people from here."

"Hunger is a good driver, my brother." Gall looked across the fire. "And we are running out of meat and flour."

"Would you be happy living on the white man's reservation?" Sitting Bull asked the elders. "Told what to do, told what to eat, told when to speak. I will never do that."

"Tell us, Red Hawk, what will your people do?" Lone Wolf looked over at the Crow Chief.

Red Hawk shrugged. "The pony soldiers do not ride against us as they do the Sioux People. But I think soon they will come and tell us what lands we will live on."

"And you will do this?" Lone Wolf studied the great chief.

Crow Killer answered for his brother. "The Crow will have no choice, my friends. The same as you will have no choice when hunger eats at your bellies."

"We can fight." Rain in the Face raised his voice.

It pained Crow Killer to tell them the truth, but they needed to know. "My brothers, I have seen the armies of the whites. They number as the leaves on the trees and the grasses on the plains. If you kill one, ten will come to replace him."

"What is your advice, Crow Killer?" Gall asked. "Tell us, what would you do?"

"If the Red Coat soldiers make you leave this land you will have no choice but to sign a treaty with the whites and move onto a reservation."

"Move onto their reservations, penned in like animals as Red Cloud and Spotted Tail have done?" The agony in the warrior's voice tore at Crow Killer's soul.

"You will have no other choice." He exhaled sadly. "I tell you, the whites are too strong. They have many guns, big and small."

Rain in the Face shook his head. "We can die like warriors."

"Do you wish this for your loved ones? For your children and your women?" Eagle Wing looked into the dark face. "You have seen the power of the whites."

"Yes, I have seen their power. The ones with long-hair Custer fell like leaves in the cold times until no more were left alive." The voice of the warrior was harsh.

Crow Killer nodded at the angry warrior. "And that is why the whites will give you no peace until they have driven you onto a reservation."

"This is a sad thing to think on." Gall shook his head. "But Crow Killer would not lie about this."

The council ended with the elders and the leaders of the Sioux talking heatedly amongst themselves. They didn't like the words they had heard, but they knew Crow Killer had spoken the truth. Their days of roaming the lands as free men were finished. If they were forced from the Canadians soon, they would be relegated to living out their lives on the reservation lands the whites designated.

Crow Killer, Eagle Wing, and Red Hawk walked out into the cool night air and stood with Gall. The stars shined brightly overhead in the northern sky as they stood in the darkness. Gall knew Crow Killer had spoken the truth. For many sleeps, he had lain awake thinking of this very thing, contemplating taking his followers and surrendering to Crook. It grieved him to know the days of the free-roaming horse people were finished. Only starvation and death awaited them if they resisted the white eyes further. He knew it was madness to stay much longer here in the Canadians. He knew reservation life would be bad, but at least the people would survive and maybe have some kind of a future.

"When will you ride south, my friends?"

"With the coming of the new sun." Crow Killer nodded. "We must finish our business and get back to our lodges."

"Your business is the one you call Lawrence, the yellow-haired one?"

"Yes, and we will speak with General Crook if we can."

"That will be dangerous." Gall shook his head. "He is

surrounded by many pony soldiers."

Eagle Wing shrugged. "We will find a way."

"I will bring the leather bags of Custer with the new day." Gall looked up at the dark sky. "Once, the mighty Sioux were numerous like the stars and went where they liked. No more, now we are trapped between two nations of whites."

Crow Killer watched the proud chief walk away. It was a sad time, the end of a way of life. He knew that Gall thought starvation here in these strange lands was pointless. Gall would probably leave Sitting Bull and Rain in the Face soon, taking his people south to Fort Robinson and into captivity.

CHAPTER 13

WITH THE COMING OF THE NEW SUN, Crow Killer, Eagle Wing, Red Hawk, and Big Smoke prepared to ride south, across the boundary, and return to U.S. soil. Blue Feather and Jumping Rabbit stood at the edge of the village, waving sadly at the departing warriors who had saved them. Eagle Wing stopped for a moment, thinking he might never see the youngsters again and wondered if one day they would wed.

Jumping Rabbit stood as tall as he could and thrust out his chest. "My father gave me a warrior's name last night."

"He is now called Pawnee Killer." Blue Feather smiled proudly at the young warrior.

"It is an honorable name for a warrior." Eagle Wing raised his hand in farewell to the two young people. "Goodbye, my friends."

Straight Arrow elected to remain behind with Sitting Bull and his people, but he rode with his friends to see them safely to the Canadian boundary. "Ride safely, my brothers. The enemy is everywhere."

Gall had also ridden with them to the border. "Remember that to the pony soldiers, any red man is a hostile."

Crow Killer nodded and looked across at the great warrior. "I hope to see Gall again one day."

"Where do you ride now?"

"We go to Fort Robinson, to see Crook. Then we will go west to our lodges."

"Thank you for what you have done. And thank you for bringing Blue Feather back to her people."

"Will Gall stay in the Canadians with Sitting Bull?"

The warrior looked to the south. "My home is out there, but for now, I cannot leave him here alone to watch over all the people. I must remain here and do what I can to help them."

"Gall knows his time here is short?" Eagle Wing looked off into the distance. "With the buffalo herds being hunted so hard, the northern tribes will grow hostile and urge the Red Coats to make you leave this land."

"You speak the truth, my friend, but for now, I will remain here."

"You have always been a great leader and protector of your people. Do not forget that, my friend." Crow Killer reached out his hand. "And thank you for the small items for Custer's squaw."

"Maybe in some way, it will soften the white eyes' hearts towards the Sioux."

"Custer got what he wanted—fame." Eagle Wing shrugged. "Maybe not quite the way he wanted it, but what is done is done."

"That day on the Greasy Grass, the day the whites call the Battle of the Little Bighorn, the pony soldiers killed my wife and small ones." Gall shook his head. "We were camped peacefully along the river. They attacked us without warning. I have no regrets for killing them."

"You were protecting your people." Red Hawk reached out his hand. "When the truth comes out, no one will blame you."

"Who will tell the truth?" Gall shook his head sadly. "Who will take the side of an Indian?"

"I would." Crow Killer turned his horse.

"I hope we will meet again one day." Gall took the hand. "Goodbye, my friends."

Straight Arrow sat his horse next to Big Smoke and looked across at his friend with sad eyes. "Stay here with your people, Big Smoke. Only bad things can happen to you on this trail."

Shaking his head, the big warrior reached out his hand. "Straight Arrow knows this I cannot do. The blood of my children calls out for vengeance. They will not rest until Bull Coat and the yellow-haired pony soldier are dead."

"I fear for you, my friend." Straight Arrow looked into the dark eyes. "We have been together since we were children. We hunted and fought side by side. But I think this hatred for the white eye could get you killed."

A hardness overcame the face of the warrior. "I am already dead. You cannot kill a dead man again."

"Go then, my friend." Straight Arrow turned his horse back to the north. "One day, we will hunt shaggies again in the big meadows above."

"When the yellow-haired pony soldier and his Pawnee dogs are dead, then I will return to my people."

"I hope so, my friend."

As Crow Killer, his son, and his brother rode away he glanced back and saw the two warriors talking and Gall watching Crow Killer and Eagle Wing ride away. It was a sad time. He knew it would be a hard road ahead for all of them, but especially for Gall and his people moving to the reservation life they were doomed to live. They would no longer ride free across the prairies, chasing the shaggies. The children might adjust to their new life, but not the older warriors who were used to roaming free and proud.

Red Hawk shook his head. "I did not get to see these Red Coat warriors you spoke of."

"Count your blessings, brother, that we got out of the Canadians with our scalps intact."

"I still would have liked to have seen such a warrior as you say the Red Coat is."

"I only told you what I have heard of them. Perhaps one day we will meet one."

Big Smoke once again took the lead as they started back to the south. Gall was right; nothing had changed. If spotted, they would be seen as hostiles and fired on. The day passed slowly as the horses plodded steadily across the grasslands which were burnt-out in places. The prairies seemed empty of any wildlife. Nothing showed as far as they could see, nary a buffalo, deer, or antelope. He saw no sign of movement even on the horizon, only miles upon miles of empty flatlands with a few wooded areas here and there.

That afternoon they sighted a small cavalry patrol, but Big Smoke had already spotted the pony soldiers and raced back to quickly guide Crow Killer and Red Hawk behind a stand of trees.

"That was close." Red Hawk watched the backs of the whites as they rode out of sight. "We must be more careful if we are to reach our lodges."

"The pony soldiers watch the boundary line closely." Crow Killer spoke quietly. "I think the farther we ride to the east and south, the fewer patrols of soldiers we will see."

"Hopefully, Crow Killer is right." Red Hawk looked around. "There is not much to hide behind here in these lands."

Almost at sundown, Big Smoke reined in on the banks of a wide river, a much larger river than the one Straight Arrow had called the Milk. This territory was unfamiliar to Crow Killer, so he had no idea what water this was. Before leaving the Canadians, Gall had told him that Big Smoke knew where Fort Robinson and General Crook would be found. So, he relied on the warrior to lead them across these vast expanses of prairies.

His thoughts returned many times to his valley as they crossed the flatlands heading east. He worried for Bright Moon and the others and wished this part of the journey was over. He pushed on, mile after mile, hoping Crook would honor the worthless treaty paper he had tucked safely in his leather pouch. The signatures of Lawrence and Crook were on the paper, but given Lawrence's sneakiness and lies, he doubted it was the General's mark.

Crow Killer figured Lawrence was out in these grasslands

somewhere. The pony soldier wanted revenge for his brother's death. He wanted Eagle Wing. Where was the man?

Since before the fight with the pony soldiers in the ravine, nothing had been seen of Lawrence and his Pawnee scouts. He figured the blond-headed one was too smart to ride into the Canadians with his Pawnee warriors. There, in the north country, he would be outnumbered. He would have Sitting Bull to fight, and he would also have the Red Coats and the Assiniboine to contend with.

No, somewhere out here on the prairie, Lawrence would be waiting for Eagle Wing to cross the boundary and return south. He knew Crow Killer wanted a reservation and a treaty for the Arapaho, and that to get them, Crow Killer would have to ride to Fort Robinson and speak with Crook. Crow Killer squinted, staring hard at the grassy expanse before them. Lawrence would not want him to reach Crook with the counterfeit treaty papers he carried.

No fire was made as they sat along the banks of the small river, chewing on the hard-jerked meat given to them by Sitting Bull's squaws. Every ear listened for the night creatures scurrying through the underbrush. The horses cropping on grass and the hushed gurgle of the river flowing by was all that broke the silence of the night. Everyone was quiet, no bantering or idle talk. They were all deeply absorbed in their own thoughts. Crow Killer thought of Bright Moon, and he figured Eagle Wing was thinking of Morning Dove and his young son.

With the coming of the new day, Big Smoke made a quick check of the land, then motioned the others to follow. Crow Killer thought of carrying a white flag but changed his mind. It would be better for Eagle Wing and Big Smoke if they avoided being seen by the pony soldiers. He didn't know if Eagle Wing was wanted by the Army, but Big Smoke would definitely be considered a hostile. At best, the big warrior would be taken prisoner and locked away in their local prison, but more than likely, he'd be shot on sight.

No, it would be better for them to ride unseen to Fort Robinson.

The day passed quietly without seeing any soldiers. Big Smoke kept them moving into the night until he finally rode up on another small stream with fresh water, trees, and good grass for the horses.

Handing out dried jerky, Red Hawk shrugged. "We must find something to eat soon."

Eagle Wing nodded. "I have never seen so much land with no four-leggeds on it."

"We will find fresh meat tomorrow." Big Smoke's strong teeth bit into the hard jerky.

Crow Killer looked over at the warrior and frowned. "How can Big Smoke be so sure?"

"Tomorrow, my friend, have faith."

Red Hawk laughed. "Oh, he's got plenty of that."

"Riding with Red Hawk." Crow Killer shook his head. "I've always needed faith."

The next day, when the sun was high overhead and the wide expanse of a river showed itself, they rode out of a timbered shelf of woods onto its banks. Crow Killer had been smelling the dampness and cooler air coming off the river as they moved through the trees. Unable to see the river itself, he knew it was nearby. Stopping under the veil of the trees, they stayed out of sight of anyone on the far bank. The river was wide, the horses would have to swim this time to make the crossing. For several minutes, the four warriors set their horses quietly, observing the other bank.

"I see nothing." Big Smoke's dark eyes searched the far bank. "I don't think any enemy waits over there."

"We will watch a little longer to be sure." Crow Killer held up his hand. "If we cross here, the swim will be a long one."

"The soldiers do not watch here much." Big Smoke shrugged. "The river stays this way everywhere. The whites do not think us hostiles would try and swim across here."

"We will cross one at a time, not bunched up." Crow Killer

looked down at his rifle. "I'll cover the rest of you as you cross."

The Sioux looked over at Red Hawk and grinned. "Can the spotted one swim?"

"We'll see." Red Hawk kicked the big Appaloosa toward the water.

"He is a magnificent animal." Big Smoke smiled appreciatively as the horse hit the deep water and swam with ease. Red Hawk slid from his horse and hung onto the mane, swimming alongside the animal. "But his spots show too brightly. An enemy could see them far off."

Watching as Red Hawk reached the far shore, Eagle Wing kicked his horse forward. The river was wide, and it was a far swim, but the current was slow and easy to cross. Almost to the bank, Eagle Wing heard the sound of a rifle and the plop of a bullet as it barely missed the swimming horse. Holding his rifle over the neck of the animal, trying to keep it from the water, he paddled, hanging onto the animal.

Shots rang out again as Crow Killer and Big Smoke fired at the unseen assailant. Red Hawk had already disappeared into the underbrush on the far bank. Again, the slap of a bullet against the water came as Eagle Wing frantically urged the horse to reach the shore. Screaming in rage, Big Smoke whipped his horse into the river despite Crow Killer yelling for him to wait.

Eagle Wing felt the bite of the next bullet grazing his arm as he led his horse into the brush. Looking back, he watched as both Big Smoke and Crow Killer hit the water.

Slipping into the thick brush, Red Hawk quietly approached where he thought the shots had come from. Crawling on his belly as another shot was fired, he located the hidden warrior. Hidden behind a large spruce, the warrior, intent on shooting the swimmers, seemed to have forgotten about the one that had already crossed.

Laying his rifle aside, Red Hawk pulled an arrow from his quiver and raised up on one knee to take aim. His arrow flew true, hitting the warrior in the side and killing him instantly. Red Hawk flattened himself on the ground and studied the brush and trees, trying to locate any others. Not seeing or hearing any more, he stood and walked to where Eagle Wing was staring down at the body.

"A youngster." Eagle Wing shook his head. "Barely more than a child."

"He may be young, but the rifle he fired almost killed you."

Walking back to where Crow Killer and Big Smoke waded up out of the river, Eagle Wing shook his head and then turned to gather up the loose horses.

"My nephew feels bad." Red Hawk shrugged. "The one I killed was a young boy."

"What tribe was he?"

"I don't know his tribe. His skin was darker than most."

"Our warriors say Crook has brought warriors from the east to fight against us." The big warrior shrugged. "I haven't seen them, but others say their skin is very dark."

Big Smoke and Eagle Wing made a pass through the tangle of brush and trees that lined the river, checking for tracks. Hopefully, the dead youngster had been alone, and no others had ridden for help. Almost an hour passed before the two warriors came back to the horses. A small doe lay across Big Smoke's shoulders.

"We will eat tonight, my friends."

"We must leave this place quickly in case any enemy heard the shots." Crow Killer swung up on his horse. "We will eat later."

"As long as we get to eat." Big Smoke patted the gutted deer. "I am so hungry my stomach thinks my mouth is dead or has forgotten about it."

"Big Smoke may not need to eat if we don't get to riding." Eagle Wing knew sound carried far on these plains. The rifle shots could have been heard for miles. "He will be dead if we get caught here."

Crow Killer took the first watch as the deer meat spattered

and sizzled over the small fire. He knew it was dangerous to make a fire, but they had no choice. They had to eat. They would just have to keep a close watch until the fire could be put out. Big Smoke said Fort Robinson was still at least ten sleeps away from where they camped. Patrols of pony soldiers rode everywhere. Danger would accompany them every mile until they reached the safety of the Fort. Maybe if Crook was at Fort Robinson and could be reasoned with, they would be able to travel back to Bridger in relative safety.

Red Hawk had checked all the horses for any sign of lameness. All were hardened to long trails and rough pastures. Eating greedily on the grass alongside the stream, they all seemed in good shape.

"It is a good night. When the moon is high, we should ride." Red Hawk said as he walked up to the fire. "I feel danger here."

Eagle Wing checked the cooking meat. "I feel a storm is coming."

"Yes, but we will be far away when it hits." Big Smoke looked up at the darkening sky. "A storm is a good thing. It will cover any tracks we leave."

"Does Big Smoke think we are being followed?"

"This I don't know. But I do think someone could be following our trail."

"Since we left the river, I have felt the same." Red Hawk shook his head. "I, too, think someone follows us."

"I don't think one boy would be out here hunting alone." Crow Killer agreed. "I think there were others with him."

Eagle Wing shrugged. "There were only tracks of one horse at the river."

"They might have ridden double as young boys sometimes do." Red Hawk shook his head. "Eat quickly. We need to leave this place."

Big Smoke grumbled. "I think we are going to get wet tonight, so fill your stomachs."

"That is a good thing. You need a bath, Sioux." Red Hawk

chuckled.

"I had a bath when we crossed the big river."

"Two in a day won't hurt you any."

Eagle Wing and Big Smoke's prediction had been right. A heavy storm with crashing thunder and blinding lightning strikes came out of the west, drenching them to the bone. The flashes lit up the sky with brilliant bolts of white fire blasting through the dark night. Soon after, a heavy deluge of blowing rain beat down on them unmercifully. The horses dropped their heads, reluctantly plodding to the south, fighting their riders, wanting to turn away from the dreaded downpour. Finally, as quickly as the storm had come up, the rain ceased, and everything calmed.

"Well, Crow Killer, you wanted our tracks hidden." Water streaked down Big Smoke's broad face. "I think now they are hidden."

"I believe you are right." Crow Killer looked up at the fading lightning flashes off to the east. "That is a good thing."

The sun found the soaked riders still moving south. The warmth of the new day was welcomed as they began to dry out. The pungent smell of the horse's wet hides hit their noses stronger than usual.

"I think my horse needs another bath." Big Smoke patted the big bay's wet neck and grinned. "He smells like a horse."

Red Hawk shook his head. "Well, Sioux, that is because he is a horse."

Topping out a rise, they saw a high ridgeback leading off to their left. Crow Killer thought it would be a good place to climb and look over the terrain for pony soldiers. Kicking their horses, they started the short climb to the top.

"Once our people did the same. They came here many times to look for the shaggies." Big Smoke chewed on a piece of dried venison. "Back then the four-leggeds covered the land making it black as far as the eye could see. Now, there is nothing but a few antelope and deer out there.”

“Shaggies must be here somewhere.” Eagle Wing stared out across the landscape. “They couldn’t have all been killed.”

“Yes, that could be. But where, my friend?” Big Smoke leaned forward, gazing at the prairie. “I think maybe the pony soldiers and the hide-hunters have run them from these lands.”

For a week, Big Smoke kept the horses in a slow trot to the southeast. Even with having to be on the watch for enemy scouts, they were making good time. As they passed farther south, they encountered a few buffalo and smaller groups of deer and antelope out on the grasslands. Crow Killer figured the pony soldiers had kept the big herds stampeded to the south so Sitting Bull and his people would have no food. They also burned the grass from the prairie to keep the buffalo from moving north. Needing fresh meat themselves, Red Hawk and Eagle Wing rode spread out, their bows ready.

Finally, as they dropped over a small rise, Red Hawk brought down a small antelope with his bow. It was a small doe, but at least it would fill their bellies for the night. Seeing a cluster of trees off in the distance, they pushed their horses into a harder trot. Two hours later, riding into the short timber, Big Smoke reined in and pointed at a small depression filled with muddy water from the recent storm that would satisfy the horses’ thirst for the night. “We will camp here tonight and cook the meat. The animals have good grass and water here, and we can see any enemies that come.”

“Where are we?” Crow Killer looked over at the warrior.

“If it hasn’t moved, two, maybe three sleeps to the south is a trader’s store.” Big Smoke shook his head. “It is a bad place. The owner is a cheat. But still, before the trouble with the white eyes started, the people used to take their furs there.”

Crow Killer nodded slowly. “A trader’s store. That’s good.”

“What is Crow Killer thinking?” Red Hawk saw the

brightened expression on his brother's face.

"If I am to ride into Fort Robinson and speak with General Crook, I'll be needing some white man's clothing. Going in dressed like an Arapaho could get me shot before I can get through the gates to explain what I want."

Big Smoke shook his head. "There are plenty of warriors at this fort dressed as you are."

"I doubt they are dressed like an Arapaho." Crow Killer shook his head. "And I doubt they would be wanting to speak with Crook."

"Crow Killer is right." Eagle Wing remembered when he and Red Horse had dressed like trappers to get into Nez Perce lands. "To go in as a trapper would be an easier thing."

"How far you figure we are from Fort Robinson?" Red Hawk looked over to where Big Smoke was skinning the antelope.

The big warrior pointed south. "Maybe four more sleeps farther than the trader's store."

"That all?" Crow Killer was surprised. They had been making good time, but he figured the fort was much farther.

"Big Smoke is sure. If we don't run into trouble before we get there, four sleeps."

Eagle Wing pushed some damp wood together for a fire and turned to his father. "Are you going in alone?"

"I figure I would. Won't have to answer so many questions that way."

"Where will we wait on you?" Red Hawk looked over at Crow Killer.

"When we get closer to Fort Robinson, we'll find a place for you to camp."

Big Smoke looked up from the carcass. "Crow Killer will find out where Lawrence and his Pawnee are?"

"If anyone at the fort knows. I'll find out."

"Someone white or Indian will know." Big Smoke frowned. "Indians know everything that the whites do."

"Then I'll find out."

"We will find the white after you leave Fort Robinson?" Big Smoke questioned. "This is why I have come here."

"I know why Big Smoke has made this trail." Crow Killer studied the cooking meat. "I'll guarantee we'll be going after him once I get the treaty paper from Crook."

"What does that word mean?"

"Guarantee means the same as you have my word."

"I don't think you will get this treaty paper from the pony soldier Chief." Red Hawk shook his head. "I think he will say no."

"I won't know until I ask. We'll just have to wait and see."

Big Smoke had been right. The morning of the third day, after riding most of the night, the small party sat on a rise overlooking a single sod building with smoke bellowing from the clay chimney. Chickens, goats, and hogs wandered freely about the filthy yard. Nearby, a pole corral held a few poor horses who stood swishing their tails alongside the building, and two saddled horses stood tied to a rickety rail in front of the ramshackle building.

Crow Killer looked over at Big Smoke. "You remember anything about this trader?"

"Yes." The big shoulders shrugged. "He cheats the Indian, and he smells worse than my horse."

"Anything else?"

"This one would not trust the white eye down there with a dead dog."

"He's that bad, huh?"

"If he is the tall white eye with a black hat, then yes, he has cheated us many times."

"Stay here. I'll ride down alone and see if I can buy clothes suitable for meeting this General Crook."

"Keep your nose shut." Big Smoke frowned. "I have been inside that white man's lodge only once."

"Just once?" Crow Killer looked over at the warrior.

"Once was enough. Even the white eye firewater couldn't get the bad taste out of my mouth." Big Smoke's nose wrinkled up as if the remembered smell still stung his nostrils. "It stunk like a buffalo had died in there."

Crow Killer smiled. Big Smoke did have a way with words. "Well, I'll go have a look at this place."

Riding into the yard, Crow Killer was greeted by three skinny hounds barking their heads off. A cuss came from inside, and then a tall man in a white apron and a top hat stepped through the door. Crow Killer wasn't sure if the apron was white, it was so filthy. Big Smoke had been right. Even from where Crow Killer sat his horse, he could smell the uncouth man.

"You got furs to trade Injun?" The voice seemed cranky and coarse. "If not, get out."

"Nope, and I ain't no Indian."

Looking at the Arapaho vest, leggings, and long hair, the tall man removed his hat and scratched on his matted hair. "You sure look Injun to me. What be you, a squaw man?"

"Name's Jedidiah Bracket." Crow Killer slid from his horse. "White trapper."

"If'n you've been trapping, where's your kit?"

"Indians stole everything I had except my horse." Crow Killer lied. "Dang near got him, too."

"They'll sure do it if'n they get the chance." The man in the dusty top hat studied the horse. "Why you here about these parts fer?"

"Be needing me an outfit, buckskins, saddle." He tried to match the man's slang speech. "Was headed for Fort Robinson when I spotted your place here. Sure, don't want the Army to take a potshot at me."

"They might just do that, 'cause you sure look Injun to me 'cepting for your speaking, that is."

"Yeah, I reckon I do at that."

"So, you're headed for Fort Robinson?"

"Figured to. I want to report the loss of my furs and traps. What be your name?"

"Ervin, Ten Penny Ervin, at your service." The tall man shook his head. "I wouldn't count on Crook helpin' you get your trappings back."

"It's nice to meet you, Mister Ervin." Crow Killer ignored the remark. "Can you be fixing me up with some duds?"

"How you fixing to pay? You look mighty down on your luck to me."

"Those scallywags didn't get my poke, just my trappings." Crow Killer pulled a leather pouch from his vest. "Like I said, they didn't get my money. I keep it on me."

"What kinda critters were they?" Ervin rubbed the stubble on his chin, eyeing the pouch greedily. "Sioux, I expect."

"Don't rightly know for sure."

"What you mean, you don't know?"

"Well, you see, they come on me at night when I was asleep."

The store-man spit and looked Crow Killer over skeptically. "You must be an awful hard sleeper to let a pack of red devils steal everything you had and not wake up."

Crow Killer smiled shamefacedly. "Well, sir, I reckon I am at that. I do like my sleep. Leastwise, I was able to grab ahold of this horse afore they got away with her, too."

"Well, tie your pony and come on in." Ervin turned for the door after giving him one last disgusting look. "I may have some leathers that'll fit you. Tell me something, pilgrim. How did you ever keep your scalp out there all alone? Sure beats me."

"Well, sir. I reckon I got lucky."

"I expect you did at that." Shaking his head, Ervin walked inside. "Well, bring your carcass on in here whilst I'm in the mood to trade."

Crow Killer followed him in slowly. He had the distinct feeling he was fixing to jump from the frying pan into the fire, as old Lige

Hatcher used to say when things were about to go bad. The trouble was he had no choice. Crow Killer needed the buckskins if he was gonna trot into the lion's den at Fort Robinson. So, there was no backing out.

The trader's yard was a pigsty, but when Crow Killer entered the adobe-style sod building, he found the place was filthier than the yard. The room reeked of filth. Only the door and two windows provided the room with light and much-needed fresh air. A rough-hewn log served as a counter for drinking or buying. Pine stumps provided places to sit. The place smelled like a goat barn. Sure enough, before Crow Killer could look the place over any closer, a musky-smelling billy-goat strutted through the open door as if he owned the place. Judging by the smell in the room, he might have at that.

"There's the duds over there, mister." Ervin pointed at a stack of clothes piled in the corner. "Better hurry afore Buster beats you to them."

"Buster?"

"Buster, that's him." Ervin pointed at the mangy goat. "That's his bed you're fixing to buy."

"Who you be, stranger?" Two men sat in the shadows at a corner table drinking. "We ain't never seen you around these parts before."

"Reckon that's cause I ain't never been around these parts before." Crow Killer looked through the leather shirts and britches while keeping a close eye on the two rough-looking customers.

"Clem, here, asked you your name."

"Well, now, if it were any of Clem's business, I'd have told him." Crow Killer held up a pair of buckskin pants.

"Kinda touchy, ain't you, pilgrim?"

Pulling the cleanest-looking hunting shirt from Buster's pile, he tossed it on the counter with the leggings. "Let's just say I like to mind my own business."

"That ain't very friendly of you."

Crow Killer turned back to Ervin. "Now, how about a saddle?"

"Outside on the corral fence, you just take your pick."

"How much I owe you, Mister Ervin."

"You want something to drink, maybe a meal?"

"Nope, just what I got laying right here and the saddle." Crow Killer pulled the pouch from his vest.

Ervin's eyes widened at the sound of the heavy gold pieces in the bag, and he scratched his head. "That comes to about fifty dollars."

"Kinda expensive buckskins, ain't they, Mister Ervin?"

Ervin shrugged and looked over at the two men who were staring hungrily at the pouch of gold. "Tell me, Mister Bracket, you seen any other places to buy duds in these parts?"

"Bracket!" The name leaped out of one of the men's mouth. "You be Jed Bracket?"

"I'm Bracket." Crow Killer turned to face the men. "Why?"

"You're a long way from home, ain't you, Mister Crow Killer?"

"Reckon, that's my business, too."

The shorter of the men stood up. "We heard about you from trappers up around Bridger's Fort. They say you're bad medicine."

Crow Killer looked over at the men. "Well, sir, I reckon that depends on who's troubling me."

"They say Bracket or Crow Killer, whatever your name is, killed some of our friends." The man rasped. "Leastways, they've up and disappeared. An' last we heard, you and your boy were dogging them across the mountains."

"And just who was I dogging?"

"Trapper named Wilde and two of his partners for starters." The other trapper rubbed his chin. "Nobody has seen hide nor hair of them since."

"Mister, I only kill someone with a big mouth that's annoying me." Crow Killer turned to face the pair. "And at the moment, you men are annoying me."

"Folks say you have some kind of real strong bear medicine that protects you." The shorter of the two, named Clem, smirked at him. "Bear medicine." He spit on the floor. "Only fools believe that Indian malarkey."

"That's right." The one called Spade rubbed his chin and grinned. "And they also said you have a beautiful squaw stashed back in those mountains somewhere."

Crow Killer felt heat rising in his neck. "An' while they were tellin' you all this, didn't they also tell you to leave me alone?"

"Well, Mister Bracket, matter of fact, they didn't."

"Well then, I'm telling you now. Sit down, have your drinks, and leave me be."

Spade ignored him. "That's a lot of money you're carrying in that bag."

Ervin spoke up from behind the counter. "I earned it for the duds I sold him, Spade." He thumped his fist on the thick log counter. "Half's mine."

Crow Killer looked curiously at the man. "Now, just how do you figure that, Mister Ervin?"

"You're in my place, that's how." Ervin swallowed hard and looked for the other two men to back him. "And those be my wares you're buying."

"Toss the little bag on the counter and ride Mister Crow Killer." The one called Spade took a step closer. "Now!"

Crow Killer smiled easily. "You reckon I don't have anything to say about it?"

"Nah, you don't. Now drop it."

"What about that Henry looking through the window at you boys?" Crow Killer looked over their shoulders. "Does that count?"

The room cast a shadow on both men, but he could see the pale look come over their faces. "You're bluffing."

The sound of the hammer cocking suddenly deafened the

room. Not a word was said as Crow Killer picked up his buckskins and started for the door.

"Now you boys have a drink on Mister Ervin. Looks like you could use one."

"What about my money?"

"Why, it's half yours, Mister Ervin." Crow Killer stopped at the door. "That's what you said, isn't it?"

"You owe me!"

"Come outside and collect if you're sure you want it. If I were you boys, I'd stay put for a spell. That rifle behind you has a hair trigger on it."

"That's robbery." Ervin squeaked.

"No, sir." Crow Killer slapped two gold dollars down on the makeshift counter. "This here is more'n you deserve."

On his way out, he glanced down at Buster, who had lain down on the pile of buckskins and butternut clothing. "Give ole Buster a drink, too. He probably needs one after smelling the three of you all day. Oh, and I wouldn't stick my head outside until you hear me ride off. You boys, just sit down and have your drinks."

Outside, Crow Killer opened the corral gate, unsaddled one of the tied horses, and spooked the animals down the trail. Leading the best of the saddled horses, he swung up on his own horse and rode back towards the high rise. Smiling, Red Hawk caught up with him after firing a couple of shots into the sod house.

Crow Killer grinned at Red Hawk. "What do you do down here, my brother?"

"I thought that goat had you." Red Hawk laughed. "You always need me to get you out of trouble."

"Well, today I did for sure." Crow Killer smiled. "Ah, which goat?"

CHAPTER 14

THE RIDE ON TO FORT ROBINSON was as Crow Killer thought it would be. Very few soldiers patrolled the area near the fort. Three times as they rode south and east, they had hidden as patrols of pony soldiers rode past, but each patrol was headed north to the Canadian border. None bothered to look for hostile enemies this far to the south. Even the usual sharp-eyed Pawnee scouts failed to look for signs on the land as they passed.

Riding into a dense stand of timber, Big Smoke reined in and studied the surrounding forests. There were no major trails showing anywhere. Only paths made by the smaller four-leggeds could be seen on the forest floor. No sign or tracks of horses passing were found on the ground. "Fort Robinson is less than a day's ride south from this place."

"That is good. With the new sun, I will ride there."

Slipping from their horses, the four warriors made camp inside a heavily timbered area. Here in this dense forest so near Fort Robinson, Crow Killer figured the pony soldiers would not expect to find enemy warriors hiding. Their orders were to patrol north, which meant they wouldn't waste their time looking here. He hoped no one out hunting for small game would accidentally find their camp while he was gone to the fort.

Soon, four freshly skinned rabbits were spitted on green limbs and roasting over a small fire that Big Smoke was tending. Dry wood was used, so hardly any smoke lifted into the air to betray their hiding place. The Sioux turned the rabbit carcasses over and looked at Crow Killer. "Crow Killer must be careful. There are warriors from many tribes at this fort. One of them could recognize you."

"With this thing on?" He pulled a Canadian Metis cap down low over his face.

Red Hawk laughed and shook his head. "Where did you get that?"

"Lone Wolf slipped it to me as we were leaving the village." Crow Killer pushed his long hair underneath the cap. "It will hide my hair."

"Will you ride the horse you took from the trader's cabin?" Eagle Wing looked over at the hobbled horses. "He could be recognized by someone at the Fort."

"I took him because none of ours are broke to a saddle. My son could be right, but I won't be there long enough for many to see him."

"I could have put the white eye saddle on one of ours as we rode here." Eagle Wing frowned. "By now, he would be ready for the saddle."

"I know, but I may be riding hard coming back here. I will need my horse to be fresh for our ride west when I return."

"Remember, my friend, it only takes one to recognize a stolen horse." Red Hawk smiled. "And this time, I will not be there to get you out of trouble."

Big Smoke laughed as he turned the spit. "Yes, from what I have heard, Red Hawk should know all about stolen horses."

"People say some things that aren't true."

"Then a lot of lies have been told about a certain Crow warrior I know."

Red Hawk nodded. "Lies, all lies."

"Red Hawk, you will not follow me to Fort Robinson." Crow Killer became serious. "And, if I don't return, you and Eagle Wing will return to our lands."

"We could not go and leave you here without knowing what has happened."

"Do not worry, I will get myself away from Fort Robinson."

"What if this pony soldier General puts you in their iron house?" Big Smoke took a bite of his rabbit. "He could, you know? He has put many warriors there."

"For what reason?"

Eagle Wing coughed. "White eyes don't need a reason. They do what they want."

"I'll be back. Do not follow me to Fort Robinson." Crow Killer set his jaw.

"If you're not back in three sleeps, we will come for you." Red Hawk flattened his hands. "I have spoken."

With Red Hawk's finality, the four warriors sat around the small fire, savoring the hot meat, each with his own thoughts. All were worried about Crow Killer walking into a trap. Outside on the plains or in the forest, they were in their element, but trapped inside the fort walls, they were at the mercy of the whites. But they all knew there was no turning back now. Crow Killer had come this far, seeking a place for his beloved Arapaho people to live in peace. He wouldn't turn back now, not when he was this close to the white Chief who could get them a reservation.

The next morning, riding out across the flat land, Crow Killer spotted the distant silhouette of the fort. He was impressed. This was the first real frontier fort he had ever seen. Bridger had seemed big to him, but Fort Robinson dwarfed the small trading post Jim Bridger had built. Several hundred lodges of Sioux were strung out around the post as far as he could see. Stopping his horse within sight of the huge fort and so near the passing mounted pony soldiers gave him an eerie feeling. For three moons and many miles, he had been avoiding these same white eyes out on the prairie. Now, they passed in plain sight of him. High gates manned by sentries stood wide open as whites, Indians, and settlers freely passed through them. Always before, he would have avoided a place such as this, but today, he rode straight into the face of danger.

Trying to look at ease like the other travelers, he wasn't even questioned by the guards. At almost sundown, he passed through the gates unchallenged. Crossing the dusty parade ground, he still expected to be stopped and questioned. He was curious when none of the soldiers looked at him or spoke a word. Dismounting in front of a building with a sign over the door that read Adjutant, Crow Killer tied his horse and stepped up onto the plank porch.

Pushing open the door, he found a three-stripe pony soldier sitting behind a scarred desk. Looking up from the papers he was writing on, the Sergeant studied the newcomer curiously. The sharp eyes of the soldier didn't miss anything from the Metis hat to the moccasins on Crow Killer's feet. Here at Robinson, white traders and trappers all dressed shabbily. Many roamed the grounds and traded at the post store, but few ever came into the post commandant's office.

"What can I do for you, mister?"

Crow Killer remembered Chalk Briggs and Alex McCord speaking about the important dispatches that pony soldiers carried between posts. Patting the leather bags on his side, he stepped to the desk.

"I have a dispatch for General Crook." He looked around the room, expecting to see Crook. "Also, I have other personal things for the General."

"I'll take them." The sergeant reached out his ham-like fist.

"I was directed to hand them personally to General Crook."

"I'm Sergeant Blake, top dog here at Robinson, and I handle all of General Crook's dispatches and correspondence." Blake stood up and reached out his hand again. "And as you say, personal things. I'll take them."

"No, sir. I can't let you have them." Crow Killer stepped back.

"Like I said, these are for the General only."

The chair scraped loudly on the plank floor as the three-stripe soldier pushed it back. "I'm telling you, whoever you are, I handle the General's dispatches."

"Not these, I reckon."

"What's going on out here, Sergeant?" A tall officer stepped through an adjoining door. "I could hear the commotion from where I was in there."

"Sorry, Major." Blake snapped to attention. "This, uh, man says he has an urgent dispatch for the General and won't turn it over to anyone but to General Crook personally."

"Out of the question." The officer seemed to look down his nose at the stranger. "I take care of all the General's correspondence."

"Now, that's just what your Sergeant told me."

"Then, I'll take them."

"No, sir." Crow Killer pulled the bags away from the outstretched hand. "My orders were to hand them directly to General Crook and no one else."

"That's not the way things are handled around here, mister." The officer looked at the beat-up leather bag. "And that's not an official Army dispatch satchel."

"Maybe it's not, but that's what they gave me to carry these dispatches to General Crook in." Crow Killer shook his head and held up the saddlebags. "You see the writing on these other bags, Mister Officer?"

The aristocratic officer studied the saddlebags with the G.C. initials closely for several seconds, then nodded his head. "Mister, are those what I think they are?"

"I wouldn't know what you think they are." Crow Killer shrugged. "But I'll guarantee the General will find them interesting."

"Come with me."

"Yes, sir."

"What's your name?"

"Jim Lewis."

"Where are you riding out of Mister Lewis?"

"East. Picked up these dispatches back on the Missouri." Crow Killer lied.

The officer nodded. "I'm Major Nelson, post adjutant."

"Nice to meet you, Major."

"You understand, this is highly unorthodox for a—" Nelson stopped speaking and shook his head. "For a dispatch rider to see General Crook personally?"

"I understand, Major, but the only way your General is gonna lay hands on these bags is if I give them to him myself."

"Like I said, it's unorthodox, but I'll see if the General will see you." Major Nelson waved Crow Killer forward. "Follow me."

Leading him past several doors, Nelson knocked at a plain wooden plank door that looked no different than the rest. Glancing down at the worn leather pouch and saddlebags, the Major nodded. "Leave your rifle out here, Mister Lewis."

"Yes, sir."

A tall, stately man with bushy eyebrows, a beard, and greying hair was sitting behind an oak desk, deeply engrossed in a map, as they entered the room. The Major stood at attention until the man looked up and nodded. "At ease, Major. What have we here?"

"A dispatch from Colonel Miles, I presume, sir." Nelson looked over at Crow Killer. "This man said it was important and says he has orders not to turn it over to anyone but you, sir."

Nodding, the tall man glanced over at the leather pouches, but his eyes widened when he spotted the G.C. on the saddle bags. "You are dismissed, Major."

"Sir?"

"You may go back to your duties, Major Nelson." Crook used a firmer tone.

"Yes, sir." Saluting sharply, Nelson exited the room.

"I'm General Crook. Now, sir, what have you got for me that's so important?"

"This, General." Crow Killer pulled out the treaty paper and unrolled it for the General to see the large signature of George Crook scrawled across the bottom.

"What is this?" Crook squinted curiously at the wording on the paper. "And who, sir, are you?"

"My name is Jedidiah Bracket, and this is a treaty paper given to me by Captain Lawrence. At least, that was the name the man gave me, but I suspect his real name may be Captain Howard. This was given to me in exchange for delivering a young girl named Blue Feather to her father, Chief Gall of the Hunkpapa Sioux."

The General listened, squinting hard at Crow Killer.

Crow Killer watched the way Crook studied the paper and frowned harder the more he read. "This Captain gave me his word that if I delivered the girl, you would honor a treaty giving the Arapaho a reservation somewhere on the Sweetwater Range in Wyoming Territory."

"He did what?" Aghast, Crook looked up from the paper. "I only see a signature of a Captain Lawrence on this paper."

"Both your signature, General, and his are right there under the wording." Crow Killer pointed at the paper.

"I don't have a Captain Lawrence in this regiment."

"What about a Captain Howard? I figure your Captain is a little loose with the truth."

Crook shook his head. "Tell me, Jedidiah Bracket, who are you exactly?"

"I'm a blood brother to the Arapaho, trying to get them an honorable peace treaty with a reservation as this paper promises."

"A squaw man?"

"If that's the term you want to use, General Crook." Crow Killer shrugged. "But, I am also a landowner and a personal friend of Jim Bridger and Chalk Briggs."

"Jim Bridger, I know that old goat." Crook traced his signature. "He's the best trapper, scout, and explorer in the West, but he's a rascal to boot."

"That may be, General, but when Jim Bridger, old Gabe, gives his word, he keeps it." Crow Killer pointed again at the treaty paper. "As most honorable men do out here."

"Sit down, Bracket. These old bones are kinda tired tonight. I've been out hunting today." Crook sat back in his cane-backed chair. "You know, sir, that my signature on your paper is counterfeit, phony, forged? Whatever you want to call it, it's definitely not my signature."

"I figured as much."

"And this Captain Howard, who you know as Lawrence, is on military leave taking care of his sick mother back in Pennsylvania." Crook studied the paper. "He's nowhere near here."

"I doubt that he's back East, General. Unless he's got himself a twin." Crow Killer shook his head. "I left your Captain just west of here, not in Pennsylvania, taking care of his sickly mother."

"Describe this man you call Lawrence."

Crow Killer quickly told him exactly what Lawrence looked like down to his height, size, and blond hair. "I left him at Bridger, but he's tracked me and my son across Wyoming and Montana Territories all the way to the Canadians."

"For what purpose would he do that, sir?"

Quickly, he told of Lawrence's promise that if he took Blue Feather back to her father and traded her for a book that Chief Gall had, he would personally guarantee a treaty with the Arapaho. "And you, sir, would give them their own reservation."

"A book?" Crook shook his head. "A guarantee. What are you talking about, Bracket?"

"Yes, sir. He claimed you wanted these saddle bags and a book holding some papers, all personal items of Custer's." He laid the bags on General Crook's desk.

"Those are Custer's saddle bags?"

"That they be, General." Crow Killer pointed at the initials on the leather flap. "Chief Gall gave them to me for bringing his daughter home."

"Where's this book?"

"I reckon that part of it was a lie. Chief Gall says he didn't have a book. He didn't even know what a book is."

"What was this book supposed to contain?"

"Lawrence said it had some orders and maps that you didn't want anyone else to see, especially the Army."

Crook stiffened, and both of his hands balled into fists. "That's a fabrication. A downright lie!" He fumed. "I have nothing to hide from the Army. Nothing!"

"Yes, sir. I finally figured that out."

"You described Captain Howard perfectly," Crook admitted. "Tell me, did you succeed in getting the girl back to her father?"

"I did."

"Did you speak with Gall or Sitting Bull while you were in Canada?"

"I spoke with both of them and their elders."

"You, sir, must be well thought of by the Bull." Crook stared at Crow Killer with genuine respect. "That old rascal wouldn't even speak with Miles in person."

"We talked alright. He's a great leader."

"Yes, he is. I'm afraid Custer found that out the hard way." Crook agreed. "When they spoke, did they seem inclined to return to the U.S. side of the boundary and move onto a reservation?"

"I may be wrong, but I believe Gall will return here in the near future. Sitting Bull, I doubt he'll come back any time soon."

"The old devil."

"His mind is set on remaining in the Canadians."

"What would it take to lure them both back?" Crook leaned forward, studying Crow Killer intently. "My scouts say they're starving up there in the north."

"Honesty and fair treatment is what Gall wants for his people. They looked pretty well-fed to me. I do not think they are starving."

"You don't lie very well, Mister Bracket."

"I do not betray my friends, either."

"That is honorable of you." Crook frowned. "But honorable doesn't get you what you want."

"What would?"

"Tell me, Mister Bracket, could you get a message to Chief Gall for me?" Crook stood and leaned on his desk, staring hard at Crow Killer. "A message that I could be sure would get into Gall's hands in my words, not a pack of lies."

"I believe so general. All I can do is try." He didn't want to ride back to the Canadians. He needed to get back to his valley. But he thought of Big Smoke. "For a price, it can be done."

"Your price is a reservation for the Arapaho?"

"That's it in a nutshell."

"A reservation." Crook paced for a moment or two. "I fear that will be hard to do."

"I don't see that it would be hard to give away land that first belonged to the Arapaho tribes."

"Who is the Chief of the Arapahos that you want this reservation for?"

"Wolf's Head, a young chief who I think will be a good and peaceful chief."

"Was he at the battle of the Little Bighorn?"

"No. I know this for the truth."

"Were his people in the battle?"

"No."

"Tell me, Mister Bracket." Crook drummed his fingers on the desk and looked across at Crow Killer. "Why would Captain Howard risk his career and time in a military prison to promise such a wild thing as this paper says?"

"First of all, I don't think he thought he would get caught." Crow Killer looked down at the floor and then back at Crook. There was the other reason, the one he'd hoped he wouldn't have to divulge, but the time had come. He took a breath and came out with it. "My son, Eagle Wing, killed this Captain Howard's brother during the battle of Skull Canyon. His brother was a scout for the military. And I think Captain Howard figured to kill us long before we could reach you with this forgery."

"Eagle Wing!" Crook jerked upright when he heard the name. "Then, sir, you are the notorious Crow Killer of the Arapaho Lance Bearers."

"I don't know much about being notorious, General." Crow Killer shrugged. "But I'm also Jedidiah Bracket, an American citizen."

"I thought Jedidiah Bracket sounded familiar." Crook's brow pinched together. "Didn't we meet years ago when I was just a young officer, and you were traveling west with Chalk Briggs and Lige Hatcher?" Crook wiped his face with his huge hand. "I believe that was in Saint Jo, Missouri."

"Yes, sir. That was indeed a long time ago." Crow Killer remembered. "I helped you up from the ground after your horse had shied from a teamster's oxen."

"As I remember it, you saved me from being badly dragged." Crook smiled, then laughed. "Fact is, you probably saved my life that day."

"Well, sir, you were hung up on the horse pretty good." Crow Killer rubbed the back of his neck and grinned at the memory.

"Chalk told me, last time he passed through Fort Robinson, how you got lost from the train and were assumed dead." Crook smiled. "Then years later, you turned up as Crow Killer, the great Lance Bearer of the Arapaho."

"Yes, sir."

"I see now why you have such a great interest in the Arapaho." Crook studied the treaty paper. "You know, I would have to get such a treaty ratified by the President and Congress?"

"The Arapaho saved my life, General. Now, I would like to do the same for them."

"Oklahoma is not a bad place, Mister Bracket."

"For a people used to the cool winds of the north, the hot Oklahoma lands would be the same as death to them."

"You believe that?"

"I know that. Have a little mercy, General. The Arapaho People are a great nation. Let them remain in their homelands with dignity."

Crook studied the papers. "Well, I do owe you, Mister Bracket."

"I'm not asking for me, General Crook. I'm asking for the Arapaho people. They're innocent men, women, and children."

"What will you do about Captain Howard?"

"If he leaves Eagle Wing in peace, then we will return to our lodges in the west."

"And if he doesn't?"

"We will defend ourselves." Crow Killer frowned. "What will the General do about him?"

Staring at the paper, Crook shook his head. "I don't know. If Gall comes in peaceably and helps us get Sitting Bull to return to Fort Robinson, then I'll have to turn a blind eye to what he has done. Captain Howard's family carries a lot of influence back in the East. His name is actually not on this paper, Lawrence's is."

"The Army seems to have many blind eyes, General."

"Perhaps, but in a way, his lies have helped your people." Crook shrugged.

"And if he attacks us when we leave Fort Robinson?"

"How can one lone man attack you and a warrior such as Eagle Wing?"

"Howard leads a band of thirty Pawnee warriors who are set on killing us as well."

"Get my letter to Gall, and I'll turn a blind eye to whatever you do as well." Crook sat back in his chair. "That way, maybe everybody wins."

"And the reservation for the Arapaho?"

"I'll send a dispatch off tonight." Crook picked up the treaty paper. "We will know in a few days."

"I cannot wait. I must return to my lodge."

"You do sound like an Indian, Mister Bracket."

"Yes, sir, I've lived most of my life with the Arapaho. I am Indian."

"And the message for Gall? How will I know if you send it?"

"Send a rider with me, and I'll send my answer back to you with him."

"Does Gall have someone who can read?"

"There are Canadian Mounted Police who can read it for him and send you his words in return."

"Rest here tonight and have a good meal."

"No, I have friends waiting for me." Crow Killer stood. "Get me a rider, and with the coming day, I'll have an answer for you."

"You know I can't promise anything." Crook stood and reached out his hand. "But I'll do the best I can for your Arapaho people."

"Your word is good enough for me." Crow Killer smiled. "Send your Major Nelson with me."

"Major Nelson?"

"He looks to me like he needs a little exercise."

"Now, see here, Bracket." Crook looked hard at him. "I don't want anything happening to my adjutant."

"The worst that could happen to the pretty Major is he might get a few saddle sores." Crow Killer grinned. "I'll make sure he returns here in one piece by late tomorrow."

"You need anything else?"

Looking over at the man, he knew the things he had heard from Briggs and Hatcher had been true. General Crook was a decent man, trying his best to help the tribes.

"Besides Nelson, I could use a little flour, coffee, sugar, and side meat. We've been riding a long way for many moons on mighty slim pickings."

"Done." Crook walked to the door and hollered for an orderly.

"Thank you, sir."

"No, sir, Mister Bracket." Crook reached out his hand. "I, thank you. I hope this works out to everybody's satisfaction."

"I hope this as well." He thought of Big Smoke. Convincing the warrior to ride back to Gall without taking revenge on Howard was going to take some real convincing. The big Sioux was dead set on Howard's blood. He had to admit that if his children and wife had been killed and mutilated, he would feel exactly the same.

"Leave Captain Howard alone if you can." Crook drew in a deep breath. "If he gets killed by Indians out here, it could mean the difference between getting your reservation or not. I'm putting my full weight behind the reservation, but it will be difficult at best."

"Even if Captain Howard dies fighting hostiles?"

"If the Army loses any more officers fighting hostiles, the politicians back east could balk at giving out reservations." Crook shook his head. "And the Arapaho are considered hostile."

"Why? You gave Red Cloud, Spotted Tail, and the Crow Nation reservations."

"I didn't, Congress did. The tribes you named weren't considered hostile to the U.S., but your Arapaho are."

"Well, I'm a thanking you, General."

Crook stepped to the door and summoned his orderly. "Take this man to the mess and get him whatever he wants. Then send Major Nelson to me."

"You know, sir." The orderly dropped his eyes from the hard stare. "Sergeant O'Toole ain't gonna like this one bit?"

"You tell that hard-headed Irishman if he wants his stripes in place come morning, he'll do as I say for once without arguing."

A sharp salute was presented as the man turned sheepishly away. "Follow me."

"Goodbye and good luck, Mister Bracket."

"Goodbye, General."

CHAPTER 15

THE SUN WAS ONLY A SOFT GLOW rising in the east when Broken Leg helped Black Bird to his feet. He could tell the warrior was in pain. The wounded leg had surely stiffened from the exertion of the long walk down the mountain, especially after lying on the bare ground during the cool of the night. They left the horse hides behind because they had dried and stiffened, becoming worthless.

Broken Leg put the walking stick in Black Bird's hand and looked down the dark trail. "We will go slowly at first." He picked up their weapons and what little meat they had left. "Maybe your leg will loosen up as we walk."

"Give me my bow and quiver."

"I will carry it for a while."

"The spirits will frown if I do not carry my own lance." Black Bird insisted.

Handing the quiver holding Black Bird's medicine lance to the warrior, Broken Leg placed his arm under the injured warrior's shoulder and supported him for a few steps. The small path was narrow, hardly big enough for the two warriors to walk side by side.

"We should hear the sound of Spotted Elk's horses if he passes soon."

"Perhaps he sleeps late." Broken Leg looked back up the trail. "Spotted Elk is no war leader. He lets his people sleep when they should be on the trail."

"I agree. He is no war leader."

"That is a good thing for us if we hope to reach the high ridge before he does."

"Then we must go fast." Black Bird pushed away from Broken Leg and relied only on the crutch to help him along the trail. Pain showed on his face as he moved on down the path. "We cannot let Spotted Elk reach the ridge before we do."

"Go slow, my friend."

Sweat broke out on the warrior's face as he limped forward. Finally, stopping to lean against a rock outcropping, Black Bird shook his head. "Broken Leg must go on without me."

"Are you sure, my friend? I hate to leave you here alone."

"The pain is too great." Black Bird gritted his teeth. "Go. I will be fine. I will follow slowly behind you."

"Be careful, Black Bird." Broken Leg handed the warrior the water flask and meat.

"I do not know this trail, but Red Horse said it can be dangerous farther down."

"I will return for you when I can."

"Do not worry for me." The warrior shook his head. "Just warn Red Horse. Go quickly."

Broken Leg moved down the narrow path, quickly disappearing from view as he turned around a bend in the sharp trail. Hitting a fast trot, he left Black Bird far behind. He hated to leave the helpless warrior, but Black Bird was right. If they were to warn Crow Killer's lodge, there was no other way.

Ahead, the trail began a rapid descent. Here, he had to be cautious. The path was covered in loose rock, creating dangerous footing that could easily cause a fatal fall. The trail narrowed in places, and the warrior had to flatten himself against the rock wall to slip by. He hoped Black Bird would wait where he was. This trail was far too dangerous for him to try and cross with his injured leg. He wondered as he moved along the trail how Red Horse had ever found this almost hidden path.

The trail was a rough and treacherous passage. It was all downhill, so at least it didn't tire a man on foot. In places, the trail became passable, allowing the warrior to move faster. Broken Leg studied the trail. The way it curved downwards it should bring him out below the high ridge.

Above, on the higher trail, horses carrying riders would have to exert a lot of energy climbing the steep mountain trail. Black Bird had said the upper trail would take a full day's ride to reach the ridge that looked down on the valley of Crow Killer. Broken Leg had no way of knowing how long this trail would take, but he could tell he was making good time. He had to reach that upper trail before Spotted Elk arrived at the ridge. Somehow, he had to warn Red Horse down in the valley. He hoped Spotted Elk would ride at a slower pace, letting the women rest, especially the woman with the new baby.

The sun was high overhead when Broken Leg crossed over a narrow ledge where a mountain stream ran shallowly over the rocks and down into the gorge. He figured the clear stream might empty into the creek running just below Crow Killer's cabin. If so, he knew it couldn't be much farther along this trail until it came into the main trail above. Kneeling to drink from the rivulet, he wiped his face and looked across the water. From where he stood, the trail started to climb back up the gorge. Carefully choosing his footing as he waded the swift running water that flowed over slippery stones, Broken Leg moved back on the dry rocky trail and started to climb.

It was mid-afternoon when the warrior recognized the huge boulder that stood just off the main trail leading down to the cabin. Stopping to rest and catch his breath, he looked back down towards the gorge. The narrow path leading up from the water crossing had been short but very steep. Drawing a deep breath, he was about to move on to the trail when he heard the unmistakable sound of a horse snorting above him. Slipping beside the boulder and crouching out of sight, he peered up at the high ridge and waited.

He had beaten Spotted Elk to the ridge, but he wasn't far enough ahead to outrun mounted warriors down the trail on foot. Armed only with a bow, he knew he couldn't stop Spotted Elk and his warriors from attacking the cabin. The bow would kill, but it wouldn't make noise to warn the ones in the valley. Studying whether to try and run or to stay and fight, he heard the sound of the little mule braying a warning from below on the valley floor. Surely, Red Horse or someone at the cabin would hear the mule warning and realize someone was on the high ridge. But he couldn't be sure. He had to try and give some kind of warning in case Spotted Elk charged down the mountain trail and took the ones below by surprise.

Moving cautiously, Broken Leg kept out of sight as he made his way to the upper trail. Reaching the trail, he moved slowly and silently up toward the ridge and the waiting warriors.

The trail down into the valley was wide, and there was only a little brush along the lower side of the trail to conceal him as he worked his way up to the ridge. Again, the mule brayed, but the cabin was out of his view. From where he lay concealed, he couldn't see any movement in the valley down below.

Broken Leg shook his head. Why were the raiders wasting time on the ridge instead of riding down the trail and attacking the valley? Surprise was what every raiding party depended on for success. Black Bird was right. Spotted Elk was not a good war leader. By waiting, Spotted Elk had squandered the advantage of a surprise attack against the cabin. Peeking cautiously through the bush he hid behind, Broken Leg studied the high ridge. Moving upward, he hoped the warriors above couldn't see him from the steep trail.

Climbing the last few feet and slipping soundlessly behind a small boulder, Broken Leg held his breath for fear that the warriors of Spotted Elk would hear his ragged breathing. He thought back on how many times Black Bird had complained of walking. He had always insisted they were horseback warriors, not made for walking. The warrior had been right again. This steep passage up the rocky trail had shown Broken Leg he was not in shape to walk as much as he had. Thankfully, he had left Black Bird on the lower trail out of harm's way. At least, if Broken Leg had to flee, he knew where the hidden passage lay. He smiled to himself. Walking made a warrior appreciate a good horse, even a sorry one.

He could plainly hear loud voices above where he lay. Spotted Elk and Wild Horse were arguing again. This was good. The longer they waited here and argued, the more time it gave the ones below to prepare for an attack. He was sure the mule had been heard by someone at the cabin, and he knew Red Horse would investigate what she was braying about.

"I say we attack now." The voice of Wild Horse was loud and sounded angry. "If we wait until after the sun leaves, it will give the ones below time to get prepared."

Spotted Elk spoke loudly. "They don't even know we are here."

"They are Lance Bearers, not foolish children." Wild Horse raised his voice even louder. "I can hear the mule talking from here. Surely Red Horse will suspect it calls to something up here."

"Wild Horse is right." Coyote Man spoke up. "If we are going to attack, let's do it now before the dark times come."

"Ei owe." Spotted Elk hissed with irritation. "We go. The women will wait here for a signal to come down."

Broken Leg notched an arrow and crouched behind the boulder. If he could capture one rifle, he could sound the alarm for the ones below. Only minutes passed before the ten riders strung out in single file and started down the steep trail. All the warriors were armed with Henry repeaters, mostly gifts from Crow Killer. Over the years, he had traded for the weapons and shells at

Bridger's so the Arapaho would be well armed and could protect the people against their enemies. Now, here they were, being turned on their benefactor and his lodge. Broken Leg shook his head. How many foolish ones had died trying to ride against the Bear Killer and his medicine?

A warrior called Fox Eyes trailed the slow-moving column as they leaned back on their ponies. Sliding down the worst part of the trail, Broken Leg eyed Fox Eyes's Henry rifle as he passed. Raising his bow, Broken Leg sent the arrow on its deadly path straight into the warrior's back. Springing forward, as the others heard the body fall, Broken Leg snatched up the rifle, fired off two rounds at the raiders, and plunged into the brush on the upper side of the trail.

This side of the trail quickly turned into a jumble of rock, brush, and mountain pine. Broken Leg remembered this rough path. It was the one Red Horse had come down from after killing the thieving trapper, Wilde. Quickly racing up the path as screams came from both the warriors of Spotted Elk and the squaws on top, Broken Leg slipped behind a large pine. Bullets ripped harmlessly through the overhead branches as he waited. He knew they were shooting foolishly. None of the bullets came close.

Stupidly, Wild Horse raced down the path on foot right into Broken Leg's waiting rifle. No others dared follow the warrior. The heavy slug of the Henry knocked the warrior backward. He crumpled in a heap on the path.

Broken Leg heard Spotted Elk barking orders and horse hooves scrambling back up the steep trail to the high ridge.

Waiting until everything quieted, Broken Leg slipped silently back down the trail, watching carefully for a hidden enemy. He doubted Spotted Elk would wait in ambush for him now that the ones below had been warned. Reaching the main trail, he trotted quickly to the ridge and stared down at the retreating horses. Raising his rifle, he was about to fire, then remembered the woman and the newborn baby. Killing Spotted Elk or his warriors would be right, but what about the baby if his shot went wild? No. He lowered the rifle.

Hearing a horse behind him, he turned as Red Horse came running his horse as fast as he could up the steep trail. The animal almost fell twice as he labored up the rocky path.

"Broken Leg." Red Horse called out to him. He stared down at the crumpled body of Fox Eyes. "What has happened?"

"Spotted Elk." Broken Leg leaned over, breathless.

"Spotted Elk is here?"

Broken Leg pointed behind him. "He flees back towards the river like a beaten dog."

Looking over where Fox Eyes's pony stood waiting beside its dead master, Red Horse pointed. "We will take Fox Eyes horse and catch them."

"No, Red Horse." Broken Leg held up his hand. "Let them go for now."

"Spotted Elk will return again to our valley if he is not punished."

"I killed Fox Eyes and Wild Horse."

"Wild Horse, too?"

Broken Leg pointed down the trail. "His body lies down there."

Red Horse remembered the white hunter Wilde. "He is in good company."

"There lies his rifle and his lance."

"The rifle is yours, my friend. The lance will go in the fire."

"Lances in the Fire." Broken Leg shook his head, remembering Two Bears burning the lance of Spotted Elk. "We have lost so many."

"You rest here, Broken Leg. I will ride back to the cabin and tell them what has happened. Then we will follow Spotted Elk and make sure he leaves these mountains."

"You warn the others. I must go after Black Bird."

"Where is Black Bird?"

Broken Leg pointed down the gorge. "He is wounded. His wounds would not let him walk here."

"How far down is he?"

"He is almost to the crooked Pine Tree at the river."

"I will warn Bright Moon and Chalk to watch carefully until we return. Then, we will go after him with the horses." Red Horse turned his horse. "The high trail will take longer, but if he cannot walk, the path through the gorge is too dangerous."

"I will wait here and watch for Spotted Elk to return." Broken Leg grabbed up the loose horses. "What will we do with Fox Eyes?"

Red Horse looked over at the body. "When I return, he will join the others that have come here to attack our valley."

Broken Leg remembered how Black Bird had dragged the white eye scout Brown away and pushed him over the ledge. "Bring food and bandages for Black Bird when you return."

"And food also for the great Lance Bearer, Broken Leg." Red Horse waved his hand. "Thank you, my friend."

Red Horse ordered Chalk to take the women and food to the fortified cave until he returned. Spotted Elk should be retreating towards Bridger, but other enemies could come into their valley from the south while he was away. He had given his word to protect the ones here in Crow Killer's lodges. Until his father returned, they were his responsibility, so he would take no chances. He had given his word not to go far from the cabin and women. But he had to go after Black Bird and make sure Spotted Elk had left the mountains and taken his people back towards Bridger. Filling his leather hunting pouch with food and bandages, he quickly switched to a fresh horse and, with a nod to Briggs, he started back up the mountain trail.

"We go." Red Horse only stopped a few minutes to let his horse blow from the long climb. Then, with Broken Leg mounted on the horse of Fox Eyes, they started down the mountain towards the Snake.

Red Horse kept the horses moving down the steep mountain and then back up through the rocky pass as fast as he could without winding the animals. Broken Leg was in a hurry to reach Black Bird. He was worried for the warrior, who was as a brother. Red Horse had no concerns that Spotted Elk might be waiting hidden along the trail. It was too narrow to hide raiders from sight.

The sun was down, darkening the narrow path as they reached another dangerous narrow gorge. Dropping from his horse, Red Horse handed Broken Leg meat and bread, then looked off into the shadows. "Now we will have to walk."

Red Horse's dark eyes could not be seen, but Broken Leg could hear the anger in his voice. "I should have killed Spotted Elk and burnt my Lance."

"That does not matter now. We must reach Black Bird quickly."

Red Horse tightened his hold on his horse's reins as they edged past a place where part of the path had washed away. "The trail here is dangerous. We will have to lead the horses until the moon rises so we can see."

"The new sun will be up before we reach the crooked tree."

"How bad is Black Bird wounded?"

Broken Leg told Red Horse of their friend's wounds. Then silence settled over the trail with only the sound of the horse's feet sliding along the gravel path making any sound. The dark now encompassed the trail completely, forcing them to move slowly and cautiously, feeling for every step.

The night passed with only the occasional sound of an owl or the howl of a wolf breaking the silence. Broken Leg kept a firm grip on the tail of the spotted horse being led by Red Horse. He had been over it only once with Crow Killer and couldn't remember the trail well enough to walk it in the dark. Anxious to reach Black Bird, he wanted to move faster, but it was not possible, not in this thick darkness.

Feeling the horse stop in front of him, Broken Leg stopped his own horse from pushing up against him. "What is wrong?"

"This is the most dangerous part of the trail. We will stay here until we can see the path." Red Horse sat down in the middle of the trail. Here, the trees and high ridges of the mountain blanketed them in complete darkness. "To move on, we will have to wait for light."

Broken Leg thought of Black Bird. "He has been alone on the trail since the sun came up this morning."

Red Horse stared out in the dark surrounding them. "We will reach him with the new sun."

The moon finally came up, letting Red Horse see well enough to start their descent down the mountain once again. Even with the dim light of the moon, for both man and horse, walking downhill on that steep rock-strewn trail was slow and torturous.

Finally, as the first ray of light broke over the mountains to the east, Red Horse stopped. "We have almost reached Black Bird. I can smell the river from here."

"He will be glad to see us."

"Come, we ride now."

The tall bent pine could be seen from where they topped a small rise, and then the mountain trail dipped back down, and the bent pine was no longer in their sight. Red Horse reined in and looked back at Broken Leg. "This is where Spotted Elk will wait for us if he dares to fight."

"I think, after losing so many, he will ride back to Bridger, where he knows we cannot follow him."

"If it weren't for Black Bird and the ones back in the valley, Bridger would not stop me from killing him." Red Horse slapped his horse. "We go. Watch carefully, my friend."

Turning a curve on the trail, both riders reined in as the sight before them took their breath. A dead horse and three bodies lay sprawled out on the trail. The Lance of a Lance Bearer stood buried in the ground, a rawhide strap tied to one of his legs.

Slipping from his horse, Broken Leg hurried to the body of Black Bird and knelt at his side. A single bullet hole showed on the bloody chest. The eyes were open in death, but the face seemed peaceful, almost smiling.

"What have you done, my brother?" Broken Leg touched the bow that lay beside the warrior.

Standing back to let Broken Leg grieve for his friend, Red Horse walked to where Spotted Elk and another warrior, Many Horns, lay. Both had been killed by the arrows of Black Bird. Looking at the rawhide tether that bound Black Bird to his lance, Red Horse saw that it had been cut. Someone from Spotted Elk's raiders had cut the rope in a final act of respect for a courageous Lance Bearer. Red Horse knew it had to be one of Spotted Elks's warriors of the Lance Bearer Society. It was taboo, bad medicine, for a squaw to touch a warrior's lance. A strange custom, but the Lance Bearers believed it would weaken their medicine if their lance was touched by anyone but another Lance Bearer.

Studying the trail, Red Horse followed the tracks down towards the river. How many of the warriors remained he couldn't know, but enough had been killed to discourage them from ever coming into these mountains again. Returning he stood beside Broken Leg.

"He died a Lance Bearer's death."

"Why didn't he wait for us?"

Red Horse shook his head. "I don't know this, but whatever his reason, he was a brave warrior. We will carry his body back to be placed near Little Antelope." He looked from his friend to the bodies of the enemies. "And I will drag Spotted Elk and Many Horns to their final resting place."

Broken Leg watched Red Horse dump the bodies over the canyon, then retrieved the lance of Many Horns. The raiders hadn't even stopped to bury their dead in fear of Red Horse catching up to them.

"Another lance to go in the fire." Looking at the carving of the horn on the lance, Broken Leg shook his head sadly. "The white eye will not have to defeat the Lance Bearers. We are killing each other off."

"Come, Broken Leg." Red Horse handed him Black Bird's Lance with the bird carved on it. "We will take our friend and brave warrior home to be raised on a scaffold with his lance."

Broken Leg shook his head slowly. "And the others that followed Spotted Elk here?"

"Spotted Elk is dead. It is finished."

CHAPTER 16

WITH THE FLAT PRAIRIE LAND behind them, Crow Killer reined in as the scrub timber turned into the beginning of heavier forest. Not a word had come from Nelson as they rode through the night. Crow Killer smiled to himself. The Major wasn't used to being an errand boy, and he didn't like it. The sun was peeking through the clouds from the east as he turned and looked back at the erect figure.

"Take your bearings, Major," Crow Killer nodded back to the southeast and the mountain peak. "I promised Crook you would get back to him by sundown tonight. So don't get yourself lost."

The face turned dark. "I'm no greenhorn, Bracket."

"No, I reckon you ain't at that. I expect you've been out here killing Indians quite a spell now."

"Hostiles."

"Whatever. You listen good, Major. We're fixing to ride into my camp. If you value your hair, keep your hands away from that pistol and in plain sight."

"I guess there's more of you heathens ahead?"

"My son, Eagle Wing, and two others."

"I've heard tales of this Eagle Wing." Nelson's voice hardened. "He killed one of my scouts named Howard at the battle of Skull Canyon."

"Well, Major, he done that, alright. But if I were you, I

wouldn't mention it while you're here in our company."

Nelson sneered at Crow Killer. "I can't believe General Crook fell for your lies."

"Lies, Major?" Crow Killer shook his head. "What would a white pony soldier know about lies?"

"Officers in the United States Army do not lie." Nelson frowned. "We are men of honor."

"Really? Well, I wouldn't say that to Big Smoke up ahead. He's just liable to pull your head off."

"Who's Big Smoke?"

"Big Smoke is a Sioux warrior who has many a grievance against your so-called honorable Army."

"Oh." Nelson got that haughty look again as if he smelled something foul. "Another hostile."

"You might say that. But if I was you, I wouldn't go sayin' it to his face. Your Captain Howard killed his whole family, including his wife and children. And then your honorable officer proceeded to mutilate them. No, sir, Major, I wouldn't call him a hostile, that is, if you value your hair. Now, let's ride."

Eagle Wing spotted them as they rode through the heavy timber and down a small game trail. Alerting Red Hawk and Big Smoke, all three warriors faded back into the foliage out of sight.

Reining in at the small stream, Crow Killer gave a short whistle and then waited for Red Hawk and Eagle Wing to appear. Keeping his eyes on Nelson to make sure he didn't do anything foolish, he slid from his borrowed horse. Dismounting the uncomfortable McClellan saddle, Crow Killer shook his head. "When you return to Robinson, you can take this animal and the saddle back with you."

"You don't want him?" The Major seemed surprised.

"Well, sir, he's not exactly mine."

"Then who does he belong to?"

"Some fellers named Spade and Clem back at Irvin's Trading

Post loaned him to me. Or, I should say Irvin's pig sty."

"I know Clem and Spade. They hunted meat for the fort a couple of years ago. Those two crooks wouldn't loan anyone the sweat off their brows." Nelson frowned. "You stole him, didn't you?" He looked around as if he couldn't believe such a thing.

"Stole him? Nah. Like I said, he was a loan. Either that or the poor animal was just so tired of the stench, he up and followed me here."

"I swear, Bracket, you're worse than the heathens you live with." Nelson shook his head.

"Well, I reckon the horse belongs to them anyway. See if you can return him."

Eagle Wing and Red Hawk walked silently up behind Nelson while Big Smoke appeared out of the woods in front of him. Nelson shifted nervously at the sight of the big Sioux, but when he noticed the other two warriors standing right behind him, he recoiled and edged back."

Crow Killer struggled to keep from smiling. "This is my son, Eagle Wing. And this is my brother, the great Red Hawk, Chief of the Crow people. This is Big Smoke, Oglala warrior." He introduced their white eye guest to his friends. "This is Major Nelson."

Nelson eyed the big warrior before him. "Oglala, huh? You must be one of Crazy Horse's Warriors?"

Big Smoke waited for Crow Killer to translate the words, and then he nodded slowly. As the fire was being rekindled, Crow Killer handed Big Smoke the supplies given to them by the supply cook at Robinson. Choice cuts of meat lay over the fire cooking. Earlier in the day, Red Hawk had killed a good-sized buck. Biscuits, side meat, and venison made the men a hearty breakfast. Nelson was famished. They hadn't eaten all day. So, the arrogant Major forgot he was amongst heathens and ate with his bare hands as the others did. Finished with their meal, Crow Killer pulled Big Smoke out of earshot of the others."

"I have an important thing to ask of my friend, Big Smoke."

"What does Crow Killer wish from this one?"

Pulling the sealed envelope Crook had given him from his leather pouch, he showed it to the big warrior. Encased in waterproof paper and sealed, he didn't bother to open it. He knew Big Smoke wouldn't be able to read it even if he did.

"This, my friend, is a paper that the whites use to speak with each other over long distances." Crow Killer watched the dark eyes as they studied the envelope. "The white chief of the pony soldiers wishes for the great warrior Big Smoke to take this message to Chief Gall in the Canadians."

Big Smoke frowned. "Then you have spoken with a forked tongue. You do not follow the trail of the killers of my family as you said you would?"

"No, I have not lied. We intend to find these killers and avenge them for our friend, Big Smoke. But this message is very important for the Arapaho people and your people."

"Nothing is important to me, except hanging the yellow hair of Howard on my scalp pole." Big Smoke flattened his hands. "Eagle Wing gave his word he would help Big Smoke hunt the white eye devil and his Pawnee dogs."

"We have not broken our word to Big Smoke." He could see the doubt in the warrior's eyes. "We will follow the pony soldier, but we need Big Smoke to get this message to Gall."

"Will the pony soldier ride with me to the Canadians?" Smoke looked over at Nelson.

"No, this one will return to Fort Robinson and give the General your decision."

"I would be the same as a Pawnee Scout doing the bidding of the white eye." The dark head shook. "Helping the whites makes my stomach sick."

"I understand how you feel, my friend. But this might help your Chief, Crazy Horse. And it will be doing a great thing for me."

"Crow Killer asks too much of this warrior."

"I am. But I give you my word; before I leave these lands, the pony soldier, Howard, and the Pawnee, Bull Coat, will taste my knife."

"It is not the same as me killing them."

"Maybe not, but I promise they will hear your name before they die." Crow Killer vowed. "I give you my word as a Lance Bearer."

"I must think on this." Big Smoke frowned gravely, and his shoulders tensed as he heaved in a deep breath. "Have Eagle Wing come council with us."

Crow Killer motioned for Eagle Wing.

"I am here, Big Smoke."

"Does my friend, Eagle Wing, know that Crow Killer has asked me to ride back to the Canadians and carry that to Gall?" The warrior pointed at the letter. "You know that from the Grandmother Lands I cannot pursue the pony soldier who killed my family."

"What has my father told you?"

Smoke glanced over to where Nelson sat talking to Red Hawk. Quickly, he told Eagle Wing all that had been said and then he stared hard at the young warrior. A strained silence settled on the three as several minutes passed. Finally, Big Smoke took one last look at the paper. "I have heard much of the war axe of Flying Cloud that Eagle Wing carries." Big Smoke pointed at the war axe. "And the war lance of the Lance Bearers. I have heard that if you swear an oath on them, you cannot break your word."

"That is true," Eagle Wing answered solemnly. "An oath is the same as our lives."

"Then Lance Bearers, place your hands on them and swear to Big Smoke that the pony soldier they call Howard and the Pawnee, Bull Coat, will be killed before you leave these lands."

"Crow Killer stared at the big warrior. "Big Smoke does not take the word of his friends?"

"You are both Big Smoke's friends, but in this, I must know. I must know the pony soldier and Bull Coat will die."

Crow Killer knew it could take some doing to locate Howard in this huge land. He wanted to ride for his valley now, but if he wanted Big Smoke's help, he had to pledge his word. To swear such a thing on his lance, a Lance Bearer must keep his pledge or die trying. As he contemplated his decision, Eagle Wing looked over at his father. He knew Crow Killer wanted a reservation for their people, and to get one, they needed Big Smoke's help. The message from Crook had to be delivered to Gall if the General was to speak with the whites back east for an Arapaho Reservation.

Pulling out his war axe, Eagle Wing placed the weapon across his chest. "Big Smoke has my pledge. The pony soldier will die for this thing he has done."

Crow Killer pushed his lance into the dirt at the warrior's feet. "Big Smoke also has my word. Howard and Bull Coat will die before I leave this land."

Big Smoke studied the two warriors for a moment and lowered his head with a brief nod. "Then I will ride back to the Canadians. But I do this only for you, my friends, and for Crazy Horse, my chief."

"We know this." Eagle Wing handed him his prized bone-handled skinning knife. "We thank Big Smoke. This knife is for you."

Big Smoke felt the heft of the beautiful knife. "What else do you wish me to tell Gall?"

"Tell him I think General Crook is a good man." Crow Killer handed Big Smoke the package. "And that I think he is a man of honor, a white Chief that can be trusted."

Eagle Wing looked at the warrior he had grown to respect. "Will you stay with Gall and Sitting Bull when you reach the Canadians?"

"No, I will return to our people and Crazy Horse." Big Smoke looked at the letter in his huge hand. "It is such a small thing to me, such a big thing to so many others."

Crow Killer had never known the warrior to be philosophical.

Normally, he was always joking. "Tell Crazy Horse we are thinking of him and his people."

"You have our word, my friend. Your family will be avenged." Eagle Wing held up his axe meaningfully and nodded at the big Sioux.

"Be careful, Big Smoke. This is a dangerous country for a lone rider," Crow Killer warned.

"They will never see me." Big Smoke laughed. "I am called Big Smoke for a reason. You see me, and then you don't."

"Put the letter in this." Crow Killer handed Big Smoke the leather satchel, and the three re-joined Red Hawk and Nelson. "You have eaten well, Major?"

"I have, and I thank you." Nelson looked over at Red Hawk. "Red Hawk and I have had a pleasant conversation. I didn't know he spoke English."

"Perhaps, Major Nelson, you should learn a little Crow and Sioux," Eagle Wing said with a half-smile. "Knowing them just might come in handy for you someday."

Nelson shook his head. "The Indian wars will be over soon, and I'm headed back to civilization."

"Why, Major, I thought you were beginning to like us heathens?" Crow Killer joked.

"Like you, Mister Bracket?" He shook his head. "I despise the West and all of you heathens along with it."

"That's too bad."

"But—" Nelson shrugged and untied his horse. "For what it's worth, you do have my respect."

"Well, thank you, Major."

"You have words for me to take back to General Crook?"

"Yes, Major Nelson, I do." Crow Killer looked over where Big Smoke was removing the hobbles from his horse. "You can tell him his letter will get into Gall's hands. Big Smoke rides to the Canadians tonight."

Saluting, Nelson swung up onto his horse. "If I'm going to

get back to Fort Robinson before the General sends out a search party, I better be riding."

"You that important to him, Major?" Eagle Wing asked. "That he would send out a hunting party?"

"Yes, Mister Eagle Wing." Nelson saluted. "I'm his adjutant." Nelson kicked his horse and rode out of sight.

"He's not such a bad sort," Eagle Wing muttered.

"What's an adjutant?" Red Hawk was curious.

"It's some kind of a lesser chief amongst the whites."

Red Hawk led his big Appaloosa Stallion to where Big Smoke was readying his sleeping robe and weapons. Offering the rawhide rein of the stallion to Big Smoke, he smiled. "He will take you swiftly back to the Canadians." Red Hawk ran his hands down the spotted neck. "Take him, my friend. No other is as fleet or as strong."

Big Smoke looked the big horse up and down. "He is a great horse, but I fear his spots would show me to my enemies, and I would not get this letter to Gall."

Red Hawk's eyebrows shot up in surprise. "I could be insulted."

"No insult, Crow. I am honored that you have offered your most prized possession to me. But I speak the truth. I must ride a horse the color of wood in the trees, a horse that blends with the shadows among the prairie grasses."

Crow Killer, Eagle Wing, and Red Hawk rode with Big Smoke out of the sheltered timber to the edge of the prairie. Reining in, they said their goodbyes and parted. Big Smoke headed north, while Crow Killer and the others turned west in their quest to find Howard and Bull Coat.

"This is an empty land, my brother." Red Hawk looked out across the flat land. "Where will we look for this pony soldier?"

"We don't look for Howard. We let his scouts look for us."

"How do we do this?"

"Howard doesn't know I have met with Crook. He still thinks he has to stop us before we reach Fort Robinson."

"If he doesn't stop us, the white eye General will find out that Howard has lied and promised the Arapaho a reservation." Eagle Wing spoke up. "The pony soldier chief would not like this."

"I think Howard will have scouts out everywhere looking for Eagle Wing." Crow Killer shrugged. "So, we will let them find us."

"This is a dangerous game we play, my brother."

"It is."

"I don't care about the danger. I want to be found quickly." Eagle Wing kicked his horse forward. "Then Howard will be dead, and I will ride for home as fast as I can."

"We ride to the southwest." Crow Killer looked out over the flats. "That is where the yellow-hair's scouts will look for us first."

Red Hawk grumbled low in his chest. "We will have to be very alert as we ride."

"Very." Crow Killer agreed. "When the dark comes, we will light fires that can be seen. This will get us found quicker."

"If we are found, our horses are strong and fleet." Eagle Wing patted the neck of the horse he rode.

"We will not be running." Crow Killer patted the Henry slung across his horse. "Our rifles will do our running."

"There will be many to kill." Eagle Wing glanced back at his father. "I counted at least twenty Pawnee warriors riding with Bull Coat. Perhaps more ride with him now."

"If we kill Howard and Bull Coat, I think the others will ride back to their people."

Red Hawk shrugged. "Like the elders say, if you cut off the head, the snake will die."

Crow Killer heeled his horse. "Let's hurry up and find this snake."

For three days, Crow Killer led Eagle Wing and Red Hawk to the west, circling across the flat plains during the day hours and making an open camp with a fire during the dark times. The bright fire was an open invitation for them to be found. Seemingly careless, Crow Killer kept a fire going, but he also kept one of them watching the camp from out in the dark. He knew no enemy would be able to sneak up on the camp without being discovered.

One always guarded the camp, but there were also the horses. Crow Killer knew no stranger could get near the Appaloosas of Eagle Wing and Red Hawk without a nervous snort or pricking of their ears. Trained from colts to give an alarm if an enemy neared, they were better than village dogs. A dog always slept, but a good horse staked near your lodge was always alert to danger. Nothing, neither the four-leggeds nor the two-leggeds, could come near the camp without being discovered. The fire was bait. Any observer could plainly see three forms asleep in their robes. Crow Killer had set his trap. Now, all he could do was wait for Howard and his Pawnee scouts to take his bait.

The prairie was empty. He saw no sign of riders on the flatlands. When the new sun came up on the morning of the fourth day, Crow Killer killed a small antelope with his Henry, and the flats reverberated with the noise.

"Does my brother think the noise was loud enough for an enemy to hear the shot?" Red Hawk shook his head. "Maybe Crow Killer should shoot again."

"I'm hungry, and now we can eat." Crow Killer jacked a fresh bullet in the Henry's belly.

Red Hawk laughed. "This one is also hungry, but not hungry enough to let every enemy on the plains know where we are."

"We have been trying to be found for three sleeps." Eagle Wing frowned. "I'm tired of playing this cat-and-mouse game with Howard or Lawrence or whatever the yellow-haired white eye's name is."

"Cat and mouse. What game is that?" Red Hawk shrugged.

Crow Killer shook his head. "It is a game where the Pawnee eat the Crow Chief."

"I think that would be a bad kind of game."

Eagle Wing interrupted their badgering. "Well, if there was anyone out here to hear anything, somebody should have heard that shot."

"We will gut the antelope, then we'll build a fire and have some fresh meat to eat." Crow Killer pointed at a stand of trees on the horizon. "Over there, that will be a good place for our fire."

Red Hawk shook his head again. "My brother, you are pointing to a ridge that can be seen from very far away."

"That's the idea, isn't it? Get their attention so they can find us."

"I think it'll get somebody's attention alright." Red Hawk laughed. "Perhaps the long knife pony soldiers."

"We'll see who comes. Let's go cook some antelope."

The fire lit up the surrounding trees brightly. Again, the trap was laid, ready and waiting for Howard to find it. Tonight, Crow Killer tended the fire while Red Hawk and Eagle Wing waited out in the dark, watching the camp like night hawks. The place they stopped late in the evening was a natural camp. Water and good grass were ample for the horses and the grove of maple trees supplied plenty of firewood to keep the fire blazing. Crow Killer knew if he was the one doing the hunting, he would quickly smell this camp out as a trick to lure him in. But he knew it would just be Pawnee scouts coming, and scouts would only be looking to see who was occupying the camp, not whether or not it could be a trap.

Long after midnight, he placed more wood on the fire as the moon showed itself. Stiffening, he noticed the ears of all three horses prick up and point off to the north side of the camp. Several minutes passed as the horses moved about in an agitated manner. Crow Killer knew one of the Pawnee Scouts had come closer to the camp as the Appaloosas snorted and raised their heads. Knowing Red Hawk and Eagle Wing were watching the camp,

Crow Killer casually ignored the warning and rolled back in his robe. He knew someone was out there. The horses wouldn't alert on a deer or coyote as they had. He had no doubt it was a two-legged moving in closer to observe the camp and find out if it was Eagle Wing.

His trap had worked. Now, the scouts would report back to Captain Howard and tell him exactly where they were. He hoped Eagle Wing or Red Hawk wouldn't have to use their weapons and warn the ones watching that they had been seen. He had set his trap. Now, all he could hope for was that Howard and his pack of Pawnee dogs would walk into it. How long it would take, he didn't know. It all depended on how far away their main camp was. Crow Killer lay still in his robes. He didn't figure there would be a confrontation tonight unless the ones out in the dark were young warriors. In every tribe, there were always hot bloods, eager for glory and foolish enough to try to kill Eagle Wing themselves.

Howard's scouts probably had orders to only find Eagle Wing and report back. No, there would be no killing tonight. Crow Killer knew the pony soldier captain would want to be in on the kill personally.

Howard probably had his warriors scattered all over the prairie searching for them. It would take time to gather the Pawnee warriors back together in a fighting force. The night passed slowly, and the eastern sky finally brightened with the coming morning. Red Hawk and Eagle Wing walked back into the camp with the new day, tired from the long night. Crow Killer had meat and biscuits heating over the flames as the two warriors set back on their robes.

Grabbing some breakfast, the two ate. "Two came in close, while more waited out on the flats."

"How many do you think?"

"We don't know. We could not leave sight of the camp." Red Hawk bit into a hot biscuit. "We were afraid they might fire on you."

"I think they will ride fast for Howard, Bull Coat, and their warriors." Crow Killer tossed more wood on the fire. "Depending on how far away their camp is, they could return with the dark."

"Crow Killer does not think they will be waiting somewhere on the trail?"

"You will sleep, then we will ride to the west. Rest, so you will be awake if they do find us on the trail."

Red Hawk finished his meal and rolled up in his blanket. "Crow Killer will wake us if the yellow-haired captain comes?"

"I will wake you when they come." Crow Killer smiled over at Red Hawk. "I sure wouldn't want you to miss the fun."

Shaking his head, the warrior rolled over, grumbling. "You are not funny, my brother."

Watching over the sleeping warriors, Crow Killer checked on the horses, then removed their hobbles and led them down for water. Nothing was seen or heard out on the flats but the waving grass and the sound of meadowlarks and doves calling. When the sun stood straight overhead, he fixed a hot meal and roused the sleeping warriors.

Eagle Wing and Red Hawk washed in the small creek and quickly ate. Rolling up their robes, the warriors removed the hobbles and swung up on their horses.

"We will ride slowly to the west." Crow Killer looked around the camp and then led out. "Keep a sharp lookout for an ambush."

"My eyes are too tired to look." Red Hawk quipped.

"If the Pawnee attack, I will warn you."

"I am too old for this."

"No." Eagle Wing shook his head. "This is what keeps you young, Uncle. You love this."

"Yes, but my body doesn't."

Crow Killer studied the surrounding flats in every direction. Nothing moved but the tall grass blown by the wind. He had deliberately kept the horses in a slow walk allowing them to plod steadily to the west. He was in no hurry, he wanted to make it easy for Howard to catch up to them. Like Eagle Wing, he was eager to confront the enemy so they could ride home to their valley and people. He knew twenty-three against three were bad odds, but to keep his word to Big Smoke, there was no other way. He was glad they would be fighting Pawnee and not Sioux.

The sooner this was finished the sooner they could return to their families, providing they were the victors and still alive. This was the longest he had ever been away from Bright Moon and he knew Red Hawk and Eagle Wing were eager to return to their own families. As the horse plodded through the tall grass Crow Killer swore to himself if he survived this fight with Howard, this would be the last time he would leave his valley.

Shaking his head, he thought back on how many times he had said this same thing. There had always been something important to pull him away from his lodge and valley.

No more. If he was victorious and lucky enough to return to Bright Moon, this would be the final trail for him.

The sun was setting in the west when the small party reined in at a watering hole and slid from their horses. Another day had passed with still no sign of Captain Howard or his warriors. Tonight, there would be no fire started. Howard and his Pawnee were probably on their trail by now, perhaps close. There was no way of knowing their whereabouts until they were spotted out on the prairie.

Tonight, Crow Killer would take the first watch, letting Eagle Wing and Red Hawk rest. The trap had been set, now the hunted would have to be on the watch for the hunters to show themselves. Sitting on the bank of the waterhole where they could survey every foot of flat lands surrounding them, the three warriors chewed silently on hard biscuits and side meat.

Red Hawk looked around. "Howard may be smarter than we think."

"Why do you say this?"

"He may smell this is a trap."

"It does not matter what he smells. His thirst for my blood is too great." Eagle Wing shook his head. "He wants my death. That will force him to come here."

"Yes, he probably will." Red Hawk agreed. "We must be wise. If he has located us, with so many warriors he could attack us from every side."

Crow Killer finished chewing on his cold meat and shook his head. "No, my brother. This one hates too much. He is too arrogant to use caution. No, he will attack us in full force as soon as he arrives."

"This is what I think, too." Eagle Wing studied the camp. "Will we remain here tonight?"

"Tonight, but if he doesn't come with the rising of the new sun, we will ride on."

"What is your plan, brother?" Red Hawk lay back on the bank and rested. "I know you ride slowly, so the pony soldier can catch up to us."

Crow Killer sipped on his water flask. "Does Red Hawk remember the deep ravine that lay hidden in the deep forest where we killed the large deer?"

"The open gorge? Yes, I remember it."

"How far away is that gorge from where we sit?"

"Maybe two sleeps. This one is not sure." Red Hawk set upright. "I know what you think, it is a perfect place to fight. The Pawnee will have to ride through it if they follow our tracks."

"How far does Eagle Wing think this place is?"

"I think my uncle is right, maybe two sleeps. It will be a good place to fight, providing we can reach it before the ones following catch up to us."

"Our animals are well-fed and strong." Crow Killer looked over at the hobbled horses. "When they find us we will stay just out of their reach and let them follow us to this place, and then."

"And then?" Red Hawk questioned.

"We will kill Howard and Bull Coat and go to our lodges." Eagle Wing spit the words out.

"Just like that?" Red Hawk shrugged. "You will kill them from ambush?"

"Yes, from ambush, just as they did Walking Horse and his son, Little Bow." Eagle Wing frowned.

"With so many coming against us, we can do nothing else." Crow Killer spoke softly, then dropped his head. "Like Eagle Wing says, just as they have done."

Eagle Wing had never known his father to be so hard, but the white eye Howard had hunted them across two territories asking for a fight. He had never known Crow Killer to lay an ambush for any enemy even the mighty Nez Perce who had ridden against them to the west. But the Crow Killer was right. With so many enemies coming against them, there was little choice. To face so many in an open battle with so few was suicidal.

They were the ones being pursued. Whatever happened ahead would be their enemy's own doing.

The trail leading into the deep gulch was the perfect place to lure Howard into and set a trap. Crow Killer remembered the deep ravine that somehow had been cut through the timbered valley. High, steep banks would give them a perfect position to ambush the oncoming Pawnee. They would leave signs where three horses had gone straight through the pass. Then they would circle and climb to the high ridge overlooking the gorge. In his eagerness to catch Eagle Wing, Crow Killer figured Howard would follow them into the gorge. They wouldn't be able to kill all the Pawnee, but they could cut down the odds without as much danger to themselves.

At one time, Crow Killer would have thought this a coward's way to fight, but not anymore. He saw no reason to fight an honorable battle with these killers of innocent women and children. Howard had brought all this on with his lies and deceptions and the massacre of Big Smoke's children and village. No, this would not be honorable. It would just be the annihilation of an enemy who, like any rabid wolf, deserved to die.

The gorge with its steep sides would be dangerous to follow an enemy into, but to bypass it and go around would be a hard climb for their already tired horses. He figured the Pawnee, intent on catching Eagle Wing and knowing they had their enemy outnumbered, would ride straight through without hesitation.

"If they ride into the deep gorge, many will never ride out." Crow Killer mumbled to himself as his big sorrel horse plodded along the next morning.

"My brother thinks much of this gorge." Red Hawk had heard the muffled words. "If I was following our trail, I would send scouts ahead before I rode into such a place."

"We will ride west as we planned and keep just in front of Howard until we near the place." Crow Killer studied the flats behind him. "Their horses have been ridden a long way, they are too tired to scout out the trails."

"The Pawnee might know of this steep pass." Eagle Wing looked across at Crow Killer. "They could warn Howard."

"The Pawnee are strangers to this land as we are." Crow Killer shook his head. "We will leave our tracks plainly for them to follow, like a wolf following a rabbit."

Red Hawk shrugged. "I think we should just find a good place to fight and kill them in open battle."

Crow Killer had thought of this too, but first, he would try to lure Howard into following their tracks through the deep ravine where they could fire down upon them from the high ridges.

"I know Red Hawks thoughts, but this is the only way to fight so many."

CHAPTER 17

LATE IN THE AFTERNOON, Eagle Wing spotted riders on the horizon far across the prairie riding towards them. Strung out in single file, Howard and his warriors had finally caught up to the small party. Kicking their horses into a faster trot to keep a safe distance between them, Crow Killer led on to the west, with Eagle Wing bringing up the rear.

For three hours, their horses kept up a sharp trot toward the setting sun. The distance between the two parties had narrowed, but trying to save the strength of their animals, the warriors following them slowed their horses down enough to stay within watching distance.

Crow Killer also slowed down enough to accurately count their numbers, yet they were still far enough apart to keep out of danger of a lucky rifle shot. He knew the Springfield rifles the Army provided for the Pawnee scouts were only single shots, but they were a good long-range weapon. They could be dangerous if an enemy got close enough to use them.

Twice, Eagle Wing slid from his horse, trotting alongside the animal, pretending the big Appaloosa stallion was crippled. The warriors hunting them must've spotted Eagle Wing running beside his horse. From clear across the prairie, a triumphant shout rang out from the Pawnee scouts.

Red Hawk shook his head when he heard the yelling. "What foolish ones these are." The big warrior laughed. "Why do we run from ones like this? Let's turn around and kill them here."

Crow Killer shook his head. "No, brother. One of us could be killed. I will not take that chance with my son's life or yours."

"But, to run like a scared coyote from such foolish dogs?"

"It means our plan is working, Uncle." Eagle Wing patted his Appaloosa. "They follow us like bees to honey."

Red Hawk grumbled and then trotted his horse up next to Crow Killer. "When we reach our lodges, not one word of this will be spoken."

"I wouldn't say a word."

"I know you, Crow Killer. You would tell anything at my expense."

"It is no different than Red Hawk telling how Comanche horses follow him home to his lodge."

"No. To flee in front of Pawnee is very different." The handsome one straightened his back. "This is embarrassing."

"Look! Three of them come this way fast." Eagle Wing swung his horse around. "They think they will stampede us into running our horses so the others can catch up when they are tired."

"See, brother, they have no problem killing us." Crow Killer shook his head as the oncoming warriors fired their rifles.

"Why do not all of them ride this way." Red Hawk studied the warriors. "Is this a trick or more foolishness?"

"Like you say, it is foolishness." Crow Killer raised his rifle. "Well, let's show them what can happen to foolish ones."

"We attack now?"

"No, not attack, but we can even the odds by three."

Eagle Wing laid his rifle barrel softly across the spotted horse's withers and sighted in on the warrior to the right. Touching the light trigger, he felt the recoil of the powerful rifle. The heavy slug knocked the Pawnee backward off of his running horse. The loud roar of his rifle fire echoed across the flats, and then the loud discharge of Crow Killer's and Red Hawk's rifles went off.

Screams of rage came from the other Pawnee as the three

attacking warriors fell from their horses. Distant gunshots were heard as the Pawnee fired their rifles in rage. The range was too great for their bullets to come close. It was a gesture of fury and futility.

Shrugging his shoulders, Crow Killer turned his big sorrel around and kicked him into a high lope. Behind them, the enraged Pawnee warriors raced their horses across the flat plains, attempting to catch up to Crow Killer and the others.

Looking behind at the oncoming warriors, Eagle Wing saw Captain Howard out in front. The furious white eye raised his rifle and shook it.

After a short chase the Pawnee reined in and gradually gave up, realizing that catching Crow Killer's powerful horses was futile. All they were doing was wearing their own animals down. But, seeing the Pawnee give up the chase, Crow Killer turned his horse, and to Red Hawk's dismay, he raced the long-legged sorrel straight at the oncoming warriors.

As bullets smacked into the grass in front of him, he fired his rifle twice, bringing down an enemy horse. The shot was long and made from the back of a moving horse; it was complete luck. Luck or not, it sent a shock through the Pawnee.

Wheeling his horse around, Crow Killer raced back to where Red Hawk and Eagle Wing were screaming and gesturing at the enraged Pawnee. Reining in beside them, Crow Killer laughed and looked back at the infuriated Pawnee. "I think we had better leave here now. Quick."

"That was a foolish thing for even the Crow Killer to do." Red Hawk frowned. "But it was something to see the hot lead hitting the ground in front of you and my brother laughing at his enemies."

"I wanted to make Howard look bad in front of his warriors." Crow Killer shrugged. "Now, he will be even more angry, and he'll follow after us without stopping."

"I don't know if you made him look bad, but you sure made

him mad." Eagle Wing raised his rifle again. "Look. Now, he waves his long knife."

Red Hawk studied the captain. "If he was smart, the yellow-haired pony soldier would take his long knife and leave this place."

Eagle Wing looked back again as his big Appaloosa loped powerfully across the prairie. "I said he was a liar and a fighter. I did not say he was smart."

Crow Killer chuckled again. "After this insult, he will follow my son, Eagle Wing, all the way to the big water in the west. His anger and pride will not let him quit this chase."

Red Hawk smiled. "Well, at this pace, I think we will get back to our lodges faster than I thought."

"Why don't we just turn and charge them?" Eagle Wing looked over at Red Hawk.

"I said they were foolish." Red Hawk shook his head. "Let's not be foolish ourselves, my nephew."

Eagle Wing grinned. "I just wanted to see what the great Chief of the Crow would say."

The handsome face frowned. "I say, no, young one. Charging them now, that is something your brother, Red Horse, might do."

"Hhmm." Eagle Wing looked back and counted twenty maddened warriors still riding after them. Two were riding double. "I do not think even Red Horse would do such a thing."

As the dark times covered the prairie, Crow Killer knew that Howard and his warriors would be forced to stop the chase. The night had no moon, and the land was shrouded in complete darkness. There was no way anyone could follow their trail through the tall grass in the dark. He figured Howard would not want to lose the trail and have to hunt for it with the coming of day. The captain would choose to make camp for the night.

After the sun went down, Crow Killer slowed their horses down to a walk to save their strength. If he guessed wrong and the Pawnee did follow through the night, if they came closer, the

Appaloosa stallions Red Hawk and Eagle Wing were riding would let them know of their presence.

Finally, Crow Killer reined in and slid from his horse at a small creek. "I think they no longer follow."

"What does my brother wish to do? Do we make camp or ride on?"

"I think we should attack their camp." Crow Killer let his horse drink. "That way, we can cut down the odds against us."

Red Hawk shook his head. "Odds. What does this mean?"

"It means dead warriors now and fewer men to chase us tomorrow, Uncle."

"Exactly." Crow Killer nodded at his son. "The ground here is level, with no holes or ravines to fall into. We can slip in and fire into their camp, then ride back here."

"It is a good plan." Eagle Wing agreed. "In the dark time, they cannot see us or catch us."

"If they do not come here soon, then we will go and find them." Crow Killer pulled cold biscuits and dried meat from his pouch. "We will give them time to fall asleep, then we will go."

"This is a bold plan." Red Hawk laughed lightly. "If it works."

"It'll work." Crow Killer kept hold of the rein while his horse grazed. It was a long-time habit of warriors on the war trail to keep their horses near them so an enemy couldn't steal them or stampede them during the night. Without horses, they would be at the mercy of Howard and his warriors.

No sound came across the flats as Crow Killer waited to see if Howard would risk trying to follow after them in the dark times. Only the quiet of the night came to him from across the huge prairie. He had figured right. The white eyes would make camp and wait for daylight.

Finally, he stood up and looked out across the vast lands. "We go."

Walking their horses slowly through the night, Eagle Wing,

Crow Killer, and Red Hawk strained their eyes in search of the orange flicker of a fire. Crow Killer didn't think Howard would make a dry camp. Most whites liked their hot coffee after a long day and at breakfast, and knowing they outnumbered Eagle Wing's small band, Crow Killer figured the long knife wouldn't worry about a surprise attack by only three warriors.

He'd kept within eyesight of Howard and his warriors throughout the afternoon, but after the sun had set, Crow Killer continued moving slowly to the west. How far ahead of the Pawnee they'd gotten, he couldn't tell. He felt sure that somewhere ahead the light of a fire would show itself to guide them to the camp.

As they topped a small rise, Eagle Wing's sharp eyes spotted the fire first. Reining in, he slipped from his Appaloosa horse. Crow Killer and Red Hawk reined in beside him, and all three looked out over the flats at the glowing fire.

Eagle Wing patted the neck of his stallion. "It was nice of them to show us where they are."

"They are foolish warriors," Red Hawk whispered.

"Very. Red Hawk will hold the horses while Eagle Wing and I go to their fire."

"I will go with Eagle Wing and visit the enemy." Red Hawk volunteered.

"Thank you, brother, but tonight I will go with my son."

"How will we do this thing?"

"If we can get by the camp watchers, we will fire into their camp and then run back here as fast as we can." Both warriors handed their reins to Red Hawk. "Stay here. We do not want to lose you in the dark."

"I'll wait here." The warrior took the reins. "Good luck, my brother."

Slipping silently through the flats, Crow Killer led the way as they moved cautiously toward the fire. Each looked warily for any sentries Howard might have posted. Laying his hand on Eagle Wing, Crow Killer motioned to a lone figure sitting at the edge of the fire's glow.

Crouching, Eagle Wing made his way up behind the nodding warrior and struck swiftly with his skinning knife. Laying the dead warrior on his side softly, Eagle Wing moved back.

"Do not kill Howard." Crow Killer whispered quietly. "Pick your targets. Fire three shots, then we will race back to Red Hawk."

"With all the noise and confusion, they won't even hear us as we leave." Eagle Wing looked at the sleeping warriors. "I am ready."

Red Hawk heard the roar of the rifles and shook his head. To kill this way was not an admirable thing to do, but he knew it had to be done. Outnumbered as they were, there was no other way. The Pawnee and Howard had carried the fight to Eagle Wing and Crow Killer, so they should've known what to expect.

Red Hawk heard the padding of feet as Eagle Wing and Crow Killer ran through the tall grass back to where he waited. No words were spoken as they mounted their horses and galloped away from the rifle slugs that were whining harmlessly around them.

Not knowing where their targets were, the Pawnee were just firing into the dark, hoping to hit something.

Riding hard until they were well out of range, Crow Killer reined in and listened behind them for any pursuit. Hearing none, he shrugged and turned the horses west in a slow walk.

As close as he and Eagle Wing had been to the enemy camp, their bullets must've hit every time they pulled the trigger. Counting to himself, he figured Howard probably had no more than fourteen warriors still able to fight, maybe even fewer. Like Red Hawk, he felt there was no honor in killing as they had, but the Pawnee were hell-bent on killing him and Eagle Wing. So, they got what he figured was justice.

Hearing no pursuit behind them, Crow Killer reined in as they crossed another running stream and slid from his horse.

Hobbling the animals where they could get water and graze, all three warriors lay down and drank from the cold stream. Red Hawk walked to a cleared place and sat down. "How many do you think you killed?"

"The watcher, and perhaps a few others." Eagle Wing shrugged. "Maybe now they will turn back."

"What of your promise to Big Smoke?"

"We will do as we promised before we leave these lands."

"I didn't see Bull Coat in that bunch." Crow Killer looked over at Eagle Wing. "Did you see him?"

"No, but they were covered in their robes." Eagle Wing shook his head. "He must've been there."

"Howard was there. I saw his yellow hair when he jumped up from his robe." Crow Killer shook his head thoughtfully. "He won't turn away. I'm sure of it. With the coming of the new sun, you'll see, they will follow our trail."

Red Hawk shrugged. "With so many dead, the odds, as you say, are better. We should wait here and meet them in open combat. That would be the honorable way to settle this."

"It would, but I want Howard farther away from Fort Robinson when he dies."

Red Hawk glanced knowingly at his brother. "You do not want the white eye General to know he has been killed?"

Crow Killer nodded, remembering what Crook had said about the reservation and not wanting Howard killed. "If any Pawnee live, they will tell Crook what has happened. But, farther out, no one will know of his death for many moons. Maybe never."

"And that is a good thing?"

"It is for my people." Crow Killer frowned. "If the whites know he has been killed, it will only harden their hearts more against the people."

"Your plan is still to lure the yellow-haired one to the gorge you spoke of?"

"Yes, if I can. There it will be finished."

Red Hawk exhaled wearily. "I will be glad when this trail is finished."

"So will I, my brother. So will I."

With the coming of the sun, Crow Killer led Eagle Wing and Red Hawk west towards the tall timber ahead, where they thought the gorge passing through the deep forest should lay. New to this country, they weren't exactly sure where the gulch was. Several times, he called a halt on a higher rise to look for Howard and his warriors. Searching from another rise, their sharp eyes finally spotted the Pawnee far behind them.

"The Pawnee take their time." Red Hawk studied the far riders. "They take no chances now. Look, they have two scouts out watching for another trick."

"Yet, they still follow." Crow Killer studied the column coming across the prairie. "That is all I want."

"How many warriors can Eagle Wing see?"

"I count fifteen. Sixteen if you count the pony soldier captain."

"Then none left the yellow-haired one." Crow Killer shrugged. "I guess he pays them well."

Eagle Wing shook his head and pointed. "Howard means nothing to them. I think they only follow Bull Coat. He will be their new chief."

"Hopefully, he will be chief in the big pasture above; they are foolish indeed."

"The heavy forest ahead is still a night's sleep away from here." Red Hawk kicked his Appaloosa. "Our horses are tiring, and they need rest."

"So are theirs."

Red Hawk stared thoughtfully at his brother. Many times, he had ridden a war trail with the Crow Killer, but this was the first time he had seen hate as he did now in the warrior's face. Normally, Crow Killer was fairly good-natured and willing to leave an enemy in peace, but not this time. This time, much blood would be on his brother's lance before this trail was finished. Every time the name Howard was mentioned, Crow Killer's face had hardened. Red Hawk knew there was no talking to him. Back at Bridger, Crow Killer had warned Howard not to speak with a false tongue, and now he blamed the yellow-haired captain for luring him away from his valley with lies. This trail would end with nothing short of death for one of them.

Reining in at a small stand of shrub Aspen trees, Red Hawk slid from his horse. "We will stop here and let the horses rest and graze until the new sun comes again."

Looking back at the warrior with a frown, Crow Killer relented with an annoyed shrug. "All right." He turned his horse and slipped to the ground. "I'll build a fire and fix some of Crook's coffee."

"Maybe the ones behind us will see the fire." Eagle Wing laughed.

"Good. If they come here, we will fight." Red Hawk hobbled the horses. "Then we can go home."

Crow Killer looked up tiredly. "Then, I hope they come."

"No, like us, they will rest until the new sun comes." Eagle Wing found wood for the small fire. "I think the Pawnee with Bull Coat and Howard are as tired of this trail as we are."

"Then why don't they go home?" Red Hawk shrugged.

"One day, Bull Coat will be their chief. None will dare to turn on him now." Eagle Wing lit the fire.

"You mean they fear his anger?"

"Pretty much."

The night passed quietly with only the occasional cry of a lonesome coyote out on the prairie. To Eagle Wing, the sound of the yipping voice was comforting. If any enemy was out there, he knew the cowardly coyote would slip away and not call out. He had taken the first watch, moving back down the trail to watch over the camp and let the others sleep.

Daylight and the new sun found the three warriors again headed west. Crow Killer led the small group, keeping the horses to a slow walk. There was no sign of Howard or his Pawnee scouts on the wide prairie. When the sun stood over their heads, and still there was no sign of their pursuers, Crow Killer reined in and looked out across their back trail.

"Something is wrong." The dark eyes stared hard out on the flats. "Howard should have caught up with us by now. He should have come in sight."

"My brother is right. As slow as we have been riding, they would have caught up much sooner."

"Where are they?" Eagle Wing scanned the open flats. "The sun is high, yet I see no sign of them."

"We should not have made camp out here." Crow Killer whirled the sorrel around and studied the prairie ahead. "The pony soldier is smart."

"He is ahead of us." Red Hawk leaned back and shook his head. "Is this what Crow Killer thinks?"

"While we slept last night, I think he rode through the night and got ahead of us," Crow Killer laughed lightly. "Yes, this one is smart."

"Can my brother tell me what is so funny?" Red Hawk shook his head.

"If I am not wrong." Crow Killer pointed behind him on their back trail. "Soon, you will see warriors coming towards us."

"You mean the pony soldier left warriors behind us to push his quarry into a trap ahead like a coyote drives a rabbit?"

"A good plan if it works."

"How many follow us?"

"My guess is only a few." Crow Killer rubbed his chin. "Just enough to make us think they still follow."

"Now, what is so funny?" Red Hawk frowned at Crow Killer.

"If this is their plan." The warrior turned serious. "It will not be so funny to the ones that follow."

"You think some will be coming from behind, and some wait up ahead in that wooded place?"

"Yes, I think that is what the white captain plans." Crow Killer studied the flats. "A clever plan to ambush and kill us. Now, brother, do you have any problem killing them the same way?"

"No." Red Hawk pulled out his rifle.

"Let's prepare to meet the ones that follow." Crow Killer slid from his horse and legged the animal onto his side. Laying across the horse's head to keep him down and out of sight in the tall grass, he motioned for Red Hawk and Eagle Wing to do the same.

"Keep a close watch in case I am wrong, and they all still follow us." Crow Killer raised up slightly so he could barely see over the grass.

"And if they all come from the east, brother?"

"Then, we will find out just how fast your great spotted horse can run. Smile, brother; this will be a good trick we pull on Captain Howard."

"And if only a few come." Eagle Wing studied the far horizon.

"Then we will see how fast their horses can run."

"Crow Killer is making a game out of this." Red Hawk shook his head. "I'm too old for playing games."

"You're only as old as you feel." Crow Killer frowned. "But you are wrong, my brother. This is no game to me. The white eye has schemed to kill my son. He has lied and cheated the Arapaho People. This is no game."

"I feel old." Red Hawk shrugged. "This trail has made me feel this way. I have realized I like my lodge more than the war trail."

Eagle Wing knew Red Hawk was just joking with his Father. "You said you wanted to finish this."

"Yes, we will finish it today." He sighted down his rifle. "Maybe; then we can ride for our lodges."

Eagle Wing glanced over at his uncle. "Does Red Hawk mean he will no longer ride against the Comanche and steal their horses?"

"I do not steal. I told you before, their horses just follow me home." The dark head shook. "No, I am not that old."

"That's what I thought." Eagle Wing laughed. "Red Hawk enjoys this game more than any of us."

"Bows, lances, or rifles." Crow Killer whispered. "Take your pick."

Red Hawk was curious at his words because he already had his rifle out. "What does Crow Killer ask?"

"My Father means, how does the great war Chief Red Hawk wish to fight the ones coming?"

"How many do you see, Nephew?"

"They are still too far away to be sure, and they ride in single file, but I think there are six riders."

"Tell us when they are almost on us." Crow Killer hovered down across his horse's head and took a strong hold on the animal's lead rope. "When you holler, we will get our horses up and charge them."

Minutes had passed by, seeming like hours, as Eagle Wing watched the unaware Pawnee move slowly towards them. With their horses down and out of sight, the oncoming warriors didn't even know that the three warriors were lying concealed in the tall grass, just feet in front of them. Eagle Wing watched as they closed to less than fifty feet, then he yipped and kicked his spotted stallion to his feet.

The three mounted warriors materialized out of nowhere right in front of the Pawnee scouts, taking them completely by surprise. The Pawnee screamed the alarm and fired wildly. Charging across the open flats, the Henrys sounded rapidly, bringing down four Pawnee as they clashed together. The others fell back in panic as the three warriors bore down on them, swinging their war clubs and screaming like crazed demons.

The surprised Pawnee Warriors crumbled under the weight and vicious ferocity of the attack. Red Hawk had been slightly grazed by a rifle slug that barely nicked his side. The other shots from the startled and frightened Pawnee had completely missed their marks as the ferocious warriors tore into them.

Eagle Wing set his horse, looking down at one of the dead. Motioning, he pointed his chin as Red Hawk and Crow Killer moved to where he waited. Before them, crumpled in death, lay a body with a shock of blond hair showing from beneath a leather hunting shirt.

"It is the yellow-haired pony soldier."

Crow Killer slipped from his horse and rolled the tall form over. Pulling back the heavy shirt to reveal what was left of the face, he shook his head. Captain Howard was dead. The heavy slug from a Henry had torn away half of his face. Except for the shock of bloody blond hair, he was unrecognizable. His long cavalry saber lay beside him in the grass.

"That is too bad." Crow Killer shook his head and stared down at the dead body. "He didn't even see it coming."

Red Hawk smiled. "If he did, I think it was the last thing this one ever saw."

"You still tired, Uncle?" Eagle Wing sat his horse.

The handsome face smiled. "No, the sting of a bullet woke me up."

Crow Killer turned to look at Red Hawk's bloody side. "You hurt bad, brother?"

"No, just a bee sting." The warrior looked down at the trickle of blood. "This is twice someone has tried to kill me on this trail."

Looking at the small skin tear, Crow Killer shook his head. "That one almost succeeded."

"What do we do now?" Eagle Wing watched as Crow Killer packed dirt onto the wound to stop the small flow of blood. "You know Bull Coat waits ahead."

"We go finish it." Red Hawk's face turned hard. "Then we go to our lodges."

Eagle Wing looked around at the scattered bodies and then out across the flats towards the forest. "I think Bull Coat will wait with what's left of his warriors somewhere ahead in the forest."

Crow Killer finished packing the wound. "By my count, Bull Coat only has eight warriors left with him."

"The pony soldier's plan was smart." Red Hawk looked down at his side. "If we had not guessed what he intended, we would have ridden into his trap."

"Why didn't he ride with Bull Coat instead of staying back with these warriors?"

"I think Howard didn't want to make such a long and difficult ride in the dark." Crow Killer shrugged. "He chose to remain behind with these warriors."

"Then the long knife made a bad choice." Red Hawk glanced down at Howard. "What will we do?"

"We will go find Bull Coat." Crow Killer looked up at the sun. "We will ride closer to the forest land and wait for the new day."

"Bull Coat may have heard the shooting." Eagle Wing looked towards the far woods. "Sound carries far out on these grasslands."

"Maybe, but he would have to ride here to find out what has happened." Red Hawk pointed at the trees in the distance. "I think he will wait somewhere ahead in that timbered land."

"Tonight, we will make a cold camp and keep a sharp lookout." Crow Killer swung upon his sorrel. "We will ride to the forests in the morning and finish this."

CHAPTER 18

THE NIGHT PASSED QUIETLY as the three sat in a circle, letting their horses graze. Tensions were high. Six or seven warriors against three were still risky odds. Crow Killer knew full well that one of the Pawnee, or maybe more, could get in a lucky shot in an ambush. He thought about the dangers throughout the night. None of the three slept much. Their senses remained keenly on edge, listening for the enemy. The little sleep they did get was fitful and light. They knew Bull Coat and his warriors could spring out of the tall grass at any minute in a surprise attack.

The mournful howl of a lonely timber wolf caused the horses to prick their ears in its direction. It also brought forth the new day. The early sun was overcast, with banked clouds casting a dark shadow over the prairie. Out of the east, another wolf answered the first, and a chorus of howls broke the prairie's silence.

Stretching from his long night sitting on the ground, Red Hawk shook his head. "This is a young man's thing. I am much too old to be sleeping on the ground."

Crow Killer smiled and shook his head. "Red Hawk will never be too old to ride against his enemies."

"Your enemies, brother." Red Hawk shrugged. "The Pawnee have always been my friends."

"Then, Uncle, why don't you ride out and tell your friend Bull Coat to ride away and leave us in peace."

"Since when are they your friends?" Crow Killer shook his

head. "They are your friends only when you are stealing their horses."

"Borrowing."

"Whatever you want to call it, but I have seen more Comanche and Pawnee horses in your herds than Appaloosas."

"Ah, brother, you grow old. Your eyes are not as good as they once were." Red Hawk un-hobbled his big Appaloosa and led him to water. "Those horses are all mine."

"Tell me." Crow Killer shook his head. "What does Red Hawk need with so many horses?"

A grin spread on the handsome face. "You know, I have asked myself the same question many times."

"And?"

"I'm just greedy, I think."

Eagle Wing rolled up his sleeping robe and then handed out some stale biscuits and hardtack. "I think it is time for us to become serious."

"Why, nephew, we are serious." Red Hawk accepted the food.

"So is Bull Coat. He sits with his warriors at the edge of the timberline as we speak."

Crow Killer, too, had already located the waiting warriors. In the dark of night, they had ridden closer to the heavy woods than they thought. Seven warriors set their horses in a line where the short prairie grass and the smaller trees and brush came together. One huge warrior wearing a large wooly bull hide vest sat in front of the others. Even at this distance, they could make out the buffalo horns decorating his skull cap.

"That is Bull Coat himself out front."

"That one is an imposing figure." Red Hawk was impressed as the Pawnee Warriors just sat there waiting motionless. "I don't remember a warrior that big back on the Blue River."

"Look." Crow Killer pointed as another warrior rode out in front and turned his horse in circles. "A warrior circles his horse."

"Well, now they want to talk." Red Hawk waved his rifle over his head.

"We are out of range for even his long shooting rifles." Eagle Wing shrugged. "Maybe he tries to lure us closer."

"No, I think he wants to talk." Crow Killer shook his head. "If it were a trick of some kind, he wouldn't have shown himself."

Red Hawk lowered his Henry. "Let only one of them come here to talk. I, too, think it could be a trick."

"Perhaps the Pawnee think Howard still follows us across the flatlands." Eagle Wing studied the warrior. "Maybe they did not hear the rifles firing from where they were."

Crow Killer stepped his horse forward and then circled him twice. "I will ride out and talk with this one. Be ready to fight if it is a trick they play."

"I stay ready." Red Hawk quipped. "For an old man."

"I thought my uncle was too old to play these games anymore?"

"Red Hawk lied. Soon, the Pawnee will find out who is old."

"Be ready." Crow Killer raised his rifle and then slowly started the sorrel forward. He knew the Pawnee could be tricky and unpredictable.

A few small birds flew up in front of his horse as he rode at a slow walk toward the oncoming warrior. Only a good horse run separated the two groups. Crow Killer didn't think Bull Coat was up to any tricks, but still, he held the Henry cocked and ready for anything the Pawnee might try. Over the years, he had ridden many times against the Pawnee tribe in battle, and he never ever took them for granted.

Slow Otter, the Pawnee Chief he had killed in his valley, had been a great warrior, but he, too, was unpredictable. Their words were as empty and unreliable as the wind. One never knew what one of these warriors might do. Crow Killer studied the slender warrior riding towards him.

Less than thirty feet separated the two warriors when they

reined in their horses and faced each other. The warrior held his rifle in his left hand and pointed it down to show Crow Killer that his intentions were only to talk.

"I know you. You are the great bear warrior, Crow Killer." The slender warrior sat atop a grey Army horse branded with the US brand.

"What is your name, warrior?"

"I am Iron Blade, brother of Bull Coat." The warrior pointed behind him. "Bull Coat sends me here with his words."

"Let Iron Blade speak."

"We heard much shooting before the dark times came."

"Your white pony soldier and the warriors who rode with him are dead."

"That is a bad thing." The shaved head nodded. "We should have ridden back to our lands many sleeps ago."

"Yes, you should have." Crow Killer agreed. "Speak, Iron Blade. Why does Bull Coat send you here to talk?"

The dark face hardened. "These are Bull Coat's words. Hear them well, Crow Killer."

"I'm listening, Iron Blade. My ears are open."

"Is that Eagle Wing sitting with another warrior there?"

"It is my son, Eagle Wing, and my brother, Red Hawk."

"Bah! A Crow and an Arapaho cannot be brothers."

"Yet, we are." Crow Killer looked over the warrior's shoulder for any tricks. "What does Bull Coat want? Speak, warrior."

"Bull Coat wishes to meet the killer of our great Chief Strong Otter in single combat." Iron Blade flattened his hand across his throat. "There."

"And if Bull Coat loses?"

"We will take his body and leave this place and go back to our lodges."

"What if I say no to Bull Coat, and we just start killing Pawnee?"

"Then we will know Crow Killer or Eagle Wing neither has

the honor or courage to meet a real warrior in battle." Iron Blade frowned. "And Bull Coat says this time there must be no tricks."

"Tricks?"

"When Strong Otter was killed, you Crow Killer were supposed to fight him, not Eagle Wing."

"My son Eagle Wing feared for my life that day as a son should fear for his father."

"Speak Crow Killer, does Eagle Wing have the courage to fight Bull Coat?"

Crow Killer knew there was no way out of this. Eagle Wing had to fight or lose face in front of a Pawnee. "I will speak with my son. Tell Bull Coat he will have his answer soon."

"No others will interfere." Iron Blade flattened his hand again. "You have our word."

"The word of a Pawnee isn't much to me."

"Your words are insulting to this one." Iron Blade's face reddened. "Maybe the Crow Killer and Iron Blade will fight after Bull Coat kills Eagle Wing. That is, if you are not too old, ancient one?"

"At your pleasure, Pawnee." Crow Killer dipped his arm at the warrior.

Turning his horse, Iron Blade rode back across the open flats to where Bull Coat and his warriors waited. Crow Killer reined in beside Eagle Wing and Red Hawk. The day seemed even more overcast and gloomy as he looked over at the two.

"Speak, brother. What did the warrior want?" Red Hawk could hear the excitement across the flats of the Pawnee warriors yelling.

"He wants to meet Eagle Wing in single combat there." Crow Killer's strong brown arm pointed to where the battle was to take place. "No rifles of the white eyes, only the war axe and knife. When one is dead, it will be finished."

Eagle Wing stared at the appointed battleground. "Do you

think it is because I killed Strong Otter or because he wants to be chief?"

Red Hawk snorted angrily. "Bull Coat doesn't care about Strong Otter. He only wants to be chief of the Pawnee."

Eagle Wing looked up at the cloudy sky and nodded slowly. Handing Red Hawk his rifle, he smiled. "It is a good day to die."

Crow Killer nudged his horse closer to Eagle Wing. "My son does not have to fight the Pawnee alone. With our Henrys, they wouldn't have a chance."

"No. I do not want the Pawnee to be able to say a Lance Bearer fears to meet Bull Coat in combat." Eagle Wing looked squarely at his father. "And I want this finished so we can ride to our lodges without fear of Bull Coat ever riding against us again."

Red Hawk laid his hand on Eagle Wing's shoulder. "Bull Coat is no different than Strong Otter was, my nephew."

"We will see soon enough."

"Remember Walking Horse and be as strong as he was." Crow Killer frowned.

"I will remember my uncle, Walking Horse, but mostly I remember Big Smoke and his children killed by this Pawnee dog."

Crow Killer and Red Hawk followed closely behind Eagle Wing and reined in behind him as the neared the heavy timber. The Pawnee, with their leader Bull Coat, rode out halfway to meet them where the grass was shorter. The huge warrior in the lead wore a bull hide vest and seemed even larger as he rode nearer. He rode a tall Army horse with a U.S. brand almost identical to the horse Iron Blade rode.

Reining in forty feet apart, the two magnificent warriors studied each other as their powerful mounts fidgeted in anticipation. The animals seemed to sense the oncoming battle. Both warriors removed their vests and leather leggings and now wore only their breechcloths. Both warriors set their horses proudly, their backs straight as ramrods, their bare torsos revealing the power they both possessed. Neither face showed any emotion, no fear, no concern. Not a muscle or an eyelash twitched on either face.

"You have come a long way to die, Arapaho dog." Bull Coat was huge, and his arm and chest muscles rolled with every move of the warrior's body. He removed the horned bull skull cap, showing his skull was shaven clean except for a top knot held in place by a Silver Concho. "Now foolish one, I Bull Coat will taste your blood."

"Stop talking, baby killer, and start fighting."

Bull Coat studied the war axe Eagle Wings held in his right hand and smiled. "When you are dead, I will have the war axe you carry. Some say that it is magical."

"Maybe it is."

"My people have heard it is the war axe of Flying Cloud, the great Arapaho warrior."

"It is." Eagle Wing lifted the axe so that the deadly blade flashed in the sunlight. "And it will be Bull Coat's death, as it was the kiss of death for your Chief Strong Otter."

"No. I do not believe this. Soon, the axe will be mine."

"Then come and take it."

Circling their horses, they closed the distance, nearing each other, each warrior ready for the other one to make his move. Suddenly, both horses whirled, and their riders heeled them into a run.

With a war scream, both warriors charged forward. The two war axes clashed together, sparks flew, the loud ringing echoed across the flats. Bull Coat laughed out hideously as he swung again and again, trying to unhorse Eagle Wing.

The war axe of Eagle Wing brought first blood when Bull Coat miscalculated and got caught by a grazing blow. Frowning, he screamed in rage and drove his grey horse forward, shouldering the Appaloosa stallion back. Both animals were well matched in size and power as they pushed and shouldered forward, trying to get closer to their opponent for a killing blow. The soft prairie sod flew in the air as the horses kicked it up, turning and charging forward.

"I think you weaken Arapaho." Bull Coat's black war paint was streaked and running down his face from the exertion of the battle. His enraged face with the smeared paint and crazed eyes was hideous to behold. "I think you die soon."

"So be it, but you have to kill your prey first before you can eat it."

"Consider it done." Screaming in rage, the Pawnee again heeled his grey horse forward.

The clanging of the axes, the snorting of the fighting horses, and the thundering of their hooves against the ground as they circled exhilarated the watching Pawnee warriors. Screams of encouragement came from the warriors as they moved in closer in anticipation of the kill.

Red Hawk looked over at Crow Killer "I think soon we will have to fight the others."

"Perhaps, my brother." But the dark eyes of Crow Killer never left the battle. "Be ready."

Reining in his horse, Eagle Wing tried several times to position his Appaloosa so that he could get a killing blow on the Pawnee. But Bull Coat was a powerful and experienced fighter, thwarting every attempt Eagle Wing made. The powerful war axes grew heavy for both warriors. Again and again, the horses pushed into each other, trying their best to overpower the other. A glancing blow from Bull Coat's axe brought a trickle of blood from the Appaloosa's neck.

Fighting and trying to kill each other was what was expected of enemy warriors, but striking your enemy's horse was considered cowardly. Warriors of the plains respected and honored the horses they rode, and even in the heat of battle, they would not intentionally hurt their enemy's horse.

Bull Coat reined in his sweating grey horse back and dipped

his war axe to show he had not hit the stallion on purpose. "I would not harm your horse, Arapaho." The big Pawnee lifted his chin arrogantly. "I will own him when this fight is finished."

"I accept your apology. Now, let us die with honor." Eagle Wing heeled his Appaloosa into the tired grey, knocking him sideways.

With the hard thrust of the Appaloosa, the horse of Bull Coat stumbled and went to his knees. Seeing his opening, Eagle Wing lunged from his stallion and landed on Bull Coat's shoulders, dragging the bigger warrior from the stumbling grey. Hitting the ground, both warriors sprang to their feet, facing each other. Eagle Wing looked at the ground. The heavy crash of the two horses had knocked the war axe from his hand and sent it tumbling to the ground.

He remembered the warning of the old medicine man Soaring Bird. "You must never let the war axe of Flying Cloud fall to the ground. That day could bring your death." The fateful words rang through Eagle Wing's mind as he looked down at the axe, then up into the grinning Pawnee's face.

Bull Coat sneered. "Your axe lays in the dirt, Arapaho. Now, you die."

Retreating before the onrushing Pawnee's swinging war axe, Eagle Wing tried to avoid the bigger man's deadly weapon. Twice, the deadly axe brushed his arm, causing a trickle of blood to flow.

"Eagle Wing's axe is on the ground." Red Hawk tensed. "We have to help him before he is killed."

"No, my brother. He would not want that."

"But the axe!" Red Hawk pointed at the axe lying in the dirt and started forward. "I will not let him die."

"We will not interfere." Crow Killer held out his hand to stop Red Hawk. "My son will kill this one without the axe."

Bull Coat and Eagle Wing faced each other, circling slowly, thrusting their weapons at one another. On foot, the Pawnee was still a formidable fighter, parrying every blow Eagle Wing tried.

"I told you, Arapaho, you are dead."

"Prove it." Eagle Wing's razor-sharp skinning knife sliced across Bull Coat's thigh. "You should be watching instead of running your mouth."

In a rage, the bigger warrior lunged forward, swiping the air with his war axe where Eagle Wing had been standing. Stumbling off balance in his rage, Bull Coat felt the sharp skinning knife as it opened up another cut on his shoulder. Blood covered the warrior as he futilely tried to catch Eagle Wing with his war axe. He charged forward but narrowly missed.

The Pawnee was tiring.

Thinking the fight was almost over, Eagle Wing slowly circled the exhausted warrior. "This is for Big Smoke. I will send your hair to him for his scalp pole."

"Who?" Bull Coat's question sounded slurred and painful.

Lunging in, Eagle Wing narrowly evaded the heavy swing of the war axe. Surprised, he realized Bull Coat had been feinting, acting like he was weaker and more tired than he actually was. Eagle Wing shook his head. The trick had almost worked.

Retreating out of harm's way, Eagle Wing counted on being faster than the larger man. Crouching like a mountain cat ready to spring, he waited for an opening to lunge underneath the deadly axe.

"Your time is near, Arapaho." Bull Coat raised his axe tiredly and lunged forward.

Slipping under the powerful arm of his opponent, Eagle Wing opened a terrible cut across Bull Coat's ribcage. Blood spurted down his side from the wound where the skin laid bare the ribs of the warrior.

"Bull Coat talks too much to be a fighter." Eagle Wing rolled sideways and grabbed up his war axe. "Now, Pawnee, you die for Big Smoke."

Lunging forward, Bull Coat grabbed Eagle Wing's wrist in a powerful grasp, forcing his arm backward. Eagle Wing knew he had misjudged the warrior as the heavier man landed atop him on the ground.

Waiting for the death blow of Bull Coat's war axe, Eagle Wing suddenly felt the big body relax. Rolling the heavy warrior away, Eagle Wing saw the hilt of his knife protruding from the Pawnee's chest. Bull Coat had landed on top of Eagle Wing, and in his eagerness to kill, the Pawnee had fallen on the sharp skinning knife.

Eagle Wing stood up and looked down into the glazing eyes of the dying Pawnee. "That was for Big Smoke."

"Who?" Bull Coat asked as his head rolled sideways.

Seeing Bull Coat fall at Eagle Wing's feet, Crow Killer and Red Hawk rushed forward with their weapons raised. Suddenly, war screams and yelling sounded from the woods, and several riders rushed from the deep woods and chased after the fleeing Pawnee. One lone warrior rode his big chestnut horse towards where Crow Killer was.

As soon as Red Hawk recognized the warrior was Straight Arrow and not a Pawnee, he turned and rushed to check on Eagle Wing's wounds.

Straight Arrow rode swiftly toward Crow Killer. As he got closer, he held up his rifle and smiled. "Don't shoot Crow Killer."

"I recognize you, Straight Arrow." Crow Killer lowered his weapon.

"Yes. It is I." The warrior looked across at Eagle Wing and yelled. "What a fight! If I live even into the next world, I will never see another such as I have just witnessed."

"What do you do here?" Crow Killer was shocked to see the warrior. "I thought you were in the Canadians?"

"No, when you rode with Big Smoke to Fort Robinson, I felt guilty." The warrior shrugged. "So, I rode back to help Crazy Horse and my people."

"How do you come to be here?" Red Hawk shook his head

in amazement. "The Canadians are so far."

"The people are starving. They need food. We were here beyond the timber hunting the shaggies when we heard the shooting last night." Straight Arrow smiled. "We rode here and waited for the new sun to see who was shooting. We watched from the timber as you and the Pawnee talked."

"It is good to see our friend Straight Arrow." Eagle Wing reached out his hand.

Looking over the bloody warrior, Straight Arrow shook his head. "Are you hurt badly, my friend?"

"No, most of this blood is his." Eagle Wing glanced down at the body of Bull Coat.

"What a fight! It will be told around our fires during the cold times."

"I am glad it is finished."

"You will ride for your lodges now?"

Crow Killer thought of Bright Moon. "Just as fast as we can get there."

"I have something for Big Smoke." Eagle Wing picked up the war axe and skinning knife of Bull Coat. Then he took the long knife of Howard from Red Hawk and handed them to Straight Arrow. "Tell him we have done what we promised him. It is finished."

"Big Smoke is not with you?"

"No." Crow Killer shook his head. "He carries a message to Gall from the white General Crook. By now, he should be in Sitting Bull's camp."

"I am surprised, as hard-headed as that one is, that he would leave the trail of the yellow-haired pony soldier and the Pawnee."

Eagle Wing nodded. "We gave our word that we would get them for him."

"Big Smoke will receive these things and your words. And I thank you for him."

"Tell him we will meet again one day." Eagle Wing leaned

tiredly up against his horse.

"It is not my kill, but I think Big Smoke would like that." Straight Arrow pointed down at Bull Coat. "It will decorate his scalp pole."

"Take it, and the yellow hair of the pony soldier, Howard. He lays just back there." Eagle Wing pointed.

As the Sioux Riders rode up brandishing their weapons ornamented with fresh scalps, Straight Arrow pointed towards the trees. "We have fresh meat. Eat with us and rest before you go to your lodges."

"We will do this, my friend." Eagle Wing nodded his head gratefully. "I need to rest a few minutes."

"What a fight." Screams went up from many throats as the words were spoken from Straight Arrow.

Bridger's Post came into view almost a full moon after Crow Killer had left the company of Straight Arrow and his warriors. No time was wasted as they were all in a hurry to reach their lodges and the deep valley. Alex Caldwell was elated and surprised to see the three back so soon from such a long trail. Shaking their hands as they dismounted, he had a young Indian lad take the tired horses to McGraw's.

"Keep the stallions separate." Red Hawk ordered as the horses were led away.

"Come in, Jedidiah." Caldwell opened the post screen. "I'll have the women make you some fixings."

Crow Killer smiled tiredly. "Thank you, Alex. Have you had word from the valley?"

Smiling, Caldwell looked over at Eagle Wing. "Red Horse and Broken Leg rode here a few moons ago. Ate them some vittles, then returned back to the valley quickly."

"What has happened for Red Horse to be here so far from the valley?"

"There was a fight. Your friend Black Bird was killed at the Snake River Crossing."

"Black Bird is dead?" Eagle Wing shook his head.

"Red Horse said he died a Lance Bearer's death." Caldwell looked over at Eagle Wing. "He killed Spotted Elk and another warrior before dying with his Lance stuck in the ground."

"Black Bird is dead?" Shocked, Eagle Wing repeated the words. "How can this be?"

Caldwell shrugged. "It would be best for Red Horse and Broken Leg to tell of this."

"Red Horse returned to the valley?" Crow Killer looked over at Caldwell.

"Yes, he and Broken Leg left as soon as they had eaten." Caldwell poured coffee for the three tired warriors. "When they found that Spotted Elk's remaining warriors and squaws rode to the south, they returned immediately."

"Thank you, Alex." Crow Killer shook his head. "We ride as soon as we eat."

"You're tired, my friend." Caldwell spread his hands. "Rest here for one night at least."

"Thank you, but no. We are all anxious to see our loved ones."

"If you ever need anything, Jedidiah, let me know."

The little mule sent up her warning bray across the valley. Alerted, Red Horse, Bright Moon, and the others greeted the trail-weary warriors as they crossed the small creek and slid from their horses. Bright Moon hugged Crow Killer and then broke out into a broad smile.

"You are home, my husband." She looked over at Eagle Wing and Red Hawk. "All of you are home safe now."

Broken Leg looked over at Red Hawk. "I have waited for you, my friend, to ride back to our lodges."

"Thank you, Broken Leg." Red Hawk shook hands with the warrior. "We will go with the coming of the new sun."

"We have much to tell Crow Killer, Eagle Wing, and Red Hawk." Red Horse took the tired horses.

"Yes, my son." Crow Killer looked out at his beloved valley and then down at Bright Moon. "But you will have many days to tell us. We are home."

Eagle Wing held Morning Dove and looked across the valley. Out of habit, he listened for the call of the old wolf. The trail had been so long that it made him appreciate the beautiful valley even more. Yes, he was home.

Hopefully, this time to stay.

–The End–

Follow Alfred Dennis on Amazon so you will be notified when the next and final novel in the **Crow Killer series** comes out.

Until then, have a look at **Slocum,** another of Alfred Dennis's exciting western novels…

This cover features a photo of the author's father, A.C. Dennis, a great cowboy with his cow dog.

Like the Crow Killer series, **Slocum** is set in the American West Frontier, full of action, adventure, and romance. A young man must battle relentless storms, treacherous rivers, and deadly confrontations with rustlers and hostile Indians, not only to save the family ranch but also to rescue a young woman from the dreaded Comancheros.

Don't miss this gripping Western adventure of courage, honor, and love. The next book in this exciting series, **Slocum's Bar S**, will be coming out soon.

Reed Slocum is relieved when he sees smoke rising from the chimneys of Sedalia, Missouri, on the horizon. The long, dusty trek driving his longhorns from Texas is nearly over. Lee Hargrove, the beautiful blonde he's fallen for, sits quietly on the wagon seat with her tired blue eyes fixed on the distant town. They've faced bloodshed, gunfights, and death at every turn, but the danger finally seems behind them.

Or so they think.

Join in the action as Reed fights his way back to Texas, with his old blue roan steer leading the way. Comancheros, Indians, and ruthless killers block his path, forcing him to draw his guns once more to protect the woman he loves.

Old West adventure, romance, and danger await around every bend. Reed has the strength to endure the hardships, but does his beautiful companion?